LESSONS IN THE WILD

by

Wendy Isaac Bergin

Publisher Information:
DartFrog Books
4697 Main Street
Manchester Center, VT 05255

www.DartFrogBooks.com

ALSO BY WENDY ISAAC BERGIN

The Piper's Story: A Tale of War, Music and the Supernatural
The Threshold of Eden

For my friends: Jane Barry, Isabelle Håkansson,
and Elizabeth Brownlee

For Nicholas, Daniel, and Lisa, who have walked where the path
was comfortless and dark. Be assured that you do not walk alone:
*Ty han skall ge sina änglar befallning om dig
att bevara dig på alla dina vägar.*

*He found him in a desert land, and in the waste howling
wilderness; He led him about, He instructed him, He kept him
as the apple of his eye.*
Deuteronomy 32:10

*Every prophet has to come from Civilization, but every prophet
has to go into the wilderness. He must have a strong impression
of a complex society and all that it has to give, and then must
serve periods of isolation and meditation. That is the process by
which psychic dynamite is made.*
Winston Churchill,
The Sunday Chronicle, November 8, 1931

CONTENTS

2009

2010

2007

PROLOGUE

He hadn't even been able to find the property at first—he'd driven right past it. Where was the For Sale sign? There was no street address, so GPS was useless. Sebastian searched left and right as he slowly followed the dusty caliche road. He drove past a handful of houses, but mostly he saw stretches of uninhabited woods. He rounded a curve and came to a sudden halt. The road dead-ended at a barbed wire fence enclosing a cow pasture. A herd of brown and white masticating Longhorns regarded him thoughtfully.

He sighed in frustration. Vogel Lane was not very long—surely he could find the property. He turned the car around and stopped to enquire at the first house where he saw life. He parked on the side of the road and approached a man cutting a sheet of plywood with a circular saw. When the man noticed him, he turned off the whining saw and removed the cigarette hanging from his lips.

Sebastian asked him if he knew where the lot for sale was located.

The man blinked a few times, his eyes almost buried between droopy lids and puffy, wrinkled bags the size of mushrooms. His seamed face had the permanent red flush of a heavy drinker, and the top half of one ear was missing, sliced off in a straight, slightly diagonal line.

Knife fight? Barroom brawl? Sebastian wondered how the other guy fared.

The man coughed and spat a yellowish glob of phlegm on the ground. "Yeah, go on back past two houses and a trailer, and you'll see the clearin' on the left."

"Thanks." *Nice to meet the neighbors.* Sebastian regained the safety of his car, retraced his route, and found the clearing.

The land didn't look like much. He parked in the shallow, semi-circular clearing beside the road and got out. Tall, untamed grass, weeds, and wildflowers ringed a few bare, stony patches of gray soil. Beyond that, a dense wall of trees—a dark green canopy of oak and cedar with an understory of saplings and thick underbrush—obscured the horizon. Sebastian could see no sign of the advertised "idyllic pond," the feature that had drawn him ninety miles away from the city in the first place. Of course, *pond* might be real estate hype for a glorified mud puddle, or worse—a stagnant, algae-covered pool.

As he waited for the realtor to arrive, the June heat bore down on his bare head with an unrelenting weight, juicing him like a citrus press. Droplets of sweat sprang up from his scalp and coursed down his face, neck, and back in steady streams. He wiped his brow with his sleeve and surveyed the area. The quiet was almost as oppressive as the heat—he wondered if he could get used to it.

A green dragonfly with transparent wings approached, stopped and hovered not far from his nose. After inspecting him closely, it flew straight up and away in search of smaller prey. Sebastian noticed delicate white and yellow moths fluttering rapidly just above the weedy grass. As he observed their erratic paths, he realized the quiet was punctuated with many sounds: birdsong, the occasional buzzing of cicadas, the sighing of wind through the trees, the distant bark of a dog. The peace always abiding in nature descended on him, but it was countered by uneasiness. With no traffic on the road and no one about, he felt forlorn, out of his element.

A grasshopper suddenly sprang up and hit him in the face, making him recoil. Almost as abruptly, a clamor of worrisome thoughts erupted in his mind. Had he wasted his time, making the long drive out here to the sweltering wilds, far from friends and city comforts? Could he turn those looming, inhospitable woods into a homestead? Did he really want to move out to the country?

He paced around the clearing and found the For Sale sign, blown over and lying flat on the ground. As he set it upright, a white pickup truck came barreling down the road, stirring up a billowing dust cloud in its wake. The driver pulled into the yard and parked next to his Honda. His realtor, he presumed. A lithe, slender woman hopped out of the cab. He walked over to introduce himself while the chalk-like road dust drifted across the land and enveloped them.

Emma Gallagher was probably in her late twenties, but with her fresh, makeup-free face and blond ponytail, she looked about sixteen. In one of their telephone conversations, she disclosed the fact that she had only worked as a realtor for six months. Her confession did not inspire confidence, but Sebastian reasoned she wasn't showing him a house, just a piece of land. As a longtime urban renter, he had never bought land or a house before. It was all new to him, but land was land, and he'd either like it or not—what could go wrong?

"The first thing we should do is walk the boundaries and find the survey pins so you can get an idea of the size of it," she told him.

It was two and a half acres of sloping, heavily wooded property, but they eventually found all the pins. Sebastian learned the size of 2.5 acres, or so he thought at the time, in addition to quite a few other things on that walk.

Emma asked him what his plans were for the property if he bought it.

"Oh, I'm probably going to move a house onto it," he told her, sounding much more confident than he felt. It was the cheapest way to own a home—if he could actually carry it off.

She nodded. "That's become common in this area. There are a lot of old German farmhouses around here that families don't use anymore, so they sell them off the property for very little—some as low as six thousand. My uncle is an ace at remodeling older houses if you ever need help. I can email you his contact information. His name is Joe Klein.

"You don't sound like you're from Houston," she added, fishing.

"No, I grew up in New Jersey. I went to graduate school in Houston and then stayed on."

"Well, in rural Texas," she told him, as she glanced down at his sneakers, "you should always wear boots. You have to be careful when you take a walk like this. We've got rattlesnakes, copperheads, cottonmouth moccasins, and coral snakes. Scorpions too."

Not the most comforting sales pitch for a city boy.

"But in all the years I've lived here," she added, "I haven't got snakebit once. For the most part, even venomous snakes avoid confrontation. So if you wear boots, especially in deep grass or around woodpiles, you should be fine."

Dressed in jeans and T-shirts, they walked the overgrown lot. Sebastian was amazed at how disoriented he became in the thick woods. They hiked uphill and down past wild grapevines and through heavy underbrush festooned here and there with immense, impressive spiderwebs. A machete would have helped clear a path through the brush, but it would have been useless against the enemies they could not see. All unaware, they wove their way between mature oaks and cedars.

They pushed pliant saplings aside and finally discovered what Sebastian had wanted to see all along—the pond. "It's about a half-acre in size," Emma told him.

Idyllic it was not, but at least it wasn't covered in algae. Ringed with briars, its edges were overshadowed by trees hung with ropy vines. It had a closed-off, secret air—unpleasant, somehow.

She seemed to read his thoughts. "Once you take down the trees and the briars around it, the pond will be beautiful. This entire property could be cleared in a day or two. I know a local guy, Edgar Rhodes, who does that type of work."

Sebastian kept his eyes on the still water. He dearly wished to own a pond. "Do you think there are fish in there?"

"Yes. When we listed it, the seller told me he stocked it. He liked to fish, but he stopped coming out here years ago. That's why the place is so overgrown. Despite what it looks like now, this property has great potential."

He tried to imagine what the land would look like when only the large trees remained and the pond, surrounded with green grass and flowers, would be opened up to sunlight and air. He pictured himself standing on its banks, casting for bass.

At the end of the tour, Sebastian told Emma he wanted to buy the property. The down payment would decimate his savings, but the monthly payments would be small. With her guidance, he settled on an offer. The decision, he realized later, was a turning point—it changed his life forever.

That evening, Sebastian discovered Emma hadn't been altogether forthcoming about rural Texas property. Although she mentioned snakes and scorpions, she failed to disclose the worst threat to life and sanity in those parts happened to be invisible. He learned the truth when the misery began. Sebastian's legs began to itch horribly, and large red lumps formed on his ankles, calves, thighs, the backs of his knees, arms, his neck, and in those hard-to-reach, unmention- able places. The itching was intense and relentless. He found out two days later that Emma had it even worse. She made a doctor's appointment and got medication. Sebastian just sipped Benadryl and plastered himself with calamine lotion.

Both were covered in chigger bites. Sebastian had had a few chigger bites before, but nothing of that magnitude. He counted seventy-two bites on one leg. The misery lasted for more than a week, and it came in waves. At times, the itching subsided, only to flare up full force later. It was sheer torment.

The chigger episode almost changed Sebastian's mind about the property. But a few days later, when Emma informed him the seller had accepted his offer, he decided to go forward with the purchase. However, in the interest of self-defense, since the land (and all its assorted wildlife) would soon be his, Sebastian did some research on chiggers.

The infernal creatures were the immature stage (larvae) of the harvest mite, most active in late spring and early summer. In the later nymph and adult stages, they ate plant material only and posed no problem to humans. But they did get one's attention in the larval stage.

Despite his direst suspicions, Sebastian learned chiggers did not eat blood—they ate liquefied skin cells. The chigger bites its victim and makes a tiny hole. Its saliva hardens the walls of the hole to create a kind of straw. Then the saliva (which later causes the intense itching) liquefies the skin cells and—*slurp!*—the little beast sucks it up through the straw. The itching, as Sebastian knew, occurred several hours after the bite.

What a modus operandi. The insidious creatures were invisible; they did their damage and departed while the victim remained completely clueless. If the US military incorporated those tactics, America would win all wars with no casualties.

At the closing in July, fully healed of all his bites, Sebastian met the seller, an Episcopal priest. Father Jack Inglewood told him he had blessed the land, which pleased Sebastian greatly. He asked the priest about the mineral rights he would own once the sale was final.

"Oh, the company sent checks regularly, but I never cashed them. I just didn't feel right about it somehow."

While Sebastian tried to figure out what was morally reprehensible about mineral rights, the priest made another equally puzzling remark. Fr. Jack had used the property as an occasional getaway, so he had kept a small trailer there. "You've heard of the TV show *The High Chaparral*," he said. "Well, I called my place The Low Chaparral."

The trailer had long since been removed, but Sebastian remembered its site was at the lowest point of the property near the pond. *Why there, when the obvious site for a house was the highest point?* He shrugged it off. Episcopal priests were known for their eccentricities.

Two weeks after the closing, heavily armed with bug spray, Sebastian went out to the lot to see the work Edgar Rhodes had done. Edgar had spared the big trees and completely cleared the area around the pond. Sebastian was delighted with the results. Although the land had a raw, scraped look, its rolling contour had emerged out of the once-faceless woods, and the pond, now clearly visible and sparkling in the sun, had become its centerpiece.

"So you're movin' out here from Houston?" Edgar asked.

"Eventually."

"What made you decide to move so far out in the country?"

Sebastian gave his stock answer, the partial truth he told anyone who asked, "I wanted to be a little closer to my work at Omega U."

"Nice piece of property," Edgar said. A slim man with a weathered face and intelligent brown eyes, he wore a T-shirt, overalls, and heavy work boots. He leaned on the bulldozer and removed his cowboy hat, revealing dark hair plastered to his skull with sweat. "How big did you say it was?"

"Two and a half acres."

"Hmmph." He wiped his brow. "Man, it's a big two and a half

acres."

Sebastian puffed out his chest in pride. After Edgar left, he stood at the highest point, where his house would one day stand, to survey his little kingdom. He congratulated himself; T. Sebastian Morrow was now the landowner of a *big* two and a half acres.

As a musician, Sebastian had spent his life in the city, the heart of civilization, home to opera houses, theaters, concert halls, cathedrals, and universities. From the age of seventeen, when he entered the conservatory, and for almost forty years thereafter, he had thrived in a metropolitan setting. But the dawn of the twenty-first century began with an ominous portent—the attack on America's greatest city, New York. Appalled, and yet transfixed, he had watched the buildings of the World Trade Center burn and collapse. In a matter of minutes, the illusion of America's security lay shattered and burning, a smoldering field of debris.

It changed everything. It forced Sebastian to reassess the world and his place in it. He watched as restless nations engaged in unending wars, and the earth itself seemed increasingly uneasy with frequent volcanic eruptions, large earthquakes, and violent, erratic weather. On the spiritual plane, he observed the rapid descent of American culture into hedonism, coarseness, and incivility. The land of his youth had become almost unrecognizable.

He wished, if it were possible, to reverse direction, to call America back from what seemed to be the edge of a precipice. Of course, that would be a monumental task for anyone, whether statesman or saint. He was neither. And sadly, he had little expectation of help or true leadership from either government or religion. It depressed him to think of the great, spineless worms who supposedly represented the people in Congress. Most of them were self-serving politicians of the worst sort, worshipers of power and money. They pledged allegiance to their pockets, not the United States of America.

On the other hand, modern-day saints like Padre Pio, who had borne the stigmata, and Mother Teresa, the humble servant of the poor, transformed hearts and minds by faith and the power of their special gifts. He admired them, but their noble work did not deflect the downward trend of the twenty-first century. Still, he did have one thing in common with them: in this most secular age he was, though not the most resolute believer, a practicing Catholic.

Sebastian ultimately decided if he could not change things, he could at least remove himself from a risky urban environment to a peaceful rural one. If disaster struck again, he did not want to face the ensuing chaos in a crowded metropolis—a rationale he divulged to absolutely no one. He made the decision to pluck himself up from Houston, his home for almost thirty years, and relocate to the hills north and west of the city, eager to start life as a country boy.

In hindsight, he might as well have parachuted blindfolded and naked into the wilderness. It was a whole new world, and he was completely unprepared.

2008

CHAPTER 1
A NIGHT AT THE OPERA

The earth is home to many peculiar creatures. Some of the strangest are nocturnal (often fur-bearing), who, in their season, exhibit extreme behaviors in rapid succession (generally in forty-five minutes or less): screaming, howling, sighing, whistling, weeping. They dwell not in forests or on lonely mountains, but primarily in cities. They are, of course, sports fans and opera lovers. Their focus may differ, but their actions are often indistinguishable. They are passionate (sometimes to the point of obsession), knowledgeable, and equally vociferous in approval or disapproval.

Most people are familiar with sports, having participated in one type or another growing up. But far fewer are acquainted with opera, and many do not understand its attraction, because they think it unrealistic. On the face of it, they are correct. Opera is life condensed (of necessity) and telescoped into art. If the plots seem implausible, they are redeemed and transcended time and again by the power of music—and therein lies the allure.

The opera audience rides on the burning intensity of the mezzo's darkly gorgeous, impassioned singing; they know triumph in the tenor's ringing high notes, and they rage with the baritone who thunders across the boards; they grieve with the soprano whose exquisite *pianissimo* shimmers and floats in heart-stopping beauty. Despite its flaws, what this contrived art reveals in its sublime moments is the ultimate reality, the very essence of life.

In the heightened, theatrical atmosphere of the opera house, passions are not only confined to the stage. In the sold-out hall, there are as many private dramas as there are people. All those who enter the house carry with them their own unfolding destinies, with outcomes yet unknown. They sit and watch, but on occasion, they too, for good or ill, may enter into the story.

❦

Leo de Graaf had a hard choice to make: he could be amorous or protective, but due to a severe lack of funds, he could not be both. His *amour*—well, actually, his hoped-for *amour*—was the violinist Stephanie Curtis. He had bought tickets for Opera D'Argento's April production of *Tosca* early in February, intending to invite her. Although he knew he hadn't yet registered as a blip on her radar, he didn't lack confidence; he already thought of her as his darling girl. Her innate thoughtfulness and kindness attracted him more powerfully than her auburn-haired, hazel-eyed charm. Like springtime, she was all bright greens and yellows.

His decision came at the end of March, when he chose duty over passion. The moment he discovered Lucas Hlavicek would be in town the weekend of the opera, he regretfully laid ardor aside and changed his plans. With his protective instincts on high alert, he invited his mother to *Tosca* instead. He intended to shield her from

Lucas, but he had to be circumspect. She didn't realize the danger, and if he wasn't careful, he would alienate her. Ideally, he would have bought her an extra ticket, so Stephanie could come as well, but he was a college student with a part-time job; penury was his lot. Two tickets were all he could afford.

On opening night, Silvie and Leo de Graaf found their seats in the center of the single balcony. Leo was delighted and secretly relieved she had come. He had preempted Lucas and asked her to the opera two weeks in advance, but she still could have canceled and gone out with the man. Leo tried not to think about him—he was murky-green and brown, precisely the color of slime. Not to be trusted, no matter how rich or charming.

Two years after his father's death, he still felt protective of his mother and responsible for her. He knew she sensed his disapproval of her new beau and thought his attitude childish and selfish. Leo did not defend himself. He rarely explained his motives to anyone, since no one would believe him if he had. He thought it natural for his mother to find a good man and eventually remarry, but he was dead certain that man should not be Lucas Hlavicek.

A far more successful and dynamic man than Leo's father Edward, Lucas had charmed and impressed Silvie. And by all appearances he was industrious, generous, and community-minded. But Leo did not fool easily. From the first, he had seen through Lucas' public persona to read the deceit hidden at the very core of the man.

Thankfully, Lucas' business required him to travel often and drew him away for days and sometimes weeks at a time. Consequently, their "romance" (the word made Leo recoil) had so far (and by virtue of his own delaying tactics) proceeded slowly.

"What a charming, intimate theater," Silvie said. "Even here in the balcony, we're really close to the stage. It reminds me of a European opera house."

Leo agreed. "Houston Grand Opera could tuck this entire hall into one corner of their building. This is David to their Goliath."

Frankau Hall gradually filled with people while the orchestra musicians warmed up in cheerful, dissonant chaos. The hall, which sat four hundred, was a former Lutheran church with large stained glass windows. With comfortable red theater seats in place of the pews, the building made a graceful transition to an intimate theater. The wide-planked hardwood floor sloped down to a raised stage with a pocket-sized space to its left for the orchestra. Theater lighting apparatus festooned the lofty ceiling, and high on the walls flanking the stage hung two large computer monitors for surtitles. Constructed in 1927, before the advent of microphones, the hall had excellent acoustics.

"The last time I saw *Tosca var på Operan i Stockholm*," Silvie said, lapsing into her native tongue without even realizing it. "*Jag var bara tjugo år. Ett år äldre än du är nu.*"

Tjugo år. It was not difficult for Leo to imagine his mother at twenty. She was a beautiful woman whose forty-seven years sat lightly on her. He thought she looked about thirty. In fact, there had been times when people had mistaken her for his older sister. They bore a strong resemblance to each other with their flaxen hair and blue-violet eyes, their short, straight noses, and full lips.

"I've never seen it before. Do you know the story?"

"*Ja*, it's an opera about an opera singer—Floria Tosca." She smiled. "Her lover, Cavaradossi, is an artist who illegally shelters a political prisoner. The villain is Scarpia, chief of the Roman secret police, who wants to have Tosca for himself. He arrests Cavaradossi, and it goes downhill from there. There's a high death toll, so be prepared, Leo." She made a gesture that took in the whole theater. "Frankau Hall is perfect for it, because the opera begins in a church where the escaped prisoner comes to hide while Cavaradossi is painting a portrait of Mary Magdalene. Tonight, the stage church is enclosed within a real one." She glanced at the walls. "But honestly, I think they should put black drapes over those stained glass windows. Then it would seem more like a theater."

He knew the remark was prompted by his mother's secular leanings. He emphatically disagreed, but he kept his opinion to himself. "Speaking of church reminds me: Mr. Mortensson thinks I should enter a major organ competition. I'll have to make a recording and submit it in June of next year. I'm the only sophomore he's ever recommended for such an important competition."

She clapped her hands together. "Wonderful, Leo!" Her delighted smile pleased him immensely. Rosy pink and blue, his mother. The gray had almost faded away. "But what does that have to do with church?"

"Oh—the finals will be held at a cathedral in Dallas in October of 2009."

"*Spännande! Jag är väldigt stolt över dig.*"

It *was* exciting, and he intended to do his absolute best to keep her very proud of him, even if he had a lot of new repertoire to learn and hours and hours of work ahead of him. "The prize for first place is $5,000, and a concert tour. And the winner will get management."

"That would launch your playing career, wouldn't it?"

"*Absolut, om jag vinner.*"

Silvie hoped he would win, but she had mixed feelings about success so early in life. Leo would be twenty in September of next year, very young to begin a concert career. Such a life sounded glamorous, but she imagined it could be very lonely to travel all the time and live in hotels. "Well, let's not get too far ahead. You have to pass the recorded round first."

"True." He pointed to the musicians warming up on the floor beside the stage. "It's nice they aren't hidden in a pit," Leo said. "Only twenty-eight players."

"They've tailored the orchestra to the hall," Silvie observed. "I don't think they could fit one more player into that cramped space." She noticed the musicians had a relaxed dress code—no tuxes, ties, or formal gowns. In fact, no one wore formal attire. Audience members dressed in business casual clothes, and food and drink were allowed in the theater. Making themselves at home, the couple seated beside her ate cookies and sipped coffee from paper cups. She rather liked the casual atmosphere.

Her glance returned to the orchestra. She had a profile view of the concertmaster, and a very handsome profile it was. His wavy black hair had touches of silver, and a lock of it fell over an angular face with strong, high cheekbones and a prominent nose. Broad-shouldered and narrow-waisted, he played with great intensity; his large hands made his violin look small.

A thin, boyish young woman dressed in black and wearing a headset walked up to the concertmaster. He immediately stood and greeted her with a warm smile, towering over her. After their brief conversation, he sat down again. Something about him held Silvie's attention. In the midst of the orchestra's cacophony, the flurry of conversations, and the movement of people being seated near him, he seemed to be an island of calm, a still point in all the commotion.

While his mother observed the activity in the hall and browsed through the program, Leo closed his eyes and breathed deeply and slowly, sensing the old church's atmosphere, the life that had been lived in it, imprinted on the very walls. He focused on his breath in practiced concentration. As the sounds around him receded, he sensed a layer of protection still hovering in the space like a sheltering mantle, present but invisible. In its covering and peace, he felt his muscles relax.

After a while, he opened his eyes and observed the four stained glass windows, two on each side. On the left, Adam and Eve clutched fig leaves in shame to hide their nakedness, as they were cast out of the Garden of Eden. The window beside it depicted the angel Gabriel's announcement to Mary. *You shall bear a Son.* On the opposite wall he saw her Son at the midpoint of his ministry, placing His hands on the eyes of a blind man to restore his sight. The final window showed another garden: Gethsemane, where the Lord knelt in agony and intense prayer on the eve of His crucifixion.

It was a long and perilous journey from the Fall of Man to mankind's hard-won redemption. Leo knew his mother wanted the images covered because they made her uneasy, but to him, they were a deep comfort.

He checked his watch—7:35, time for the show to begin. It seemed a little warm in the balcony, maybe because there were so many people. Leo glanced around and couldn't see a single empty seat; the hall appeared to be sold out. The house lights dimmed, conversations hushed, and the concertmaster stood while the orchestra tuned.

As he gazed down at the musicians, Leo suddenly straightened his back, startled.

"There's an angel in the house." The words slipped out before he could stop them.

Silvie smiled wryly. "*Ja, precis—han heter Gabriel.*" She pointed to the Annunciation window and then fanned herself with the program.

Leo had no idea if it was Gabriel or not, but he kept his eyes riveted on the tall, shining being who stood beside the concertmaster. As the tuning faded away, for just an instant, the angel turned his gaze on Leo. The glance pierced him and altered his world with the instantaneous imperative of a *fiat lux*. At once, Leo knew there would be an entwining of his destiny with that of the man standing beside the angel. How or why, he did not know, but with an unshakable certainty at his very core, he knew it would come to pass.

Leo drew in his breath, wondering what it all meant. At the same moment, a brilliant spotlight (though dimmer than the angel's visage) split the darkness of the hall and illuminated the conductor as he strode in. The orchestra musicians stood, and the audience erupted into applause. The vision disappeared as quickly as it had come.

Squinting in the dim light, he quickly checked the program for the list of musicians. *Concertmaster, T. Sebastian Morrow.* As he read it, the name seemed to engrave itself on his heart.

He glanced at his mother as she applauded and saw her lovely smile of anticipation. He wanted to tell her what he had just experienced, but he knew her skepticism all too well. She wouldn't want to hear it, and she certainly wouldn't believe it. So, as he had with similar experiences throughout his life, he kept it to himself. With practiced skill, as though he handled a glowing, mysterious jewel, he placed the vision in the innermost vault of his mind, the private chamber where he kept his true treasures. Only after he mentally locked the door was he able to concentrate on the evening at hand.

He drew a deep breath and focused on the things he had to be thankful for. His mother had consented to come with him; they were about to see a marvelous Puccini opera, and lying Lucas was nowhere to be found.

CHAPTER 2

RISKY BUSINESS

In performance, at full throttle, an opera is more complex than an engine, and it has more moving parts. Unlike an engine's cylinders and pistons, firing mechanically, an opera runs on human energy, which is unfortunately flawed, prone to variance, and therefore not entirely reliable. This creates a pervasive, elastic tension. The coming together of singers, orchestra, lighting, and staging is kinetic, fluid, and changes subtly from night to night, all the parts being responsive to each other and to the prevailing communal energy. As veteran musicians can affirm, an opera performance is akin to a living, breathing organism, and on some nights, it's a beast.

Sebastian hoped this would not be one of them.

It was Opera D'Argento's opening night of *Tosca*, and the small theater crackled with the energy and electricity of first-night nerves and anticipation. Sebastian took his violin out of the case, quickly tuned it, and stowed his case on the floor beside his chair. As he warmed up, it was easy to feel the exuberance of the audience; the first row of seats was only an arm's length away. He heard bits of animated conversations, bursts of laughter, and the sounds of people moving around the theater and settling in for the performance.

He was as keyed up as the audience, partly due to the fact that the everlasting money crises of a small opera company resulted in too few orchestra rehearsals. That plus the presence of critics lent a real edge to the performance. But this night, April 17, 2008, he had his own extra-musical reasons for excitement. All this ran through his head as he practiced a few of the thorniest passages in his part.

When Jessica, the stage manager, approached from the back of the house down the near aisle, he stopped playing and glanced at the clock on the balcony wall. It was only 7:15. He stood to greet her. "Sebastian, we're going to hold for five minutes," she said. "The house is sold out, but there are some stragglers. There was a major accident on the West Loop, which may delay some ticket holders. We'll dim the lights at 7:35 and you can tune then. Have a good show."

"Thanks, Jessica." He glanced at the orchestra and counted heads. He caught the eye of his university colleague, Miles Greenfield the flutist, who gave him a cheerful wave. Only three people missing. The strings, harp, woodwinds, horns, and percussionists were all present; only the trumpets and trombone chairs sat empty. Brass players, typically nonchalant, usually glided in with five minutes left to go.

He sat down and felt beads of perspiration spring out on his brow. From fifteen years' experience as concertmaster in this hall, he knew it would only get hotter as the night went on, due in part to the temperamental air conditioning system which blustered and blew like a diva and occasionally tanked altogether. Thankfully, the twin tenets of the orchestra dress code were comfort and survival. Sebastian wore a black short-sleeved, open-collar shirt with black slacks.

He tucked his violin under his arm and listened to the house, abuzz with conversation and laughter. Despite its small stage and lack of a pit, he loved the little theatre, so intimate and beautiful.

Nice that those pesky protestants had had the good sense to invest in stained glass windows. It made a Catholic like him feel at home. Though they said not a word, the beautiful images told the story of a Creator and his creation to an increasingly secular world.

When the house lights dimmed, Sebastian stood and nodded to the oboist, who gave the A. As soon as the sounds of tuning strings died away, he sat down, and Peter Storgis, bathed in a brilliant spotlight, charged down the nearest aisle. As was customary, the orchestra stood. Storgis stepped onto the podium and shook Sebastian's hand. The conductor acknowledged the exuberant applause with a half-bow, and then turned to the musicians, who took their seats. He waited until the hall settled into an expectant silence, and then he lifted his baton to give the first downbeat of Puccini's *Tosca*. They were in for quite a ride.

Somehow, despite the dearth of rehearsals, everything clicked that night at Opera D'Argento. The excellent singers rose to the occasion; the lively, heat-tolerant audience responded, and Storgis, a dynamic conductor, led with unstoppable energy. The scaled-down orchestra ratcheted up its intensity to a new level, practically seething with passion.

Sebastian loved the music, but the story was one of jealousy, cruelty, and betrayal. In Act II, Scarpia has imprisoned and tortured Tosca's lover Cavaradossi for harboring a political prisoner. Scarpia promises to spare Cavaradossi's life if Tosca gives herself to him. In response, she sings the exquisite aria "*Vissi d'arte*." She has dedicated her whole life to art and to love, and she has prayed in true faith. "Why, O Lord," she asks, "do you reward me with grief and misfortune?"

Then Scarpia tells her Cavaradossi must be executed, but if she submits to him, he will stage a mock execution. She agrees, but when Scarpia approaches to take her, Tosca draws out a knife and kills him.

In Act III, Scarpia's malice betrays Tosca even after his death. To Sebastian, the sweet beginning to the third act, with solo horns, then woodwinds, and a shepherd boy's song, made the ending even more cruel. What Tosca believes is the mock execution of her lover takes place, but unbeknownst to her, Scarpia previously ordered the firing squad to use real bullets, and Cavaradossi dies. Wild with grief, she commits suicide to escape capture for Scarpia's murder. She cries out, "*O Scarpia, avanti a Dio!*" ("O Scarpia, we meet before God!"), and hurls herself down from a parapet. The brief play-out was a burst of sound, full orchestra, then curtain.

During the ensuing thunderous applause, Sebastian breathed a sigh of relief. His back ached, and his bow arm felt heavy. The lights came back on, and the cast, beginning with the lesser roles, took their bows. Expectation rose until finally, as happens frequently in the theatre, the heroine magically reappeared. The soprano beamed and curtsied as whistles, shouts, and calls of *Brava!* shook the house. Sebastian wiped his brow and waited for the conductor's acknowledgement to lead the orchestra's bow. He deemed it a good omen that the performance had gone so well.

Fifteen minutes later, as his orchestra colleagues departed to their favorite bars for post-show Chardonnay and Shiner Bocks, Sebastian headed toward the freeway with a lot on his mind. This was the night it was going to happen.

He drove onto Interstate 10 and beheld not the worst traffic jam of his life, but the most memorable. It was a cool spring night, around 10:45 p.m. Traffic jams in Houston are like hay fever in spring—the congestion is frequent, irritating, and lingering. They often occur during rush hour or in one of the blinding downpours typical of the city. But it was a clear night and well past the time for heavy traffic when the five westbound lanes of Interstate 10, opposite from Sebastian, backed up just a few miles west of downtown.

As he drove on the free-flowing eastbound side, he had a strong hunch about what had caused the traffic jam. He glanced back and saw precisely what he suspected. A trailer truck, escorted by two police cars with flashing lights, slowly labored down the freeway bearing an oversized load.

He smiled. "Well, thar she blows!"

Sebastian offered a silent apology to his fellow Houstonians, who no doubt fumed and cursed in frustration as they crawled along behind the truck. The huge load was his latest purchase, an eighty-eight-year-old Craftsman cottage removed from its site, not two miles away.

As he drove east, back to the barrio, his house rode west on its ninety-mile journey to the plot of undeveloped land he owned in hilly, picturesque Helprin County. He prayed it wouldn't fall off the truck. It was the largest purchase he had ever made and the biggest risk he had ever taken in his life. He tried to relax, but if the steering wheel had been a snake, the force of his grip would have crushed the life out of it.

CHAPTER 3

AN UPSET STOMACH

The reason a musician takes up a particular instrument in childhood may seem to be happenstance, but there are no accidents. Some think that over the years, the instruments musicians play shape their personalities, but from long observation, Sebastian concluded that in some mysterious way, children choose instruments that actually correspond to their natures.

Low brass players tend to be large people, relaxed, nonchalant, easy-going. Opinionated trumpet players think themselves strong leaders, when the truth is, they're simply bossy people who adore loud music. Never cross oboists and bassoonists—they are touchy, and they come armed with thousand-dollar knives. They alternate between tedium, in the hours they whittle away at their reeds, and terror in performance, when their success or failure is determined by the effect of the prevailing temperature and humidity on the quirks and vagaries of two pieces of unreliable cane. Introverted horn players have excellent ears and particularly virtuosic lips; they are rumored to be amazing kissers. Those in the hot-seats, who face the greatest technical demands, play high-pitched instruments: flutists and violinists. Euphemistically labeled high-strung, they are in fact nervous wrecks.

Sebastian belonged to the latter category. His tension translated itself into neck and back aches, and an easily upset digestive system. Tired as he was after the opening night performance of *Tosca*, he slept badly. He had played well, but his anxiety about the transport of the house kept him awake. The next night was no better, even though Murphy the house-mover called him on Friday to tell him the house had arrived intact at two o'clock in the morning. They had left it on the truck overnight and would unload it onto the site that day.

He couldn't go out to his property because of the Friday night performance of *Tosca*, but he had Saturday off. That morning, he ate a late breakfast and drove out to see his house. On the drive, he pictured the two-bedroom cottage set at the highest point on his sloping two and a half acres. The western windows would have a view of the pond, while the sunroom overlooked the front yard. Sebastian loved the oak floors, the crown molding, and the many windows. He could hardly wait to see it.

Ninety minutes later, with a quickening pulse, he drove down unpaved Vogel Lane. Trees obscured his view until the moment he turned into the yard.

Holy Mary, Mother of God. Stunned by the scene before him, his mouth dropped open. First, a large swathe of the property was covered in bluebonnets, which he had not expected. He had never seen the land in springtime before, and the flowers delighted him. But the trailer truck had gouged huge, ugly ruts through the blooms, and the moving crew had cut down an oak tree to reach the prepared site. Secondly, it was obvious that the word *intact* meant one thing to Murphy and something entirely different to him. The house had been beheaded and butchered like a lamb. They had sawed it into two parts, and the roof was missing.

Intact? Really?

Sebastian knew they had to cut it in order to travel under the overpasses between Houston and Helprin County, but seeing it in that condition shocked his digestive system. As he got out of the car, Murphy, a stocky man with thinning red hair, hurried over to greet him. "You all right, Sebastian?" he asked. "You look a little pale." He hooked his thumbs under the bib of his blue overalls.

Sebastian laid one hand on his queasy stomach. His breakfast was in the process of deciding which end to exit. He hoped it would stay put, since his destroyed house obviously had no facilities. He didn't want to squat in the bushes.

"Ohhh," he gasped, "I'm fine."

When his eyes met Murphy's, Sebastian read the word *bullshit* there, plain as a headline in the *Houston Chronicle*.

Murphy spat a stream of brown tobacco juice onto the dusty ground, which did nothing to help Sebastian's roiling guts. Then he wiped his mouth with the back of his hand. "Now don't worry about the roof," he said.

The roof—hell, the house was split in two.

"Once we get the sunroom reattached, we're gonna level the house, and then we'll put up the rafters. Your contractor'll dry it in with plywood."

A black pickup truck, moving too fast, pulled into the yard and kicked up a cloud of dust.

There was no driveway.

"Speak of the devil," said Murphy.

Two men climbed out of the cab. Joe Klein, the contractor, wore a white, sweat-stained cowboy hat, a khaki shirt, jeans, and boots. He was Emma's uncle, the ace. His long neck and shifty eyes somehow reminded Sebastian of a weasel. Tall, thin, and sunburned, he spoke with a high-pitched, nasal Texas twang.

"Howdy, Sebastian. This is Fidencio Montemayor, my foreman."

Fidencio's name was longer than he was. A squat, burly guy with black hair tied back in a ponytail, he reached out a thick, tattooed arm and solemnly announced, "You can call me JR."

While Sebastian attempted to figure that one out, Murphy said, "Well, I'll get back to work."

"What time will you guys get the rafters up?" asked Joe.

Murphy spat again. "Five or 5:30."

"Okay, Fidencio and the crew will be back with the plywood then."

Sebastian glanced up at the towering white cumulonimbus clouds gathering from the west. "It looks like we might get a thunderstorm," he pointed out.

"Nah," said Joe, with an air of complete certainty, "Only twenty percent chance today."

He clapped Sebastian on the back with a little more force than necessary. "Ha, don't look so worried, man. We'll get that roof on tonight, no sweat. I been doin' this for twenty years and ain't had a problem yet."

He seemed too hearty and too cocky. Fidencio—JR—stuck his hands in his pockets and stared at the ground.

Joe nudged Sebastian with his elbow. "Hey, man, I wanna show you something." Joe led him over to the house. It sat about four feet above the ground on piers Murphy had set up.

"When was this built?" Joe asked.

"In 1920."

The contractor tapped the narrow wood siding. "Man, this old stuff won't even hold paint. Now if I was you, I'd tear all this siding off, rip it down to the studs, and replace it with Hardiplank."

"All of it?" The entire house was covered in siding.

"Yeah."

He was out of his mind. It would be cheaper to tear it down and start over. *Which I'll do over your dead body, Mr. Klein.*

"Look, Joe, I don't have the funds or the desire to do that. I bought the house because I liked it the way it was, siding and all."

Joe shrugged. "Just sayin' what I'd do if it was mine."

Well, buddy, it ain't. "Let me know how it goes with the plywood," Sebastian said. "I'm looking forward to seeing the metal roof go up." With the former roof of conventional shingles gone, he had decided on silver AP panels that would reflect the Central Texas sunlight and last for decades.

"We'll get to that by the end of next week," Joe said.

Sebastian's gut cramped alarmingly. As there was nothing more he could do at the site, he left them to their business and sped away to his own, at the nearest gas station, where he occupied the men's room for quite some time.

CHAPTER 4
THE KOLACHE KING

On a gray, blustery day in March, he came calling at de Graaf's because of the coffee bar. He wanted the bookshop to agree to sell only his brand of pastries. It surprised Silvie that the founder of Hlavicek's Bakeries would even care about such a small operation as her tiny coffee bar. But of course, he would expect to dominate the local market, since tiny Bullinger, home of the original pastry factory, remained the Kolache King's headquarters.

They sat at a table in the small seating area near the door, and Lucas made Silvie an excellent offer. For her exclusive use of Hlavicek pastries, he agreed to use de Graaf's Bookshop in his television and online marketing. "Quite a quaint place, inside and out," he said, making a sweeping gesture that took in the interior of the historic two-story building. "I'll send a photographer and film crew here next week. The ads ought to send people your way, boost your sales, and increase the tourist traffic in downtown Bullinger."

After they settled on the terms of the contract, she asked him, "Would you like to look around the shop, maybe choose a book or two, Lucas?"

"I don't read books," he replied bluntly, and rose to go. He had dark hair, slicked back neatly on his head, and he smelled faintly of cloves. "No time for it. Besides, I have dyslexia, and reading is always difficult for me. But I like sports." He smiled down at her. "So what sports do you like?"

Silvie could tell he was interested in her by the way he prolonged the conversation. She stood just under six feet, but he was a head taller than she. Though not a handsome man, his sharply creased, expensive clothes, his coiled energy and self-confidence drew one's attention. His high cheekbones, somewhat pitted by acne from his teenage years, framed a long, sharp nose and a jutting chin. There was a blade-like quality about him, an aggressive air. As she regarded him, Shakespeare's words came to mind: *He has a lean and hungry look*. His commanding presence seemed to fill the small space of the coffee bar. "Football is my favorite," she replied.

When his green eyes lit up, she hurried to say, "I mean European football, your soccer."

"Ah-ha. I heard you were Swedish." He chuckled and shook his head. "I like American football—you know, the kind where teams actually score points. What other sports do you like?"

"Well, I like cross-country skiing, hiking, and cycling."

He sighed. "You're a European girl, all right. How about baseball? I've got tickets to the Astros' opening game next weekend. Got my own box in the stadium down in Houston. Why don't you come with me?"

Silvie's eyes widened at the straightforward proposal. If he knew she was Swedish, he had probably done some digging and discovered she was a widow. Easily accomplished, since gossip in tiny Bullinger was just as alive, fecund, and stinging as poison ivy.

When she hesitated, he grinned. "You know it's hopeless to refuse. Baseball season runs for another seven months, and I'll just keep comin' back and askin' until I secure the pleasure of your company. Whaddya say?"

She laughed and succumbed without protest, happy to provide breaking news for the tongue-waggers.

Satisfied, Lucas started for the door. "Well, Silvie, I can tell you right now, I'm gonna have some very jealous buddies at that game."

As she got to know him better during the next few months, Silvie discovered that politics was another of Lucas' strong interests. She told him how she had come to question Sweden's stance on immigration. Compared to America and the rest of Europe, the Scandinavian countries had been a quiet backwater, peaceful and prosperous. Then, in the eighties, Sweden began to accept refugees from the Iran-Iraq war. Some Swedes hated the infusion of Middle-Easterners into the homogeneous blond, blue-eyed population. They saw it as a threat to the country's strong national identity and traditions. The foreigners didn't look kindly on the Swedes either. They settled in low-cost housing enclaves on the outskirts of Stockholm, Malmö, and Gothenburg where the graffiti on the bunker-like buildings proclaimed their point of view: *Utvisa svenskarna!* (Deport the Swedes!)

Back then, Silvie hadn't worried about it. But now, twenty years later, on visiting her homeland, she found the number of immigrants, their crimes, and their refusal to assimilate shocking. The "refugees," mostly young men, seemed more like the soldiers of an invading army. She feared that Sweden, like the UK, and much of Western Europe, was on the verge of committing cultural suicide.

Lucas held the exact opposite view. "Immigrants make a country stronger. They provide a cheap workforce. Where would American employers be without Mexican laborers?"

She later learned that Lucas employed a large number of illegal immigrants. Their fear of discovery made exploitation easy. They worked long hours for little pay, and they dared not complain. When she questioned him about it, he shrugged. "It's just good business, darlin'. To make a profit, you gotta cut costs. And business is about making a profit. It's better they work for a living than burden the system by being on welfare."

He definitely made big profits; he was a wealthy man. He owned a beautiful house in the country outside of Bullinger, set on two hundred acres and the highest elevation in the area. As far as she could tell, he seemed generous with his money. He took her to expensive Houston restaurants and gave extravagant tips. He was also community-minded. He helped finance the restoration of The Arcade, a decaying vaudeville theatre in the historic downtown. The Hlavicek Foundation gave grants to schools and scholarships to area students. Lucas was a financial pillar of St. Michael's, the oldest and most prominent Lutheran church in Bullinger, but he didn't attend on a regular basis.

But neither she nor Edward, her late husband, had been church-go-ers. And, like a true Dutchman, Edward had been tight with his dollars. They seldom ate out, and he rarely spent money on concerts or sporting events. He was a model bookshop owner, a quiet introvert, content with reading nonfiction and taking walks or cycling with her. Lucas' appetite and budget for entertainment were much more flamboyant.

On their first date, Silvie had watched the Astros play the San Diego Padres with some interest, although she knew little about the sport. She had been more curious about Lucas' private box and his well-heeled friends, Texans in their fifties and sixties who had made their fortunes in the oil and gas industry. While the men drank scotch or beer and watched the game, Silvie sat with their wives, Evelyn, Barbara, and Paige, who knew each other well. The women, perfumed, expensively clothed, and well made-up, paid intermittent attention to the game. They ate boiled shrimp with salad and French bread and imbibed what seemed like gallons of cold white wine. As they chattered together, they surreptitiously sized up Silvie, who was at least a decade younger. She noticed a few sidelong glances from the men as well.

For her part, Silvie added little to their conversation about clothes shopping, house renovations, and patron parties at Houston Grand Opera and the Museum of Natural Science. She might have enjoyed the game if Lucas had provided her some explanation, but despite the fact that she was his guest, he paid her scant attention, simply throwing a comment her way ever so often, like a man tossing a treat to his new puppy. Annoyed, she divided her attention three ways. She peered occasionally at the playing field and participated now and again in the wives' conversation while quietly observing Lucas.

He drank scotch on the rocks steadily, but slowly, as he kept up a lively, running commentary on the game with his friends. By the ninth inning, the Astros held a lead of three runs. Silvie noticed Lucas' glad patter dwindled and then ceased altogether. While his friends chuckled and whooped, he seemed anything but jubilant.

She had felt like a conspicuous outsider the whole time, so the game's end came as a relief. On the drive home, she noticed Lucas' mood seemed to darken. To counteract the silence in the car, she prodded him, "Hurray for the Astros! They won 9-6, but you don't seem happy about it."

"Naw, well, their win was my loss. I bet five thousand on the Padres at 3 to 1 odds."

Why the Padres? "Can you explain that? I don't know about betting."

He sighed. "It means I just lost five grand when I could've won fifteen."

She raised her eyebrows—no wonder he seemed irritated. But why he had bet against the Astros? Where was his loyalty to the home team? "Goodness, that's a lot to lose."

He waved a dismissive hand in the air. "It's not the money—it's the principle of the thing. I really like to win." He eyed her suggestively and smiled. "At everything."

The innuendo unnerved her for a moment. She knew where business was concerned, Lucas had a relentless hunger to dominate the market—he wanted Bullinger's businesses, groceries, coffee shops, and restaurants saturated with his products. But if he thought he could dominate her as well, he was mistaken. Looking straight ahead at the road before them, she clenched her teeth and set her jaw—that would never happen.

She had a much more enjoyable time when Lucas took her sailing on Lake Travis in Austin one day in early summer. He rented an eighteen-foot sailboat at the lake. Silvie hoped he knew what he was doing, because she certainly didn't know how to sail. To her relief, he handled the boat skillfully. After they spent two hours skimming over the sparkling water, he dropped anchor and they swam a little. Long-legged and quite fit, Lucas was a good swimmer, and Silvie found herself more than a little attracted to him.

Afterward, they ate an early dinner of fajitas at a popular Mexican restaurant. Silvie drank one margarita, while Lucas had three. He told her about Hlavicek's Bakeries, the business he had built. He smiled. "I have my mother and my grandmother to thank for that. My grandmother emigrated from Czechoslovakia, and she and my mother baked traditional Czech pastries. I grew up loving those pastries, and I learned to bake them myself. After I got a business degree from Texas A&M, I decided to create my own company. I used my family recipes and started small in Bullinger. It's grown into quite a big business, thanks to an excellent product and very effective advertising. You know our slogan, don't you?"

"Everybody knows your slogan: *The only bakeries with authentic Czech pastries!*"

Lucas beamed at her. "Exactly." He finished off his third margarita. "It was really hard work for the first few years, but it's paid off in the end."

As they drove away from the restaurant in his silver Lexus, Lucas checked his handwritten directions.

"Don't you use GPS?" Silvie asked.

"No, I don't trust it. If I have a visual map in my head, I am in control, not some computer." He made a left turn into heavy traffic on a two-lane boulevard. "We have to turn right at the next light."

He pulled into the right lane immediately without checking his blind spot. The car already in the lane jumped the curb to avoid a collision. "Shit!" He slammed on the brakes and stopped abruptly. The older model blue Buick managed to bypass them on the grass and then clanked down heavily into the roadway just ahead. The impact blew out the Buick's front right tire.

As the Buick came to a stop, Silvie said, "Oh my goodness, Lucas, the driver is an old woman. She had amazing reflexes to avoid hitting us!"

As the white-haired woman climbed out of the car to come and talk to Lucas, he glanced in the rearview mirror, saw an opening in the traffic, turned the wheel sharply to the left, and sped away before the woman had time to approach.

"Lucas, stop!" cried Silvie. "She has a flat tire. We should help her."

"Never mind that. If she recognized me, she'd probably try to get a whole lot of money out of me."

"We should help her," Silvie insisted. "She's the reason we didn't have a wreck. If she hadn't reacted so quickly, you could have major damage to your car and all of us could have been injured."

"Well, darlin', as you say, there was no wreck and nobody's hurt. The little old lady will get help—some nice Texan will stop and fix her flat. As for us, we're not leavin' the scene of an accident." He glanced in the rearview mirror and sped up. "We're just leavin'."

Silvie fretted silently in displeasure. *Edward would have got out to see if the woman was all right, and he would have fixed her flat.* Lucas had money, and money had its charms indeed, but Edward's wealth had been kindness, a coin that never tarnished.

CHAPTER 5

OMEGA U

As part of his duties as an associate professor at Omega U, Sebastian taught violin, viola, and directed the orchestra, but his biggest challenge lay in teaching the required music theory courses. All music majors took his classes, which gave him ample time to observe their struggles over two or three years.

There were those who passed through the harrowing journey unscathed, but for a select few, music theory was the gateway to Hell. *Abandon all hope, ye who enter here* might as well have been inscribed above the classroom door. The Music Theory Netherworld included the torments and inscrutable mystery (apparently akin to quantum physics) of writing harmonies and fugues, building and inverting tonal intervals, and deciphering the symbols for lead sheets and figured bass. (No matter how careful and clear Sebastian's explanations, the behavior of chord tones remained as unknowable to some as that of quarks—they moved according to certain rules with all sorts of exceptions and anomalies.) Understanding seemed to elude certain students like a will-o'-the-wisp in the marsh—ever receding the closer they came.

Sheer frustration propelled them into outer darkness where there was a good deal of wailing and gnashing of teeth.

But perhaps their learning problems weren't entirely their fault. In Sebastian's opinion, the real culprit was the current dependence on technology. The notorious iPhone in particular made this last generation almost incapable of logical or critical thinking. Crack cocaine was less addictive than instant answers pulled up on a tiny video screen. With sadness, he observed young people wear out their thumbs, shrink their brains, and rarely experience the pleasure of real live person-to-person conversation.

Accustomed to retrieve information immediately without effort, students baffled by theory could find no instant answers. They couldn't look up solutions on their iPhones; calculators were of no avail, and to read just two scintillating paragraphs in a theory textbook plunged them like Shakespeare's Juliet into a comatose state resembling death.

Sebastian realized students no longer knew how to study. They photographed his written explanations on the classroom whiteboard with their phones (very easy and wholly ineffective) instead of taking notes the old-fashioned way, by hand. Writing had become a lost art. He encouraged his students to manually copy his explanations as part of their study regime, but few did.

Although he made it a rule to be merciful (in order to obtain mercy himself), he couldn't study for them. At exam time, many threw up their hands and took the inevitable F, which Sebastian was obliged to dole out. Of course, there were exceptions, but it seemed to him over the course of his two decades as an instructor that the work ethic and the standard of previous years had shot downhill like a ride on a soaped-up slip-n-slide at a forty-five-degree angle.

The Monday after his house had been moved, Sebastian administered an exam to his Advanced Theory class. While he monitored the test, he thought about his career at Omega. His dismay in teaching theory was offset by his enormous love for conducting the university orchestra and working with the violin and viola students. Well, all save Miss Alicia Borden, a talented girl with as much dedication and diligence as a decapod crustacean. Her violin didn't know how to respond when played—it suffered from instrument dysphoria—convinced it was a hermit crab meant to stay in its borrowed shell.

Originally a Catholic school, Alpha and Omega College had gone broke and been bought by the state in 1951. Renamed Omega University, it was one of thirty-eight state universities in Texas. The Music Department had hired Sebastian full-time when he was a single father, desperate for a job after getting his doctorate. When his euphoria at winning the position faded, and the reality of his situation set in, he had serious second thoughts. He envied his graduate school peers, who all seemed to have better positions at more prestigious colleges, while he labored at a small, rural campus with an 89 percent admission rate. In Sebastian's opinion, the university lived up to its name; it was surely the last place any professional musician would want to work. Even the football team upheld the tradition. In dead last place, they owned the record for the most consecutive losses of any team in their conference.

At the end of the period, he collected all the exams and returned to his studio thinking of losses, which led him to his financial worries. He laid the test papers on his desk, sat down, and put his head in his hands. He had tried to get a low-interest bank loan to buy the house, but although his credit was fine, no bank would take a chance on a house to be moved. It had seemed like serendipity when he got an offer in the mail for a line of credit up to $60,000, to be used however one wanted—no application necessary. The catch was the interest rate: a heart-stopping 29 percent. At the moment the house went up for sale, it had been his only recourse, courtesy of one of America's largest financial institutions, a.k.a. the Bank of Hades: Happy Home of Usury and Grinding Oppression of the Common Man.

Woe is me. His stomach felt unsettled. Like Orpheus, he had descended into the underworld—of major debt. Just thinking about the accumulating interest made the perspiration pop out on his furrowed brow. He did have a recovery plan, though. Now that the house was moved and back on solid ground, he could get a low-interest home equity loan at a Houston bank to pay off the Bank of Hades.

His mobile phone rang, interrupting his thoughts.

"Dr. Morrow, it's JR. Are you comin' out here today? We got a problem."

Wonderful. All he needed was another problem. He could see where this would lead. *Problem* translated to *money*, which equaled *more debt*. He rolled his eyes. "Yes, I'm about to leave work. I should be there in about forty-five minutes."

"Okay, I'll show you when you get here."

The line went dead.

"Thank you, Mr. Laconic," Sebastian muttered to himself. He felt a tightening in his gut and a drop of sweat trickled down his temple.

He hurriedly packed his violin, locked the studio, and hustled out to the parking lot.

When he arrived at the property, the plywood was up on the roof, and they had reattached the sunroom. Now the house did look intact. There it sat, beige with white trim, small but pleasing to the eye. Of course, they had not yet installed the metal roofing he had chosen, but at least the place resembled the house he had bought. What could be the problem? Maybe JR was a worrywart who fretted over minor issues.

Wearing faded jeans and a Dallas Cowboys T-shirt, JR emerged out of the house to greet him.

"It looks good!" Sebastian said.

"Well, we just finished drying in the roof."

"I thought you did that on Saturday."

He shook his head and flicked his ponytail back. "By the time Murphy got the rafters up, the weather turned nasty. We climbed up there anyway and nailed the plywood as fast as we could, but then a really bad thunderstorm came up with lightning and high winds. We couldn't finish. Joe told me to get the crew down. It was dangerous."

"And?"

"We threw some tarps over the open part, but the wind came up, and well, it rained for several hours. The ceiling collapsed."

"In what room?"

"All of them."

His stomach lurched, and he tasted bile in his mouth.

"Come see."

He followed JR into the house. The interior resembled a demolition in progress. The beautiful oak floors were almost hidden beneath the ceiling wreckage—piles of broken, crumbling sheetrock overlaid with sodden, dirty pink fiberglass insulation from the attic. When he looked up, he could see the rafters. He sighed and shook his head, feeling nauseated and completely defeated. "Now what?"

"I can replace the sheetrock and rebuild your ceilings, paint and spackle them. I'm good at that—I can make it look great. We can buy new insulation for the attic. See that pink stuff?" He pushed a piece of wet fiberglass with his toe. "It was old anyway. Just tell Joe if you want to do that."

Well, what the hell else could he do? It might damn well break the bank.

"Where is Joe?" Sebastian had a sudden suspicion he had called off the crew on purpose. The more repairs he did on the house, the more money he made.

"He's working another job north of town."

Cocky Joe—Mr. Twenty-percent-chance-of-rain. "Does he do any of the work?"

"No, I do the work. He deals with the clients and tells me what they want done. Then he buys the lumber and supplies. He'll invoice you. If you wanna talk to him about it, you can call him after six tonight."

"Oh, yes, indeed, I do want to talk to him."

Sebastian took a deep breath. "JR, was it absolutely necessary for you guys to get off the roof and leave it unfinished on Saturday?"

"Yes, sir. It got real dark. I had to use the headlights on my truck so we could see. It was blowin' so hard the rain was comin' in sideways, with bad lightning."

He seemed completely sincere. Sebastian hoped he was telling the truth.

"Okay, JR. What's your phone number, just in case I need to contact you?"

JR told him and Sebastian entered the number into his phone. He had a plan in mind, but first he had to talk to Joe Klein.

CHAPTER 6

THE SEARCH COMMITTEE

Sebastian did have a conversation with his contractor Joe Klein. It was brief: he fired him.

Joe was Emma Gallagher's recommendation, her uncle. That should have warned him about her judgment, not to mention her pedigree. But Joe was a minor problem, a flesh wound, quickly healed. He had no idea that the ramifications of Emma's inexperience and faulty guidance were two strands of a slow-burning fuse soon to ignite a near-fatal explosion.

On Thursday, May first, the day after he fired Joe Klein, the new search committee met at Omega U. The previous department head had departed, taking a substantial amount of unearned funds with him. The administration had skillfully covered up the scandal, but now five committee members had the task of finding a replacement for the fall term. The group was a cross-section of the faculty: Roscoe Boyle, the band director; Philip Washington, the choir director; flute instructor, Miles Greenfield; the pianist, Abbie Goldberg; and Sebastian. Naturally, the band director chaired the committee.

Sebastian had a theory about band directors. He suspected as undergraduates, they minored in music and majored in tyranny. They tended to play brass or percussion instruments, not particularly well, but they were virtuosi when it came to domination. They exerted total control over band members and yearned passionately for total dominion over the entire department, if not the world. Since they were usually the biggest university recruiters, they were paid accordingly. They basked in the unending adulation of alumni and grateful administrators.

In addition to his six-figure salary, Roscoe had something even the department head lacked: a reserved parking place. A rectangular sign with BAND DIRECTOR in large white letters, marked the spot for his BMW convertible.

Recently, however, someone had painted over the N.

Perhaps that explained his scowl. Roscoe, with his out-of-date buzzcut and jutting jaw thrust into the air, sat at the head of the conference room table, looming large with a military air. Abbie sat to his left, a sweet-faced, bespectacled dumpling who nervously drummed her plump, nicotine-stained fingers on the table. Philip Washington, a big-boned black man, with a rich, bass voice and a penchant for bright bow ties, sat on Roscoe's right, humming to himself. The flutist Miles Greenfield, Sebastian's colleague and friend from Opera D'Argento, sat across from him beside Abbie. He was a dapper, ruddy-cheeked Englishman who had studied at the Royal Academy of Music. Luckily for the school and the opera orchestra, he had married an American businesswoman and moved to Houston.

Each committee member had been given a folder of twenty-four résumés and cover letters, which everyone had reviewed prior to the meeting.

"Let me tell you how this works," said Roscoe. No hale and hearty "Good afternoon!" from him. The other faculty on the committee were not anywhere near his pay grade, and none of them numbered among the four assistant band directors and one full-time arranger who comprised his staff, so courtesy was simply not an issue.

"We have to narrow the number down to five," he announced. "From there, we'll choose three finalists. But you realize, we don't have the final say. We recommend the finalists to the dean and the provost, and they make the decision."

Sebastian didn't believe it for an instant. Roscoe, the administration's Golden Boy, ate lunch several times a week with the president, the provost, and the dean. He carried a lot of clout in any decision affecting the department, and everyone knew it.

The group dug in and quickly eliminated the Hail Mary applicants, the poorly qualified ones who applied knowing they had little-to-zero chance for the job. Thereafter, partisan colors flew openly. Roscoe's favorite applicant was a band director he knew from his alma mater, Ole Miss. Abbie favored hiring a pianist who could help with the accompanying in the department. Philip wanted another singer, a soprano from New York, and Miles had his hopes set on an oboist who would complete the woodwind area. Sebastian wanted the lone cellist who had chaired a department at a college in Oklahoma for twenty years.

Ninety minutes later, after some lively arguments, the committee had achieved its goal and narrowed the field down to five. At that point, Roscoe dismissed them. "Good work, everyone. That'll be all for today." As soon as Betsy Bloom, the Administrative Assistant, could set up back-to-back Skype interviews with the five semifinal candidates, the committee would meet again.

As he left the meeting, Sebastian got a call from JR, who was now his contractor. JR and his son had replaced the ceilings and spackled them. They wanted Sebastian to inspect the job. Since he owed JR for the materials and labor, he said he would come and bring his checkbook.

As he drove the thirty miles from the university to his property, Sebastian thought about his new foreman. JR had won Sebastian's trust when he took him up into the attic to show him the shoddy job Murphy's crew had done the day they put up the rafters.

"It's flimsy," JR said. "They just tacked it up and left. I was afraid the roof might fall in, so I shored it up with these 2x6s." He had buttressed the roof on his own initiative, a very good sign. It also meant JR knew what he was doing. He told Sebastian he had worked construction jobs for twenty-seven years, from the age of thirteen. He had loved the work and the money was so good he had dropped out of school. "It was a mistake; I shoulda stayed in school."

"Would you have chosen a different career path?"

"Maybe." He pulled on the bill of his baseball cap. "I like doin' hair."

"Hair?"

"Yeah, you know, cuttin' and stylin' hair."

Sebastian couldn't suppress a smile. *Was he serious?*

He was. "I love the feel of it, you know, smooth and silky." He gently stroked his own black ponytail.

"Did you ever think about trade school or college?"

"Nah, I quit school at sixteen. I thought I was hot stuff, makin' all kinds of money in construction. Big mistake. I got married at eighteen, and now I'm not even forty, and I've got three grandkids."

"Whoa, I got married at twenty-two," Sebastian remarked. "I'm a slow starter compared to you."

JR brought to his mind the medieval lads who served long apprenticeships with established artisans. Many of them later became artists in their own right. JR was a workman who wanted to do a good job and took pride in his work. As a musician, so did Sebastian. That was why, despite their differences in age, background, and education, he felt a kinship and a respect for JR.

Everything he wanted done to the house, JR was able to do. When Sebastian told him he wanted to build a large open deck on the west side of the house and a smaller covered deck on the north side, which faced the road, JR nodded. "No problem, Dr. Morrow."

Sebastian arrived at the house in the late afternoon. JR's red pickup truck was parked in the yard near the fading bluebonnets. Well past their prime, the wildflowers still gave Sebastian pleasure. He knew they would bloom in spring, year after year. His was the only yard on Vogel Lane with a profusion of the violet-blue, white-tipped lupines, one of the most photographed, iconic symbols of Central Texas. There were so many, he could smell their sweet fragrance as he walked to the house.

His foreman met him at the door. Sebastian walked in and glanced around. The floor had been cleared of all the debris and cleaned, and the repaired ceilings gleamed, pristine. "It looks brand new, JR." He couldn't see any flaws. They toured all the rooms and returned to the living room. He admired the skill it took to replace all the ruined sheetrock, spackle it, and paint it. It was impossible to tell that the ceilings had ever been damaged.

"Now the ceilings are done, I'll put all new insulation in the attic," JR said. "See? It's gonna be better than before."

"True. What do I owe you for the ceilings?" JR showed him the invoices for material and the hourly labor. He groaned inwardly, but he wrote the check to Fidencio Montemayor.

As he handed him the check, Sebastian decided to satisfy his curiosity. "I have to ask, Mr. Montemayor, why do you go by JR? Does it mean *Junior*?"

JR gave a sheepish grin. "Nah, it's 'cause I watched the TV show *Dallas,* and I liked the main character JR Ewing a lot."

Sebastian had only seen one or two episodes, but he knew JR Ewing was a hard-dealing, conniving character. It surprised him that

JR admired such a person. What a quirky guy.

JR glanced at the check and counterpunched, "So what does the *T* in T. Sebastian Morrow stand for?"

"Well, my mother loved dinosaurs, so she named me Tyrannosaurus."

JR's mouth fell open, but then his eyes narrowed. "No, she didn't."

"All right, I'm named after one of the presidents of the United States."

"Which one?"

"Well, one that begins with a T of course." Sebastian grinned. "I'm a teacher—I'm going to make you do some research."

"First name or last name?"

"Could be either."

JR pointed to the name on the check. "Okay, I'm gonna figure this out."

Sebastian turned his attention back to the interior. The materials and labor cost a bundle, but the improvements to the house were worth it. Unfortunately, the clean white ceilings made the drab walls look dingy. "Look at those walls, JR. Why would anyone want to live surrounded by this wretched shit-brown?"

"*Wretched.*" The word made JR laugh. "Especially in a dining room."

"Turns your stomach, doesn't it? If I don't brighten it up, I can't live here."

"You pick out the colors and I'll paint."

"What will that cost?"

After a little thought, JR gave Sebastian a reasonable estimate. Sebastian breathed a sigh of relief that he still had room on his credit cards. He himself could paint, but with so little free time between his teaching job and the opera, it would take him months to finish the interior. And, honestly, JR would do a much better job. "All right, when do you need to know the colors?"

"No hurry—think about it. I'm gonna build the decks first."

JR tapped the wall and glanced around the room. "This house is so well made. Good materials and good workmanship." He nodded his head in approval. "You got gold here, Dr. Morrow."

Sebastian met his dark brown eyes and smiled. He thought so, too.

CHAPTER 7

THE WEDDING

Sebastian Morrow kept a mental catalogue of great wedding failures. He had forgotten 90 percent of the ceremonies he had played in his career, simply because they went according to plan. Those he remembered, the real screw-ups, often took place outdoors. He fondly recalled the Italian wedding on top of a high-rise in Maryland, a really bad idea. The building happened to be in the flight path for Dulles International Airport. The howling gale-force winds and the minute-by-minute roar of low-flying passenger planes made the wedding vows and the music practically inaudible. To add insult to injury, he got robbed in the middle of the ceremony. The wind ripped the music right off his quivering wire stand. As he tried to continue from memory, he watched the first violin part to a Mozart quartet sail up and flap away to the east. He sometimes wondered if it still transited the globe, borne on high by the jet stream.

Two weeks before Christmas one year, a couple got married in a gazebo in Houston's Hermann Park. Yuletide in Houston can be fairly warm, but on this particular day, an arctic front descended on the city. The wind and the damp, piercing cold forced Sebastian to wear a cap with earflaps, a heavy coat over his suit, and gloves with the fingers cut off. The gloves looked ridiculous, but without them his hands grew stiff. The bride wore a bare-backed gown despite the weather. Sebastian could read her mind; she had spent a fortune on the darned dress, and by golly, she was going to wear it. For the length of the ceremony, thirty interminable minutes, she shook like a woman in the throes of her own personal earthquake.

The wedding he was most ashamed of took place in a Houston shop that sold occult books and New Age paraphernalia, a Wiccan ceremony. He let his single-father financial woes override his misgivings, and he found himself in a back room of the shop, standing beside a keyboard player in a chalk circle someone had drawn on the floor.

"Stay in the circle, and you'll be safe," the presiding witch solemnly assured him. He bit his lip to keep from contradicting her. At the time, he thought she was the most deluded person he'd ever met. What utter crap: Demons would manifest (supposedly), and a stupid circle would protect him? These people didn't know what dangers they were summoning. Unfortunately, Sebastian did. Before the ceremony began, he silently prayed the Lord would enclose him in a seal of protection. All the while he played, a persistent voice in his head screamed: *Leave! You should leave! You know you shouldn't be doing this.*

Something equally unforgettable occurred at the wedding Sebastian played in southwest Houston the weekend after the search committee met. He did recount some of it to his colleagues later on, but one part of the experience he never spoke of to anyone, ever.

When he exited the South Loop just after four o'clock, Sebastian realized something was wrong with the CRV's power steering. In order to turn the wheel, he had to use great force, as though he was manually turning the tires. He groaned due to the physical effort and his sudden apprehensions. First of all, he didn't know if he could make it to the wedding, and secondly, another car repair meant another blasted expense, the result of owning a ten-year-old Honda with close to 150,000 miles on it.

The Baptist church was not far from the freeway exit, but it was extremely difficult to steer the car, and he was barely able to pull into the parking lot. Relieved he finally got the car parked, he turned off the ignition and rested his forehead on the steering wheel. He certainly couldn't drive all the way home in traffic without power steering. He got out, opened the hood, and peered at the engine, but he couldn't see anything obviously wrong. He didn't poke around because he had to keep his hands and his tux clean. He slammed the hood shut and got his violin out of the car. There was nothing he could do at the moment, except go in and play the gig. He would deal with the car problem afterward. The wedding would end by 6:00 or so, but unfortunately, no repair shops would be open that late on a Saturday.

It was Philip Washington's church, and on his recommendation, Ron Chapman, the organist, had hired Sebastian and two other string players, a violist and cellist, for the young black couple's wedding. The large Baptist church was almost full when Sebastian entered. He walked up the aisle to the raised dais in front where the organ console was centered. Chairs and music stands had been set up on the right side for the string trio. He greeted the cellist and violist, a married couple, Mischa and Sally Orlov. Sebastian had worked with them a few times previously. Philip, Sebastian's colleague from Omega, was there to sing "The Lord's Prayer." Ron, the organist, and Susan, the wedding coordinator, came over and discussed the order of music. There was no rehearsal, just a brief talk-through.

The musicians began on time. After twenty minutes of prelude, the wedding was supposed to begin at 5:00, but at that time, Susan the coordinator, who stood at the back of the church, frantically signaled them to keep playing prelude music. Apparently, the bride wasn't ready . . . and wasn't ready. And wasn't ready. The twenty-minute prelude stretched to fifty minutes. Sebastian's back ached from the continuous playing. Finally, they got the go-ahead hand signal from Susan, and they launched into the music for parents, the bridesmaids, and Miss Ultra Tardy, the bride.

The musicians got a rest when the actual ceremony began. Sebastian laid the violin and bow in his lap and let both arms hang down to let the blood flow back into his fingers. He discreetly rolled his shoulders and stretched his back. As he rested, he observed the young couple, the pastor, and the predominantly black congregation. Of the dozen or so Caucasians and Hispanics scattered throughout the congregation, it was particularly hard to miss a flaxen-haired young man who sat on the groom's side. Sebastian's rest ended after Philip and Ron performed "The Lord's Prayer." The pastor pronounced the couple husband and wife, and the musicians played the recessional. They finished half an hour late, at 6:30.

As he paid the musicians, Ron apologized. Sebastian nodded his thanks, pocketed the check and hurriedly packed up his violin, impatient to go take care of his car. He strode quickly out of the church and wove his way through the crowd of people standing just outside the double doors. As he walked toward the parking lot, he heard someone behind him calling, "Mr. Morrow, Mr. Morrow!"

He stopped and turned. The flaxen-haired boy waved at him and walked rapidly to close the distance between them. The boy must have read his name in the program; Sebastian had never met him before. He might have been college age, tall and slender, dressed in navy slacks and a pale yellow shirt. The wind ruffled his longish hair and his blue tie flapped in the breeze as he hurried to catch up with Sebastian. "There was something so magnificent . . ."

Well, that was overkill. Adequate, maybe, but nothing special.

The young man read his thoughts. "Oh, not the music. Well, I mean it was fine, but I had to speak to you before you left. It's you."

"Me?"

"Yes, there's a light around you that is so magnificent." He spread his long arms out and shook his head with an expression that combined bafflement with wonder.

Was this a joke? Sebastian frowned and searched the boy's eyes intently. They were an unusual sapphire blue, with hints of violet, and they radiated sincerity. He was entirely serious. Sebastian tried to fathom what he meant.

"Every now and then I see a person like you, but not very often. I can see there's some kind of burden on you. You're bearing a lot right now. But you're surrounded by peace. You are very special to God."

Sebastian raised his eyebrows. "I am?"

He nodded emphatically. "Yes, you are." He smiled in a kindly way. "And you don't even know it."

The boy's certainty and the matter-of-fact way he made his astonishing pronouncements left Sebastian at a loss for words. He gazed at the young man in disbelief. Three possibilities came to mind: He was nuts; he was the reincarnation of the Delphic oracle; or he was telling the truth.

"And I can assure you, Mr. Morrow, it's going to be all right. Don't worry. God is in control, and it's going to be all right."

The kid wasn't frothing at the mouth, and he seemed completely sensible. How had he sensed Sebastian's inner anxieties? Was his financial angst over the house as apparent as sunburn? They walked together into the busy parking lot, dodging cars heading for the exit. When they reached Sebastian's car, the boy turned to leave. "I'm a friend of the groom, and I've gotta catch my ride to the reception. I just had to tell you before I left."

Before Sebastian could say a word, the boy sprinted off toward the other end of the parking lot, all elbows and knees, blond hair flying in the wind.

Sebastian returned to the problem at hand. He took out his mobile phone and called roadside assistance. If he could at least get a wrecker to tow the car to a repair shop, he could leave it over the weekend. Then he would have to take a cab home, which would cost another forty bucks, if not more. Hopefully, his insurance would cover the towing, but he dreaded the cost of the looming repair.

He removed his jacket and tie and sat in the CRV while he waited for the wrecker. To mitigate the heat of the day, which felt more like midsummer than early May, he rolled down all the windows to let the evening breeze flow through the car. After twenty minutes, the wedding guests had all gone, and the parking lot was a deserted asphalt plain except for his Honda. As he faced west, a beautiful sunset unfolded before him. The red-gold fire of the sun burned low on the horizon, contrasting with the deepening velvety blue of the sky.

In the quiet, Sebastian pondered what the boy had said. He suddenly realized he didn't even know the young man's name. He had never consulted a psychic or a fortune teller, a practice expressly forbidden. The worst he had done, to his regret, was to play the Wiccan wedding. But this boy was no fortune teller or witch. His manner had been earnest and sincere. He had encouraged and reassured Sebastian; he hadn't predicted his future. Had the boy spoken truth? If not, why would he made such an effort to single Sebastian out and lie to him? What would be the point? If what he said *was* true, he apparently had the gift of clairvoyance.

Clairvoyance, clear seeing. Seeing the invisible.

The powerful vision had spurred the boy to chase after him and tell him about it. But still, Sebastian couldn't quite believe it—he hesitated to think he was surrounded by a magnificent light. True or not, he knew right then and there, he could never tell the tale. It would sound completely ridiculous and self-aggrandizing. *Saint Sebastian.*

But as he watched the day dissolve into night, he held onto the young man's words. *It's going to be all right.*

The wrecker, driven by a thin, middle-aged black man, arrived at 7:30. He shook hands with Sebastian and introduced himself as David. Sebastian explained his plan to tow the car to a repair shop.

"Well, what's wrong with it?" The black pools of his eyes contrasted with the reddish-brown mahogany of his skin.

When Sebastian described the steering problem, David said, "Open up the hood, and let's take a look."

After poking about in the front of the engine, he lifted his head and said, "The serpentine belt is broken. It's a simple fix. We can get one at an auto parts shop, and I'll put it on for you."

Sebastian's jaw dropped. "Really?"

"Sure. Let's go."

With Sebastian riding shotgun in the cab of the wrecker, David towed the car to a nearby auto parts store. Sebastian bought the belt, and David took off the old one and replaced it right there in the parking lot in less than thirty minutes. "You're good to go," he said.

Sebastian could hardly believe it: no towing, no cab, no repair costs. "What do I owe you, David?"

"Twenty bucks is fine."

What a blessing. Sebastian knew it would have cost him well over a hundred bucks if a repair shop mechanic had fixed it. He handed David thirty dollars, all the cash he had. He shook the man's hand and thanked him. As he drove home, he remembered the boy's words: *I can assure you, Mr. Morrow, it's going to be all right.*

Apparently, he had told the truth. Sebastian had just experienced his first confirmation.

CHAPTER 8

NARROWING THE FIELD

State universities are usually affordable, they often have pleasant campuses, and their acceptance rates are fairly high. Those attributes attract many students. As big businesses, they are also bastions of bureaucracy. For every faculty action, some bureaucrat has devised at least fourteen governing regulations and a minimum of three forms to fill out. Never mind teaching: *documentation is all.* The bureaucracy is secretly run by bean-counters who never sleep. They sit hunched over calculators in hidden control rooms, counting, counting, counting. Their calculations control the priorities and the direction universities take.

Increasingly, that direction is determined by quantity rather than quality. The emphasis is on numbers: increased enrollment and decreased expenditure. The trend is to cut small classes, courses and curricula that are not moneymakers for the university. Another strategy is to encourage experienced, tenured faculty (those with the highest salaries) to retire and replace them with adjuncts and inexperienced faculty who will work for less money. Profit, not quality of education, is paramount.

The top administrators contrive to retain six-figure salaries for themselves and for those who are the public face of the university: football coaches and the marching band director. They allot generous sports and band scholarships, and they reserve the highest faculty salaries for professors in science, technology, engineering, and math. The arts (except for marching band, the fraternal twin of the football program) are as important as broccoli. Music, art, theatre, and dance are tolerated, but unlike football, one can live without them, and of course they are, and ever shall be, last on the funding list.

This financial reality was the basis for Sebastian's never-ending battle to fund the orchestra. He created campaigns to target alumni, local businesses, and various foundations. He wrote proposals to three Houston foundations, two businesses (Lonestar Oil and Hlavicek's Bakeries), and the Helprin County Arts Commission. In addition, he submitted yearly requests to the dean for scholarship money. The dean had a sizable budget he could distribute as he saw fit, but Sebastian could only send his request via the department head. It was taboo for a faculty member (other than Roscoe) to approach Dean Ezra Faul directly, a horrifying breach of protocol punishable by vitriolic emails and shunning. Entry to the provost's or president's offices required a dispensation from the Archangel Michael. However, anyone who came with a donation in hand obtained an immediate audience.

If the department head did not advocate strongly and convincingly for the orchestra's funding, the dean denied the request. Sebastian had even worked out a three-year plan showing the increased recruitment potential of orchestra scholarships. He felt sure it would be a winner with the secretive bean-counters. But, according to the former department head, Scott Woolrich, Sebastian's detailed plan elicited a cluck of Dean Faul's tongue followed by the rousing comment, "Persistent, isn't he?" Whether the dean threw it immediately into the circular file, or let it petrify on his desk, the upshot was the same:

no increase in funding for the orchestra. So far Sebastian had lost every battle; he tried not to think about the outcome of the war.

Within the music department, there was a clear funding demarcation between Them That Had—the band and its staff, and Them That Didn't—the choir, orchestra, and piano faculty. The band's budget, circa $1.5 million, allowed them to give lucrative scholarships competitive with other universities. The latter group operated on a pittance with no hope of recruiting the best students. Peanuts and charm only went so far.

It was mid-May, the last day of finals, and Sebastian eagerly looked forward to the freedom of the summer, when he did not teach. The opera season had ended with *Tosca*. Except for the department head search, and JR's work on his house, everything was winding down. Sebastian had given the music theory final exam that morning. Some had prepared, and some had not. It was easy to tell the difference by the cold sweat, frustration, and stricken stares on a few faces. It was both poetry and truth that the wages of sin is death, and the grade for half-assed studying is F.

His own sin, ignorance of country life, had paid him in wages almost worse than death. He had miscalculated badly; he forgot chigger season began already in May rather than at the peak of summer. He had gone out to Vogel Lane to see JR's progress in building the decks and to meet the man who would put in the septic tank. Like an idiot, he had wandered about in his yard unprotected by bug spray. One stroll through the tall grass sufficed to produce persistent, torturous itching. Hours later, his legs and arms were covered in chigger bites, *again*.

At 4:30, the search committee met for the Skype interviews. Sebastian wanted to go home and coat himself in calamine lotion, but he couldn't. Time for a stiff upper lip.

"Thanks for setting this up, Betsy," Sebastian told the administrative assistant as he walked into the conference room. She was adjusting the large monitor for the Skype interviews. A tall, buxom woman, she had raised two children as a single mother. She was meticulous, reliable, and opinionated as hell. She dipped her chin and peered at him over her bifocals. "This department would disintegrate without me. How 'bout giving me a raise?"

Abbie Goldberg laughed. "You're priceless, Betsy, and if it was in our power, we'd do it. But whether you get a pay hike or not depends on which one of these candidates gets the job."

"We'll see about that," intoned Roscoe.

Yeah, I bet we will. Sebastian took a seat beside Miles. He wore a short-sleeved shirt, and he couldn't refrain from scratching the lines of red, lumpy bites on his arms, running north and south like miniature mountain ranges. Twenty-three on one side and fourteen on the other. He tried to ignore the fierce itching around his ankles and knees.

Miles glanced at the red bumps on Sebastian's arms. "Crikey, what happened to you?"

"Chiggers."

"What's that?"

"Invisible creatures from hell that inhabit the country. Mites that bite, and their bites seem to itch for months."

"Blimey!" He picked up his iPhone. "Let me take a photograph of your war wounds."

Sebastian held out his arm and Miles took a close-up. "I have to show Julia the cost of country living."

Sebastian smiled. "Send me a copy. I'll forward it to Helen for sympathy."

"How do you treat those bites?"

"I've contemplated amputation, but that makes it hard to play the violin, so I use calamine lotion. It's pink and messy, but it gives some blessed relief."

At that point, Roscoe handed everyone a list of the prepared questions they would ask the candidates. After a brief discussion about protocol, he dialed the first person on the list, his college crony, now band director at a university in Nevada, Ferris Duck.

Great moniker, thought Sebastian. If he got the job, the students would have fun with it. At least his mother hadn't named him Daffy.

The screen came to life, and they beheld the pale, expectant face of Dr. Duck, smiling behind his bushy black goatee. Roscoe turned up the volume and introduced everyone around the table. Then Philip Washington adjusted his green bow tie and asked the first question in his rumbling bass. "Dr. Duck, what are the qualifications that make you a good fit for this position?"

And the first horse—duck—one could say, shot out of the gate.

They went through the process four more times. At the end of the day, they ranked the candidates by points. They voted, and the final list, from highest score to lowest was as follows:

1) Soprano Marjorie Matthews, chair of a music department in upstate New York
2) Cellist Bruce Riker, chair of the department at a private college in Oklahoma
3) Samuel Nudelman, oboist and chair of a department in Pennsylvania
4) Soren Lind, professor of piano at a large university in Washington state
5) Ferris Duck, band director at a comparably-sized university in Nevada

The first three had administrative experience as department heads, but the last two, including Ferris Duck, did not. This only confirmed Sebastian's distrust of Roscoe's judgment, musical or otherwise. He was a good recruiter and an outstanding tyrant, but his positive professional qualities ended there. Sebastian was delighted that Roscoe's favorite had garnered the least points.

After a moment's silence, his face impassive, Roscoe cleared his throat and said, "We'll invite these five to come here in person for more in-depth interviews with us, the dean, and the provost when

Betsy can arrange it—hopefully sometime within the next three weeks. At that time, we'll vote again and narrow the field to three finalists. We'll recommend those to the dean and the provost, who will make the final decision."

Sebastian knew Roscoe had to be disappointed about the current standing of his favored candidate, although he showed no emotion. Well, score one for the music department and zero for the band and their million-dollar budget. The choir got $25,000 a year from the university, and the orchestra $10,000, a clear demonstration of their respective worth in the eyes of the administration.

As he left the conference room, Sebastian's bites flared up again. He and Miles greeted two of their students in the hallway, Keisha Williams and Alicia Borden. As they passed the girls, Sebastian exhaled forcefully in annoyance and scratched the inside of his arm violently. "I *hate* those damn chiggers!"

Miles laughed and said, "Beastly buggers they are."

They walked quickly out of the building to the parking lot, refraining from conversation until they had privacy. Despite Sebastian's physical discomfort, he felt elated. The majority of the faculty didn't want Duck, a band director, to lead the department. Roscoe clearly wanted him to win the job, but the man didn't have the requisite experience. For once, almost unbelievably, Sebastian and Miles had hopes that music interests would prevail over band interests. That would only be ensured if Roscoe's candidate was eliminated. Duck had made the cut, but he was ranked dead last.

When they got to the parking lot, Sebastian and Miles traded high fives in great good humor. "Here's hoping Roscoe's canard just won't fly," said Miles. "Any one of the top three candidates would be good. I'm relieved. And hungry. Let's eat Chinese."

"Excellent idea," replied Sebastian. "Calamine lotion can wait. I feel like celebrating."

CHAPTER 9

MARY CATHERINE

It was always in the evenings when Sebastian thought of his wife. Maybe it had to do with the setting of the sun and darkness descending, the slow quenching of the light. She entered the stage of his mind like a ghost in an opera, her music as sad and lonely as the memories haunting a ruined city. The music of emptiness, the music of regret always became the music of his own guilt, as he remembered how he had failed her.

Mary Catherine was the seventh and youngest child of an Irish-Catholic family. Her father, Patrick Flynn, was a blunt, hard-drinking Baltimore cop, and her mother, Fiona, worked for a dry cleaning company. He met Mary Catherine when they both sang in the choir at St. Ignatius Church in the Mt. Vernon neighborhood of Baltimore. At that time, Sebastian studied violin at the Peabody Conservatory, and Mary Catherine taught second grade at a public school.

Although Mary Catherine was eight years older than he, it wasn't obvious. Sebastian was a tall man, and he'd always appeared older than his actual age. (Although, at this point, he feared his age and his appearance had caught up with each other.) Anyway, his mother knew about the age difference, and she tried to discourage the relationship. But it's a proven fact that twenty-two-year-olds always know better than their mothers. He married Mary Catherine the summer after he graduated from college. He auditioned for and won a long-term substitute job in the first violin section of the Baltimore Symphony, and their daughter Helen was born a year later.

Helen inherited Mary Catherine's fair skin and his dark hair. They expected her eyes would be blue, like both her parents. But her startlingly gray eyes were her own. Perhaps, Sebastian thought, she entered the world with the foreknowledge of her mother's decline, which descended like a veil to mute the color of her eyes.

In any case, she was a solemn child who didn't speak until she was two and a half years old. Both Sebastian and Mary Catherine feared there might be something wrong with her until one Saturday morning when she announced, "Hehwwy is tirsty. Dere's no watah in his bowl."

Mary Catherine froze with her beer bottle lifted halfway to her mouth. Sebastian smiled with relief, but his knees felt weak. He was almost afraid to speak in case it might startle her back into silence. "You're right, Helen," he said quietly. "Would you like to help me give Harry some water?"

"Yes, Daddy."

Although they didn't know it at the time, Helen's first speech was significant. It showed her love for animals and her concern for their welfare, and it indicated the path she would follow.

It is fair to say that Helen dogged the dog. She toddled alongside patient Harry, their five-year-old Irish Setter, with one hand gripping his long red fur, and she often took naps with him on the living room rug. She lay between Harry's front and back legs and rested her head on his ribs. At night, Harry slept at the foot of her bed, and he quietly placed himself between Helen and any visitors who entered the Morrow home.

The past seemed so clear in Sebastian's mind that night, he could hardly believe Harry had died twenty-odd years ago, and his little girl Helen was now a thirty-two-year-old married woman.

The telephone rang and startled Sebastian out of his reverie. He had to remove Frank, the ailing cat, from his lap before he could get up. On the fourth ring, he picked up the receiver. It was Helen, with bad news. Mary Catherine had had a stroke and was taken to Johns Hopkins Hospital in Baltimore. "Her prognosis isn't good, Dad. They think it's an intracerebral hemorrhage."

"What's that in layman's terms?"

"There's bleeding from the blood vessels inside the brain. She's in a coma, and they don't know if she'll come out of it."

He sighed. "Helen, I'm so sorry. Are you there at the hospital?"

"We're on the way. Kieran and I drove down from Lancaster as soon as we heard. Will you be able to come up here, Dad?"

"Well, I'd like to, but right now, I have search committee meetings at Omega, and the final work on the house is going on. I have to be on the site several times a week to consult with the electrician, the plumber, and JR about what to do next. There seem to be a thousand decisions to make every week, from what kind of pipe for the plumbing to what color to paint the walls. I should be able to move in by June twenty-first, in about three weeks. After that, I'll be able to travel. I hope your mother will come out of the coma before then. In the meantime, keep me informed."

"I will, Dad."

Of course, the news shook him, but there was something inevitable about it. It seemed like the hammer blow Sebastian had expected for the past thirty years.

He got a glass of water and sat down again. Two seconds later, the scarred red tabby hopped up in his lap, settled down, and purred. As he stroked the cat, Sebastian recalled a defining experience with

Mary Catherine, one of the most shocking events of his life. It lasted a matter of seconds, and it took place in total silence, yet it changed his view of the world forever.

It happened in Baltimore during the third year of their marriage. They lay in bed one evening, with the lamp on. Mary Catherine reclined on her back, eyes closed, with her head propped on a plump pillow. Sebastian watched her, unsure if she was already asleep or not. He loved her milky skin, the scattered freckles across her nose. Worried as usual about her drinking, he suddenly decided to pray for her. Trying not to disturb her, he gently placed his hand on the soft blond curls crowning her head. He prayed soundlessly, *Mary Catherine, be healed in the name of Jesus.*

With an odd, abrupt motion, she turned her head toward him and opened her eyes. They lay face-to-face, only inches apart. But it wasn't Mary Catherine who gazed at him with white-eyed malevolence—it was a demon. Something ancient and evil lived in her eyes. His breath caught in his throat at the pure hatred and stunning malice directed at him. He stiffened, his pulse jumped, and he drew his hand away from her head. Without a word, Mary Catherine closed her eyes and turned away from him to lie on her side.

Dumbfounded, he lay on his back, hands at his sides, rigid, staring at the ceiling. He couldn't explain it, but he knew the thing he had seen in her eyes was not Mary Catherine. He believed the prayer caused it to manifest. Beyond that, he had no idea what to make of it or what to do about it. But the experience changed his view of the world forever.

Demons existed. Human beings walked in a world they could see, surrounded by beings they could not see. He had just looked into the eyes of an ancient, intelligent, calculating entity, shockingly malevolent.

He knew Jesus cast out demons, but he had never truly understood what that meant. Now he had an inkling. It was one thing to read about a tiger, but a shocking reality to meet one face-to-face: to tremble in utter fear before a great, feral beast with bared yellow teeth, whose rank odor and hot, fetid breath filled one's nostrils.

Shaken, he turned off the lamp and lay still, wide awake in the darkness. After what seemed like hours, he suddenly remembered the prayer everyone had recited at the end of Mass in the years before Vatican II. He had said it automatically then, but now he knew why it had been written in the first place. He whispered it with intensity to still his anxiety:

St. Michael the Archangel, defend us in battle. Be our protector against the wickedness and snares of the Devil. May God rebuke him, we humbly pray, and do thou, O Prince of the heavenly hosts, by the power of God, thrust into hell Satan, and all the evil spirits, who prowl the world seeking the ruin of souls. Amen.

He crossed himself, turned on his side, and lay awake until morning light.

✷❦✷

Not long after, he played a Friday night subscription concert with the Baltimore Symphony. Afterward, he took the bus home. He enjoyed the two-block walk from the bus stop in the brisk air. When he entered the apartment a little after ten o'clock, all was quiet. Too quiet.

First, he checked on his daughter. Helen lay asleep in her room, with Harry the Irish Setter keeping a bedside vigil. Mary Catherine was nowhere to be found. He double-checked their bedroom, the bathroom, the kitchen, the living room, even the closets, as if he looked for lost keys instead of a lost wife. *Where was she?*

He tried to stave off the blind fury building behind his eyes. Maybe she had just stepped out for a moment. Maybe she had a valid reason for leaving a four-year-old child alone in a third-floor Baltimore walkup. He tried to calm himself down. *Wait and see. Wait and see. Give her a chance to explain.*

He quickly changed out of his tux into a T-shirt and pajama bottoms, and then he checked on his daughter once more. As Sebastian entered the room, Harry, lying on the oval rag rug beside Helen's bed, lifted his burnished, silken head and gave a doggy smile, tongue hanging out to the side. The sight of the tail-thumping, protective dog warmed Sebastian's heart and helped calm his anger. He patted Harry's head. "Faithful Harry, keeping watch. Good dog."

The elephant nightlight on Helen's bedside table illuminated the sleeping child. Small and vulnerable, she lay on her left side in the narrow bed, strands of her hair strewn like dark ribbons across her pale cheek and onto the white pillowcase. Sebastian watched the rise and fall of her chest. Her mouth was slightly open, and he listened to the music of her breathing, its tempo slow and regular and gentle as a heartbreaking Adagio. His eyes traveled down the perfection of her arm as it narrowed to a delicate wrist, and then flared out to the hand that lay palm up to one side, the small fingers relaxed and gently curved. He knelt beside the bed and drank in the beauty of her delicate eyebrows and long lashes, the ridge of her nose, the labyrinth of her tiny ear, the smooth pearl of her cheek.

She was a miracle of creation, and his love for her swelled until he thought it would burst his chest. He leaned down and brushed his lips against her cheek. She stirred slightly but did not wake. She was his daughter, his joy, and his solemn responsibility. No one, including her mother, had the right to put her life in jeopardy. He murmured a prayer of blessing and protection over her, patted the head of Harry, her loyal guardian, and then left the room.

Hungry as always after a concert, he went to the refrigerator and took out some smoked gouda and a tomato. He put a thin smear of mayonnaise on a piece of rye bread and made an open-faced sandwich with cheese and tomato slices. He checked the refrigerator for a beer, but there was none. He decided on red wine instead, but, just his luck, the liquor cabinet was empty. He settled on a tall glass of orange juice.

He sat down at the table in the eat-in kitchen and ate like a half-starved wolf, consuming most of his sandwich in two big bites. He took a sip of the orange juice, and in the moment he swallowed it, he realized where Mary Catherine had gone. She had run out of booze. No beer, no wine. No problem. Just leave your sleeping four-year-old alone while you dash out to the liquor store.

He heard the rattle of the key in the lock and the sound of the door opening and closing. "Sebastian?"

"I'm here, in the kitchen."

She walked in with a lopsided smile and two cloth shopping bags. "You're home early." She looked angelic with her tousled blond hair and cheeks rosy from the cold.

"Yes, the last piece on the program was for winds and chorus only, no strings." He watched her unload the bags. She set a six-pack of beer, two bottles of red wine, and one bottle of white on the counter. He was appalled at his overwhelming desire to stand up and strike her across the face. It took all his self-control to remain seated.

Enraged, with a pounding pulse, he barely opened his mouth as he spoke, "You left Helen alone in the apartment to buy beer and wine? That couldn't wait until I came home?"

Surprised by his tone of voice, she turned to face him. "I was only gone for ten minutes."

"The hell you were. I've been here for at least half an hour." He drew in a deep breath and continued, his voice shaking with anger. "Listen to me, Mary Catherine. You cannot ever leave that child alone at night or any other time." He sharpened his tone. "*Do you hear me?*"

Even as he uttered the words, Sebastian wondered how many times she had already done it, unbeknownst to him.

A deep flush burned Mary Catherine's cheeks, and she stepped back against the counter as if he had physically threatened her. "She wasn't alone. Harry was with her."

"The dog?" he spluttered. "What if there was a fire or a break-in? Do you expect Harry to call 911 or unlock the door so she could escape?" He stood up and pointed a finger at her. "I'm telling you, Mary Catherine, this cannot happen again."

Unable to hold his gaze, she dropped her eyes. They stood frozen in a tense silence punctuated by the muted sounds of traffic on the avenue, a door closing somewhere in the building. Sebastian held his breath and waited for the apology that never came.

He exhaled, feeling deflated and suffused suddenly by a great fatigue. He could not comprehend her negligence, nor could he easily forgive her. At a loss for words, he simply said, "Goodnight, Mary Catherine."

As he walked out of the room, he heard her reply: a loud *pop-hiss* from the beer can she opened. It startled him as badly as a gunshot, and he froze in the doorway. With terrible clarity and a sense of doom, he knew it to be the sound of rebellion, not repentance. Like a declaration of war, it changed everything.

CHAPTER 10
RUPTURE

After that, there seemed to be a wall in the middle of their bed; they hardly touched each other. He counted six weeks before they made love again. On the evenings he was home, she contrived to go out more and more. She had always been more social and outgoing than he, and as a Baltimore native, she had a network of girlfriends from high school and college who still lived in the city. She went out to meet them for dinner, "coffee," or a movie. When she came home, he could smell alcohol on her breath.

As far as he could tell, she never got drunk, but evenings at home, she always had a beer, a mixed drink, or a glass of wine in hand. The steady drinking made Sebastian uneasy. "Look, you don't have to have a drink every night."

"What does it hurt?" she replied. "I don't get drunk. I never miss work. I'm a stellar citizen." She twirled the red wine in her glass and smirked.

"It hurts our pocketbook. We're spending a lot more on alcohol than we need to." He opened a cabinet in the kitchen. "Look at that." Rows of empty wine bottles stood at attention. "Sixteen bottles at twelve dollars minimum a pop, that's close to two hundred dollars right there." He opened another cabinet which served as their bar. "Two bottles of scotch, three bottles of red wine, some gin, and a bottle of Amaretto." He looked at Mary Catherine. "What do you estimate? Another hundred-fifty or so?"

He fixed his gaze on her. "Three hundred-fifty a month is way more than we can afford, whether we get drunk or not. That's more than we pay for childcare." Her benefits kept them all insured, but teachers were not wealthy people. Sebastian's income consisted of his regular substitute job with the symphony, private violin students, and occasional freelance work playing weddings, parties, and church concerts. Rent, childcare, and the monthly payments for Sebastian's student loans were their greatest expenses. They didn't own a car. With very little savings, they lived as many Americans did, from paycheck to paycheck.

She didn't put up a fight about it. She shrugged her shoulders. "Sure, I can buy less."

As time went by, despite her agreement, he didn't observe any change in Mary Catherine's habits. The bar stayed stocked and the empties kept coming. He did note a marked decrease in their communication. They passed each other in the apartment, hardly speaking, while their sex life dwindled and finally came to a halt.

Often, Mary Catherine seemed to be gripped by some sort of malaise. She seemed to fade into the background, either absent or absent-minded, a nonparticipant in their family life. She left more and more of Helen's care to him. He laundered Helen's clothes, changed her bed, made sure she bathed and brushed her teeth. With increasing frequency, it was he who cooked their meals. He dropped Helen off and picked her up at the daycare; he took her with him on walks with Harry. Where once Mary Catherine had accompanied them, she came no more.

Sebastian grew annoyed with her growing apathy and withdrawal from family life and his increasing role as a dogsbody. He complained and asked her to share the load. She agreed to help more, but it seemed that whatever tasks he asked her to do rarely got done. She "forgot" to clean the kitchen or pick up his tux from the dry cleaners. She didn't remember to buy milk and cereal for Helen. Once, at the first of the month, he gave her the utility bills, stamped and ready to be mailed, and found out the next month, by the doubled charges and threats of interrupted service, she had taken the envelopes to school, put them in her desk, and forgotten to post them. But her memory seemed sharp in one direction: she never forgot to stop by the liquor store.

Frustrated and unable to fix the problems, Sebastian realized he was rapidly becoming an angry, resentful man. He even snapped at Helen. He didn't recognize himself, and he truly didn't want to live that way. Finally, he suggested marriage counseling, although he knew they couldn't afford it for long. Mary Catherine went, and agreed to follow all the therapist's suggestions during the sessions, but as soon as they left the office, she treated it as a joke. After two months, Sebastian realized it was pointless, and he canceled the therapy.

In November, as the days grew colder and darker, it seemed to him they inhabited a gray twilight world, hopeless and directionless as Purgatory. Helen, his only ray of sunshine, seemed subdued as well, touched by melancholy. Sebastian grew increasingly restless; he felt an urge to make a change in his life.

A year earlier, his friend Rob Davidowsky, a cellist in the BSO, won the principal job with the Houston Symphony. For a while, Sebastian considered following Rob's lead and auditioning else-where for a position. But as much as he loved playing the violin, he decided he didn't want to spend his life buried in the string section of a major symphony orchestra. During his five years with the BSO, he had witnessed the heavy toll stress and constant playing took on the bodies of string players. Two of his colleagues, twenty-year vet-erans, struggled with chronic shoulder pain. They spent thousands of dollars on physical therapy and massages just to keep going. Love of the job had almost evaporated in the face of the pain they endured, and they grimly held on, counting the years until retirement. Another colleague lost feeling in three fingers of his left hand. Despite two surgeries and a long stint in rehab, he had to retire early because his ring finger remained numb and useless.

Sebastian devised an alternate plan. When he explained it to Mary Catherine, she listened, but seemed noncommittal. With a doctorate, he told her, it was possible to get a tenured teaching position at a university. He was only twenty-eight years old, and after a four-year program, he would be in his prime. He told her he wanted a job where he could be at home more often on nights and weekends. He didn't want Helen to grow up without him. When she brought up the cost, he told her scholarships and teaching fellowships made it very possible to get a free ride in graduate school.

He spent hours researching various graduate programs. He considered the excellent schools in New York and on the West Coast but ruled them out due to their exorbitant tuitions and the high costs of living in those cities. He refused to go any deeper in debt. He finally focused on the two major universities in Houston, a city where he already had contacts: Rob and Miriam and his aunt and uncle, Nancy and Bear Leaton. It was the fourth largest city in the United States, with a warm climate and a relatively low cost of living.

In late November, he applied to both universities, and in January, he flew there to audition. He stayed in the Heights area with Rob and Miriam. He took one audition on a Thursday and the other the next day. That Friday night, Aunt Nancy and Uncle Bear drove in from the country to have dinner with him, and on the weekend, Rob and Miriam gave him a driving tour of the city.

Houston surprised him—he was impressed by the city's energy and optimistic, bold atmosphere. He'd half expected the place to be overrun with cowboys, and he did see a few Stetsons and boots, but he was pleasantly surprised by the city's ethnic diversity and international flavor. Rob told him there were more than a hundred foreign languages spoken in the city, with the top ones being Spanish, Chinese, Vietnamese, French, and Arabic. Sebastian scanned newspaper ads for rentals and real estate and was heartened to find the cost of living substantially lower than that of Baltimore. After he got his degree, when they had two fulltime jobs, he and Mary Catherine would be able to afford a house.

From Rob, he discovered Houston was a real arts town with many playing opportunities for musicians. There were at least five professional orchestras in town, the Houston Symphony, Houston Grand Opera, and its smaller counterpart, Opera D'Argento, a ballet orchestra, and Theatre Under the Stars, which mounted Broadway musicals. A center of the petroleum industry and a major port, Houston was one of the fastest-growing cities in the nation, second only to New York in Fortune 500 headquarters. It also had one of the youngest populations. Tacky in places, and sprawling over six hundred square miles, it had a rambunctious, raw energy that he found enormously appealing after the decaying urban blight of Baltimore.

In April, Sebastian received acceptance letters and offers from both schools. As he had hoped, they offered him enough scholarships to cover all tuition. The University of Houston also offered him a teaching fellowship with a stipend. He wasn't worried about housing, which would cost less than their rent in Baltimore, but they would need to purchase a car, since Houston's public transit system couldn't compare to those of the older East Coast cities.

He had the future all laid out in his head when he sat Mary Catherine down to plan what he hoped would be their new life. He waited until Helen had gone to sleep, and then he set out two servings of tiramisu he had bought from the Italian bakery on the avenue and brewed a half pot of coffee. He had a hope, naïve, he realized later, that a change of scene would rejuvenate their marriage and jolt Mary Catherine out of the doldrums. As they sat at the kitchen table, his enthusiasm overflowed, and he excitedly described Houston and his vision of their new life.

She ate the tiramisu slowly, taking her time with each bite. She drank small sips of black coffee, as if she pondered his every word. "What about a job for me?" she asked.

"It shouldn't be a problem." Encouraged by her question, Sebastian washed down the rich dessert with a gulp of hot, milky coffee. "There must be hundreds of elementary schools in the city. Houston is four times bigger than Baltimore, and Texas teachers' salaries are slightly higher than here." He searched her eyes, hoping for a positive reaction. "I also think it would be a better place to raise Helen." He leaned forward. "In a few years, we could buy a house."

The corners of her mouth drooped. She stared at her half-eaten dessert, chin in hand, animated as a tombstone. "But all my friends are here."

Sebastian smiled. "We'll make new friends. The Texans I met were very welcoming."

"Yes, but my parents are here, also, and they're getting older. I really don't want to leave them."

Sebastian read between the lines; he knew his wife. Unwilling to confront him head-on, Mary Catherine conjured up thin excuses because she didn't want to move.

"I see," he said. And he did—he visualized a roadblock, like a gray stone wall. Faced with an impasse, he thought it wise to turn around, for the moment at least. "Well, I want the best for your parents—I always have. We can always discuss this with them." He drank the last of his now lukewarm coffee. "Look, we don't have to make a decision tonight. Let's research elementary school positions in Houston, and then we'll do the math and see if this move is right for us."

All conversation ceased. Mary Catherine poured herself a glass of white wine and disappeared into the living room while Sebastian cleaned up the kitchen.

The next day, while she was at work, he called the Houston Independent School District and asked them to send notices of elementary school openings to Mary Catherine Morrow at their Baltimore address. Three weeks later, she had received four listings, and Sebastian asked her if she had applied to any of the job openings.

"Not yet."

The next week, the same question drew the same answer. Sebastian told himself there was still plenty of time. But it seemed to him that Mary Catherine drifted further and further away. She stopped attending Mass with them, and she often ate dinner out, so they rarely had any family time together. It was a strategy: avoid discussion, delay action.

Her game plan was effective, but he couldn't let it go on. He was convinced their marriage needed a jump-start, as he himself certainly did, and Houston had the electricity to do it. The moment of decision loomed.

He waited until mid-June, the end of the school term, to broach the subject again. This time they sat on the living room sofa as he carefully laid out his case. He emphasized the long-term economic advantages, the better environment for Helen, the warmer winters, and the lower crime rate. When she brought up her parents again, he said, "Mary Catherine, this is about us, our immediate family, not Patrick and Fiona. Once we make the decision, we'll talk with them."

"Well, they need my help. Dad has diabetes and Mom is going to have knee replacement surgery."

"Yes, and they live a hop, skip, and a jump from Johns Hopkins Hospital, one of the best in this country. They also have six other healthy children in town who are ready and willing to help them."

Mary Catherine pursed her lips and turned her head away.

"Believe me, they'll have all the help they need." Sebastian took a deep breath. "What is really holding you back, Mary Catherine? Can't you talk to me?"

She gazed at him, with an unhappy expression. "Baltimore is my home, Sebastian. All my family is here, and all my friends are here. I like the school where I work. I don't want to start from scratch. I don't want to move to Houston."

Just as he suspected, but at least now the truth was out in the open. Sebastian took her hands in his and tried to persuade her. "Mary Catherine, Houston's a better place, with better opportunities, and we'll be there together. We won't lose contact with your family and friends here. We'll visit each other." He searched her blue eyes, willing away the doubt in them. "Baltimore was once a fine city, but you know what it's like now—it's a crime-ridden, depressing place. You haven't been to Houston, but the atmosphere there is positive and full of energy. It will be better for us, for our marriage, and for Helen too." He rubbed the backs of her hands with his thumbs. "I know we've been going through a difficult time, but that happens in all marriages. I married you because I loved you, and I love you still. I think we should make this move. What do you say?"

He saw a glimmer of the old light in her blue eyes and held his breath, hopeful. She lowered her gaze and sat with head bowed in a silent struggle. He could feel the tension in her hands.

"Mary Catherine, this is something I really want to do. Let's try it out for a year. Baltimore's not going anywhere; we can always move back. Isn't it worth a try?"

She drew in a deep breath and exhaled. "All right, I'll try."

So much pressure had built up inside Sebastian, that when she agreed to move, it was akin to popping the cork on a champagne bottle. His energy shot out in all directions, bubbling and effervescent. He gave his notice to the BSO. He bought a used Chevy Malibu with 58,000 miles on it. Then he contacted Rob and Miriam to ask if he could stay with them for a few days in July while he looked for a place to live. They were delighted to hear he was moving to Houston, and they welcomed him into their home once again. He found a roomy two-bedroom duplex with a garage and a large, fenced backyard, only five minutes from the University of Houston. He called Mary Catherine and told her to contact their landlord and give notice that they would be out of the apartment by the first week in August.

Houston did not exactly roll out the welcome mat for them. The city did, however, give them a foretaste of the inferno. They moved into the duplex the first week of August in the midst of a searing heat wave. The high temperature for each day that week topped 100 degrees and climaxed at 104. To the delight of children and stray dogs, people could, and did, fry eggs on the sidewalks.

He bore the oppressive heat as best he could, with air conditioners in the house and car set on the lowest temperatures and highest fan speeds. Aside from the weather, he had a lot to think about: school, furniture, the hole in his pocketbook, and the naked fear that he had made a colossal mistake. He was on his own with Helen in a strange, scorching city, reeling from a stinging, unexpected blow—at the last minute, Mary Catherine had refused to come.

He enrolled Helen in kindergarten at St. Jude's School, just a mile away from their new home on Lewis Street and registered for his doctoral classes at the university. They both began school on August twentieth.

Their neighborhood, just east of downtown Houston, was a quiet

Hispanic enclave, decidedly lower middle class. The smell of fresh coffee from the local Maxwell House plant permeated the air. In a block of one-family frame homes built on small lots, their duplex was the only rental, and they were the only *gringos*.

They inhabited the ground floor of a slowly declining, but unique two-story building, built in the forties. *Declining* was the literal truth. Over time, the back of the house had settled six inches lower than the front, which created a noticeable upward bow in the living room's wooden floor—quite likely the only hill in Houston. The wiring had its own quirks. Before Sebastian ran the microwave, he had to turn off his bedroom air conditioner or it tripped the breaker. The two-bedroom apartment had a detached garage, and for the first time in their lives, Harry and Helen had the freedom of a large backyard, enclosed by a wooden privacy fence and shaded by a very large oak tree.

From August to October, Sebastian could not afford furniture, so he slept on the floor in a sleeping bag. He had intended to haul all their worldly goods to Houston, but when Mary Catherine made her decision, he left everything but clothes, his books and music, Helen's bed and her toys. And Harry, of course. Helen would not leave without Harry, and Sebastian would not leave without Helen.

In the new apartment, Helen and the dog latched onto him for security; for weeks, they followed him from room to room. He comforted them as best he could, while the last scene with Mary Catherine played over and over in his mind in a hellish loop.

When he returned from house-hunting in Houston, he had called Marco Ricci, their Baltimore landlord, to ask when they could expect a refund of their security deposit. They would need every penny for the move. Marco answered, "I had no idea you were moving."

"What? You didn't get a notice from my wife?"

"No."

Sebastian's heart flipped over. "All right, let me call you back."

When he confronted Mary Catherine, she said she didn't tell Marco because she couldn't bear to leave. "I'm sorry, Sebastian, I can't do it. I'm not going."

Stunned and furious, he stood speechless, his mind whirling. He had already left his BSO job, paid his fees to the university, and put down the first month's rent and a security deposit for the new apartment. He had bought the car. At that moment, something inside him ruptured. He was done with patience and persuasion. He made up his mind—let the consequences be damned—he was going. And Helen was going with him.

"Suit yourself, but I've cut all my ties here and set everything up for a new life in Houston. I'm going, and I'm taking Helen." He stiffened and braced himself for the explosion.

Mary Catherine shrugged and turned her head away.

In the silence, Sebastian could hear his own heart beating. He waited until he couldn't bear it anymore. "Well?"

She shrugged again.

That was it? A shrug? As a dramatic moment it fell flat, but like an earthquake, it rocked Sebastian's world. There would be no fight. His relief at her surrender was dwarfed by his shock at her indifference. He stared at her in disbelief. He wanted to scream at her. *Why aren't you fighting to keep your daughter? What is wrong with you?*

The awful gesture, the lift and fall of Mary Catherine's shoulders, haunted him over the course of the two days and 1,445 miles he drove to Houston. In fact, it stayed with him the rest of his life. Swift and soundless as a guillotine, it divided them forever.

Thrown into the role of a single parent with a single income, he struggled to keep afloat financially. His only steady income was the stipend from his teaching fellowship. But thanks to university referrals, he acquired a goodly number of private students by mid-semester. He transferred his music union membership to the Houston local, and

Rob recommended him to a number of area music contractors. When they discovered he had played five years in the Baltimore Symphony, they made him first-call for freelance jobs. Little by little, he pieced an income together. It was a patchwork quilt, but as the damp and chilly winter came on, it kept them warm.

Years later, when he looked at his income tax returns, he realized he and Helen had survived on $12,000 a year. Thankfully, she never knew how poor they were.

By December, after their uncertain and almost frantic beginning, he and Helen hit their stride. He had bought a bed for himself, a kitchen table and chairs, and a sofa from Goodwill. The apartment actually resembled a home instead of an abandoned warehouse. Most importantly, Sebastian found a good babysitter for Helen for the evenings he taught lessons or played concerts. Valeria Marquez, a stay-at-home mother, lived at the very end of the block. She had a son, Hector, who was Helen's age, and a three-year-old daughter, Isabella. Valeria's husband, the taciturn Ernesto, worked for the Budweiser plant on Interstate 10.

The Marquez home was simple but very clean, and Sebastian and Helen immediately liked Valeria. She was a plump, engaging woman in her thirties who made them feel at home. Affectionate, with a warm smile, she was just the motherly influence Helen needed. She spoke with a strong accent, but her English was good, and her hourly fee was affordable.

Helen was Sebastian's biggest worry. Although Valeria was wonderful, no one could fill the vacuum Mary Catherine's absence made in Helen's life. Despite his deep and abiding anger at her indifference, Sebastian telephoned Mary Catherine every weekend so Helen could talk to her mother. He maintained a neutral exterior, never speaking against Mary Catherine in Helen's presence. But his anger simmered.

As time went on, Sebastian realized that as difficult as the breakup of his marriage had been for him and Helen, its effect on Mary Catherine was worse. She saw herself as a victim. Having been abandoned, she now had a standing excuse to drink. With Sebastian gone and all restraints removed, she drank nightly until the wee hours. Somehow, she managed to hold onto her job. But if the ocean had been made of wine, like Thor, she would have created an ebb tide. Unlike the god, who gave up at the end, she would have asked for more.

He finally accepted the truth—Mary Catherine was an alcoholic.

There are many medicines for illnesses, and they often work, if the patient takes them. There are cures for alcoholism, and they also work. But in their own eyes, alcoholics are not alcoholics. They don't have a problem. They can always stop drinking; they just don't want to. Simple.

How could he help a person who didn't want help, one who denied her own illness? The question haunted him down all the years. He wanted to see her well; he wanted to reclaim their marriage and give his daughter the mother she should have. How could he help Mary Catherine? Like a mathematician seeking the solution to a seemingly insoluble problem, Sebastian kept at it for decades. He couldn't let it go. He prayed for her daily, sometimes fervently, sometimes in rote phrases, sometimes doggedly, but not a day passed that he didn't assail Heaven on her behalf.

When Heaven did not respond, he grew impatient. He tried another tack: healers. There were those, he knew, who had the power of healing. Mary Catherine would never submit to the laying on of hands, so it had to be someone who had the power of remote healing.

He approached the world of remote healers cautiously, wary of frauds. There certainly was no shortage of websites advertising people with names like Madame Luna or Sir Maximilian. There were female healers with provocative photographs, tarot card readers, Masters of Indian Healing with pictures of Hindu gods and goddesses, Chinese healers, African shamans, channelers, mediums, and a "love healer" from New Jersey. Their fees varied from $50 to $3,000, depending on the length and number of sessions.

By this time, eight years had passed since he left Mary Catherine. Helen was thirteen years old. Sebastian had finished his doctorate and was in his fourth year at Omega. His vision of a healed Mary Catherine moving to Texas had begun to fade, but who knew what could happen if she finally stopped drinking?

At last he found a healer with a normal name: Rosalind Harper. She offered her services for free. Sebastian could have afforded a reasonable fee, but he believed a person who didn't charge anything was more likely to be genuine. He contacted her. All she required was a name, the illness, and a location. Sebastian provided it all, crossed his fingers, and waited.

CHAPTER 11

THE RECORDING SESSION

Life and death seem to be opposing states, separated by a wide gulf, but truly, Sebastian thought, they are not. The quick become the dead at the exhaling of a single breath, the cessation of a single heartbeat, moving as wind through an opaque, delicate veil made of the finest gossamer. In a mere instant, the incorruptible takes flight and only the earthbound, corruptible flesh remains. The veil is a subtle, mysterious partition, but porous; there are those who have passed through it and returned.

As a teenager, Sebastian had watched over his paternal grandfather Jacob for days as he died of lung cancer. Sebastian's parents had taken in the old man when he became incapacitated. Jacob had loved gardening, and for many years Sebastian had worked with him in his garden every summer. But Jacob had smoked unfiltered Lucky Strikes his whole life, a very costly habit.

Sebastian learned many things as he sat beside his grandfather. At the point of death, the body works very hard. Fever may accompany this effort. Even in a cold room, a person may throw off the covers and lie exposed, completely unselfconscious. The breathing can alternate from rapid panting to long lulls where the breath stops. Sometimes there is a rattle in the throat. A dying person wants no food or water. There is no desire to speak or answer questions, although the sense of hearing is usually intact. The person withdraws to an interior place, physically and spiritually preoccupied with the ongoing transition from this life to the next.

On a Thursday at the end of May, Sebastian recalled the experience vividly as he sat vigil with Helen's red tabby cat Frank. He found the approaching signs of death almost the same. Over the last twenty-four hours, Frank's condition had rapidly deteriorated. He lay on his side, emaciated and weak, suffering from kidney failure. He took shallow, panting, irregular breaths. He didn't want to lie on a soft, warm blanket; he preferred the cool bedroom floor. At a certain point, Frank's breaths became deep gasps, and brief, hard spasms shook his body. With a surprised look in his large green eyes, he gave a sharp cry, and then he was gone. The body, emptied of life, lay still on the floor.

Sebastian stroked Frank's soft red fur for the last time.

> *In articulo mortis*
> *Caelitus mihi vires,*
> *Deo adjuvante non timendum.*

Why the Latin poetry suddenly surfaced in his mind, he didn't know. Nor could he recall its provenance. He was only certain of one thing—he'd recited it for himself as a defense against all death—that of the cat, of his grandfather Jacob, and what he feared was the impending demise of Mary Catherine.

> *At the moment of death*
> *My strength is from heaven.*
> *God helping, nothing should I fear.*

He made an entry in his day planner: ***Thursday, May 29.*** *Frank died this evening at 6:35 p.m. Will call Helen later.*

He glanced at the next entry: ***Friday, May 30.*** *Recording session 9:00–5:00, Willow Studios.* Tomorrow would be a grueling, tiring day, but easier than this one. Fatigue was easier to bear than sorrow. Sebastian sighed—now he had to bury the cat.

In lieu of a coffin, Sebastian enfolded Frank in one of his old T-shirts. He buried the eighteen-year-old cat in the backyard of his duplex. The image of the limp, dead cat contrasted sharply in Sebastian's mind with the picture of Frank in his prime, Frank the Fighter. A neighborhood stray his daughter Helen befriended and brought home, Frank had one notched ear from a long-ago fight, a huge rumbling purr, and an unrelenting appetite born of near-starvation. A dominant male, he had impregnated most of the females on the block. Thanks to Frank in his pre-surgery days, red tabby cats and kittens abounded in the barrio.

In the midst of the recording session the next day, Sebastian battled fatigue. His sadness about Mary Catherine's stroke and Frank's death had translated itself to insomnia during the night. His violin felt like it was made out of lead, and his eyelids seemed to be lined with sandpaper. His mind wandered: he wondered how Helen could bear to be a vet. The sight of suffering animals tore his heart, and she worked with them every day. He wondered if there would be any change in Mary Catherine's condition. He wondered if he would ever see her again.

With a great effort, he tried to focus on the recording session. Studio work was lucrative, and he would receive royalties from the CD later on. He was lucky the contractor had hired him, and if he didn't concentrate and play well, he wouldn't be hired again.

He sat in the first violin section of a thirty-piece orchestra, mostly strings with a few woodwinds, brass, and one percussionist. The orchestra, a mishmash of players from the symphony, the ballet, and the opera, had been put together by Aaron Tanner, a well-known Houston contractor, to record an album of inspirational songs with a female singer. Due to the high cost of the orchestra and studio time, the project had to be completed in one day. Wearing earphones, the singer stood alone in a small sound booth, adjacent to the large room for the orchestra and conductor.

They played the music at sight. The conductor rehearsed each song once, made corrections and comments to the orchestra, and then they recorded it. If a glaring error occurred, they would record a second take. At noon, after the three-hour morning session, Aaron called a two-hour break for lunch before the afternoon session from two to five.

Mischa Orlov, one of the cellists who lived near the recording studio in West Houston and knew the area, suggested they eat lunch at Khalil's, a Middle Eastern restaurant nearby. He gave Sebastian and several others directions.

In the restaurant, the musicians sat together at a large round table. Although Mischa's wife Sally, a violist, didn't play the recording session, she joined him for lunch with their seven-month-old son since the restaurant was so close to their home. Sebastian had last seen them at the black couple's wedding earlier that year. Mischa and Sally, with the baby on her lap, sat to Sebastian's left. Two other violinists, Jane Decker and Christine Brown, sat directly across from him, while the oboist Bruce McCracken and Kim Knudsen, a flutist, sat to his right.

The physical exertions of performing burn up a lot of calories, especially after hours of playing. Sebastian and the other musicians loaded up their plates at the buffet. Despite his sadness about Mary Catherine and the cat, Sebastian had a fierce appetite. His meager breakfast of coffee and one piece of toast five hours ago had not sustained him. As he ate his chicken shawarma sandwich, he tried to shake off the mantle of depression. He contributed almost nothing to the conversation at the table, which rattled on steadily, mostly shop talk and gossip.

After a while, Sally addressed him, "Sebastian, Sasha seems fascinated by you. He's watched you ever since we sat down."

Sebastian had paid little attention to the baby. He glanced at the baldish child sitting in his mother's lap. Sasha's blue eyes gazed at him, but not with a fixed stare. It was a moving glance, as if he observed something above and around Sebastian's head. The baby's lips parted in a wet, gummy smile of delight. He gurgled and stretched out his chubby arms toward Sebastian.

How odd, Sebastian thought. Sasha focused steadily on him; his attention did not wander.

"Here," Sally said, "you hold him."

Sebastian put down his sandwich, wiped his hands, and with some trepidation, took the baby from Sally. It had been a long time since he had held such a young child. Sasha was definitely well-fed. With his rolls of fat, he resembled a miniature sumo wrestler, although it was doubtful that sumo wrestlers smelled like milk and baby powder. As Sebastian held him in his lap, Sasha kept his eyes on Sebastian's head. The baby warbled and cooed like a dove; he seemed completely at ease. Sasha's reaction to him made no sense, but it cheered Sebastian's heart and made him smile.

The moment was short-lived. Sebastian suddenly realized all conversation had ceased; he and Sasha had become the center of attention. All at once, the women asserted their maternal rights. Each one wanted to hold the baby. Kim took Sasha first and prattled to him a while. Then she passed the baby to Christine and Jane. After he had made the rounds and charmed the company, Sasha returned to his mother.

While Sebastian finished off his sandwich, he recalled another curious incident with a child. It occurred the Saturday afternoon he and Helen had moved out of the Baltimore apartment. He had carried suitcases of clothes, Helen's bed and mattresses, and boxes of books and music out to the rented trailer in the summer heat. Tuckered out from climbing up and down the stoop plus three flights of stairs, he had sat down to rest on the bumper of the trailer, parked parallel to the curb of St. Paul Street.

As he wiped his brow and caught his breath, many people passed by on the wide sidewalk to his left, but no one paid him any heed until a woman pushing a toddler in a stroller walked by. As they passed the back of the trailer where Sebastian rested, the child turned his head abruptly and stared at Sebastian as if he saw something remarkable, like Santa Claus or a fireworks display. As the stroller moved away, the child bent forward and craned his neck backward to keep Sebastian in view. He almost fell out of the stroller. Finally, the mother stopped, fussed at her child, and pushed him back inside.

Twenty-eight years ago, and he still remembered it.

His thoughts broke off when he realized the other musicians were leaving. Everyone had finished eating, and it was time to go back to the recording studio for the afternoon session. Sasha's reaction still puzzled him, but thanks to the child, the burden of heaviness on Sebastian had lifted.

That night, despite his fatigue, he lay in bed wide awake, thinking about the way Sasha and the nameless Baltimore child had watched him. Then he remembered the fair-haired young man at the wedding who had seen, or so he said, a magnificent light around Sebastian. Had Sasha and the other child seen that light too? Maybe little ones, still pure and not too far removed from heaven, could see as a matter of course what only sensitives and clairvoyants were able to see. Were clairvoyants those who had somehow retained their spiritual vision into adulthood?

More importantly, what did it all mean? He had felt both fatigued and depressed all day. Did that supposed light shine despite the state of his emotions? He had been upset about his car at the wedding when he had the encounter with the clairvoyant young man. And even if the child had seen a light around him too, what was the point? He was no saint.

"Maybe," he muttered, "as the song says, *it don't mean a thing.*" He clicked his tongue. "Hmmph," he grunted, feeling puzzled and dissatisfied at the same time, "maybe I'll never know."

He tossed and turned for a long while, but finally his fatigue overwhelmed him, and he slept. He dreamed his Houston duplex had become a tall concrete bunker sunk halfway into the ground. The walls were the height of a two-story building, but he stood at the lowest level looking up. Only the top half stood above ground, and for some reason, there was no roof. Someone wearing a large, wide-brimmed black hat slowly circled the outside perimeter with an ominous air, seeking entrance. Sebastian could only see the flat, circular brim of the hat over the top of the wall, but it terrified him. He knew it was the devil prowling, hoping to harm him. The bunker had no windows, and only one door. A staircase led up to an open door on the top level. The open doorway frightened him, but to his everlasting relief, he saw it was guarded from the inside by a gigantic lion. The enormous, tawny lion lay on its haunches, alert, but relaxed, facing the door. Sebastian knew that as long as the lion was there, the devil could never enter his house; no harm could come to him. All his fear left him, and he knew he was safe. He laughed in relief.

When he awoke the next morning, the dream was still vivid in his mind. In the months to come he would remember it often.

CHAPTER 12

FAR FROM CIVILIZATION

Although it was a presidential election year, Sebastian had been so preoccupied with the house, his work, and his financial worries, he had paid scant attention to the campaign speeches. When he finally did, he regretted it.

The house improvements, his main concern, took place in rapid succession. So did the charges on Sebastian's three credit cards. Like a marathon runner holding level with the pack, he felt confident he was keeping pace with the national debt.

In addition to JR and his son, Sebastian also had to employ a plumber, an electrician, and two different firms to install the septic tank and propane tank. The workmen crawled over, under, and inside the house like swarming termites. Before the cottage was moved from its original site, the plumbing had to be disconnected and the pipes cut. Sebastian's plumber replaced all the old galvanized pipes with PVC, and then connected the house to the water line at the edge of the road. When a local company installed the septic tank, the most critical feature of the house—the toilet—worked. Splendid—no more peeing in the bushes. *Sayonara* to chigger bites on his privates.

After the power company installed a pole at the front of the property, the electrician connected the electrical line to the house and rewired it top to bottom. Two months after the house had been moved, Sebastian finally had power and water. Once the gas company installed a large propane tank and hooked it up to the house, he bought a refrigerator, a stove, and gas heaters for the living room and bathroom. For cooling, he put in three window air conditioners.

During the same time, JR and his son built the two decks Sebastian had requested. The larger one was open and faced the pond, while the smaller one, with its sloping roof, faced the road. When that was done, they were going to paint the interior. JR estimated it would only take two weeks before he finished. That meant Sebastian would be able to make the move out to the country as planned, around the summer solstice.

Although Sebastian had not divulged his precarious financial situation, he had kept his friends informed about the progress on the house. Miles Greenfield was particularly curious to see the property, so Sebastian invited the Englishman to join him one afternoon. "You can ride out with me after work, and we can eat dinner in Bullinger. Then I'll drop you off at Omega so you can get your car. I have to drive past there anyway on my way back to Houston."

"Sounds lovely. Let me ring Julia." After Miles checked with his wife, they set out toward Sebastian's house.

"You know, Sebastian, I'm staggered by all the driving you do, commuting from the east side of Houston to work, and then driving out to your land afterward." Miles lived in one of the northwest suburbs, only twenty minutes from the university.

"My true home is the highway. The commute to Omega plus the extra mileage to the house is about ninety miles one way, and I go out to the house about twice a week. I've put about 15,000 miles on this car in less than six months."

Suddenly, in a blur, a low-flying object passed them with a *whoosh* of air that rocked the vehicle.

Miles blurted, "What the hell was that?" just as another one whizzed by. They watched a red Mustang tailgate a blue Corvette in a wild chase through three lanes of traffic at ninety miles per hour or better.

"One of the last vestiges of the Wild West. On Texas roadways, the same rules apply as in buffalo stampedes: go fast or get outta the way." Sebastian pointed backward with his thumb. "Take a look at the buddy they left behind."

Miles glanced at the rear of the car and saw the grill of a white pickup truck filling the back windshield. "Good Lord—he's about four inches behind us. I think I see steam coming out his ears."

"Now he's pulling over to the left and flashing his lights in my mirror."

Miles glanced back. "He has a few choice words for us, Sebastian—I can read his lips."

"And there he goes!" The pickup truck driver pulled over abruptly and passed them on the right, narrowly missing Sebastian's rear bumper. As he roared by, he stuck his arm out the window with a one-finger salute, punctuating the air with it at least three times.

"Ah, sign language. Just in case we weren't sure what he said," remarked Miles. "So thoughtful of him."

"My personal favorites," he added, "are the music lovers. You know, the ones with custom sound systems set at the decibel level known as *annihilate*. They want to share their delightful tunes with the world." He played air guitar and sang a rhythmic bass line, "*Boom, boom, ba-doom-boom, boom-boom-boom!*" He laughed. "Those idjits are all deaf as stones. They can only feel the vibrations, which probably register 3.5 on the Richter scale."

"They're the worst," said Sebastian.

"Yeah, and they're the ones who always end up right behind you in a traffic jam."

Sebastian had actually considered buying a pickup truck for self-defense. It would also be useful to haul around the truckloads of money he was dumping on the house and its improvements. But buying a new vehicle was simply out of the question. As he waded through knee-deep financial *merde*, he had to ignore the 165,000 miles on his battered Honda, trust to Providence, and just keep going.

To remedy the situation, he'd applied for a low-interest loan from a big Houston bank. Of course, the bank required full disclosure of everything, practically down to his boxer shorts: bank statements, tax returns, and a list of all his current debts and assets. His assets consisted of his teacher retirement, one grand piano, and one violin. Together, the two instruments were worth at least $300,000. (Too bad he couldn't drive one and live in the other.) If the loan was approved as he expected, he could pay off the Bank of Hades. He was currently racking up about $1,300 a month in interest.

Just thinking about it set his bowels in motion.

In the meantime, there was the ongoing major suction on his bank account for the repairs, the cost of an appraisal and a survey. He kept telling himself it would all work out in the end. But he was growing very, very nervous.

Sebastian turned off the highway onto a two-lane farm-to-market road. The gently rolling land was sparsely inhabited, mostly open pastures interspersed with wooded areas.

"Looks like there are more cows than people hereabouts," Miles remarked, "and so many wildflowers."

"The wildflowers draw a lot of tourists. About one-third of my property is covered with bluebonnets in March and April. But I didn't discover that until this year, since their bloom time had ended when I bought the land last July. My yard—the tourist attraction. That was the Band-Aid on the trauma of seeing the house decapitated and sawn in two."

"Yes," said Miles, "I remember the tale."

As Sebastian turned onto a narrower lane, the land began to roll even more. As they crested a hill, Miles could see a ridge looming hazy and purple in the far distance. He felt himself relax in the peace of the pastoral landscape. They traveled downhill and crossed a narrow bridge over a shallow, rocky creek. The land began to climb again, and at last, Sebastian turned right onto a dusty, unpaved road.

"Vogel Lane," said Miles, "a good street for a musician."

"Speaking of birds," replied Sebastian, "there's a roadrunner."

"Ah, yes. I recognize him from the cartoons on the telly."

Sebastian glanced at his friend. "Watching cartoons, are you, Miles?"

"Yes, Looney Tunes. Omega has driven me to it." He smiled. "No, actually Simon watches them. I simply provide moral support and a lap to sit on."

"How old is Simon now?"

"He's five. He'll start kindergarten this fall." Miles yawned and shifted in his seat. "I hate to sound like a five-year-old, but are we there yet?"

"A quarter mile to go."

"Sebastian, couldn't you have bought land a little closer to civilization? Do you have hermit tendencies?"

He grinned. "Probably, but they're justified. Civilization, as you may have noticed, if you dare to watch the news, is growing increasingly uncivil. It's unraveling."

"True."

"Actually, Miles, this area was what I could afford. Real estate here is relatively cheap because sane people don't live this far out." He glanced at Miles. "I have discovered one advantage to inaccessibility, however. Even the Mormons and Jehovah's Witnesses haven't found me yet."

Miles laughed. "Is that possible? They're as omnipresent as dust. Your house must be covered with hyperstealth invisibility paint."

"Let's hope it works with the IRS as well."

"Ha! Not bloody likely, I'm afraid. When do you expect to move in?"

"In two weeks or so, once the interior is painted."

When they finally turned into the yard and parked, Miles smiled broadly and gave his friend the thumbs-up sign. "Well done, Sebastian. It's a charming cottage. Looks like it's been here for ages."

"Come in and I'll give you the tour."

Miles stepped out of the car and inhaled deeply. "Mmm, it smells so fresh—the scent of pine and cedar. What a relief from Houston. Maybe I'll become a hermit too." He glanced at the back perimeter of the property and stopped in his tracks. "Good Lord, what is that?" He pointed to a gigantic debris pile.

"Those are the small trees and underbrush that had to be cleared from the land. Gives you an idea of how thickly wooded it was."

Sebastian led Miles up a short set of stairs to a small covered deck. He unlocked one of the double glass doors and they entered the house.

Standing in the archway between the dining room and living room, Miles smiled. "Ah, these old houses have character, don't they? Real oak floors, crown molding, generous windows. What's its area?"

"Including the decks, it's about 1,200 square feet."

"Small, but charming. The dining room flows right into the living area and the sunroom. It really feels quite spacious, and it's full of light. Almost like a miniature concert hall."

"Once the piano's in place," said Sebastian, "we'll bring Abbie over and play some chamber music here."

"Good idea." Miles paused a moment, and added, "I like the atmosphere—it's warm and inviting. Except for one thing."

Sebastian rolled his eyes. "I know what you're gonna say."

Miles grimaced. "The wall color. Do you think the former owner was suicidal?"

"Possibly. If I don't paint over the turd-brown, *I'll* be suicidal."

In the bedrooms, Miles peered out the windows. "Every room has nice views," he said, "with no neighbors in sight. Private—I like it."

"Take a look at this," Sebastian said. They walked through the living room and then outside onto an elevated, spacious deck that ran the entire length of the house. They stood at the railing next to a wide staircase that descended to the yard.

"Ah, here is your whole motivation laid bare," said Miles, gesturing at the vista before them. "No wonder you fled civilization—this view is worth it all. I'd spend all my time out here. Let's walk down to the pond."

"But first, put on your armor." Sebastian picked up a handy container of bug spray and doused his shoes, pants, legs, and arms.

Miles did the same. "Chiggers. I remember your war wounds."

"I would laugh," said Sebastian, "but the memory is too painful."

They descended the wide steps and walked out through the untamed yard of rough, uncut grass interspersed with tall black-eyed Susans, Indian blanket, and purple verbena. They startled a great blue heron hunting at the edge of the water. It bent its thin, bony knees, flapped its wings, and vaulted up, launching itself laboriously into flight with a loud and most unmusical croak—*braaak!* The ripples from the bird's departure spread across the oblong pond, which lay in a bowl-like depression with sloping sides. The surface glimmered like an opal in the late afternoon light, with streaks of pinks and blues.

"It's so peaceful out here, Sebastian, it's affecting my body. My pulse must be around sixty, and my blood pressure is in the rarely experienced realm of normal." Miles grinned. "Highly unusual for a flutist."

Sebastian nodded. "This place has the same effect on me."

"You should put a bench here by the pond," Miles suggested, "so the next time I come, we can sit beside the water, have a pint together, and gloat about getting a competent, fair department head at Omega U."

"We're so close, I almost can't believe it," replied Sebastian. "It's like a perfect dream, too good to be true. Roscoe always gets his way, but this time it looks like we might prevail. His candidate is in fifth place, and we'll only recommend the top three."

"Do you think if he loses, he'll self-destruct?"

"Doubtful. Go ballistic is more likely. We may all have to lay low until the fall semester."

"Well, we shall soon see. Thanks for showing me your lovely place," said Miles, "but all this country air makes me hungry. Ready to get something to eat? It's on me—no protests allowed. I imagine this must have cost a bomb—moving the house, the repairs and all. You don't need the added expense of taking me to dinner."

Sebastian did not protest.

They ate at Alexander's Steakhouse in the quaint downtown area. After they ordered dinner, Sebastian steered the conversation toward something that had happened the previous night, which still weighed on his mind. He asked Miles, "How long have you lived here in the United States?"

"I moved here when Julia and I got married, in September of 2001, just before the attack on the World Trade Center. Seven years."

"Do you intend to become a citizen?"

"I may. Haven't taken the plunge yet. There are some advantages to keeping my British passport. Why do you ask?"

"Well, are you at all interested in American politics? The presidential primaries and all that? This is an election year."

"Yes, I find it fascinating." Miles removed his spectacles and cleaned them with his cloth napkin.

"Have you heard any of the candidates speak?"

"Snippets on the telly—news reports." He donned his glasses.

The waiter brought their mugs of beer, and Sebastian drank gladly from his. "Well, I've been so busy working and running the roads between my house and Houston that I hadn't heard them at all. But last night I actually listened to the news, and I heard one of the candidates speak—Robby Mara, who's supposed to be so eloquent—Mr. Silver Tongue."

"Ah, yes." Miles nodded. "The media darling. Highly overrated in my opinion. Not worthy to light Winston Churchill's cigar. What did you think?"

"Well, it was a very strange experience for me. I found his delivery odd, rather flat and mechanical. But the most bizarre thing was the way he spoke. His voice sounded low and husky, more like a whisper than true speech. It had a hissing quality: sibilant with drawn-out S-sounds. I could understand the words, but it sounded like a serpent speaking, malevolent really." Sebastian laughed in embarrassment.

Miles wrinkled up his forehead. "Blimey. Well, he does have a slight lisp sometimes, I noticed. It might seem more pronounced if you didn't expect it."

"Could be." But Sebastian didn't really think so; it had been more than a lisp. He didn't tell Miles the hissing, seductive voice had horrified him so much he turned off the TV. He had looked up the meaning of the name *Mara* and found two interesting definitions. In Hebrew, it was a feminine name which meant *bitter*. In Buddhist lore, Mara was a demon who tried to hinder, obstruct, and corrupt those on the way to enlightenment.

In addition to being shocked by what he heard, Sebastian was baffled. Was it another type of encounter with the demonic—auditory instead of visual as it had been with Mary Catherine? Had the serpent-like voice revealed the true character of the man? (Whether or not it had, it upset him so much he would never vote for Robby Mara.) He wished there was someone he could ask, but that type of encounter seemed to be outside the realm of most people's experience.

Or was it? Maybe, as he had, others chose to keep quiet about their unusual experiences, like aging veterans who never spoke of the wartime atrocities they witnessed. He decided to file it away for the time being until he could do some research on the demonic. Once he moved into the house, he would have two months before the fall semester. After all his strange encounters, maybe it was time; maybe God was nudging him in that direction.

The waiter arrived with their entrées, and Sebastian welcomed the diversion. He carved out a piece of his ribeye, while Miles tasted his roast beef.

"Delicious. I'll have to come back to Bullinger!" Miles grinned at him, and then conveniently changed course. "To talk shop a little, are you having any luck with the orchestra funding? How does it look for next fall?"

"Well, I'll get nothing from Omega. If the money's purpose is not for band, the dean couldn't care less. Since I can't count on any extra funding from the administration, I applied early this year for grants or donations from Lonestar Oil, Hlavicek's Bakeries, and the Helprin County Arts Commission."

"Hlavicek's Bakeries?"

"Yes, the original Czech bakery is here in Bullinger, and the owner has a foundation that gives education grants. I struck gold—the foundation awarded our orchestra $8,000 for the fall of 2009."

"Congratulations, Sebastian! If Hlavicek likes music, tell him the orchestra will program *The Moldau*, any Dvořák symphony he wants, and a whole concert of polka music in his honor. Maybe in 2010, he'll raise it to ten thousand."

"Good thinking, Miles, but the closest I'll get to him is to eat one of his kolaches. I doubt I'll ever meet him."

"Who knows?" said Miles. "It's a very small town indeed."

CHAPTER 13

UNEXPECTED ENCOUNTERS

By Tuesday, the tenth of June, to Sebastian's everlasting relief, JR finished painting the interior of the house. Drab brown had given way to bone white, pale and creamy against the stark white of the crown molding. The change created a very calm, restful effect, and the dining room walls, painted blue-green, made a bright contrast. The place was cheerful and just about move-in ready.

Sebastian met the appraiser who came out in the morning to take pictures on all sides and walk through the house. He told Sebastian he would send him a report later, since he could only estimate its value after he researched the neighborhood and the sales of similar houses in the area.

The final hurdle to satisfy the bank was the survey. Sebastian had contacted the surveyors, but they couldn't come out until later in the month. By that time, he would have moved in. He'd have to cross that bridge later.

After the appraiser left, it was only one o'clock, so he decided to explore the town before heading home to Houston. The industrious German immigrants to Helprin County had planted a dozen Lutheran churches in a town with a population of ten thousand. He wanted to visit St. Mark's, the only Catholic church. And secondly, in order to research the demonic as he intended, he decided to visit the one bookstore in the hope that he might find *Encounters with the Diabolical,* a book on exorcism by a renowned priest from Rome.

Sebastian drove to the quiet, residential neighborhood where St. Mark's was located and parked on the street. As he entered the church, he caught the faint, familiar scent of incense and candles. The beauty of the Baroque interior surprised him—the marble floors, limestone pillars, and soaring, vaulted ceiling. Clearly, the Germans had been more prolific, but with this richly ornamented space, the Czech and Polish immigrants had done the Catholics proud. The twelve stained glass windows featured the apostles, and the dark wooden pews made a strong contrast with the light-colored stone. He gazed up at the painting behind and above the altar, where Christ ascended in billowing robes, surrounded by angels.

Alone in the cool, quiet church, Sebastian crossed himself and knelt to pray, albeit with a slight reluctance. As a believer, he went to Mass regularly, but for a long time he'd felt his faith was just the go-through-the-motions variety. Over the years, doubts had crept in when his endless prayers for Mary Catherine had gone unanswered. With a sigh, he determined to keep trying. He prayed for healing for his estranged wife, who still lay unconscious in Johns Hopkins Hospital, for comfort for his daughter Helen, and for his own rescue from crushing debt.

By the time he got to the debt part, he heard rustlings above him in the loft, and then a grand music rolled out from the organ. That ended his prayers. When he heard music, he had to focus on it to the exclusion of all else.

He crossed himself and sat back in the pew. The organ needed tuning, but the music was well played. It was a free form, improvisatory Baroque piece played with dramatic flair. He tried to guess the name and composer of the piece. Thanks to his perfect pitch, he knew it was in D Major. After several minutes, the piece came to an end, and then a dancelike piece in strict rhythm followed. He was fairly certain it was a staple of the repertoire, a J. S. Bach Prelude and Fugue.

It surprised him to hear such inspired playing in a small town. He noticed a few blurred notes and minor mistakes, but overall the organist was in control. Hidden in the loft at the back of the church, he (or she) played with technical ease and a mature musicality. Probably a fifty-year-old conservatory graduate who'd been doing this all his life, Sebastian guessed.

He leaned back against the pew and listened as the sparkling notes rippled and cascaded in the beautiful space. In Baroque music, if one finds the exact right tempo, there is a kind of hyperbeat that takes over; the music rolls and dances in waves like the sea—naturally and inevitably as if planned by God. This organist had nailed it. *Whoa*—Sebastian looked forward to going to church here, with this level of music-making to enhance the Mass.

He was sorry when the piece came to an end. He hoped to hear another, but it was not to be. St. Mark's had a good acoustic and sound carried very well, so in a minute or two, he heard the clatter of the organist's shoes as he descended the wooden stairs at the back of the church. Sebastian rose, genuflected, and walked quickly to intercept the musician out of curiosity.

The organist was at least three decades shy of fifty. A young boy, not yet out of adolescence, long-legged, gangly, all bones and little meat headed for the door. His straight, white-blond hair shone in the dimness under the loft. Was he even sixteen?

"Excellent playing," Sebastian said.

The young man stopped short and snapped his head around in surprise. "Oh, I didn't realize anyone was here." Dressed in a T-shirt, shorts, and sandals, he shifted the weight of his worn backpack, and mumbled belatedly, "Uh, well thanks."

The boy seemed so familiar. Then it struck Sebastian. "I remember you—we met at the wedding in southwest Houston, and uh . . . well, I didn't get your name." His voice trailed off and a sudden self-consciousness overcame him. To cover his discomfort, he held out his hand. "My name's Sebastian."

The young man seemed unperturbed. Sebastian saw recognition followed by relaxation, a kind of lightening and opening up, take place in the blue-violet eyes, and the boy smiled. "As in, Bach?" He clasped Sebastian's hand firmly and shook it. "I'm Leo."

Sebastian had the distinct impression the young man was quite glad to see him again. "Leo. Do you remember the day I mean?"

"At the Baptist church, my friend's wedding. Yes, I do. You're the violinist."

Sebastian couldn't bring himself to follow up on their earlier meeting—especially not the "magnificent light" remark. "Yes, I teach at Omega University and I play with Opera D'Argento."

Leo raised his eyebrows. "Oh, yes, my mother and I saw a performance of *Tosca* there in April. You're the concertmaster, aren't you? T. Sebastian Morrow—I remember your name."

"That's me." Sebastian nodded, surprised. "By the way, were you playing the D Major Prelude and Fugue just now?"

"Yeah, it's one of the pieces I'm working on for a competition next year. Are you a fan of organ music?"

"I like organ music, but I'm no expert. I just made an educated guess. Do you study organ with someone locally, Leo?"

"Not anyone from Bullinger. My teacher is Tobias Mortensson at the University of Houston. I'm about to start my sophomore year."

Nineteen or twenty, and already playing like a pro. "Well, keep up the good work. Are you the organist here?"

"Yes, it's a part-time job."

"I wondered because I'm moving here later this month, and I'll be attending Mass at St. Mark's. I look forward to hearing you in the future."

"Nice to meet you again," the boy said and turned to go.

"Oh, by the way, I heard there's a really good bookstore in town called de Graaf's. Can you tell me how to get there from here?"

He grinned. "That's easy. I'm going there now, so you can follow me."

As they walked out of the dim, cool church into brilliant sun and shocking heat, Sebastian wondered what the odds were that he should meet this remarkable boy again in this little town, far from their first encounter. He didn't believe in coincidences. There must be a reason Leo had come into his life.

The temperature in Sebastian's car had reached *broil*, so he turned the AC on high. He followed Leo's battered black Jeep about two miles north and then west as the boy turned left onto Zeiss Street, which ran through the heart of Bullinger's quaint downtown. It was dominated by the dignified courthouse, which took up a whole block. There were several restaurants, two bakeries, clothes shops, and at least five antique stores.

They parked on the street, and Leo pointed at a corner building painted a cheery yellow. "That's de Graaf's," he said.

"Are you going there too?"

"Later. Right now, I've got a date with a big banana split at the ice cream bar across the street."

Ah, youth. For the first forty years of his life, Sebastian consumed as many calories as he wished and stayed skinny as a single strand of spaghetti. Now in his mid-fifties, he was not overweight, but he would be if he ate with the wild abandon of a teenager. He wiped his brow in the heat and thought with envy of Leo's cold, delicious dessert.

As he entered the bookstore, the cool air refreshed him. Sebastian was pleasantly assailed by the aroma of fresh-brewed coffee and a faint, musty undertone of books and old wood. He knew from his research about Bullinger that the downtown had been built in the late nineteenth-century. This particular building was two stories tall with an oak floor, high ceilings, and ancient ceiling fans that oscillated lazily, stirring the air.

There was a small, unattended coffee bar to the right of the entrance with a few tables and a comfortable-looking white sofa against the wall. At the only occupied table, a young mother shared a thick purple smoothie with a placid toddler and a very energetic little boy, about five years old. The checkout counter was to the left, and the wooden staircase to the second floor was straight ahead. The rest of the large downstairs was taken up by shelves and shelves of books, both new and used.

"May I help you?" asked a feminine voice.

Sebastian detected a slight accent which he couldn't place. The owner of the voice, tall, lithe and blond as a Nordic queen, emerged from behind the staircase. Cheeks flushed with effort, she carried a large, heavy cardboard box of books as she walked quickly and purposefully toward him, closing the gap between them.

The box looked so heavy, Sebastian stepped toward her and said, "Let me help—"

But the mother's shout cut him off. "Come back here, Jeremy!"

The little boy darted right across the path of the Nordic queen. She stopped short to avoid hitting him, but her momentum and the weight of the box caused her upper body to pitch forward. As the little boy ran past, she and the box of books hit Sebastian in the center of his chest. The force of the blow knocked him backward, and he lost his balance. He fell heavily on his back with the box and the Nordic queen on his chest. It knocked the wind out of him.

While he lay wide-eyed in pain, paralyzed and unable to breathe, the woman immediately rolled off of him and lifted the box off his chest. She leaned over him and spoke rapidly in a low voice in what seemed like gibberish.

He heard another female voice. "Mamma, speak English. He can't understand you."

"Oh, sir, are you all right? I'm so sorry! Can you get up?"

Sebastian closed his eyes, clutched his chest, and grimaced in pain, unable to speak. The only thing he wanted to do at that moment was breathe.

"Do you think he's having a heart attack, Kristin?" the woman asked. "Should we call an ambulance?"

He shook his head vehemently. Hell no, he didn't want an ambulance. Medical costs on top of all his house debt—no way! Finally, he gasped for breath and opened his eyes.

The woman leaning over him gave the impression of light—long white-blond hair framing the fair skin of her face; a white, sleeveless blouse; a sky-blue cotton skirt. Even in his distress, he noticed a fragrance about her. He didn't know if it was her skin or her hair, or a combination of both—but it was sweet and clean, a fresh smell with a hint of orange blossoms. The worried eyes that searched his own seemed familiar, large and a deep blue-violet. She had a short straight nose and rather full lips. "Do you think you can sit up?"

Kristin, blond as her mother, extended a shapely arm covered in fine white hairs. "Let me help you."

As Sebastian gripped her hand, her mother put an arm around his back—not a bad feeling at all. Together, they helped him sit up. Chest heaving, he began to catch his breath. He glanced at the two women bending over him and wondered if he had opened a magic door to Scandinavia.

In the meantime, the wayward Jeremy had been captured by his frazzled mother. Firmly grasping the hands of both children, she appeared beside them. "I'm so sorry, Silvie. My son just got away from me before I could catch him."

Silvie, the Nordic queen.

"Well, I know it was an accident," Silvie said rather sternly, "but you see what can happen."

"I promise you he won't get away from me again. Say you're sorry, Jeremy."

Jeremy's chin dropped, his lower lip shot out, and his eyes welled up with tears. "I'm sorry."

The mother bit her lip and looked at Sebastian. "Are you all right, sir?"

All he could muster was a whisper. "Don't worry, I'm okay."

"Oh, thank goodness. I'm taking these two home right now." She and her two children stepped around them and made a quick exit.

"If we help you, do you think you could walk over to the sofa and sit down?" asked Silvie.

Good Lord, she talked to him as if he were a hundred-year-old geezer. The man in him decided to get up even if it killed him. Sebastian shook his head and rose on his own with some effort. They walked with him to the sofa.

He sat down and finally got his voice back. "Oh, it knocked the wind out of me. I'm really all right. Just give me a few minutes."

"Would you like something to drink?" asked Kristin, pointing to the coffee bar.

"Actually, some hot coffee with cream would be great. I need a jump-start."

"Coming up!" She smiled and disappeared behind the coffee bar.

Sebastian looked up at Silvie and held out his hand. "I'm Sebastian Morrow."

"Oh," her eyes widened. "I forgot my manners in the uproar—or was it a downroar?" The corners of her mouth pulled back in a most charming smile. "I'm Silvie de Graaf."

"The owner?"

"Yes, and that's my daughter Kristin who's helping me out this summer."

Kristin returned with two cups of coffee and a poppy seed kolache wrapped in a paper napkin for Sebastian. "Extra jump-starting," she said as she handed it to him. He sipped the strong brew gratefully.

"Here, Mamma, I thought you might like a cup of coffee, too."

"Thank you."

At that moment, a customer descended the stairs and walked to the checkout counter.

"Sit down, Mamma. I'll take care of it."

"I think I will," said Silvie. "My knees feel a little weak."

As she sat beside Sebastian on the sofa, he remarked, "That sounds a little Old World."

"What does?"

"The use of the word *mamma* instead of *mom*."

She sipped her coffee, and then said, "In Sweden, children—even grown ones—say Mamma."

"Were you speaking Swedish just now in the downroar?"

There was that smile again. "Yes, I was. I speak it with my children at home, and I lapse into it when I get upset or very tired."

"I thought I noticed a slight accent. How long have you lived in America?" He took a bite of the kolache and chased it with coffee.

"About twenty-five years now."

"Do you have other children besides Kristin?"

"Just one," she said and glanced at the entrance. "And here he comes."

The shop door opened, the bell jangled, and in walked Leo.

"Hey, Mamma! I see you met Sebastian."

The resemblance between mother and son was so strong, Leo could have been her twin. No wonder her eyes had seemed so familiar. Now surprise filled those sapphire eyes as she glanced from her son to him, but she asked no questions. She simply answered, "Yes, I did, and what a meeting it was."

CHAPTER 14

MOVED

During the week of June sixteenth, as the summer heat ratcheted up in earnest and the chiggers continued their assault on humankind, Sebastian spent every day at Omega attending interviews with the five candidates for the department head position. Evenings, he packed and sorted through all his worldly goods for the move to the country.

The committee interviewed one candidate per day, and they also observed each one teach a class in his or her specialty. Marjorie Matthews did a stellar job teaching music history—she captivated the students. Roscoe's choice followed her the next day. Ferris Duck might as well have been Lame Duck; he was the amateur to her professional. The students fidgeted and rolled their eyes—he never gained their attention, much less held it.

Of course, for the faculty, the highlight was lunch with the candidates at Christo's, a local seafood restaurant. The meals, to Sebastian's great relief, were paid for by Omega U. Tending toward the methodical, he tried fried shrimp, fried catfish, fried oysters, fried frog legs, and fried alligator. When Miles asked him which one he liked best, he replied, "Fried shrimp, of course. But in the barrio, we don't eat shrimp." He smiled. "We eat *trimps*."

On Friday afternoon, the committee voted again and narrowed the field to three finalists. They eliminated the pianist Soren Lind, although Sebastian thought he might make a good administrator even without prior experience. And thankfully, Ferris Duck got cut. That dashed Roscoe's hopes of course, probably the first time he was ever thwarted in his career at Omega U. What were the odds of that? Normally he prevailed like Godzilla over Bambi.

The search committee's job ended with their final recommendations: Marjorie Matthews, Bruce Riker, and Samuel Nudelman—good choices all, though dynamic Marjorie was Sebastian's favorite. Now the committee had to wait for the dean and provost to make the final decision.

Sebastian and Miles had hoped for a good department head for years, so even though it was premature, they celebrated in advance. Since all the finalists had had successful administrative experience, and most importantly, not one of them was a band director, they thought they couldn't lose. They felt sure the focus in the department would shift from its narrow, almost total emphasis (financial and otherwise) on the band program to a share-the-wealth/share-the-spotlight mentality supportive of the choir, orchestra, and pianists. Band and marching band were important—certainly some graduates would become band directors—but many others would teach choir or orchestra, and a few would become performers in symphony orchestras, dance bands, opera, ballet, and musical theater orchestras.

With an enormous sense of relief that his work with the search committee had ended, Sebastian made the move to the country the next day, the longest day of the year, and he needed every hour of it. His departure from Baltimore years ago had taught him one important fact: moving is hell. He found it ironic that his emotional stress then and now, almost thirty years later, still centered on Mary Catherine. Previously, he and Helen had left her; this time, unless she recovered from the coma, she would leave them.

On Thursday, the piano movers transported his six-foot grand. Sebastian followed on Saturday morning. Thankful for the hot, clear weather, he made the move the cheapest way possible: with JR's open trailer. Rain would have been disastrous, but the sunny weather held. JR hauled the trailer to Houston, and with his help, Sebastian loaded his furniture and all the boxes he had packed. They tied everything down, and then JR towed it back to the country with his pickup truck. Sebastian followed with his CRV stuffed to the roof. After they unloaded at the house, JR left.

By the time Sebastian had set up some of his furniture and moved all the boxes into the appropriate rooms, it was nearing midnight. As he reassembled his bed and made it, his arm muscles trembled with fatigue, and his eyelids threatened to descend like a third-act curtain. He showered and then crawled into bed and lay flat on his back. He woke up in the same position eight hours later.

The first thing he noticed the next morning was the quiet—no traffic noise or sirens, no car radios blaring Tejano or rap music, no kids shouting, not even a barking dog. He didn't get up immediately; he allowed himself a few lazy minutes to rest. For the first time in his life, he had awakened in his own house on his own property. After a few exultant minutes, Sebastian heaved himself out of bed, with a grimace and a long, loud groan. There are many muscles in the human body, and Sebastian could have sworn every one of them was on fire. He opened the blinds in all four windows to let in the morning light and looked out at his land. A cardinal and two black-capped chickadees in the cedar tree outside his window greeted him with their cheerful songs.

He stretched, wincing at the pain and then hobbled to the bathroom to pee. Even the bathroom had a large window. While he stood at the toilet, he glanced out at the expanse of cleared land that ended in a narrow perimeter of cedar and oak trees. No neighbors or prying eyes that way—just pastures. He spied two wild rabbits nibbling the greenery near the edge of the property. Movement caught his eye, and to his delight, he saw three white-tailed deer glide out of the woods and walk on his land, parallel to the barbed-wire fence.

He could have gazed out the window all day, but his growling stomach urged him into the kitchen. He unearthed his toaster and a small cast iron frying pan from two of the boxes. Next, he found the coffee and coffee pot and made himself a strong brew. In the refrigerator he had the supplies he'd brought in a cooler the previous day—cheese, eggs, bread, butter, a carton of milk, strawberry jam, and three bottled beers. He set to work making a cheese omelet with toast.

He decided that clearing off the boxes on the dining table could wait. He sighed, looking at stacks of cartons everywhere. It could all wait—he intended to have a leisurely breakfast before unpacking. With his plate in one hand and a mug of coffee in the other, he threaded his way through the living room between the boxes on one side and the piano on the other and took his breakfast out to the big deck.

The deck sat four feet above the ground, giving a high vantage point to survey the scene. He sat in one of his two Adirondack chairs with his plate on his lap, enjoying the cool breeze. Straight ahead, the cleared land, dotted by large trees, sloped down to the pond. The morning sun sparkled on the ruffled blue surface of the water. He sipped the hot coffee and watched a great white egret stalk the pond's perimeter, hunting. He was so pleased, he didn't even notice how leathery the omelet was.

A few puffy white clouds scudded across the sky, and the trees teemed with birds, singing for all they were worth. A red-tailed hawk sailed above him, and Sebastian laughed. Ha! All he lacked was a scepter and he could have been an Old Testament king on a high throne, viewing his kingdom. His T-shirt, pajama bottoms, and bare feet didn't really fit the image, but, nonetheless, the fact was, he owned (with the current backing of the Bank of Hades) a goodly two and a half acres of Texas.

Beyond the pond, another acre of heavily wooded land sloped up again, a pathless, tangled wildlife sanctuary. Two black vultures glided in large circles above the woods, which served as a buffer to hide Daniel and Meg Doyle's house from sight.

The road lay eighty feet to the right, but the horizon was houseless, although he did have two other neighbors nearby. Bart Bidler lived across the road, but he owned seventy-five acres, and his house was set far back from the road, hidden by an encircling forest. The property adjacent to Sebastian's on the opposite side of the house was owned by a young couple, Roy and Lilian Greiner, who had a two-year-old son. They lived in a single-wide trailer, but a natural hedge of live oaks, cedars, and pine trees on Sebastian's land created a privacy fence between them. Even though he had three neighbors, he couldn't see them, and they couldn't see him—perfect for a man who wanted to distance himself from the rest of humanity. Or so he thought.

Twenty seconds later, in the midst of chewing a mouthful of buttered toast and jam, Sebastian glanced up at the distant vultures, and then at the empty chair beside him. With a pang, he remembered Mary Catherine. Suddenly the sun seemed dimmer. He had made flight reservations to Baltimore for the following week, per Helen's suggestion. *She may only have days left, Dad. If you want to see her, you'd better come soon.*

With the committee's work done and the move accomplished, he could travel, but he didn't look forward to it. He hadn't seen Mary Catherine since Helen's college graduation twelve years ago. The change in her would be enormous, and not for the good. "She's just skin-covered bones," Helen had said. His stomach tensed as he imagined her lying in a coma, her wasted body fed by tubes and attached to cold, blinking machines. He set down his coffee mug. He hated the fact that neither he nor Helen could communicate with her now, and, worse, that every intervention he had tried had failed to halt her headlong flight into self-destruction.

In fact, one of his interventions had backfired badly. Mary Catherine told him she had been sitting on the sofa in her apartment one day, when she heard a rush of wind. A goddess (Sebastian took it to mean some sort of apparition) wearing a red gown entered through the open window and touched her. She felt the addiction pass out of her—she literally felt limp and slumped over. She no longer felt the need for alcohol.

She had three halcyon weeks. Then one Friday night she went out with her girlfriends and temptation overcame her. She resumed drinking and went on a binge. Six days later, she woke up fully clothed on her bed, with dried vomit all over her chest. Her shoes were missing, and her hair was matted. She could not account for the lost time—she had no recall of what happened or where she had been.

Sebastian realized it was all his fault. The remote healer had removed one demon, but apparently a host of others had taken its place. Whatever the good intentions of the healer, she dealt in witchcraft. He hadn't understood the danger, and he regretted his action the rest of his life.

The empty chair beside him would never hold Mary Catherine— her story was coming to its end. She would never see this house or hear the birds' exuberant morning chorus. She would never sit with him and breathe in the sharp, fresh smell of pine and cedar woods or feel the morning breeze ruffle her hair. She would never delight in the play of sun and wind on the pond.

He sighed and sipped his coffee. And then, unbidden, another image came to mind. Guilt raised its head and contended with sorrow.

He was in life, not death, he reasoned; he had years yet to live. Mary Catherine's story was ending, but he was only midway in his. Sebastian couldn't help it—his caffeine-fueled imagination filled the empty chair beside him with the long-legged presence of another woman, she of the blue-violet eyes—Silvie the Nordic queen.

CHAPTER 15

DANCING DAY

Oftentimes people, including his Aunt Nancy (who knew better), asked Sebastian why he had never remarried. His mother's younger sister by twelve years, Nancy Leaton was only eight years older than he, the same age as Mary Catherine. Long considered the family outlaw, she'd married an attorney, left New Jersey for Houston, and truly infuriated her parents with her final betrayal: she converted to Protestantism, the Episcopal Church to be exact.

Though she'd taken up Anglican ways and practically memorized the Book of Common Prayer, Aunt Nancy still came armed with a rosary. Warm and cheerful, she was one of the reasons Sebastian had decided to move to Houston for graduate school. And she deserved his everlasting thanks for all the weekends she had babysat Helen while Sebastian played his gigs. She had also given pre-adolescent Helen "the talk." The female reproductive system, although wondrous, was not something he felt comfortable explaining to a twelve-year-old girl.

A small woman with the same salt and pepper hair as his, Aunt Nancy called him regularly and always began the same way.

"Sebastian, any girlfriend yet? Why should a handsome man like you stay single all these years?"

Handsome, he didn't know. But he had enough anti-marriage excuses to fill a cookie jar, and maybe a couple of them were true. He tried them all out on Aunt Nancy:

I'm too picky.
I'm too busy working to meet women.
Raising Helen alone, I had to focus all my energy on her
and my job. Now she's grown, the energy's gone.
I'm too set in my ways.
I snore and I'm too damn old.

Her answer was always the same: "Nonsense! I'll keep praying for you."

Of course, some people didn't ask; they were the ones who suspected he was gay. *He's fifty-something years old and lives alone—what else could he be? Artists like him are all fruitcakes.* And speaking of his work, this was his favorite comment: *A violinist? Really? No wonder his wife left him. He should grow up and get a real job.*

The worst was when his well-meaning friends tried to remedy the situation. "Why don't you come over for dinner on Saturday? My wife's friend Susan is coming. She's a really nice woman."

A really nice woman—code words. Translation: 1) she probably resembles a truck, 2) she's a female wrestler who's built like a truck, or 3) she's a pale, scrawny vegan who looks like she was run over by a truck.

Sebastian, you should sign up for one of those dating services.

Never. He didn't like shopping for anything, much less a date.

Speaking of dates, today was the Fourth of July and the fourth day after his return from Baltimore. It was not only America's birthday; it was Helen's too. July 4, 1975. He would call her later. She entered the world thirty-three years ago on a Friday at 6:12 p.m. Sebastian played an outdoor concert less than two hours later with the Baltimore Symphony and smoked his first cigar immediately after. He was a father at the advanced age of twenty-three.

He adored his daughter. *Children and the fruit of the womb are a heritage and a gift from the Lord. They are like arrows in the hand of a giant.* He remembered the Bible quote, but like most good Catholics, he couldn't cite chapter and verse. Bible study was for Protestants—it kept them busy. Catholics had no time for that; like clockwork, they attended Mass, received the Eucharist, and brought their sins to confession.

All right, here was his confession: the reason he never remarried was because he and Mary Catherine never divorced. Clear and simple, but if he told the truth, he would have to answer a million more questions about why two people who hadn't lived together in twenty-eight years never got divorced. That was the rub about being Catholic. Or maybe it was just the rub about being T. Sebastian Morrow.

Ah, Mary Catherine. For decades, he and Helen observed her long descent into the vortex of addiction, a slow-motion suicide.

He recalled his sad trip to Baltimore. They had buried her on Monday, the last day of June. With the singing of the first hymn, Helen sobbed, and Sebastian's own tears surprised him. He grieved for what might have been if his wife had loved her husband and child more than her next drink. That a human being, made in the image of God, could willfully and single-mindedly destroy her own body, alienate her family, and bind herself like a slave to a bottle was sad beyond words.

The funeral took place in St. Ignatius Church, where Sebastian and Mary Catherine had met in the choir, where they married, and the place now where they would part forever. Outside, the rain poured down in a gray curtain. Sebastian sat in the first pew between Helen and his Aunt Nancy. Kieran sat on the aisle with his arm around Helen. Aunt Nancy had traveled from Houston at short notice, and Sebastian was very glad for her company and her prayers. Mary Catherine's six siblings and their families took up the rest of the first row and three more pews behind them. Thankfully, both her parents had passed away and didn't have to endure the death of their troubled daughter.

As Sebastian kept his eye on the pall-covered casket, he wondered about the state of Mary Catherine's soul. He hoped she might be with the Lord, but he didn't know. Where had she gone at the moment of death? Had she been afraid? Had her faith comforted her?

In articulo mortis
Caelitus mihi vires.
Deo adjuvante non timendum.

At the moment of death
My strength is from heaven.
God helping, nothing should I fear.

Even as he hoped for her salvation, his sadness swelled. Lost in his thoughts, he barely heard the readings and prayers throughout the Mass. It seemed to end very quickly. Riding together in Kieran's car, they followed the hearse to the cemetery in the pouring rain. The family and the priest huddled under a large canopy beside the open grave for the burial rites.

Afterward, Helen, Kieran, Sebastian, and Aunt Nancy ate lunch at a seafood restaurant near the harbor in Baltimore. A subdued group, they sat in a booth and ordered salad, crab cakes, and beer. The rain had stopped, but the city steamed, hot and humid as Houston. After the meal, they would all go their separate ways. Kieran and Helen would drive Sebastian and Aunt Nancy to the airport, and then they would head back home to Lancaster.

Over the course of the meal, Sebastian and Helen talked about their last moments with Mary Catherine. "You know," Sebastian remarked, "Mary Catherine was a cheerful drunk. She once told me that alcohol was her best friend. In the end, it was her only friend, false and deceitful, but she had driven everyone else away."

He described how he and Helen had sat beside her bed several hours a day for three days. The first time they entered the room together, Helen began to weep silently. Sebastian stared in shock at a woman he hardly recognized. She bore only the faintest resemblance to the attractive, lively girl he had married long ago.

Unconscious, she lay like a stick figure in the bed. It was as though someone had sucked all the meat from her body and left only the skin, intact and clinging to the bones. "Aunt Nancy, I covered her with the knitted prayer shawl, the one in blue-green sea tones you sent with me. It was the only color in the room. With her poor, thin arms resting by her sides, she looked bloodless, withered, and old enough to be my grandmother instead of my wife.

"Her eyes were sunken, and she breathed very slowly and shallowly. She had an oxygen tube attached to her nose, a monitor clipped to her forefinger, and a tube inserted in her arm to feed her intravenously." The room had been chilly, but not as cold as the ice at the pit of Sebastian's stomach.

Helen said, "We sat on either side of her bed. I told her who I was and that Dad had come to see her."

"I saw Mary Catherine's eyes move under the closed lids and wondered if that was recognition or just a random reaction," Sebastian said. "I spoke to her myself, and told her who I was. I took her hand in both of mine—it was very cold—and gently chafed it. I asked her if she could hear me.

"She didn't react, and I didn't know what to do next," Sebastian continued. "Helen and I sat without speaking for a while. Then, partly to break the awful silence, and partly to comfort myself, I sang a song she had loved." He sang it softly in the restaurant, while the others nodded in recognition:

> *Tomorrow shall be my dancing day;*
> *I would my true love did so chance*
> *To see the legend of my play,*
> *To call my true love to my dance.*
> *Sing, oh! my love, oh! my love, my love, my love,*
> *This have I done for my true love.*

"Why did you sing that particular song, Sebastian?" asked Nancy.

He shrugged. "I don't really know." Perhaps it recalled the beginning of their courtship, when he and Mary Catherine had often attended dances. Unlike many trained musicians who move awkwardly and self-consciously on the dance floor, he had always enjoyed dancing. Or maybe he sang it to comfort himself, because music was always his refuge, or because he stared into the face of death and wanted so badly to call her back, to affirm life—no matter what.

They suspended the conversation when the waiter brought the food. Aunt Nancy said a prayer to bless the meal, and they ate in silence for a few minutes. During the lull in the conversation, Sebastian wondered what they would not have done, he and Helen, to snatch Mary Catherine from the jaws of addiction. He went with her to AA meetings, and later on, so did Helen. He suggested therapy and paid her psychologist. They found a faith-based treatment center for female addicts in Baltimore. The program included a one-year residency followed by a halfway house at the end of the twelve months. And they prayed for her daily through all the years.

Any one of those solutions would have worked had not the essential thing been lacking—Mary Catherine's will, her desire to stay sober. Sometimes she stayed sober for a month, six weeks, and once six months, a record indeed, but she always relapsed.

Their last attempt was the residential treatment center in Baltimore, nine years ago. By that time, Helen had married Kieran and moved to Pennsylvania. She had researched the year-long, faith-based program and found it to be one of the more successful facilities, with a very low recidivism rate. After interviews with the staff of the treatment center, Mary Catherine had been accepted for the program. She agreed to move in during the summer of 1999.

He and Helen rejoiced. They traveled to Baltimore and the three of them had dinner together on the eve of Mary Catherine's admittance to the center. They congratulated her on her brave choice. They encouraged her and promised to visit each month. They laughed together and felt like a family again after so many years. At the end of the evening, they dropped Mary Catherine off at her apartment and returned to the hotel.

When they arrived to pick her up early the next morning, she didn't answer the door. She didn't answer her phone either. Finally, they convinced the superintendent of the building to let them in. They did not find her passed out drunk as they feared. They simply did not find her. The next day, they filed a missing person's report and then waited. Two weeks later, the police arrested her along with several homeless people for forcing entry into an unoccupied building and lighting a fire. They put her in jail.

Sebastian refused to post bail.

The ugly memories, the disappointments and betrayals were as stark and endless as the badlands, a barren wilderness, where they had wandered for many years. As they sat at her bedside, they did not dwell on the memories, but they talked instead of the difficulty in understanding her determined self-destruction, a theme repeated in different ways over many years: *Why, Mary Catherine, could you not love life and love us more than the oblivion decanted from a bottle? Was it really worth it? To trade ten minutes of euphoria for hours and days of 200-proof misery?*

Sebastian resumed his story. He told Nancy and Kieran about the third day of the bedside vigil. By then, he had arrived at the cliff where the highway of rational thought ended. Faith took over. "I decided to pray for my wife." Before Nancy could say anything, he held up one hand and said, "Aunt Nancy, I prayed privately for her every day all these years. But this time I held her hand and prayed aloud for peace and healing for her if it was God's will. I said if it wasn't God's will, then might she at last enter into the Lord's kingdom. In Jesus' name."

"The prayer had an immediate effect." Helen took over the tale. "Mom stirred. Her eyelids fluttered and she turned her head. We hadn't seen her change position the whole time we were there. Except for her shallow breathing, she had lain completely still, white-faced and unresponsive.

"I asked if she could hear me and I rubbed her hand and arm. 'We love you, Mom,' I said." Helen's voice broke and tears flooded her gray eyes, magnifying them. She took out a tissue and dabbed them away. "Mom opened her eyes and moved her head from side to side as if she were searching for something. I couldn't tell if her eyes were focused or not. Her mouth worked as if to speak, but only a groan emerged."

Sebastian winced at the memory. "I wondered if she was hurting. I took hold of her hand and asked her to squeeze my hand if she could hear me. Her fingers tightened slightly. My heart jumped and I nodded at Helen.

"I asked her if she was in pain. 'Squeeze my hand again if you are.' But she didn't.

"When Helen asked her if she wanted some water, she tightened her grip," said Sebastian.

Helen continued, "I took a small green sponge on a stick, dipped it into a glass of water on the bedside table, and placed it in her mouth. After Mom sucked on the sponge, I gave her water a second time. She opened and closed her eyes several times, but she seemed unable to speak. We told her we had been by her side for three days, and we wanted her to get well."

Sebastian didn't even remember all he said. "She closed her eyes and lay motionless again. I still held her hand in mine, but after a moment, I decided to release it. Then a curious thing happened. I relaxed my grip, but she tightened hers, as if she didn't want to let me go. I held her hand for a very long time."

He had tried in vain to remember the last time he had held Mary Catherine's hand. It must have been thirty years ago.

"Then she tried to speak again, but her voice was almost inaudible. I couldn't understand her." In truth, Sebastian thought he heard the word *sorry*, repeated three times, but he couldn't be sure. Perhaps it was his own wishful thinking. He hoped it was a sign of Mary Catherine's last-minute repentance, but he would never know.

"Very softly, I sang another verse of *Tomorrow Shall Be His Dancing Day*.

> *Then on the cross hanged I was,*
> *Where a spear my heart did glance;*
> *There issued forth both water and blood,*
> *To call my true love to my dance.*
> *Sing, oh! my love, oh! my love, my love, my love,*
> *This have I done for my true love.*

Kieran encircled Helen with his arm, while Aunt Nancy removed her glasses and wiped her eyes.

"After a while, her fingers went slack, and I laid her hand by her side. It was six o'clock in the evening. Helen and I were tired and hungry, so we left to get something to eat. Ten minutes later, the nurse called. Mary Catherine had passed away."

CHAPTER 16
STUNNER

If a tree don't bear fruit, it ain't worth a damn. So said Jacob Morrow, Sebastian's paternal grandfather. And Sebastian wholeheartedly agreed. His mouth watered as he remembered eating the apples, pears, and sweet cherries his grandpa grew. On a sunny afternoon in mid-July, Sebastian visited one of the local plant nurseries in Bullinger. As a lifelong renter, he had never been able to create an orchard like his grandpa, but now that he owned land, he could plant whatever he wished. As he walked the nursery grounds, he smiled, remembering Jacob's oft-repeated maxim.

Although it wasn't certain why New Jersey's nickname came to be "The Garden State," in Sebastian's mind it was because of farmers like Jacob. He had been one of the devoted and gifted gardeners whose efforts made the state—well, at least the southern and western part—green, flourishing, and beautiful. Sebastian had fond memories of helping him plant the vegetable garden. (Mostly he had just played in the dirt and thrown clods at the birds.)

Sebastian browsed among the potted plants and trees, as his imagination transformed his raw land into Eden. He didn't make any purchases that day, since it was best to plant fruit trees in the fall, but he asked the proprietor a number of questions about what thrived best in Central Texas and made some mental plans. He drove away in a state of eager anticipation. He would begin in October with persimmon, fig, and blueberry. And maybe satsuma.

He also made a run by de Graaf's Books. Since he didn't teach in the summer, he had a lot more time for reading, which naturally gave him a good reason to visit to Silvie's store. He bought a biography of Handel by Paul Henry Lang, Sibley's book on North American birds, and a small book called *Stand Against the Adversary* by a Pentecostal preacher educated in England. Sebastian had already bought the Catholic exorcist's book, but he wanted a different point of view.

To his chagrin, Silvie was out. While he nursed a cup of coffee for thirty minutes in the hope she'd return, he chatted with her daughter Kristin, who was about to begin her senior year as an English major at University of Texas.

"What will you do when you graduate?"

"Probably enroll in law school," she laughed. "There aren't any jobs for English majors."

Sebastian fished, "What kind of work does your dad do?"

An odd look crossed her face, and she glanced down at the table. "Well, Pappa started the bookshop, but he passed away two years ago. He had a heart attack."

"Oh, sorry to hear that," a statement both true and false. He was sorry Kristin lost her father, but secretly delighted that Silvie was no longer married.

"Mamma runs it now. She likes the work, and she's a good businesswoman."

Feeling suddenly lighthearted, Sebastian drank the last sip of coffee and said, "Well, give her my regards. After a run by the grocery store, I'm going home to read my books."

He kept an eye out for Silvie as he shopped for groceries, but he had no luck there either. When he arrived home, he set the books down on the dining table and put his groceries away. He mopped his damp brow and poured himself a glass of ice water. He noticed the blinking message indicator on the answering machine. Two messages. He had the landline installed as disaster insurance. If in a catastrophic situation his mobile phone ceased to work, he would have another option.

He didn't count on disaster coming via the telephone, but that's exactly what happened.

The first message was from Roscoe. "The dean wants to meet with the search committee in his office at ten o'clock tomorrow. Call me and let me know ASAP if you can be there."

Naturally, he didn't bother with a greeting. Sebastian blew out a burst of air. What was that all about? The search committee's job was done—what did the dean want? The fact that weeks had gone by and he had not yet announced the name of the new department head made Sebastian uneasy.

He pressed a button and the machine played the second message, which seemed innocuous enough. "Dr. Morrow, this is Charles Schneider, the surveyor. Please give me a call."

First, Sebastian dutifully called Roscoe and told him he would be there in the morning.

He asked him if he knew the purpose of the meeting.

"No idea," he said and hung up.

Thank you, Mr. Abrupt.

Next he called the surveyor. Schneider's loud, gravelly voice hurt his ear; he held the phone four inches away from his head. "Uh, Mr. Morrow, we surveyed your property yesterday, and I have to tell you your house is not on your land."

"What!" Sebastian shook his head—that couldn't be right. "No, I put this house on my lot. The realtor showed me the survey pins the

first day I came out here. My land extends all the way from Doyle's property to Greiner's."

"Well, sir, it does not. There's a one-acre lot between your property and Greiner, and that's where you put the house."

Sebastian's stomach knotted up and he held his breath. "Then who owns the lot?"

"I don't know. You'll have to call the Helprin County Office and ask them."

He laid the receiver down with a shaking hand. His heart hammered, his palms sweated, and he felt sudden nausea. *He had moved the house onto someone else's land.*

"Ohhh!" The word came out in a burst of air as if someone had punched him in the stomach.

Suddenly the Episcopal priest's words sprang into his mind. *You've heard of the TV show* The High Chaparral? *Well, I called my place The Low Chaparral.* And the statement of Edgar Rhodes, who bulldozed the property: *Man, it's a big two and a half acres.*

Fr. Jack had put his trailer down in the low part of the property because that was all he had owned. He hadn't owned the high ground. And Edgar Rhodes had hinted that the property Sebastian bought was more than two and a half acres.

God, he was the biggest fool in the world. T. Sebastian Morrow: the consummate ass, a *dummkopf extraordinaire.* What a blunder.

What could he do? His worst nightmare would be to move the house all over again, fifty feet down the slope where he never wanted it to be in the first place. That would cost another ten grand, and the plumbing, electricity, septic tank, and propane tank would all have to be torn out and reinstalled. It made his bowels loose just to think about it.

He could make an offer and try to buy the property from the rightful owner, whoever that was. That person hadn't been out to see the land in at least a year. He, or she, didn't even know someone had cleared the lot and moved a house onto it. Surprise!

And who had got Sebastian into this mother of all disasters? Emma Gallagher, rookie real estate agent and . . . and . . . boy, he had some rich adjectives to describe her. He could turn the air blue, but it would be a waste of energy. The damage was done.

It dawned on him then that he could sue her and her real estate firm for misrepresentation. Maybe they should pay the costs involved. That would be his last choice; he really didn't want to resort to litigation. But he really did want to talk to Emma.

It was only four o'clock; she would still be at work. Sebastian called and she answered on the third ring. He told her the lot where his house sat did not belong to him and was not included in the property he had bought.

"What?"

He felt a grim satisfaction at her shocked tone.

"How do you know that, Sebastian?"

"The surveyor just confirmed it."

Silence reigned at the other end of the line.

"Emma, can you find out who owns the lot?"

"Uh, yes. Let me look it up online."

A little task she had failed to do a year ago.

After about thirty seconds, she said, "It belongs to Sharon Obermann. She's an older woman who lives in Humble."

Well, that explained why Ms. Obermann didn't visit her property very often. Humble was about two hours away, a long drive to see a piece of undeveloped land. Well, formerly undeveloped.

"Do you have a phone number for her?"

"Hold on."

After another short wait, Emma gave him the number.

"Sebastian, I'm very sorry. I thought the property went all the way to Greiner's land."

He didn't utter a word; he just let her stew.

"Umm, what are you going to do?"

Did he detect a slight quaver in her voice? Did she realize he could sue the hell out of her and her firm?

"I'm going to call Sharon Obermann and offer her a very good price for the lot."

"Well, let me know if I can help you in any way."

Oh, hell no. She had done enough damage as it was.

He told her goodbye and hung up.

The next question was, how much should he offer? The amount had to be high enough to convince Sharon Obermann to sell. He divided the total price he had paid for the land by 2.5 and came up with $9,600. Then he checked land prices online to see what the going price of an acre was locally. Some acreage was higher, some lower. He decided to offer $8,000.

Of course, Sebastian didn't have $8,000. He would have to borrow it. The Houston bank could probably roll that sum into the final loan amount. He'd have to call his banker tomorrow. But everything hinged on whether Ms. Obermann would sell or not.

He decided to call her as soon as he could calm himself down. His pulse pounded at march tempo, close to 120 beats per minute, and he breathed as rapidly as if he had just run a race. It was 4:30. He would wait until 7:30 to call—not too early and not too late.

In the interim, he took a shower to relax. He stood under the shower head for ten minutes, letting the hot water do its work. He dried off, shaved, and ate a slice of buttered toast. Then, big-time squatter that he was, he got down on his knees and prayed. "Lord, let Sharon Obermann be receptive to the idea of selling. Please let her understand what happened was a horrible mistake. Please let her be reasonable. Lord, give me the right words and strengthen me for what I am about to do. And, Lord, please don't make me move this house again."

At 7:30 sharp, heart hammering, Sebastian called Sharon Obermann.

She answered.

"Ms. Obermann, my name is T. Sebastian Morrow, and I bought property last summer on Vogel Lane near Bullinger. I moved a house onto the land, and today the surveyor told me that I moved the house onto your property, not mine."

He could hear the quaver in his own voice.

"Oh, my goodness."

He swallowed. "Ms. Obermann, please know that I never in my life would have done such a thing on purpose. The real estate agent who sold me the land misled me. She said the property extended all the way from Daniel Doyle's lot to Roy Greiner's land."

Sebastian took a breath and launched himself out onto a high wire with no net. "I'm calling to ask if you would be willing to sell your lot."

"For how much?"

"Eight thousand."

"Yes," she said, "I will, but I don't want to pay any closing costs, and I want to retain the mineral rights."

In that instant he knew that prayer worked. His mouth fell open and he nearly levitated in relief. He would pay whatever, as long as she agreed to sell and he didn't have to move the house again.

"Oh, thank you!" His dance on a high wire had ended in life, not death.

She told him she had no use for the land. She would give three thousand to her church's capital campaign and divide the rest amongst her grandchildren. She asked Sebastian to describe the house, which he did, and then she said she would probably drive out to see it one day. The conversation went on a little longer, but he hardly heard what she said.

They shared their contact information, and she told him to draw up a buy-sell agreement for eight thousand dollars and to bring it to her when it was ready to sign.

When Sebastian hung up the phone, he dropped to his knees and thanked his Maker. Then he sprang up, danced two circuits around the living room, and whooped at the top of his lungs like a crazy man.

CHAPTER 17

DOUBLE-CROSS

First thing the next morning, Sebastian called James Givens, the Houston banker who was handling his loan. He quickly told him how he had put his house on Sharon Obermann's property. "She agreed to sell me the lot for eight thousand."

"Whoa, Sebastian, you dodged a major bullet there."

"Oh, I know it. If she had refused to sell, I intended to dine on cyanide."

James laughed, but Sebastian felt cold sweat pop out on his brow just thinking of it. With tension straining his voice, he asked the banker, "Can we roll the extra $8,000 into the loan?"

"Yes, we can."

Sebastian blew out a rush of air. "Oh, thank goodness. And one more matter—she asked me to provide a buy-sell agreement, but I don't know what that is."

"I'll email you a form," he said. "It's just a simple contract with the amount of the sale and any other stipulations. You both have to sign it."

James cleared his throat. "Sebastian, on another matter, our mortgage underwriter wants you to install central air and heat in your house."

"Why? What's wrong with what I've got?" It really irked him that the mortgage company wanted to dictate how he should heat and cool his own house.

"Nothing's wrong with it, but they have certain stipulations if they're gonna give out the loan. And after looking at photos of the house, they want you to tie it down. They think it sits too high off the ground."

"Well, that I could do, but can you explain to them that I've already got a propane tank and window units installed?"

"I can try."

"When do you think they'll make the decision on the loan?"

"I would guess by the end of the week."

"The sooner the better in my book." The rate of interest accumulating on his Bank of Hades loan rivaled the speed of reproducing bacteria; in his imagination it seemed to double itself every four to twenty minutes.

He clicked off the phone. By then it was 9:15, time to leave for his meeting with the dean at Omega. Surely by now, after a month had gone by, Ezra Faul and Provost Corrotto had decided who the department head would be, and the dean would announce the winning candidate to them. Perhaps he wanted to tell the search committee first out of courtesy before the university made a public announcement. Would it be Matthews, Riker, or Nudelman? Any one of them would be a good administrator. But as he drove to the university, a persistent uneasiness gnawed at him. Why had the decision taken so long?

The search committee assembled in the third-floor conference room adjacent to Dean Faul's office. Miles and Sebastian sat on one side of the large oval table across from Roscoe, Abbie, and Philip Washington. They left the chair at the head of the table vacant. They were not a talkative crew. No one knew why the dean had called the meeting, and they wouldn't find out until he told them. Nervous tension hung in the room like a yellow fog.

At 10:10, Dean Ezra Faul entered the room and sat at the head of the table. Impeccably dressed in a tailor-made suit, with a full head of curly salt-and-pepper hair, he had the groomed good looks and the confidence of a talking head on network television or the star pastor of a mega church. The son of a pig farmer in Missouri had done very well for himself. His salary equaled three of theirs.

"Good morning and thank you all for meeting with me on such short notice. Sorry I'm late, but as you know, my office is quite busy year-round." He placed his elbows on the table, clasped his hands together and rested his chin on his knuckles. "And thank you for all the work you have done as a search committee in narrowing the field to three candidates." He made eye contact with each person, to show how much he valued them.

He paused and pursed his lips. "After careful consideration of all the candidates, Provost Corrotto and I have chosen Ferris Duck as your new department head."

Abbie jerked involuntarily, as though she had touched a live wire. Sebastian gritted his teeth and glanced at Miles. Two bright red spots appeared in the Englishman's fair cheeks. Philip Washington cleared his throat and straightened his perfectly straight pink bow tie. Only Roscoe sat immovable and expressionless, his eyes fixed on the dean.

Having destroyed their hopes (Roscoe exempted) and negated all their work, Ezra Faul launched into a speech designed to justify the unjustifiable. It was remarkable, a performance worthy of an Academy Award.

He took each well-qualified finalist in turn, Marjorie Matthews, Bruce Riker, and Samuel Nudelman, and explained why they were unacceptable. Under Matthew's leadership, enrollment shrank so badly her department had to let two faculty members go in the last two years. Riker had never worked at a state university and therefore his experience at a private Methodist college was irrelevant. Nudelman had only chaired the department for two years and was looking for a big increase in salary. Dean Faul didn't trust his motives.

The crowning moment came when he sang the praises of Ferris Duck. "He is a hard worker. Of all the candidates, Ferris Duck is the one who really wants to be here."

Oh, yes, that is one soaring qualification. Just the kind of thinking that ensures the continued greatness of Omega U.

Having made his brilliant case, Dean Ezra Faul asked if anyone had questions.

They were as chatty as the corpses in a Cambodian killing field.

"Excellent," he said in a hearty voice, dismissing them. "I know you will do everything in your power to welcome Dr. Duck and make him feel at home."

❦

"Bloody fucking hell," spat Miles, as he, Sebastian, and Abbie piled into the elevator.

"Couldn't have said it better myself," remarked Abbie. She lit a cigarette as soon as the doors closed. It was a no-smoking building.

"Why the hell did we go through the motions if those two pompous asses had already made the choice?" blurted Miles.

"Three pompous asses," said Abbie. "You forgot Golden Boy."

"So you think he was in on it?" Miles asked.

The elevator came to a halt and the doors opened. Abbie blew out a stream of smoke. Neither the Red Sea nor the Jordan parted as quickly as the group of students waiting for the lift. They stepped aside and stared at her in amazement as she walked past them, oblivious, waving her lit cigarette.

"Of course," she answered. "They're all bosom buddies. That's why the band has so much money. That's why a non-major second trombone player gets a $15,000 band scholarship while the best pianist in the school gets a whopping $1,500. God forbid we should change the status quo."

They charged across campus at such a clip, Sebastian had trouble keeping up with them. At 6'2", he was four inches taller than Miles and at least a foot taller than chubby Abbie, but rage propelled them, and their legs churned like eggbeaters.

"This makes Faul and Corrotto zero for two," Sebastian said.

"What do you mean?" Miles asked.

"They're the same ones who hired Woolrich, our late, great embezzler."

"What a winner he was," said Miles.

"You know they concocted a cover story for him. First, they said he went on medical leave for his worsening diabetes. Then they said he decided to take early retirement. Nary a word about the theft of funds."

"Woolrich was no loss, but personally, I mourn Marjorie Matthews," said Abbie. "With her at the helm we might have had a chance for great things. We could have arisen from our current state of substandard performance to the heights of upper-echelon mediocrity. But, alas, that's all down the tubes now."

When they got back to the music office, Betsy Bloom pounced. "Okay, who is my new boss? I'm betting on Marjorie Matthews."

Miles broke the news. "It's Ferris Duck."

"What! He wasn't even in the running."

"Well, superior beings like the dean and the provost have the ability to overlook little details like that," said Abbie.

Betsy smiled. "I hope I don't slip up and call him Derris F—"

"Betsy!" Sebastian hissed, pointing to the open door. "You never know where students may lurk."

"Okay, already." She dropped her voice. "I'll refer to him in code as Quack-Quack."

"Right," agreed Abbie. "It'll be our little secret."

Sebastian's rage took a long time to cool. About the time his blood pressure had returned to normal, nine days later, he was searching in his studio library for the Debussy Sonata, a piece he intended to perform in the fall. James Givens called him to tell him the bank's decision. "Sebastian," he said, "they dropped you. They're not going to loan you the money."

Alone in his studio, Sebastian went into free fall. He felt himself plummet; his mind whirled and his muscles contracted in sheer panic as if he skydived from eighteen thousand feet without a parachute.

"It's not our bank, it's our mortgage underwriter."

James' voice sounded faint and tinny through the roar in his ears. Sebastian could hardly concentrate as James explained the under-writer would not finance the house unless Sebastian tied it down like a house trailer because it sat so high up on piers. In addition, they insisted he install central air and heat instead of the room air conditioners and large propane heaters he already had set up. He hadn't had the money to do either, but he thought the matters could be negotiated. He was wrong.

He spoke through the cotton in his mouth. "James, I've got to get a loan at a reasonable interest rate and soon, or I'll go under. What am I gonna do?"

"I think your best bet is to talk to some of the smaller banks in your area. If you go to another large bank in Houston, you're very likely to get turned down again."

After his conversation with the banker, Sebastian walked to the studio window on shaky legs. The bright sunrays reflected off the lake hurt his eyes. He had to act and he had to act quickly. He had already photocopied the buy-sell agreement and taken it to Sharon Obermann to sign. She was expecting her eight thousand dollars very soon.

Widowed, she lived alone in the piney woods outside of Humble, not too far from Intercontinental Airport. She was thin and frail, but bright-eyed and sharp concerning business. She told Sebastian she and her sister had driven out to Vogel Lane to see the house he had moved onto her property. They passed by but didn't stop.

"Well, I like your house, and it looks good on the land," she told him.

He didn't dare tell Sharon Obermann what had happened. Now that they had both signed the agreement, Sebastian had to come up with the money. He had to find a bank to give him a loan as quickly as possible. Feeling sick at his stomach, he left. Never mind the Debussy—it could wait.

There were two local banks in Bullinger: the Bank of Bullinger and Farmers Bank. He tried the Bank of Bullinger first. He drove there with sweating hands and an uneasy stomach. After a ten-minute wait, he talked to a female loan officer and explained the situation. A middle-aged woman with watery blue eyes and dyed black hair falling out of its bun, she seemed doubtful. She left Sebastian sitting at her desk while she conferred with the manager. Sebastian could see them in an adjoining glassed-in office, but he couldn't hear their conversation. The manager glanced at him, then quickly turned back to his female colleague.

After a few more minutes, she returned. "I wish we could help you, Mr. Morrow, but my manager said our bank couldn't approve such a loan." She peered at him over the top of her half-glasses. "I'm so sorry."

Panic rose within him like a post-nuke mushroom cloud; he fought for control of himself. Aside from the $8,000 he needed immediately, the exorbitant interest accruing daily was unsustainable—he would lose everything if he didn't get a low-interest loan. As a musician, he faced performance anxiety on a regular basis. He knew what it was to bear with a pounding heart, shaking knees, sweaty palms, dry mouth, or trembling fingers. Usually it was one or the other, but now he had them all with nausea. He couldn't think straight. He managed to walk to his car and drive home, although he hardly saw the road. He drove into his yard, stepped out of the car, and vomited on the grass.

By the time he cleaned himself up, it was already 4:30. Sebastian forced himself to call Farmers Bank. He asked to speak to a loan officer.

"Lee Prager speaking."

Sebastian gave him a short version of his story. Prager asked him a few questions and then said, "Mr. Morrow, I think we can help you out. Bring your appraisal and all your documents and let's meet tomorrow at 10:30."

Hope glimmered faintly, but it did little to quell his anxiety. He poured himself a scotch on the rocks to settle his stomach and sat down in his recliner to drink it. After a while, his stomach calmed down. He put his feet up and leaned back in the chair.

When he awoke two hours later, it was 6:30. He drank a tall glass of water, ate some cheese and crackers, and then went out to the big deck. The heat of the day had begun to dissipate, and the low humidity in rural Helprin County (unlike Houston's perpetual sauna) made it quite pleasant to sit there. The evening breeze cooled him, ruffled his hair, and stirred the surface of the pond. But best of all, it breathed a melody as blessed and holy as any that ever sprang from David's harp. Sebastian closed his eyes and listened to one of the most soothing, beautiful sounds on earth, the sighing of the wind in the trees. For a long time, he focused on the rise and fall of the susurrating music. Gradually, he felt his breathing and his heart rate slow until he seemed to float on a tide of peace.

He laid his head back against the chair and opened his eyes. The dark blue, cloudless sky seemed so serene. Movement caught his eye to his right. With outspread wings, a large, black bird glided slowly and silently over his deck, a vulture. Its shadow passed over him. It made him uneasy—a bad omen.

Would Farmers Bank turn him down tomorrow? He tried to fend off the thought.

Then, right behind the vulture, flying swift, low, and clean as an arrow, a falcon passed overhead. Small and streamlined, its determined flight chased the vulture away. Sebastian sat up straight and followed its aerial path. It had to be a sign. He had a sudden inexplicable knowing that, somehow, it would be all right.

He stayed on the deck while the sun went down. The wind sang its husky lullaby, and at dusk, the crickets and cicadas joined the chorus, *fortissimo*, sawing away like an enthusiastic horde of beginner violinists. Unfortunately, as the sound rose and fell in waves, the mosquitoes arrived to add their tiny, irritating buzzing and devilish bites. No matter: Sebastian set his face like flint and kept his eyes on the deepening blue of the sky. He refused to go in until the first stars came out.

CHAPTER 18

WIN ONE, LOSE ONE

Before he headed for the bank on Friday morning, Sebastian walked out to check his mail. With all the uproar the day before, he had completely forgotten to collect it. He reached into the narrow white box atop its wooden post and found two credit card statements, his electric bill, and one bulky business envelope addressed to him from Trinemark Resources, a company he had never heard of. He took the mail inside and put the bills in a folder he kept for his monthly expenses. He had no idea how he was going to pay them—his bank account currently registered *empty*. He suspected the other envelope was junk mail. He tossed it on the table in the dining room. It could wait until after his meeting at the bank.

Twenty minutes later, Sebastian sat across the desk from Lee Prager, the CEO of Farmers Bank, in his spacious, sunny office. Curly wisps of white hair wreathed his head. He had rosy cheeks, a well-fed look, and a confident but low-key demeanor.

Sebastian's confident demeanor was total theatre. As a performer, he knew how to veil his internal quaking. And as a precaution against the workings of his volatile stomach, he had forgone breakfast. It was a good thing—at the moment, his guts churned like white-hot lava in a volcano ready to blow.

He took a deep breath and told Lee Prager about the high-interest line of credit which he had to pay off, plus the fiasco of moving his house onto someone else's land. "Now I need $8,000 more to buy Sharon Obermann's property. Here's the buy-sell agreement we signed."

Prager took it and smiled. "Out here in the country, these things happen more often than you would imagine. You're not the only one who's made such an error. I happen to know of two other cases."

Well, he wasn't the only idiot in the area. Sebastian handed him the appraisal and the survey of his original 2.5 acres, as well as the loan application he had recently filled out for the Houston bank, so Prager could see his income, debts, and assets.

"The bank in Houston didn't have a problem with my credit. Their underwriter demanded I install central air and heat and tie the house down like a trailer. I didn't want to do it, and when I asked the loan officer to try to negotiate with them, they turned me down."

The next thing Prager said slayed Sebastian.

"I wish you had come here first. We do refinancing loans for local folks all the time."

He could have buried his face in his hands and wept. All this grief for nothing, not to mention the five months' exorbitant interest he would have to pay. His blunders followed him like a trail of debris left by a tornado. He decided to search Bullinger's antique shops for a cat-o'nine-tails and commence a course in self-flagellation.

Prager took his time and studied all the documents carefully.

It's hard to keep a straight face when one's guts are exploding. Sebastian decided to distract himself and appeal to Heaven simultaneously. He put a hand in his pocket, fingered the beads of the rosary he had brought, and prayed silently.

After Sebastian's tenth Hail Mary, Prager looked up, nodded, and laid the appraisal down on the desk. "Your house is valued at about $40,000 over the amount you want to borrow, and your credit looks good. Those two things make it easy to accept. I'll write you a ten-year home equity loan, so you'll actually borrow money based on the value of your home. This will be a good investment for the bank, actually."

"What will the interest rate be?"

"Seven percent."

Hallelujah!

By lunchtime, they had worked out the details, and Sebastian filled out a Farmers Bank loan application. Prager told him he would have to resurvey the property.

Another survey at $700—what was that to Sebastian? He was so elated he could have frolicked silly-happy and loose-limbed as a puppy. He wanted to leap up in Lee Prager's lap and lick his face in gratitude. Somehow, he managed to restrain his exuberance and simply shook the man's hand instead.

"Come back on Tuesday," said the banker. "I'll have the papers ready to sign, and I'll issue the check for Sharon Obermann. We'll pay off your credit line next week, as well."

As he practically floated out of Lee Prager's office, Sebastian saw the Nordic queen rapidly exiting the bank. What a lucky day! He put his long legs in high gear and gave chase. She made it easy, though. When she got to her car she came to a dead stop.

"Damn!"

"Hello, Silvie."

She looked up, startled. "Oh, hello, Sebastian." She sighed and grimaced. "That's a brand new tire." She pointed to the flat on the driver's side of her Volvo—what else would she drive?

He knelt and looked carefully at the treads. "There's the problem. See the nail head?"

"What rotten luck."

Sebastian glanced up at her. "If you have a spare, I can put it on for you."

She did, and after thirty minutes or so, he had got the spare on and laid the punctured tire in the trunk.

"Thank you so much, Sebastian! I'd better drive the car over to Bruno's Tires now. Hopefully they can patch it."

"Where is Bruno's? I still don't know the town very well."

"Across from Sammy's Mediterranean Grill on the east side."

"What good news—a Mediterranean restaurant in little Bullinger!" That triggered the next question, which shot out of his mouth before he knew what he was going to say. "Look, Silvie, why don't you have lunch with me while you wait for the tire to be repaired?" Half afraid of the answer, he hurried on, "I was going to eat out," (a bald-faced lie) "and it would be nice to have company."

She smiled. "That's kind of you, but only if you'll let me pay."

"I would, but two entities dear to my heart, Mrs. Felicity Morrow and my manly honor, prevent me."

"Is Felicity your wife?"

"My darling mother."

She crossed her arms and squinted at him in the bright sunlight. "You realize you're an anachronism, don't you?"

He laughed. "With a capital A, and quite a hungry one at that."

"By the way, *is* there a Mrs. Sebastian Morrow?"

A sign of interest, maybe? "No," he answered. He decided to keep it simple. Now was not the time to elaborate.

There were several cars in the service queue ahead of Silvie's at Bruno's Tires. The manager told her she had at least an hour's wait before the car would be ready. That gave them enough time for lunch at Sammy's.

They crossed the street and entered the crowded restaurant.

Sebastian took it as a good sign that the restaurant was so busy. After he washed the tire dirt off his hands in the restroom, he and Silvie sat at a booth and ordered lamb kebabs and tabbouleh, with baklava and coffee for dessert. The waitress immediately brought them a plate of four complimentary stuffed grape leaves.

"Good choice of restaurant," Sebastian said.

"Thanks." She glanced at him with those beautiful blue-violet eyes. "Leo tells me you're a musician."

"He's an unusual person, your son." He picked up one of the stuffed grape leaves dripping with olive oil.

"He just submitted a recording for an organ competition. If he qualifies for the final round, it will take place in Dallas in October of next year." She smiled. "We'll see what happens."

"I wouldn't be surprised if he makes it through to the finals. But aside from being an excellent musician, he seems to be a very perceptive person."

"That he is. He notices everything, and he has an uncanny ability to read people. He doesn't talk a lot, but when he does, it's a very good idea to listen. But back to you—you're a musician?"

Sebastian swallowed a mouthful of stuffed grape leaves. "Mmmh, delicious. Yes, I'm a violinist with Opera D'Argento in Houston and I teach music theory, upper strings, and direct the orchestra at Omega U."

"Opera D'Argento? Leo and I saw your production of *Tosca*." She snapped her fingers. "I remember you—you're the concertmaster."

Sebastian was pleased. "Yes, I am."

"We thoroughly enjoyed it. I love opera. You know, one of my favorite films is Ingmar Bergman's *Trollflöjten*."

Sebastian wrinkled his brow, puzzled for a moment by her pronunciation and the use of a foreign word. Berrymann—who was that? Trollfloyten? But then he quickly realized what she meant. "*The*

Magic Flute," he guessed, "with Hakan Hagegard as Papageno?"

"Who?"

"Hakan Hagegard or Papageno?"

Silvie laughed and the sound was melodious. "I know who Papageno is, but Hackin' Hagegard? I didn't understand you at first because in Swedish, the singer's name is pronounced Hoh-kaan Hah-ga-gourd."

"Sounds like a phrase of music when you say it. But you said *Berrymann* instead of *Bergman,* didn't you?"

"*Ja,* in Swedish the *–rg* is pronounced *–ry.* For example, the word spelled *v-a-r-g* means *wolf.* We pronounce it *varry.* Swedish is a tonal language, with lots of ups and downs."

"*Varg,*" Sebastian echoed.

She nodded. "Perfect pronunciation. You have a good ear."

He took a bite of the lamb kebab. "Do you miss Sweden?"

"Some things, certain foods and seasonal traditions. But Stockholm sees a lot of gray, cloudy weather. I don't miss that or the winter darkness. In December there is light for only about five hours a day."

"How do you like our Texas summers?"

She rolled her eyes. "I'd like to trade those in for the Swedish variety."

"D'you think we could convince Sweden to export its summers?"

"Hmm. For enough money, probably. But for the time being, I think they'll stick with Volvos, vodka, and au pairs."

"Were you an au pair?"

"Yes, I was with a family in Houston for one year. I met Edward de Graaf that year and later married him."

She ate the lamb kebab in the European manner with fork in the left hand and knife in the right. She turned the tables on Sebastian. "Why did you move to Bullinger?"

"I longed for the adventure of country life."

"And has country life measured up to your expectations?"

"Well, actually it's been almost more adventure than I can stand." He told her about buying the property and moving the house, omitting the fact that he had put it on someone else's land. That wound still bled. Besides, Sebastian didn't really want to talk about himself. He wanted to extract Silvie's story; he wanted to know all about her.

Just then a shadow fell across the table. A tall, wiry man loomed over them. His thin brown hair was slicked close to his skull. His gaze was intense, with pale green eyes in a face pitted by acne scars. He seemed familiar somehow. Silvie looked up at him with a nervous smile.

To Sebastian's astonishment, the man bent down and kissed Silvie on the mouth—exactly what Sebastian wanted to do, not at all what he wanted to observe. It was a lingering, possessive kiss.

Silvie broke away. Flustered, she reached for the tall man's hand. "Lucas, this is Sebastian . . . uh . . ."

"Morrow." Sebastian stretched out his hand.

"Lucas Hlavicek." His deep, booming voice seemed to dominate all other sounds in the restaurant. His mouth drew back in a grin as he fixed his unsmiling eyes on Sebastian and attempted to crush the violinist's hand.

The bastard. Hurting, and taken by surprise, Sebastian silently fought back with pressure of his own until Lucas finally released his hand. Then it clicked. The Kolache King. Sebastian had seen him often in the ubiquitous television commercials for Hlavicek's Bakeries. *The only bakeries with authentic Czech pastries!* Hlavicek's was a central Texas institution, with a growing national market. The business was Bullinger's claim to fame, and Lucas Hlavicek was the local star whose foundation had granted the Omega University Orchestra eight thousand dollars.

From the gold Rolex encircling his wrist and the diamond encrusted pinky ring to his thousand-dollar alligator boots, Lucas oozed wealth. He wore a blue silk shirt with gray trousers creased so sharp they could have sliced strudel. His outfit probably cost more than Sebastian's car.

Ah, hell. She would have a boyfriend—and a rich one at that.

Lucas addressed Silvie, "Saw the Volvo at Bruno's and stopped in. They told me you were over here eating lunch." He dragged out the words in a thick Texas drawl.

"Yes, when I came out of the bank, I had a flat, and Sebastian was kind enough to put the spare on for me so I could drive over to Bruno's. We decided to have lunch while they fixed it."

"Well, they've got it patched," replied Lucas.

Silvie rose quickly. She hadn't finished her coffee or the baklava. "I guess I should go," she said. "Do you mind, Sebastian? I really should get back to the bookshop."

Sebastian rose. "Sure, Silvie, go on." He waved her off.

"Thank you again." She gave him a last glance with those lustrous sapphire eyes. Over her head, Lucas met his eye and smiled smugly as he put his arm around Silvie's waist with the air of a property owner.

Sebastian's enormous, unwavering smile hid abject disappointment. His hope of courting the Nordic queen had been shot out of the air and shattered like a clay pigeon. As he watched her walk out of the restaurant, he knew two things: Lucas Hlavicek was a *varg*, and Silvie was afraid of him. He was certain of it.

He sat down heavily and drank the last of his lukewarm coffee. His heart ached as much as his hand. He took out a worn credit card to pay the bill.

When he got home, the first thing he noticed was the bulky white business envelope lying on the dining room table. He picked it up and started to toss it into the trash, but something held him back.

"All right Trinemark Resources, what do you want?" Reluctantly, he opened the envelope. He found six sheets of paper, each labeled

Revenue Summary Statement. His name and address stood at the top of each. He stared at endless columns of incomprehensible figures in microscopic print. Every entry was dated. When he saw the word GAS, he realized the figures had to do with the mineral rights to his property. The dates spanned the time period 1987–2008. As he tried to make sense of the figures, he shifted the sheets of paper, and a check fluttered to the floor. He picked it up and, to his astonishment, read the words that weakened his knees: *Pay to the order of T. Sebastian Morrow: $1,567.80.*

He almost cried. He needed the money that badly.

Several thoughts ran through his mind almost instantaneously. He remembered the Episcopal priest had never cashed the monthly checks for the mineral rights. That was a mystery—whyever not? The small amounts must have accrued for over twenty years. "Thank you, Fr. Jack."

At the same time, he suddenly understood why Sharon Obermann retained the mineral rights to the one acre she sold him. And then, in gratitude, he remembered Leo de Graaf's remark after the wedding: *I can assure you, Mr. Morrow, it's going to be all right.*

Well, Leo had spoken the truth. Sebastian looked at the check again. He held in his hand a gift, direct from the storehouse of God.

2009

CHAPTER 19

PREPARING FOR BATTLE

If fruit trees could talk (and who's to say they do not), they would counsel their owners: *Patience and pruning, not to mention fertilizer, reap rich rewards. And in the meantime, get some chickens.* Whether he heard their rustling, dulcet voices or not, Sebastian got the message. The trees he planted in the fall of 2008, save one, survived into 2009. The satsuma, made for warmer climes, froze in its first winter.

His two persimmon trees grew eight inches in the first year, and the three blueberry bushes grew well despite the heat. He planted them fifty feet from the house on the left side of the pond. He set the fig tree next to the house on the south side where it would be protected from the north wind. The persimmons and the fig tree were still too immature to produce fruit, but he did harvest a few blueberries.

When he went out to inspect the trees one morning in July, he found many of the leaves either missing or half-chewed. Each day the damage grew worse. Chiggers, who had previously headlined his Mortal Enemy List, had to move over for grasshoppers. If he let them, the infernal insects would kill off his fruit trees.

Sebastian declared war.

At first, he considered chemical weapons, but eventually he ruled them out because he didn't want pesticide residue on the (future) fruit, the land, or in the pond. He wanted a natural solution—either guinea hens or chickens. Guineas made great watch-birds because they screeched at predators, they didn't scratch up the land, and they were topnotch at bug control. Chickens were also excellent bug-catchers, but it was the thought of fresh eggs daily that sold Sebastian on chickens.

Keeping chickens was to give him a real course in country living. But before he could buy any hens, he had to have a coop. He called Kieran about it, and his son-in-law the builder promised to help him.

Helen and Kieran visited him the last week of July, and they came bearing gifts. He had been forewarned. "Dad, we thought it might be good for you to have a dog for protection out there in the wild. We're bringing you Penny, a Great Pyrenees puppy. The breed is very gentle, and they make wonderful guardians for goats or chickens. They even get along with cats, just in case you have any strays that show up."

(His daughter the prophet. By mid-September, three female cats appeared at his house: a tiny, almost mute tortoiseshell with a rumbling purr; a large, fluffy pinkish-orange cat; and a black and white tuxedo cat. He named them Tortie, Plush, and Jemmers.)

Helen and Kieran drove down from Pennsylvania with the puppy taking up the backseat. When they arrived, Helen opened the door and Penny lumbered out. Even though she had sent him a picture, Sebastian could hardly believe his eyes. "That's not a dog—it's a horse. How old is she?"

"Ten months. I've already spayed her and given her her shots."

Penny, the ninety-five pound puppy. Though she was a beautiful dog, white with longish wavy fur, a curling, feathered tail and feathered legs, Sebastian's immediate reaction was: *No! She's too big—I don't want her.* She was not at all agile; in fact, she moved like an old dog. With a peculiar, heavy gait, she slowly made her way over to him and sat on her haunches at his feet. She gazed at him with liquid brown eyes, smiled, and offered him one giant paw. That single disarming gesture sealed his fate. Sebastian took her paw in his hand and fell in love on the spot.

"She's not through growing yet, Dad."

"Well, if my car gives out, I can ride her to work." He stroked her head. "Where did you get her?"

"The local shelter in Lancaster rescued her from a bad breeder. He kept the dog locked in a cage all the time and only let her out twice a day to do her business. She was so inactive her muscles atrophied. Her gait is odd because she can't even lift her back legs; she drags them. She'll strengthen with exercise and a large area to roam. Your place will be perfect." Helen laughed. "The chickens will guard the fruit trees, and the dog will guard the chickens."

Kieran's gift was a .22. He handed it to Sebastian while they still stood out in the yard. "For you."

"A rifle? Do you have one at home in Lancaster?"

"Sure."

"What do you use it for?"

"To keep the Amish at bay."

"Yeah, I've heard they're pretty aggressive."

His green eyes sparkled. "I figure I'd better be prepared in case the crop fails. They go berserk when they run out of food."

He pointed to the woods. "But seriously, Sebastian, there are a lot of wild critters out there. With a rifle you can defend yourself and the livestock if you come eye to eye with bobcats or coyotes."

Sebastian knew he was right, so he accepted the rifle. "Thanks, Kieran. Some nights out here I've heard packs of coyotes yipping and howling, and I actually saw a six-foot rat snake climb that post oak tree not ten feet from the deck."

"How'd you know it was a rat snake?"

"I went out and bought a book on Texas snakes the same afternoon. We've got a great bookshop in town, by the way. I figured I'd better be able to identify the poisonous snakes. Rat snakes aren't venomous, but they can still deliver a fearsome bite if they're cornered."

"Well, it's too hot out here. Come in and see the house." Sebastian gave them the tour, Penny included.

Kieran, who restored old houses for a living, appreciated the workmanship of Sebastian's cottage. "It's as solid as can be, Sebastian. They made houses to last in 1920. Someone updated the kitchen lighting and the doors, but the floors, the bathroom tile, and the wavy glass in your windows are original."

"I love these pointed arches," Helen added. She stood in the living room and outlined the inverted V with one finger extended. There's something sort of Arabian about them. Unusual."

In the meantime, Penny made herself at home. With a loud thump, she flopped down on the wood floor underneath the piano and lay panting on her side. She seemed ready to stay for the long haul; she obviously preferred the seventy degrees inside to the ninety-eight-degree Texas summer heat outside.

While Helen admired the house, Sebastian riveted his whole attention on her. He hadn't seen her since Mary Catherine's funeral the previous summer. For so many years, he and Helen had only had each other. She had been his heart, the center of his life. They had endured so much together; they were bound perhaps closer than most fathers and daughters. During her college years at Texas A&M, she lived less than two hours away, and she came home for summers and holidays. But once she married Kieran and moved to Pennsylvania, Sebastian saw her maybe twice a year, and he missed her greatly.

He had tried to create a stable home for her, but he knew he had fallen short, which he sorely regretted. Had he been able to bilocate and be present at work and home simultaneously, Helen would not have been a latchkey kid. But he was only one flawed person; he couldn't be both mother and father. And of course, over the years, Mary Catherine had been the very model of instability. Treacherous as a bog, she appeared to offer solid ground, but one step onto it and the bottom dropped out; one sank chest-deep in the quicksand of disappointments and broken promises.

That Helen enjoyed a happy marriage pleased him mightily. She had found an excellent match in Kieran O'Neill, and Sebastian respected and liked his son-in-law. Kieran was steadfast, unflappable. Wise, but rather brusque, he told the truth whether one wanted to hear it or not. Consequently, some liked him and some didn't, but people instinctively trusted him. That, plus his good work and integrity on the job, resulted in more clients than any other restorer in Lancaster County.

Sebastian believed Kieran's calm and integrity had drawn Helen to him. Once she met Kieran, like the dove that left the Ark after many days adrift, she found a tree to nest in. A solid, muscular, red-haired Irishman with green eyes, freckles, and a crooked smile, he was only slightly taller than his wife. Dark-haired Helen, with her solemn gray eyes, was slender and lithe, ethereal as a creature of the air. Sebastian imagined his grandchildren (forthcoming soon, he hoped) with their double Irish ancestry might well be a bevy of leprechauns.

That week, in addition to a fair amount of target shooting and gun instruction, Kieran helped Sebastian build a 4x4 chicken coop out of pine posts and plywood. They built it about twenty feet behind the house. The coop was four feet off the ground with three laying boxes and two roosts. A ramp led from the ground to the coop, and Kieran made a lockable door. Later on, Sebastian surrounded the coop with a tall picket fence.

He would have done the fencing himself, but he learned an interesting fact about the land when he tried. He couldn't dig down more than two inches. The shallow topsoil covered a layer of limestone. His house quite literally stood upon a rock. The fencing company he hired had to use high-powered drills to sink the posts.

On the last day of their visit, Sebastian took Helen and Kieran with him to a local farm where they bought a rooster and three young hens—a yellow Buff Orpington, a White Leghorn, and a black Copper Maran. The large and lively rooster was a mixed breed—white with a fountain of iridescent blue-green tail feathers. Sebastian named the yellow hen Buff and the other two, Olympia and Antonia, after characters in *The Tales of Hoffmann,* the first opera of the upcoming season. The rooster he named Newt the Mute. For weeks when he didn't crow, Sebastian guessed he was either bashful or defective. But the day did come when the rooster found his voice. Depending on the time of sunrise, or when the spirit moved him, Newt let out godawful, ear-splitting crows guaranteed to wake the neighborhood, if not the dead.

When Helen and Kieran departed, the silence in the house assailed him. Though Sebastian had lived in solitude for many years, he found the sudden absence of his family oppressive. The dog seemed to sense his mood, and she often rubbed against his legs and gazed up at him as if to say, *I'm still here with you; don't grieve.* Penny's concern had a limit, however. She followed him around the yard mornings and evenings only; midday she reserved for siesta time under the piano. She heartily endorsed Kipling's maxim: she was neither a mad dog nor an Englishman—not even for Sebastian would she go out in the noonday sun.

In the lull after Helen and Kieran left, before the fall semester and the opera season began, the topic he had pondered for three decades began to weigh on his mind—the existence of demons. He had never revealed his experience with Mary Catherine to anyone, not to Helen, not even to a priest. In researching the subject, he hoped to validate his experience of the dark side of the supernatural. He thought it wise to study the enemy—the more he learned, the more prepared he would be for any future confrontations. And confrontations would occur—demons were disembodied spirits, intelligent entities, at war with human beings, whom they wished to deceive and destroy. Mary Catherine was a case in point. But Sebastian also knew her destruction could not have happened without her consent. Both those facts enraged him.

He found the two books he had bought the previous summer and dusted them off. When the heat dissipated around seven that evening, he brought them out to the deck. It took him two evenings to read *Encounters with the Diabolical,* written by a Catholic exorcist. He read the Pentecostal pastor's slim volume entitled *Stand Against the Adversary* in a single go. On subsequent evenings, he used his laptop to study the life and ministry of Francesco Forgione, later canonized and known as Padre Pio.

The exorcist and the Pentecostal pastor wrote from long experience, and their testimony agreed on many points. First, the most common activity of demons is temptation, but other characteristic actions include harassment, torment, compulsion, and enslavement (addictions being a prime example, as he knew), defilement, deception, and even physical attacks to weaken, sicken, and to kill.

Secondly, they emphasized the fact that Jesus cast out demons everywhere He went. Rather than a rare or exceptional occurrence, it was an integral, ongoing part of His ministry. Many illnesses he cured were caused by demons, particularly in the cases of those who were blind, deaf, and mute. There was also the woman bent double, deformed by what Luke called a spirit of infirmity. But when the Lord laid His hands on her, she immediately stood up straight.

Clearly, there were different kinds of demons. In Matthew Chapter 17, when the disciples failed to heal an epileptic boy who suffered terrible seizures, the boy's father asked Jesus to heal him. After the Lord cast out the demon, the disciples asked their Rabbi why they had failed. He explained: *This kind can come forth by nothing, but by prayer and fasting.*

Sebastian's reading brought to mind again the eerie dream he had had. He clearly recalled his extreme fear when the ominous black-hatted figure circled his house, stalking him and seeking entry. And likewise, he remembered his immense relief when he saw the great lion, his protector, lying on its haunches facing the open door. He believed it meant that though the devil watches and waits, ready to pounce, he cannot override the Lord's protection.

He learned that chronic restlessness and the inability to be at peace were often signs of demonic oppression. Complete possession could happen, but it was rare. It was more likely that demons occupied or oppressed specific areas of an individual's personality. Sebastian believed Mary Catherine belonged to the latter category.

As he read, a gradual relief stole over Sebastian. The writers did not recount lurid ghost stories—the stuff of horror movies or scary campfire tales. They cited example after example of their own experiences in delivering people from demonic oppression, simply and without sensationalism. They acknowledged demons had real power, but they emphasized how much greater God's power was to overcome them.

Aside from willful sin and any occult practices (including yoga), the exorcist mentioned two causes for demonic oppression which surprised Sebastian: one was by God's permission, for His purposes, which meant the human being was blameless, and the other was through evil spells and curses. The author defined curses as the intentional harm of another through the intervention of the devil, as practiced in witchcraft or sorcery. Even objects could be cursed through satanic rites performed by witch doctors or shamans. The black magic with the greatest evil power included the original from Africa, the Haitian variety, and the Brazilian type, called *macumba*. To counteract the curses, the Roman Catholic rite of exorcism consisted of prayers and blessings and most powerfully, the name of Jesus.

"Of course!" Sebastian exclaimed and slapped his thigh for emphasis, startling the dog, who barked, and the lounging cats who fled the deck in panic. The demon in Mary Catherine had manifested immediately after he ended his prayer with the words *in Jesus' name.* Then in the hospital, when he concluded his prayer the same way, she had awakened briefly out of her coma.

That was the other point on which both writers agreed: the centrality and authority of Jesus over all creation and created beings. Sebastian wished he had understood that earlier, but he guessed it would not have helped Mary Catherine simply because she spent her life in denial. No one, including God Himself, could help an unwilling person.

Sebastian was fascinated by Padre Pio, the twentieth-century Capuchin monk from Italy, who bore the stigmata from 1918 until his death in 1968. For fifty years, he endured the excruciating pain caused by the open wounds in his hands, feet, and side. Known for all manner of healing and miracles, Padre Pio confirmed the existence of demons. One of his statements stunned Sebastian: *The number of devils active in the world is greater than all the people who have been alive since Adam.* How many billions or trillions would that be? On another occasion, the monk explained his ministry: *I don't have a minute of free time; it is all spent releasing my brothers from the grip of Satan.*

Padre Pio certainly had the gift of discernment. He was a confessor, and it was said that if a person in the confession booth omitted certain sins, the good priest would enumerate them to the astonishment of the sinner. Clearly, the closer one was to God, the keener one's sight.

Sebastian looked up the root of the word *discernment*. *Discern* came from Old French: *dis* (apart) + *cernere* (to separate). It meant to distinguish, divide, or separate (a thing) mentally from another or others; to recognize or determine; to use keen perception or judgment.

He knew keen perception was necessary in this world because it was often very difficult to know the true from the false and the good from the evil. The problem arose because to be credible, evil must closely imitate good. Antichrist must mimic Christ, and therefore, in a superficial way, they resemble each other. But only the latter had true power and authority; the former was but a sham.

Thinking of discernment, Sebastian's thoughts shifted to Leo de Graaf. After Mass the previous Sunday, Leo had informed him he had been selected as one of five finalists for a major organ competition. He was going to give a preparatory recital in early October, and he asked Sebastian to attend. Sebastian promised to do so and to invite Abbie Goldberg as well. He knew Leo was a good musician, but he was equally impressed by his spiritual acumen. Although Leo was an adult, somehow, like the small child Sasha, he had retained the purity of sight that cuts to the heart of things.

For himself, Sebastian mused, discernment might take time. Its essence was careful consideration. One had to gather all the facts and then sift and weigh them, using sound judgment. But it was more complex than that. He knew intuition played a major role, but how could he amplify that in himself? Maybe the key to it all lay in the practices followed by saints, exorcists, and the Lord Himself—prayer and fasting. Spiritual power didn't come by wishing. He guessed it was time to make a steady effort, time to take the rust off his spiritual life.

That, Sebastian decided, would be his ongoing task. The world consisted of the visible and the invisible. The Lord had opened his eyes to see the demon in Mary Catherine, and the Lord had brought him into contact with Leo, whose vision had revealed a light around him. The Creator of all things had a plan, and perhaps, Sebastian thought, little by little, He was teaching him, guiding him, preparing him for some future deed or purpose that he alone could fulfill.

As August ended in searing heat, Sebastian steeled himself for the start of the fall semester. He thought of September as back-in-the-saddle month. With excitement contending with trepidation, he prepared to ride into the fray. The opera season would soon open with *Tales of Hoffmann*, the fall term was set to begin at Omega, and even in Texas the blistering heat couldn't last forever.

Omega was always the rub. The opening ordeal would be an ice cream social Dean Ezra Faul had organized for the faculty to meet and mingle with Ferris Duck, the newly appointed department head, and his Brazilian wife Eloa. Along with the ice cream, Sebastian would have to swallow his great resentment toward the unqualified Duck and the dean himself, who had overridden all the rules to appoint him. That fact loomed large as an irritant in the chapped-butt department. But as it happened, Sebastian had no idea that a second problem would arise, a burr so sharp and painful it would affect the rest of his life.

CHAPTER 20

PRIVATE LESSON

Hardcore Texans think there is no better place to live than the Lone Star State. However, in September, when they have survived the dreaded furnace of August, and the daytime thermometer still tops ninety-eight degrees Fahrenheit, they secretly fantasize about moving to Colorado or Oregon, or even (God forbid) California. Sebastian, a Yankee by birth, and Penny, a canine bred for the high mountains, likely suffered more than everyone else.

After decades of living in Houston, Sebastian finally realized that Texas, unlike northern states, has only two and a half seasons instead of four: the heat from May to September, the cool from October to April, plus the superimposed roulette of hurricane season, June to November. In the latter season one hoped for good odds, never knowing if the Gulf Coast might be walloped by a huge storm or not.

One benefit of Sebastian's move inland was his protection from hurricanes. The previous year, on September 13, 2008, a little over two months after he moved from Houston, Hurricane Ike made landfall on the east end of Galveston Island in the wee hours of the morning. It had been a Category 2 storm with winds of 110 mph, but its storm surge reached somewhere between fifteen and twenty feet, like a Category 5. It traveled north up Galveston Bay, along the east side of Houston, right into his old neighborhood, causing flood damage and spawning tornados.

Not even a hurricane, however, could equal the havoc of one fifty-minute lesson with Alicia Borden. Sebastian wondered if she might drop out after her lusterless performance in the spring semester, when she received a D in violin and a C in orchestra. But no, she reappeared for the fall term. He had assigned her the Preludio of the Bach E Major Partita, the Beethoven Romance in F Major and the Kreutzer Étude No. 2 at her first lesson. She called in sick on the day of her second lesson, and now it was already the sixteenth of the month, and he'd only heard her once.

Alicia's lesson was scheduled for one o'clock on Wednesdays. As he waited for her in his spacious studio in Berman Hall, Sebastian kept his eye on the clock. His large desk and computer stood against one wall, flanked by floor-to-ceiling built-in bookcases filled with his personal music library. A seven-foot grand piano stood against the other wall, and there was a large window directly opposite the door. The window admitted a great amount of natural light, and it overlooked a field where wildflowers grew in the spring. At the end of the field, near the road, was a small lake with a central fountain. He loved the view, and he resorted to it often when he felt frustrated by the bureaucracy and funding inequities of Omega U.

Sitting tensely at his desk, he felt on edge for more reasons than one. He had risen at 5:30 for an hour of prayer before breakfast, and he hadn't eaten lunch as part of his new spiritual regimen. He was down to two meals a day, a newcomer to the discipline of ignoring hunger pangs. As his stomach grumbled in protest, he heard a light tap on the door. Sebastian braced himself. He hoped she was prepared for the lesson, ready for a new start, but her previous record made it doubtful. She was a classic underachiever, frustrating to work with. Despite her talent, in the two years he had known her, she had made no sustained attempt to develop it.

Alicia entered, bearing a backpack and her violin in its case. She was a buxom, pretty girl, of medium height, with closely cropped curls and large, flamboyant gold hoops in her ears. She wore a long, brilliantly colored dress printed with splashes of orange tropical birds and green palm trees.

"Good afternoon, Alicia."

"Good afternoon, Dr. Morrow." She laid the backpack on the floor and put the violin case on a chair. She didn't smile, and she didn't open the case. She remained standing. "Dr. Morrow, I'm gonna get right to the point. I don't think you treat me like all your other violin students."

She caught him by surprise. "Really? In what way do you think I treat you differently?"

"You grade me lower because I'm black."

Sebastian raised his eyebrows and gave a brief laugh. "Are you kidding me, Alicia? We've worked together for a year now, and you know me better than that."

"No, I don't. All your white students got As or Bs last semester, and I got a D, and the semester before that you gave me a C."

"I grade on merit, Alicia, and merit has no color. The grading criteria for violin majors is the same for all, and it's clearly spelled out in the syllabus. I grade on the preparation for each lesson, the effort each student makes. There has to be improvement from week to week."

Sebastian thought for a moment. "You know, we had a similar conversation at the end of your first semester last fall when you got a C. I gave you a pep talk, if you recall. I emphasized how much potential you have and told you that I expected more work from you, which you agreed to do, by the way. But instead of working harder in the spring, Alicia, your practice time declined."

She avoided eye contact and gazed at the floor. She shook her head in mute contradiction.

"During your jury exam at the end of last semester, you played the étude as if you had never seen it before, stopping repeatedly. You didn't memorize the one movement of the Bach concerto I had assigned, which was a requirement, and you played it quite under-tempo. Mr. Chang, the cello teacher, also gave you a D. There was almost no improvement from the day I assigned you the pieces at the beginning of the semester to the day you performed them. In addition, you missed several lessons last semester, with no valid excuse."

Sebastian was beginning to wonder if her accusation was an elaborate smokescreen to hide the fact that she was completely unprepared again.

He went on, in the hope of reaching her, "In my opinion, your purpose and mine should be the same. I'm here to help you improve, and you're here to become a better violinist. We have the same goal. But no one can improve without proper practice."

"I do practice. I'm in the practice rooms two hours a day."

"Alicia, whatever you're doing in the practice rooms doesn't seem to involve the violin."

She frowned and pinched her lips together. "Yes, it does."

"All right, then take out your instrument, and let's hear what you've done this week. Let's start with the Bach."

She shook her head. "I'm not ready to play it, 'cause I've been so upset about the way you treat me."

Sebastian raised his palms skyward. "The D was in May—now it's September. Why didn't you speak to me sooner?"

"You don't teach in the summer."

"That's true, but you know you can reach me anytime by email or telephone. I'm always happy to speak to students."

Her tone hardened. "Dr. Morrow, I want you to change my grade. I should have gotten at least a B for last semester."

Sebastian tried another tack. "Alicia, have you ever watched the Olympic games?"

She rolled her eyes. "Yes."

"The athletes who win those races don't win because they happen to be white or black, or any shade in between. Those who win have trained the hardest and run the fastest. They deserve to win, and they win on merit alone.

"Your grade last spring indicated the quality of work you did *then*. And I emphasize the word *then*. You have the potential to be a fine violinist, but that potential must be developed. If you're serious about being a musician, you have to put some sweat into it, starting now. The professional music world is highly competitive, and it's my responsibility to prepare all my students to compete in that world."

"I don't want to play in a professional orchestra. I'm going to be a teacher."

"Nonetheless, the university and I, as the violin teacher, have certain performance standards that students must meet to graduate. We have high standards, and we want students to rise to those standards." He leaned toward her. "Alicia, don't you want to be the best violinist you can be?"

She crossed her arms over her chest and cocked her head to the side. "I need you to raise my grade."

"Honestly, to reward you for poor work and let you slide by would be a real disservice, and I won't do that. I happen to think your mind and ability are as good as anyone else's, and I expect a lot of you. The D should have woken you up. I know you can do better, and so do you."

"So you're not gonna change my grade?"

"No, I'm not."

She drew the corners of her mouth down and pressed her lips

together. "All right, then. I'm going to speak to Dr. Duck about this."

As she picked up her backpack and violin to leave, Sebastian said, "What you should do is play your lesson today, and make a new, committed start. You can talk to Dr. Duck after the lesson."

She didn't answer him or make eye contact—she walked out and slammed the door.

Sebastian stared at the closed door for a minute, trying to get his bearings. He had never been accused of racism in his life. How could she be so wrong and so convinced she was right at the same time? He didn't understand her at all.

His office telephone rang, and the sound startled him. Could that be Dr. Duck already?

It was Abbie. "Sebastian, can we start our rehearsal earlier today? One of my students is ill, and we can use his time and finish earlier if you're free at three."

"That works."

"Okay, meet you in Conroy Hall then."

Sebastian replaced the receiver and then rose and walked to the window. He stood there with his hands in his pockets. Some days he had a real grudge against Adam and Eve, and this was one of them. If they had just obeyed God, humanity would dwell in Paradise, without strife, accusations, anger, or self-justification for sins and shortcomings, because there would be no sins or shortcomings. "Dear Adam and Eve, my ancient forbears," he muttered, "you've got a whole lot to answer for."

CHAPTER 21
CLARIFICATION

Music departments always seem to live on the edge in more ways than one, and Berman Hall, home of the music department at Omega U, was no exception. It sat ostracized at the edge of the campus, a stone's throw from the football stadium. It was a two-story red brick building built in the early part of the twentieth century. Two recital halls, the band hall (also used by the university orchestra), the choir room, the percussion studio, and the music office occupied the ground floor. The second floor housed four classrooms, a music library, the teaching studios, and twenty practice rooms. There was a lounge for the students, but none for the faculty.

The recital halls sat left and right of the entrance foyer. Godden Hall, the larger one on the left, could accommodate seven hundred people and was well-suited for band, orchestra, choir concerts, as well as operas and musical productions. The intimate Conroy Hall held only three hundred seats and was used for student and faculty recitals, as well as chamber music concerts.

At three o'clock, Sebastian met Abbie on the stage of Conroy Hall to rehearse their recital program scheduled for the end of October.

They had chosen a Mozart Sonata, five of the Brahms Hungarian Dances, and the Debussy Sonata. As Sebastian helped Abbie remove the large cover from the nine-foot Steinway, he remembered the organ recital Leo had invited him to attend.

"Abbie, there's a young organist named Leo de Graaf who plays at St. Mark's, my church in the teeming metropolis of Bullinger."

"Ha! Ten thousand people—some metropolis." While she listened, Abbie rummaged in the shapeless cloth bag she carried everywhere, and took out a pack of cigarettes, a lighter, an ashtray, a slim packet of stick incense, and its wooden holder. Eventually she found her music scores.

"As a sophomore at the University of Houston last year, he entered a competition and made it into the finals, which take place in Dallas next month. After Mass on Sunday, he invited me to a preparatory recital he's giving at Christ Church Cathedral in Houston next weekend. I thought you might like to come with me and hear him. He's remarkable, really."

"Sounds interesting, and not too far from our house. Hold on," she said. She lit a cigarette, took a deep drag, and placed the ashtray on the piano. Then she reached into her bag again and pulled out a badly worn day planner.

"Date?"

"Sunday, October fourth."

"Time?"

"Four o'clock sharp."

"Who's driving?"

Sebastian laughed. "I am, with dinner afterward for all my guests."

"Approved and noted." She made a notation in her planner. "Looking forward to it. If he's free, Rafa might like to come, too."

"I hope he can; I'd like to see him, and the larger the audience, the better for Leo." After Sebastian raised the heavy piano lid and propped it on the long stick, he took out his violin and rosined the bow. He set his violin parts on a music stand and moved it next to the keyboard.

Abbie placed her scores on the piano rack while the cigarette dangled from her lips. She squinted as smoke curled up toward the bright stage lights. Sebastian had grown so accustomed to her addiction, he didn't react anymore. She was having a better year in that regard; so far, she had only set off the building's smoke alarms once. The previous year it had happened twice, but no one had ratted on her, so they hadn't caught her yet. She told the fire department she had burned some incense to dissipate the smell of the new carpet in her studio, not realizing that the smoke would set off the alarm. On the second occasion, one of her loyal students covered for her by deliberately incinerating his lunch in the student lounge's microwave. After that episode, she brought a ladder into her studio ostensibly to hang pictures, which she did, but she also gained access to the smoke alarm and removed the battery.

Abbie quickly and expertly turned the knobs on the sides of the padded piano bench to raise it. When she had it adjusted properly, she played an A for Sebastian. While he tuned, she finished her cigarette and stubbed it out in the ashtray.

Sebastian loved working with Abbie. She was a keen-eared, sensitive pianist who could accompany discreetly, or play boldly in solo passages, and she had the technical and musical chops to hold her own with anyone. He trusted her musical judgment completely. In his opinion, she was the best musician in the department, and yet she never took herself too seriously.

Her chubby, unprepossessing appearance hid a brilliant intellect and a sharp wit, which often came to the fore in faculty meetings. He found her frankness and honesty refreshing in the stuffy world of academia; she always found a way to cut through to the heart of the matter. As a full professor who had taught at Omega for thirty years, she kept the bar high, and she fought for the good of the students. Sebastian considered her the de facto leader of the department. The other side of the coin was the uncanny way she bent the rules and operated in gleeful disregard of the regulations.

Her husband Rafa was a well-known Houston heart surgeon and an amateur pianist. They owned a house in West University, not far from the medical center. Both native New Yorkers, they had met when she was in graduate school at Juilliard and he was in his residency at Mount Sinai. "We ended up sitting side by side at the top of the house at a concert in Carnegie Hall. Afterward, between us, we had enough money to order coffee and one lox and bagel sandwich at a nearby deli. That was it. Thirty-five years later, we're still together, but now we can afford one sandwich each."

They could afford a lot more than that. They were gracious hosts, and Sebastian had eaten dinner with them often at their beautiful home. Maybe her irreverent attitude about university rules derived partly from the fact that she didn't really need the job at all.

Sebastian said, "Well, I guess we'd better get down to business, Abbie. Let's take the pieces in order." They began with the Mozart Sonata, followed by Brahms and then Debussy. The two-hour rehearsal passed very quickly.

At the end of the rehearsal, as Abbie lit another cigarette, Sebastian decided to tell her about Alicia Borden's accusation against him. He related the whole conversation.

"What a crock," Abbie said. "I remember her jury clearly. I accompanied her and all the string students. Very poor preparation—on her part, I mean. You did a fine job preparing your other students. You always do. She was the only dud. In my book she deserved an F."

She tapped the ashes into the ashtray. "You know, Sebastian, this whole thing may really be about money."

"Money?"

"Yes. If she had a scholarship of some sort, she could have lost it if her GPA dipped too low."

Sebastian slapped himself in the forehead. "She shocked me so badly, the thought never occurred to me. You're probably right. And if I change the grade to a B, she might retain the scholarship."

"Correct."

"Well, why accuse me of being racist? Why not just tell the truth about the scholarship?"

Abbie blew out a stream of smoke. "The truth won't get her what she wants. She lost her scholarship due to her own laziness. If she were honest, she'd have to admit that and take the consequences, but she doesn't want to do that. So, in order to get the scholarship back, she's chosen to lie and shift the blame to you. If she can make the racist label stick, she'll get what she wants without ever having to admit her own shortcomings." Abbie played a glum-sounding F minor chord on the piano. "It's worrisome, Sebastian. An accusation of racism could be tricky."

"Abbie, I did nothing wrong. The grade had nothing to do with race and Alicia knows it. She deserved a D."

"I'm perfectly aware of that, and I'll back you up. But we're living in a highly charged, politically correct atmosphere, and generally speaking, marshmallows have more backbone than administrators. We'll see if Q defends you or not."

By Abbie's logic, Ferris Duck's name had been transformed from Duck to Quack-Quack to Q. "I hope he does," she continued, "but there's the question of human nature. He knows you and me and everyone on the search committee except for Golden Boy voted against him."

"He does?"

"Well, sure he does. You know his buddy Roscoe must have filled him in on all the dirt. Consequently, if Q is like most people, he'll be biased against us and not very predisposed go to bat for us. It will be a measure of the man to see if he does what's right in this case, or what's politically expedient for him."

She blew a smoke ring that wobbled and ascended in the air. Behind her spectacles, her merry brown eyes crinkled as she smiled at Sebastian. "In other words, my friend, we'll see whether or not the man has balls."

In certain ways, musicians are just like the general population. Some tell the truth, and some are skillful, convincing liars. But when musicians perform, they cannot lie; they are as pure and transparent as the gold that paves the streets of heaven. Alicia hadn't worked at all during the spring semester, and her jury performance proved it. No matter how vehemently she swore she had practiced, her playing manifestly contradicted her word. It had been painfully apparent, and Sebastian had witnesses in Abbie Goldberg and Alfred Chang.

Abbie had advised Sebastian to bring documentation to the inevitable conference with Q. He made a file consisting of copies from his gradebook showing the individual lesson grades he had given Alicia, and a separate attendance record for her violin lessons and the orchestra rehearsals. He intended to add departmental copies of her jury evaluation sheets.

The summons came the following week. On Monday, September twenty-first, Ferris Duck emailed Sebastian and told him they needed to discuss Alicia Borden's complaint. He asked Sebastian to schedule an appointment with Betsy Bloom. Sebastian called her and she scheduled him for Wednesday at one. "Betsy, that's Alicia Borden's lesson time."

"You mean Pinocchio?"

Sebastian laughed. "Somehow, I don't think Pinocchio is Alicia's nickname."

"It is now. You know—the nose phenomenon."

"Ah, you must have heard the accusation."

"Oh, yes. She's spreading it around with a tractor, like manure on the north forty."

"Lovely."

"Ain't it? Dr. Morrow, Q specified the one o'clock time. Pinocchio will not attend any more lessons until the matter is settled."

"I see. By the way, Betsy, can you please make me copies of her spring jury sheets?"

"Glad to. I'll put them in your mailbox."

On the day of his appointment to see the department head, Sebastian had a free half-hour beforehand. After his lunch, a cup of hot tea, he went to the restroom to pee and wash his hands. Back in his studio, he combed his hair, knotted his sky-blue tie, and donned a sports jacket. He said a "Hail Mary" under his breath as he hustled downstairs to the music office with Alicia's file in hand.

He had no idea how the conference would go; Ferris Duck was still an unknown. He had met with the faculty three times. The first event, the ice cream social, held in the foyer of Berman Hall the week before the fall semester began, had gone unexpectedly well. Duck and his ebullient wife Eloa, a Brazilian, dark-haired beauty, had been quite cordial. Recently returned from three weeks in Rio de Janeiro with her family, Duck had brought back small handmade gifts for the faculty, surprising them all: a green stone frog for Sebastian, a wooden keyless flute for Miles, a carved wooden mermaid for Abbie, and for Philip, the hand-carved bust of an open-mouthed male figure with red thread wound around its neck.

Roscoe and Dean Faul, being a different category altogether, got four packages each of specialty coffee grown in various regions of Brazil.

"Tokens of gratitude," remarked Abbie, "for ushering him into a job over the heads of candidates who were actually qualified."

"Quite," remarked Miles. "What would life be without liquid energy, otherwise known as *quid pro quo*?"

The next day they met for a working lunch in the conference room adjacent to the department head's office. There had been a smattering of chitchat and a whole lot of dedicated eating. Then Q gave them the administrative goals and directives for the semester. None of them were his own; they had all come from the dean and the president. During the second faculty meeting at the end of the week, Q had explained his own goals for the department. He emphasized recruiting, the usual blather. "It's each person's responsibility, not just that of the band director and staff."

For the umpteenth time, Philip Washington suggested it would be easier to recruit if they had better funding. "I mean, what would the band do if they all they had to offer were three-hundred dollar scholarships? The choir and orchestra aren't even competitive with middle schools, much less other universities."

"True," he agreed. "That's an issue I intend to address with the dean."

Sebastian mentally rolled his eyes. *Good luck on that one, friend.*

Duck had seemed matter-of-fact, congenial, and almost as dynamic as Kool-Aid. His strongest characteristic seemed to be his fashion sense. He dressed formally, as though at any minute he expected photographers from *GQ* to burst through the door and blind him with banks of flashing cameras.

If he had lingering resentment against the search committee for voting against him, he showed no sign of it. But, Sebastian reasoned, no matter how the committee voted, Duck had won the job and the six-figure salary that went with it. He had got the last laugh; maybe that was enough for him.

When Sebastian walked into the music office for his appointment, Betsy greeted him and notified Q he had arrived. She also handed him an envelope from the Hlavicek Foundation. Sebastian's heart thumped in expectation of the $8,000 check for the orchestra.

"Have a seat, Dr. Morrow," said Betsy. "He said it'll be a few minutes." The office phone rang, and she engaged in a long conversation with someone from the scholarship office.

Apparently, Q was going to make him wait. Eager to see the check, Sebastian tore open the envelope from the Hlavicek Foundation. But all he found was a letter from Fred Margolis, Executive Director, informing him that the Hlavicek Foundation had chosen to rescind the grant. In the intervening months between the award and its distribution, the Foundation had changed its focus from the arts to business and education programs only. Sebastian grimaced and muttered, "What?" Thwarted again—no money for the orchestra.

He leaned his head back against the wall in frustration. Why would the foundation switch its emphasis with no forewarning? It simply didn't ring true, or if it was true, the action was very peculiar. He suddenly wondered if Lucas Hlavicek, who surely had the final say on all the grants, had decided to swat him like a fly, simply because he had eaten lunch with Silvie. It would not have surprised him; in the restaurant, the man had shown himself to be aggressive and possessive. Vindictiveness could not be far behind.

He wadded up the letter and threw it into the trash. Bad news was all he needed right before his conference with—

The door to the inner sanctum opened, and Q beckoned him in.

Sebastian walked into the office and sat in a large armchair, feeling discouraged and half-asphyxiated by a cloud of Duck's pungent cologne. He regarded the man across the vast, shiny expanse of an ultra-clean, uncluttered desk. If Ferris Duck did any work at all, he hid it well: no documents, no notebooks, not even a stray pen or a coffee mug marred the desk's mirror-like surface.

It struck a wrong note with Sebastian. There was something phony about the man. Perfectly groomed as always, he seemed counterfeit—like an actor in a commercial for "Careers in Academia" posing as a working administrator. Sebastian noted the studied, careful image—the tailored blue suit, the expensive shirt, creamy white, with French cuffs and tiger eye cufflinks, the yellow power tie. Duck's black goatee and eyebrows had not a hair out of place. He laid his huge, pale hands flat on the desk, as if to show off the diamond-studded wedding ring. His nails caught the light.

Fingernail polish? Mr. Immaculate Appearance.

Duck's computer monitor dwarfed Sebastian's, and his office had banks of windows on two sides. The other walls were littered with photos of him and his college bands; Duck and the president of the United States; Duck and Rocky Lipinsky, the famous football coach; Duck and his band at the Rose Bowl Parade. Sebastian wondered what any of it had to do with music.

"As you know, Dr. Morrow, to get right to the point, the charge of racism is quite serious."

Sebastian's head snapped away from the Rose Bowl Parade to face his boss, Dr. Poseur.

"I've heard Alicia's story, and now I'd like to hear what you have to say." Duck's cushy chair creaked as he leaned back into it and knitted his manicured hands together.

Sebastian produced copies of her grades, her spotty attendance record, and the jury evaluation sheets for the last semester and slid them across the desk to Dr. Duck. "Her performance exam was clearly substandard, as Mr. Chang noted on his sheet. He gave her a

D for the jury, as I did. Both he and I graded Alicia on the basis of how she played and nothing else. Dr. Goldberg accompanied her in the exam, and she can also vouch for the poor level of this student's preparation and performance.

"As you can see, she missed five of fourteen lessons. That's about 35 percent, and the absences marked U were unexcused. All but one. When she did come to her lessons, she was not prepared. There again, you can see her grades hover between C and F levels.

"Dr. Duck, Alicia has potential, and I have told her so. But until she actually commits to a regular practice regimen, she will not improve. Unfortunately, I cannot give her grades based on unrealized potential."

Ferris Duck looked over the evidence and seemed to ponder Sebastian's words. "She's your only African American violin student?"

"Yes, she is."

"And all your other students received As and Bs?"

"All my students received the grades they *earned*, just as Alicia did."

"Did you seat her last in the second violin section in orchestra?"

"She was seated last based on her audition. Both Alfred Chang and I heard all the string students' auditions. We made the seating decisions together."

"I see." There was a brief silence. Then Duck opened a desk drawer and pulled out a single sheet of paper which he laid before him. He stroked his chin twice, and then bowed his head.

His manner was so dramatic, Sebastian wondered if Duck was about to read him his execution orders: firing squad or electric chair?

After a moment, he raised his head and pierced Sebastian with an intense gaze. He spoke with an air of gravity and quiet distaste. "Dr. Morrow, there is also the matter of the racial slur you used against her."

Sebastian blinked in disbelief. "What?" The accusation was so ludicrous, he felt an impulse to laugh. "What racial slur?"

"I'll read Alicia's account of the incident." He consulted the paper before him on the desk. "These are her words: *I overheard Dr. Morrow talking to Mr. Greenfield just outside the music office. As Dr. Morrow and Mr. Greenfield passed me and another African American student in the hallway, Dr. Morrow clearly said, 'I hate those damn niggers,' with emphasis on the word 'hate.' Mr. Greenfield laughed.*"

Sebastian's mouth fell open. "That is *absurd.* I would never say something like that." He shook his head. "Not ever."

Duck sat silently and observed Sebastian.

Sebastian's mind whirled. He was so blindsided by the accusation that his thoughts splintered and speech left him. Alicia had not mentioned a racial slur when she spoke to him in his office. He finally blurted out, "When did this so-called incident happen?"

"At the end of the spring semester, just after you gave her the D. Your remark confirmed to her that the grade was based on racial discrimination." He clasped his manicured hands together and laid them on the desk. "Dr. Morrow, Alicia's mother has called me to complain. She has also spoken to the dean and the president of the university. She's threatening to bring in national news organizations." He paused and placed his hands together in a position of prayer with the index fingers pressed against his lips. "What are your thoughts?"

"Aside from the fact that this is a blatant lie, I'd dearly like to know why Alicia is doing this."

"Her grade point average has dropped below a 2.0, and she will lose her scholarship."

Right-o, Abbie. "What scholarship is that?"

"The Isaiah Yates Scholarship, an academic scholarship for African American undergraduates. Without it, she can't afford to stay in school. Her mother is unable to pay for her college education."

"What grades did she receive in her other classes last spring?"

"She got three Cs, one B, and an F in English Composition. However, the English instructor made a clerical error. The F should have been a D, and she has corrected that error. If her violin grade is changed to a B, the GPA goes up to a 2.0, and she retains the scholarship."

"Well, that explains it. But I didn't make a clerical error."

"Have you re-averaged her grades?"

"I can, but I double-check the grades at the time I give them. I think it's very important to be accurate."

Ferris Duck nodded. "Dr. Morrow, I've conferred with Dean Faul on this matter, and we think the wisest course would be to change the grade."

Sebastian felt heat rising to his face. "On what basis? There has to be a valid reason for changing a grade. The only reason I see in this instance is that the student wants it changed, which is not a valid reason at all."

"There is still the matter of the racial slur. She has a case, you know. And the charge of racism is not good public relations for the university. The dean and I intend to keep the university's reputation clean."

Sebastian leaned forward in his chair. "May I remind you, Dr. Duck, the charge of racism is just that—a charge, an accusation. It isn't founded on facts or reality. As a citizen of these United States, am I not presumed innocent until proven guilty?"

Ferris Duck ignored the question. "Dr. Morrow, please consider changing the student's grade. If you do what is right, the student will forgive the racial epithet, and the matter will be resolved."

Unable to fully control his temper, he replied, "First of all, I believe you mean *the imaginary* racial epithet. Secondly, if I change this grade solely because that's what the student wants, will she then dictate each semester what final grade I should give her? I mean, I won't know how to grade her otherwise. And thirdly, what happens if I decide not to comply?"

"Dr. Morrow, this is a one-time situation."

"Is it? I don't think so. It would be if this was stopped right here, which would be in the best interest of the student. She needs to bear the consequences of her actions."

Duck smiled, leaned back in his chair, and crossed his arms over his chest. "Well, it cuts both ways—the student might say the same of you."

Sebastian could see the man was enjoying himself. "That could very well be. But she, and any who agree with her," he smiled at Duck, "would be wrong. I cannot be faulted for something I did not say. And as all the evidence shows, she deserved the D."

Duck dropped his gaze and hurried on. "In any event, if you choose not to change the grade, the university will suspend you with pay until the matter can be resolved, hopefully in six weeks or less. During that time, we will follow the protocol for dismissal. At the end of that period, the final decision on your employment will be made."

Interesting how they had it all worked out. "Who will teach all my string students, the ones who work hard and earn their good grades? Who will conduct the orchestra and teach my theory classes in the meantime?" *And do you think I'll just go meekly along without defending myself?*

"We may hire a graduate student from Rice."

"I see." *Wonderful—a surefire way to improve public relations and maintain a reputation. Omega U, home of great customer service and quality education, where associate professors are replaced by graduate students.*

"Why don't you think about it tonight and give me your answer in the morning?"

Sebastian couldn't remain seated any longer. He rose and looked down at Ferris Duck. "This has been very informative, Dr. Duck. Thank you for the clarification." He turned and walked out.

Betsy Bloom's smile faded when she saw his high color and the thunder on his face. She grimaced, and murmured, "Oh, boy."

Too angry to speak, he simply nodded and strode out the door. Charged with adrenaline, he bolted up the stairs two at a time. He unlocked his studio and sat down at the computer to send an email:

Dear Abbie,
Just back from my conference with Q. There is a second false accusation against me, which I will tell you about later. Due to this situation, we may have to cancel our recital. They're prepared to suspend me with pay and possibly terminate me if I don't change the grade. I'll inform Q of my decision tomorrow morning.
Sebastian

He fired off a second email to Miles.

Dear Miles,
There's an important matter I must discuss with you. Please call me this evening any time after 8 p.m. Also, I lost the orchestra grant from the Hlavicek Foundation. Will tell you about that when we talk later.
Sebastian

He leaned back in his chair and tried to think. He took a few deep breaths to slow his pounding heart and his racing, scattered thoughts. It took him some time to finally calm himself enough to sort through his options.

To change the grade would give everyone what they wanted. Alicia would retain the scholarship and a 2.0 GPA. The department head and the dean would avoid a public relations embarrassment, and the charge of racism would be dropped. He would be "forgiven." He would keep his job.

On the other hand, to do that would reward the student for poor performance and teach her that not only was it profitable to lie, but that her lies had the power to intimidate others and force them to do her will. For his part, if he did what he knew to be wrong, he would pay a very steep price: the loss of his self-respect.

What does it profit a man to gain the whole world, but lose his own soul? He picked up the green stone frog Duck had given him and weighed it in his hand. He decided to return it to nature—he would fling it into the Brazos River on the way home.

He glanced at the computer monitor, still open to his email. Abbie had replied.

> *Sebastian,*
> *We should play the recital no matter what. If you are sus-pended, we'll find another venue in Houston.*
> *If you decide to fight this, Rafa and I will help you find a lawyer. Just let me know. And if you want to talk, give me a call later tonight. I know you must be very upset right now, but just remember, the truth is the only thing that's unshakable. In the end, it's the only thing that stands.*
> *Abbie*

Well, as usual, she got right to the heart of the matter—the truth. Sebastian rocked back in his chair and looked at the ceiling. It wasn't about a grade; it wasn't about stirring up trouble. He had to decide: Who would he serve: falsehood or truth? Who would he please: God or man?

CHAPTER 22

UNCHARTED TERRITORY

Sebastian had played a concert at the Episcopal Cathedral years ago, but Abbie had never visited it before. He had forgotten how beautiful it was. Standing beside her in the center aisle, his eye followed the piers and rising lines of the nave's architecture to the great beams and rafters supporting the high, peaked wooden ceiling. The pews, floor, walls, and ceiling were all made of dark wood. Spacious, yet somehow intimate, the cathedral had an air of warmth and protection. Sebastian felt as though he rode amidships in a great sailing vessel, enclosed and shielded from the sea. He could almost imagine motion: waves slapping at the hull and the creaking of the timbers. As he and the Church sailed into the perilous and uncharted territory of the twenty-first century, he prayed the Captain of the Ship had his hand on the rudder.

He took heart from the beauty and peace of the space. Its physical presence testified that evil did not have the field to itself, nor would it ultimately prevail. Immensely powerful, benevolent forces worked in the world to defend and help human beings. Despite his own sufferings and discouragements, Sebastian knew he did not walk or fight alone: *the battle is the Lord's.* A plainchant melody, probably sung in this very cathedral, came into his mind, but he could only remember fragments of the words: *Humbly I adore Thee, Verity unseen . . .* As the serene melody flowed through his mind, he recalled one verse:

Taste, and touch, and vision, to discern thee fail;
Faith, that comes by hearing, pierces through the veil.
I believe whate'er the Son of God hath told;
What the Truth hath spoken, that for truth I hold.

There was the solution to life: have faith and hold fast.

And have good friends. To his right stood a pillar of truth, albeit a short one. Abbie appeared entranced by the glorious stained glass windows. The images of angels and archangels, the apostles, the Lord and His mother, in vibrant shades of crimson, blue, purple, green, and gold, glowed and came to life in the late afternoon sunlight. Glancing down at her tousled curls, Sebastian wondered what a Jewish woman made of the images. "You know, Abbie," he said, "we follow the greatest Rabbi of all time."

"That he was," she replied. "I can't think of any other life that affected the world so profoundly as his."

She glanced at the group of young men conversing quietly in the transept. "Is Leo one of those guys?" She'd heard Sebastian talk about him, but she'd never met him.

"No, I haven't seen him yet." *Nor his beautiful mother.* Surely, she would be here, and hopefully without the Kolache King. "Maybe he's up there." Sebastian pointed to the elevated chancel and altar, separated from the nave by an elaborately carved rood screen. "That's where the organ console is."

A man, possibly in his early sixties, wearing a gray blazer and black trousers, appeared from behind the rood screen. He had a round head with wispy, fly-away hair the color of wheat. He addressed the audience members from the top of the chancel steps. "Good afternoon, everyone, and welcome to Christ Church Cathedral. I'm Tobias Mortensson, the cathedral organist and Leo's teacher. Thank you all for coming to his pre-competition recital. We're about ready to begin. It's an informal recital, so please come up and sit in the choir stalls on the left where you can see Leo."

His spoken English had a peculiar sound; it combined his native Swedish lilt with a British accent. "The organ console is situated against the wall to the right of the altar, and unfortunately, from the nave, the organist is quite invisible." He seemed very jolly, and his toothy grin made his blue eyes crinkle up behind his round spectacles.

Sebastian had never met the man, but the music world was small, and Mortensson had a fine reputation. He was a graduate of the Royal Swedish Conservatory and had also held positions in Uppsala and London.

When everyone had ascended the stairs, Mortensson turned off all the lights in the nave and left only a few lights on in the chancel. The dimness and the small cluster of people in the enclosed space created a very intimate atmosphere. Sebastian and Abbie sat in the second row, with six organ students behind them.

At the last minute, to Sebastian's delight, Silvie de Graaf and her daughter Kristin hurried up the chancel steps. They smiled and greeted him briefly before they sat in the first row. To his relief, there was no sign of Lucas Hlavicek. He hoped Silvie had come to her senses and broken up with him.

Abbie produced a yellow legal pad and pen from the depths of her shapeless cloth bag on the pew beside her. "I thought I'd jot down any helpful comments that come to mind," she told Sebastian in a low voice.

"Good idea, Abbie." She was a wonderful musician, and it was generous of her to make notes for Leo. Sebastian had read her comments on jury exams at Omega many times, and he knew how skillfully she could sum up the adjustments necessary to improve a student's performance. Lucky Leo.

Leo, dressed in a dark blue blazer, white shirt, blue tie, and gray trousers, entered from a side door to stand before them. When everyone applauded, he smiled, bowed a little awkwardly, and blushed. He thanked everyone for coming and handed out a simple program with the titles and composers' names and then invited them to a reception in the courtyard after the concert. Although the atmosphere was informal, Sebastian sensed a certain tension in the boy. He knew it was Leo's first public performance of these particular pieces, and of course, he was playing for his peers from the university—a harrowing but necessary experience, as Sebastian remembered from his conservatory days.

Leo walked to the console, slid onto the long bench, and set the stops. His teacher stood beside him to turn pages. He played Bach's D Major Prelude and Fugue first, the piece Sebastian had heard him play the day they met in St. Mark's. Sebastian enjoyed watching him play. He had a focused, palpable intensity about him, and somehow it added to the effect of the music. His hands shifted back and forth over the three manuals, while his feet danced on the pedals in a marvel of coordination.

Leo's performance had markedly improved. The cathedral organ was larger and better suited to the Bach than the small instrument at St. Mark's, and also, in the intervening months, he had eliminated the minor errors. He played the piece even more musically than before.

Afterward, Abbie murmured, "Wow, not too much to say about that other than *bravo!*"

Sebastian's attention was divided between the glorious music and the close proximity of Silvie. He had only seen her briefly in the bookshop a few times since the previous summer, but she had never been far from his mind. He listened to Leo play with the keen ear of a professional musician, but his eyes feasted on the shape of Silvie's head and her hair, unadorned and lovely as light itself. It shone flaxen in the dimness of the chancel. He could smell her perfume—so fresh and light. When she turned her head left to gaze at the altar, he saw the lovely straight line of her nose and the long white lashes. He wanted to kiss those eyes and caress her cheek.

So it went through the entire forty-minute recital. Afterward, Mortensson shooed them all out to the courtyard while he turned off the lights and locked the cathedral. Sebastian and Abbie bypassed the card table bearing refreshments at the edge of the courtyard. They walked over to Leo, who stood beside the central fountain, wiping his brow with a handkerchief. They had him all to themselves for a few minutes, since the students' first priority was food. Sebastian introduced Abbie and they both congratulated him. When Abbie handed him her notes, Leo was quite surprised and pleased that she had made the effort, and he thanked her profusely.

As much as he disliked himself for doing it, Sebastian fished for information. "I thought I might see Lucas Hlavicek, your mom's friend, here tonight," he said. "I met him last summer one day when she and I ate lunch together. I applied to his foundation for a grant for the Omega orchestra, and I wanted to talk to him about that." *And why the louse rescinded it.*

"Well, I didn't invite him, but I think Mamma did," said Leo.

The statement hit Sebastian like a torpedo; his heart burned and sank faster than the *Lusitania*. Silvie was still dating the schmuck.

"But he's such a busy man, he rarely comes to small events like this," Leo added.

"Well, you can tell him for me he missed out," replied Sebastian. "The quality of your playing made it a big event. Congratulations, and I expect you'll have very good results at the competition."

As his fellow organists surrounded Leo, Sebastian and Abbie retreated to the refreshment table. Silvie and Tobias Mortensson stood on the far side of it conversing with each other. As he drew near, Sebastian realized they were speaking Swedish. Mortensson was another man who had a common bond and a level of intimacy he could not share with Silvie. Added to what he had just learned, it irritated the hell out of him, and he felt a stab of jealousy.

Kristin tended the table, which bore simple refreshments: pastries, a thermos of coffee, and bottles of sparkling water. She greeted Sebastian cheerfully, and he introduced her to Abbie. To his chagrin, he counted three different kinds of kolaches on the table, the unmistakable sign of the effing Czech bastard Lucas. Abbie chose one with a poppy seed center. "Aren't you going to have one of these?" she asked him.

Sebastian would just as soon have eaten dirt. He shook his head. "Don't want to spoil my dinner."

Kristin poured Abbie a cup of coffee, while Sebastian opened a bottle of sparkling water.

He drank greedily, wishing it was a liter of single malt scotch, so he could get pie-eyed.

"Dr. Morrow, I got accepted to law school at UT," Kristin said. "So, you can see where all this is going."

"Not sure I can, Kristin."

"Well, Leo will graduate in two years with his music degree, about the same time I graduate from law school. I won't have to look for a job—I'll just be the manager of his big-time career and negotiate his contracts for him."

Sebastian smiled. "You could be right, Kristin—time will tell. But you may be destined for a big-time career of your own. Congratulations on getting into law school."

Silvie suddenly switched to English and turned to him with a bright smile. "Sebastian, it's so good to see you here. Thank you for coming."

"I'm glad I did. Leo played wonderfully." He gestured toward Abbie. "Silvie, this is my friend, the pianist Abbie Goldberg."

Silvie took Abbie's hand in hers. "I'm Leo's mother."

"Yes, the resemblance is quite unmistakable," replied Abbie. "And in addition to his good looks, your son is extremely talented."

"Yes, he is." Silvie beamed with pleasure at the double compliment. Then she brought Mortensson into the conversation. "Tobias, this is Sebastian Morrow. He's the concertmaster at Opera D'Argento, and he teaches at Omega University."

Taught, rather. Sebastian didn't correct her, mostly because he didn't want to broach the subject while his job was in limbo. Instead, he congratulated Mortensson on the fine playing of his student.

After a little more chat, they wished everyone goodnight and then left for dinner. Sebastian had promised to treat Abbie, so they drove a short way to a Thai restaurant in Midtown. It was a large, simply decorated place, busy with mostly Asian diners. They ordered green tea and spring roll appetizers. Abbie had a shrimp dish, and Sebastian decided on Pad Kee Mao with beef. (At least his noodles were drunken.)

"How are you holding up?" Abbie asked. She hadn't seen him for over a week, and he had lost weight—shadows played in the hollows under his cheekbones.

Sebastian smiled ruefully. "Other than feeling completely at sea?"

It was the tenth day of his suspension. He had refused to change Alicia Borden's grade, which gave Ferris Duck the unalloyed pleasure of booting him out the day after their conference, September twenty-fourth. "Well, the opera kept me busy through the end of September. Currently, I'm tackling some home improvement projects and practicing a lot for our concert. Which reminds me, I got word today from Peter Storgis, the Artistic Director at Opera D'Argento, that he and the board agreed to let us play the recital at Frankau Hall on the date we had scheduled it for Omega. No charge for the hall."

Abbie smiled. "Excellent, we don't even have to postpone it—at least I hope not." Her face grew clouded. "I've been having some shooting pains in my hands the last few weeks. There are days when I can't play." She glanced down at her hands and flexed her fingers.

"Does aspirin help?"

"No. I've even gone to a hand specialist at Methodist Hospital, and after X-rays and an MRI, they can't find anything physically wrong. It's a bit of a puzzle. Maybe it's age-related or even weather-related." She smiled and showed Sebastian her hands. "*Voilà*, my personal barometers—I now get twinges when it's going to rain." She ate a bite of her spring roll. "But what about you—are you eating, Sebastian? You've lost a lot of weight."

His self-imposed fasting, now in its third month, had begun to lighten his physical body. His clothes fit more loosely—he had to fasten his belt one notch higher, and he could see his ribs in the mirror when he undressed. But he wanted to keep that aspect of his life private. He feared discussing it would somehow nullify any good effect. With a grin, he tried to pass over it lightly. "Oh, for that I blame the cook." He pointed to his chest. "Me."

Abbie's smile didn't erase the look of concern in her eyes.

Sebastian hurried on. "In other news, I've filed a grievance with the university, in the hope that this dispute can be resolved in-house by a faculty panel. The student and I will testify at a formal hearing. This whole thing can be stopped dead in the water then, I hope."

"Do you know when the hearing will take place?"

"Probably by the end of October." Sebastian dipped his spring roll into a tiny tub of sweet sauce and ate a bite.

"Have you hired Katzberger yet?" Rafa Goldberg, Abbie's husband, had suggested Martin Katzberger, a well-known Houston lawyer.

"No. I might not need him if the hearing goes my way." He hadn't acted on the suggestion, primarily because he feared the enormous cost of retaining a high-powered attorney.

Abbie's eyes were grave. "Sebastian, I really think you should hire him now. I'm certain the university will have their own counsel on hand at the hearing. Katzberger can guide you through the process and help you avoid any pitfalls. There's so much riding on the outcome."

He sighed. "Maybe you're right. Well, I'll think about it." Maybe he could convince the Federal Reserve to add credit to his bank account the way it added credit to its member banks' deposits. *Please stretch my economy, kind sirs. It's all for a good cause: my survival.*

The waiter brought their food, and they ate with the practiced concentration of hungry musicians. After a few minutes, Abbie's thoughts reverted to the recital. "Leo might truly have a big career ahead of him. He's certainly got the talent. I wrote a few notes for him on the Tournemire and the Petr Eben piece. He tends to revel in the technique, which he commands well. But he'll reach a higher level of music-making when his technique becomes a vehicle for artistic expression and not an end in itself."

Sebastian nodded. "True. He's got a lot to learn. I think it's easy at the beginning for young musicians to focus too much on technique. Everyone wants to play all the notes and be perfect . . . except, of course, my student Alicia." He rolled his eyes and smiled.

Abbie chuckled and shook her head. "In her case, striving for excellence seems to be a completely alien concept."

"I have to agree. But, you're right—great artists go far beyond the technical level, and if they miss notes, no one minds, because they transcend the medium, whether it be organ, piano, or violin; they take us to a spiritual place."

"Like Arthur Rubenstein. Listening to him play Chopin was a revelation."

"Exactly. But Leo is quite an unusual person, and he's very young."

"And very intense, it seemed to me."

"Yes." Sebastian thought a moment. "No one can tell the future, but given the right kind of teaching, Leo might reach those heights."

Abbie gazed at him with a knowing expression. "I also noticed Leo's mother seems to captivate you."

Sebastian felt heat in his cheeks. "Damn, Abbie. You notice everything."

"Well, she's beautiful." She pursed her lips in mock frustration. "What is it about those Scandinavian women, anyway? How did they get all the good looks?" She smiled at Sebastian. "I thought her quite warm and lovely—why wouldn't she captivate you? You know, Sebastian, your friends would like to see you happy and fulfilled. Haven't you had enough of the single life?"

"I would love to be happy and fulfilled, Abbie, but unfortunately, she has a rich boyfriend. The Kolache King."

Abbie sat back in her chair. "The Czech pastry guy on TV?"

"That's the one."

She burst into laughter. "No wonder you wouldn't eat a kolache. You had the most sour expression on your face."

"And now you know why."

"Well, cheer up. He's only her boyfriend, not her husband. And if she's as intelligent as she is beautiful—and why wouldn't she be if she produced a son like Leo?—she'll value virtue and valor—that's you, my friend—over fame and hard cash: him."

"I hope you're right."

With her customary humility, she replied, "I usually am." She laid her napkin on the table. "And now, Dr. Morrow, I must depart and go home this minute—it's an emergency."

He widened his eyes in alarm. "What's wrong?"

"I haven't smoked a cigarette in over four hours."

CHAPTER 23

COMPETITION

Tired and a little stiff from his four-hour drive to Dallas, Leo climbed out of the Jeep, thankful to have reached his destination. He had driven to the site of the competition first, before he checked into the hotel, and he was quite pleased he had. The photos he had seen of the cathedral did not compare with its reality.

Situated at the heart of the city, the cathedral in all its grandeur was a perfect metaphor. The transept's horizontal axis intersected the vertical axis of the chancel and nave to form a three-dimensional gray stone cross. A powerful symbol, its Gothic spires and slate roof reached up toward Heaven. Like a man, the cathedral was body and spirit, the intersection of Heaven with Earth. And, like a man, it was the image of something greater.

The spires drew the eye up to the deep blue of the sky. Somewhere above, hidden in light, was the place Leo called *There*. He wished he could see through that sky into the pure, timeless realm above it. It was a place as real and glorious as the incandescent sun that warmed him, a place free from the darkness of fear, pride, deception, anger, jealousy—the home of unimaginable peace, of landscapes and beings enclosed in a height, breadth, and depth of love that was at once its source, its light, and its reason for existence. If he could have, he would have flown there on the instant with speed and power, like the flock of pigeons rising up and banking into the wind above the cathedral, all swiftness and grace.

After a moment, he dropped his gaze back to the cathedral. Though impressive, the fortress-like granite walls rising seventy feet from the ground had merely the strength of stone, no match for the silent, elemental force of continual prayer that radiated outward from the cathedral, spreading its blessing over and around the city, drawing down the influence of the Divine upon humanity.

The traffic of the oblivious city rushed on, noisily, ceaselessly, grinding away like a wheel spinning around a still point. As the city and the world teetered more and more off-kilter, the cathedral was a steadying, benevolent influence. A thousand years ago, that fact would have been taken for granted. But now, ironically, in the Information Age, much was forgotten; much was obscured.

It was difficult for a young man like Leo to discuss such thoughts with his peers, who had roundly mocked him whenever he had tried. Few weapons are as effective and devastating as ridicule. Hoping he might have more success with a mature person, Leo had broached the subject with an amiable history professor at the university. Smiling, the professor scratched his head, the hairs of which were numbered, and derided the thought that any city had a need for a temple. Cities prospered or faltered due to the prevailing economic policies, the available workforce, the influence of climate and geography, and so on, the litany of the modern world.

But Leo did not agree.

He drove to the hotel, only five minutes away, checked in, and ate a light supper at a sandwich shop across the street. He had come on Thursday in order to rest and be fresh for his Friday practice session. He would have only one chance to get used to the cathedral organ before Saturday, the day of the competition.

Like a major airport in the days just before Thanksgiving, the hotel teemed with people. The Dallas Cowboys were set to play the Falcons on Sunday, and rowdy Atlanta fans clogged the elevators, roamed the halls in packs, and thronged the restaurant and bar. That night, to get his mind off their loud voices and raucous laughter, Leo distracted himself by reading about European cathedrals.

He connected his laptop and found an interesting article detailing the history of Dresden's cathedral, the *Frauenkirche*. At the end of World War II, in 1945, the allies dropped 650,000 incendiary bombs on the city, creating a firestorm. For two days and nights, the cathedral's eight interior sandstone pillars held up the great weight of the dome until the temperature in and around the church reached 1,000 degrees Celsius. The pillars, glowing red as logs in a fire, exploded, and the outer walls shattered. Six thousand tons of stone fell, creating a smoldering pile of rubble forty-two feet high. But the chancel and the altar, with its relief of Jesus' agony in the Garden of Gethsemane, remained standing. For sixty years the heap of ruins served as a war memorial. But from 1994 through 2005, the *Frauenkirche* rose from its ruins, resurrected and rebuilt with the fire-blackened original stones interspersed with new, lighter ones.

By the time he finished the article, it was almost eleven, and the noise in the hotel had begun to fade. He showered, got into bed, and fell asleep. He dreamed of Gothic cathedrals.

On Friday, just before two o'clock, Leo returned to the cathedral for his three-hour practice session. As he walked up to the building, he noticed a gargoyle crouched on a neighboring high-rise. It surprised him, since he associated gargoyles with Gothic buildings, not modern ones. The demonic face seemed to glare down at the church as if the sight was repellent. Nowadays, no one believed in demons either. But it was a fact that in Jesus' lifetime, though human beings refused to acknowledge His divinity, the malicious, watchful demons knew precisely who He was.

Fifteen minutes later, in the center of the darkened cathedral, Leo sat at the organ. It took him a few minutes to register the first piece. He sat at the console in the choir loft, just behind and above the stone altar, and set the stops. The cavernous nave was dark, and Leo appeared to float in an island of light, a slender figure with white-blond hair. He was alone, or so he thought, and he began by playing Bach. His long, finely made fingers moved deftly over the manuals, while his feet danced over the pedalboard. His back was straight, and his eyes were focused on the music. He did not notice the angels beside him.

He had to make the most of his three hours before the next competitor came in for his turn. As soon as he finished with the D Major Prelude and Fugue, Leo set the stops for Petr Eben's piece, *Laudes*. He smiled to himself, thinking of the story Kristin told him she created when he had played the piece for the small audience at his preparatory recital.

Slow moving pedal duet. "There's an enormous, creeping monster pulling itself lugubriously across the earth."

2' flute stop. "And suddenly a little bird appears floating and singing high above it."

"Kristin," he had told her, "the pedals and the flute stop are supposed to represent Earth and Heaven."

"Oh." Undeterred, she continued, "And then the evil army attacks, loud and angry!"

Leo set the reed stops for the evil army.

"But they're defeated in the end, and the bird . . . well, maybe it's an angel," she amended, "comes back, and all is peace."

Stops set, Leo straightened his back, took a deep breath, and then gripped the organ bench with both hands. He placed his feet on the pedals and played the opening measures of *Laudes,* heels and toes of both feet moving deftly, with precision. The deep, rumbling pedal tones vibrated the bench. With his right hand he brought in the flute stop, a high, ethereal sound that fluttered and soared above the plodding bass notes. The music of Heaven and Earth floated out into the darkened nave. *Heaven and Earth. There and Here.*

He played with great concentration, the corners of his mouth pulled back, completely absorbed. There was a purity, a kind of innocence about him as he played, of which he was entirely unaware. After a while, as it sometimes happened, he sensed rather than saw the two angels beside him, protective presences burning like two immense candle flames in still air. He played on.

He took a brief break before he began the Tournemire piece, an improvisation on the Easter plainchant *Victimae paschali laudes.* He still had an hour of his practice time left. He took a bottle of water, an apple, a chunk of cheddar, and some crackers out of his backpack. *Praise to the paschal victim.* He sat in the great and beautiful cathedral, erected for just that purpose. And so, before he drank or ate, he gave silent thanks. The apple was sweet and juicy; practice was going well, and he felt confident. He just wanted to do his best, whether he won or not.

He admired the carved wooden angels that stood like brown sentinels around the choir loft. He counted them. Eleven to the left, eleven on his right, and four on the railing behind him. Twenty-six? Two times thirteen? Somehow that didn't seem right. He stood up to get a better view. Ah, there were two more, one carved in the center of each wall to the left and right.

Twenty-eight—four times seven. Seven, the number of spiritual perfection.

As he sat down again in the pew, his mind shifted to the article about the Dresden cathedral he had read the previous night. He was certain each cathedral had an effect on its surroundings. He stretched out his legs and crossed them at the ankles. He rested his arms on the back of the choir pew to either side and laid his head back to look up at the vaulted ceiling. Reclining, he mirrored the sacred geometry of the cathedral even as he regarded it. The perfect proportions of the vault, the arches, the great and noble height produced a quiet peace in him. It pointed him heavenward—*There*. The closest he could come to that indescribable beauty here, was music. All anxiety left him, and at the same time, Bach's magnificent fugue resounded in his head. The inner music played perfect counterpoint to the echoes of all the prayers, past and ever-present in that place.

Refreshed, Leo spent his remaining time working on the Tournemire piece. Forty minutes later, he left the cathedral. The sun glinted off the high-rise across the street, and he noticed something different about the building. Hadn't there been a gargoyle on the west side, right on the corner? He squinted into the glare, but he didn't see it now. Surely it had been there earlier. Had it been a shadow or a trick of the light? Had his preoccupation with Gothic cathedrals caused a fanciful hallucination?

He shrugged it off, climbed into his Jeep, and drove back to the hotel. He walked through the elegant lobby and picked up a brochure advertising local restaurants and entertainment. Then, smashed in with rah-rah Falcon fans, he took the elevator to his fifth-floor room. He dropped his backpack on the table, sat in an armchair, propped up his feet, and studied the list of restaurants with his natural intensity. He weighed the pleasures of seafood vs. steak, Asian vs. Italian, balanced against what he could afford. He narrowed it down to a highly rated Chinese restaurant, "elegant, quiet dining," and a landmark Dallas steakhouse.

He chose the steakhouse. He didn't want elegance—he wanted a high-calorie, high-carbohydrate meal for energy. Besides, he just loved red meat. After a quick shower, he changed into dressier clothes than the jeans and polo shirt he had worn to practice. He checked his phone for directions, and with his stomach growling almost as loudly as the Jeep's engine, he headed for MacKenzie's.

Outside, the temperature had dropped precipitously. A norther was blowing through Dallas and it felt refreshing. It was late October, about time for the heat to break in Texas. He found the restaurant easily and parked in the crowded lot.

The two dining areas lay to either side of a handsome, mirrored bar. The hostess seated him to the left of the bar at a small table in a corner. No diners sat near him yet, and he had a clear view of the bar where two couples and three lone men sat. The snowy-white table-cloths added brightness in contrast to the dark wood of the interior. After the hotel chaos, he enjoyed the calm of the restaurant, the quiet conversations underscored by the clinking of glasses and utensils. The smell of grilled beef made his mouth water.

At twenty, he was still legally underage to drink. When the waiter came, Leo opted for a non-alcoholic beer. He ordered a twenty-ounce ribeye, medium rare, with a baked potato and the largest green salad on the menu.

To eat alone in a restaurant was a novel experience for Leo. He felt a little self-conscious, unaccompanied by family or friends. He was glad he had changed into black slacks, a white shirt, and a blue wool pullover. MacKenzie's clientele were of the business and pro-fessional class and most had just come from work. Many of the men wore suits or sports jackets, and the women wore dressy pantsuits or dresses with spiky-heeled shoes.

The waiter returned with Leo's beer, the huge salad, a basket of warm crusty bread, and a small white saucer with chunks of yellow butter. Feeling quite grown up, Leo buttered a slice of bread and ate his salad. At the same time, he surreptitiously spied on a newcomer at the bar.

She sat alone, drinking a margarita. Wearing a clingy purple dress, she appeared to have stepped off the cover of a fashion magazine. She had the endlessly long legs and willowy body of a model. Her dark straight hair, cut Cleopatra-style with long bangs, emphasized her huge brown eyes. Her pale, flawless skin, sculpted cheekbones and straight nose were striking. She could have been twenty-five or thirty-five, it was hard to tell. Whatever her age, she did not go unnoticed by any of the men at the bar.

She didn't speak to anyone except the bartender, but every now and then she checked the watch on her narrow wrist. Leo guessed she expected to meet someone who was apparently late.

The waiter returned and cleared away his salad plate. He set an oval platter with the sizzling ribeye and a large split baked potato before Leo. There was also a separate serving dish with toppings for the potato. Leo ate a piece of the ribeye and smiled with pleasure. Perfect! Then he mounded the potato with layers of crumbled bacon, sour cream, grated cheddar, topped with chives. It could have been three thousand calories by itself—Leo certainly hoped so. He dug in happily.

In the meantime, two middle-aged couples had been seated at the table to his left, and four young businessmen sat to the right. He was glad for company in his corner of the restaurant; he felt less conspicuous.

After making good progress on the steak and the potato, Leo's hunger eased. He returned his attention to the bar just in time to see the model's boyfriend arrive. Apparently, she saw him approach in the mirror, because she turned on the barstool as he reached for her. He was a tall, lean man with slicked-back hair, and he wore a black suit with the jacket unbuttoned. He swooped down and enveloped her like Count Dracula. Bending his head, he kissed her with a long, open-mouthed kiss that somehow offended Leo. It seemed inappropriate in public, and less a sign of affection than a display of ownership by a dominant male.

When the man finally lifted his head, Leo inhaled so sharply and audibly that one of the women at the table next to him turned and asked him if he was all right.

"I'm fine," he lied. He pointed to his mouth. "Just bit my tongue."

In truth, he thought he would never be fine again. He had just recognized Lucas Hlavicek.

"You slimy, two-timing bastard," Leo hissed through clenched teeth. So, this was what lying Lucas did on his business trips. Leo felt himself flush with a swirl of conflicting emotions: fury for the betrayal of his mother, an impulse to rise and smack the bastard's ugly face, and an ashen, bitter satisfaction that his instincts about Lucas had been confirmed.

Leo laid down his fork and knife. He had lost his appetite.

As Lucas and the model began to walk away from the bar to the other side of the dining area, Leo realized there was one thing he could do. He grabbed his iPhone and snapped a picture of them. They were laughing, and Lucas had his arm snaked around her waist. Leo's photo captured the back of her head, but a clear shot of Lucas in profile.

If anyone required proof, Leo had it.

CHAPTER 24
EXPOSURE

After the competition ended, Leo drove home to Bullinger late on Saturday. He had won third place, which thoroughly surprised him, considering the skill and experience of the other organists. The first and second place winners were ten and eight years older than he. Pleased and excited, he immediately texted the news to his mother and his teacher, Tobias Mortensson. He emailed the results to Sebastian and asked him to forward it to Abbie Goldberg. He especially thanked Dr. Goldberg for her detailed notes, which had helped him improve the Eben piece and the Tournemire.

When his mother called to congratulate him, he smiled—he could hear the pleasure and pride in her voice. She was going to make a really nice meal for him the next day, and as usual, she told him to drive carefully. A little later, he got texted congratulations from Kristin and his teacher Mr. Mortensson. Sebastian Morrow congratulated him by email and also invited him to a violin-piano recital he and Abbie Goldberg were performing the following weekend on Friday, October thirtieth.

He began the drive home in a euphoric daze, but his elation faded after a couple of hours on the road. He was more fatigued than he should have been, primarily because he had not slept well the night before the competition, after he had seen philandering Lucas. To boost his flagging energy, he stopped for a quick meal at a fast food restaurant as he traveled south.

When he finally arrived home at midnight, he found his mother had waited up for him as always. She hugged him and they talked briefly, but Leo didn't broach the subject of Lucas—he just went to bed.

He didn't sleep well that night either. He knew he had to tell her the news about Lucas, but he kept wondering *how* he should tell her. Bleary-eyed, he rose at 6:30 on Sunday morning to get ready to play Mass at St. Mark's.

When he came home from church, his mother had a special Swedish lunch ready for him and Kristin, who was home for the weekend from UT. They ate smoked salmon, boiled potatoes, and hard-boiled eggs, with *knäckebröd* (a flat crispbread), *Västerbottensost* (a sharp cheese), and a green salad. For dessert, his mother made a *princesstårta*, a Swedish cake with of layers of sponge cake, vanilla cream, and raspberry jam under a dome of green marzipan. And, of course, she brewed Swedish coffee, the battlefield elixir that in ancient times was guaranteed to raise the Viking dead.

Naturally, his mother and Kristin wanted to hear all about the competition. Leo described the cathedral, the organ, and he told them a little about the other finalists. He even described the hotel chaos with all the Falcon fans. He showed them his prize for third place, a check for $1,000. As he rattled on, he kept trying to find a way to broach the subject of Lucas with his mother. Then he remembered Sebastian's concert invitation. He asked Silvie if she wanted to go the following Friday.

"It's a violin and piano recital. I'll take you out to eat afterward, Mamma, now that I'm a thousandaire."

She laughed. "A very generous offer, Leo, but Lucas asked me to go see the Pompeii exhibit at a museum in Houston that evening."

There was the opening, and Leo charged through it. "Mamma, don't go with him."

Silvie drew her chin down and pulled her head back, puzzled. "Why not?"

Leo plunged in, "Because I saw Lucas in Dallas—"

"Did you?" she smiled. "He had to handle some problem that came up at his bakery there."

"He handled more than a bakery problem, Mamma. I saw him at a steakhouse the night before the competition, and . . . well, he met a very beautiful young woman at the bar, and he kissed her in a way that made it clear she was his girlfriend."

Silvie's brow furrowed, and her lips parted, but she did not speak.

Kristin broke the tense silence. "Could the woman have been a friend or a relative?"

"No, not the way he kissed her. It was a very, uh, 'make out' kind of kiss. They obviously had a romantic relationship; it couldn't have been construed any other way."

Leo glanced at his mother to gauge her reaction. He saw a flush rising under her pale skin from her throat to her cheeks. He could see the news had wounded her. "Mamma, it made me so angry, I wanted to punch him." Leo sighed and added, "I thought you should know."

She drew in a deep breath and lowered her eyes. "Thank you, Leo. To know the truth is always best, even if it hurts."

He hated to see the light dimmed in her eyes. At least she hadn't cried. He never knew what to do when women cried.

"Better to know now than later," said Kristin quietly. "No wonder he was twice-divorced."

"I took a photo of them," Leo said, "in case you want to see it."

"I do," said Kristin.

Leo took out his iPhone and found the photo.

Caught completely by surprise, Silvie could hardly think straight. Her mind reeled with images of Lucas. She mentally replayed the lying words he had spoken. She felt shamed and embarrassed, as though Lucas' betrayal was somehow her fault. And she knew, in a way, it was. Leo, with his keen discernment, had never liked Lucas. He hadn't spoken against him, but he had made his distaste clear in other ways. She should have paid attention to her son's instincts and her own misgivings, but she had been blinded by Lucas' attention and flattery, his prominence in the community.

After a few moments, anger flared within her, as sudden and out of control as a grease fire. She hated dishonesty. If the man wanted to date younger women, fine. All he had to do was tell her. Instead, he had misled her all these months. What a fool she had been.

At least she hadn't gone to bed with him. Ha! But maybe that was why he had another girlfriend. In fact, who knew how many women he was stringing along? Maybe he had a different girl in every Hlavicek bakery town. And if he was promiscuous, he could have given her a disease—ugh. He had certainly kept up the pressure on her, but something had held her back. Probably everyone in gossipy Bullinger suspected she was sleeping with him, but they were quite wrong.

She had hesitated because in her heart she hadn't trusted him. He was wealthy and he had flattered her. She was middle-aged, after all, and his compliments had made her feel younger and more beautiful than she really was. He was so sure of himself, so forceful and dynamic. But his aggressive, unpredictable edge always created a certain tension in her and made her wary. Like a painstakingly trained wolf-dog, Lucas seemed well-behaved, but one never knew if or when his wild nature might erupt in ferocity.

But the man knew how to wine and dine a woman. She remembered the sailing trip on Lake Travis one brilliant afternoon last

May. They had rented a boat, and she had been impressed with his sailing skills on the water. She had loved the feeling of speed, the sparkling water, the smooth motion of the boat, the wind ruffling her hair. Afterward, they had fajitas and margaritas at a Mexican restaurant. To cap the day, he took her to Austin City Limits to hear Nyckelharpa, a Swedish pop/folk group touring the US.

But she also recalled the near car wreck on the way to the concert. The poor old woman had swerved to avoid hitting them and got a flat tire in the bargain. Instead of helping her, Lucas had fled the scene. That had been a snapshot of his character, and she knew it. She should have ended the relationship then.

Later in the spring, he had taken her down to Galveston, before the heat of summer. They had had the beach almost to themselves. It was too chilly to swim, but they walked for a long time, waded in the water, looked for seashells, and watched the brown pelicans gliding parallel to the shore. After a seafood dinner at Hotel Galvez, Lucas took her to the Grand 1894 Opera House for a performance of *The Merry Widow.* Though they had spent the night at the hotel, Silvie had reserved her own room. Her decision had royally ticked off Lucas, who was sure he was going to take her to bed that night.

He'd even promised to take her on a winter ski trip to Colorado. Well, that would never happen. At this point, she wouldn't go with him to the dry cleaners.

How seductive it had been to imagine a life of pleasures, free of financial worries. Lucas would take care of her; she would live in his mansion north of Bullinger, and they would fly occasionally to the house in Aspen. She could sell the bookshop and live a life of ease.

But the catch had been Lucas himself. The truth was she didn't love him. And she had feared his ruthlessness—his determination to have whatever he set his mind on. Perhaps that very determination had sparked her resistance—she didn't want to be owned. But his deception and dishonesty shocked her. Now she knew what kind of a man he really was.

"Let me see that photo, Leo." He handed her the iPhone. Silvie gazed thoughtfully at a slender, beautiful young woman, and the tall, narrow man who clutched her waist, a man who was the biggest mistake she had almost made.

CHAPTER 25
CONCERT

An unoccupied theater has an air of loneliness and abandonment. All the lively players have departed; the darkened stage is vacant of life, the seats are empty, dust motes float in pools of dim light, and silence settles heavily where once bright music reigned. Standing alone on the Frankau Hall stage, Sebastian's inner desolation matched that of his surroundings. He had refused to change Alicia's grade, and a month had gone by, thirty torturous days, since his suspension from Omega. He still smarted from the false accusations leveled against him and the betrayal of the administrators who should have defended him. In disbelief, like a man caught in an ambush, he sought to comprehend what had happened. It was as if his daily walk through the park had suddenly routed him into a war zone.

Because Sebastian was the orchestra's concertmaster, the management of Opera D'Argento allowed him to use Frankau Hall for his violin recital with Abbie Goldberg. The hall was as intimate and familiar to him as Omega's Conroy Recital Hall, and the acoustics were even better. Thrust out of his normal work routine, he would have felt lost without his morning prayers and his daily practice for the recital. Together they kept him grounded and provided an emotional and mental escape from his troubles.

Jessica, the stage manager, and her four-man crew had moved the seven-foot Steinway onto the stage. The opera company had just finished the run of *Tales of Hoffman,* and Jessica suggested he and Abbie use four potted palms from the set so the stage wouldn't look so bare. Although there were some vocal rehearsals in the hall in October, the next opera, Puccini's *Madama Butterfly* wouldn't open until mid-November. The hall happened to be available on Friday, October thirtieth.

Abbie met Sebastian at the hall for their dress rehearsal on Thursday, the day before the recital. She drove in on her way home from Omega. She parked in the small adjacent lot, and he led her in through the stage entrance, a shabby metal door and dim hallway at the side of the building. They walked through another door to the right, into the hall itself. The stage manager met them, and Sebastian made the introductions.

Jessica had set the stage lights to spotlight the center where the piano stood. "Sebastian, let me know if the lights are too bright or too dim, so I can adjust them before I leave."

"What do you think, Abbie?"

"Let me take out my scores and sit at the keyboard before I answer."

He followed her up a short set of stairs to the raised stage. Abbie rummaged in her large cloth bag, and felt a hard, bulky thing in the bottom. Surprised, she grasped it and took it out. It was the bare-breasted mermaid Q had given her. She had completely forgotten about it. It was rather crude folk art carved out of light wood with black threads wrapped around its waist and wrists, like a belt and cuffs. Ugh, Q was the last person she wanted to think about. She shoved the object back into the bag, took out her scores, and set them on the music rack. Sebastian put his music on the stand beside the piano to test the lighting.

"Perfect." Abbie gave the thumbs-up sign to Jessica, as did Sebastian.

"Good," said Jessica. "Sebastian, come up to the lighting console so I can show you how to turn them off when you're finished. The staff is gone for the day, and I'm about to leave too."

He met her in the back of the balcony and she showed him what to do. "When you leave," she said, "just close the stage door; it will lock behind you."

In the meantime, to get a feel for the instrument, Abbie played a set of rapid arpeggios and scales that ran the gamut from low to high on the piano. She had had two bad days earlier in the week, but thankfully, she had no shooting pains today. Hopefully, she would be pain-free for the concert. She kept her thoughts to herself; she didn't want to worry Sebastian.

When he returned to the stage, he asked her how she liked the piano. It had been tuned that morning.

"It's much better than I expected."

He rosined his bow, tuned, and then they played through the program, stopping occasionally to work on passages where the ensemble was rocky or to fix other small problems. They finished the rehearsal in less than two hours.

"It's going to be a good performance," Abbie assured him.

"I hope so."

"Listen, Sebastian, I'm dying for a cigarette." She had behaved herself and abstained from nicotine for the duration of the rehearsal. "It's 5:30, and I'm also starving. Is there a restaurant nearby where we could eat and I can smoke?"

"There's a Greek restaurant with an outside terrace two blocks from here. We could walk there."

"Let's do that, and I'll have a smoke on the way."

After Sebastian turned out the lights and made sure the stage door was locked, they stowed the music in their separate cars, but Sebastian took the violin with him. It was far too valuable to leave in a car. Abbie lit her cigarette before they left the parking lot. She took a deep drag and sighed, "Oh, Lord, that feels good."

The weather was cool and not too humid for a change. It was a pleasant stroll through one of the older neighborhoods in Houston, the same area where Sebastian's house had originally stood. Like his, most of the houses were Craftsman cottages, built in the early years of the twentieth century. The small, well-tended yards were shaded by live oaks and sycamores. Sebastian and Abbie shared the sidewalk with joggers, dog walkers, and a few mothers pushing baby strollers.

"Fall and spring are the best times of year in Houston," Sebastian remarked.

"I couldn't agree more," said Abbie. "Summer's sheer hell. But the southern winter is diabolical too, because it comes in waves, so you never have a chance to adjust to the cold. I swear, thirty degrees in this damp climate is more bone-chilling than ten below in New York."

"As a veteran of East Coast winters, I have to agree." At the restaurant, they chose an outside table. They ordered Greek salads, spanakopita, and moussaka.

As they ate their salads, Sebastian asked, "How's my replacement doing?" They had brought in a doctoral student from Rice to teach theory.

"Apparently it's not going so well—there are a lot of student complaints. And this is rich—Q is conducting the orchestra himself—a grand disaster, I hear." Abbie took a sip of water.

"You know, Abbie, there are two faculty members I haven't heard from since I was suspended: Roscoe and Philip Washington. I didn't expect any support or sympathy from Roscoe, but I had hoped to hear from Philip."

Abbie nodded. "Well, at the moment, Philip can't even talk. He's had a persistent case of laryngitis and had to postpone his faculty recital indefinitely. But politically, his situation is complicated. As the only black faculty member, he may have divided loyalties. I think he's trying to maintain a neutral stance and not tread on anyone's toes. He hasn't broached the subject with me."

She ate an olive and changed course. "Have you met with Martin?"

Martin Katzberger was the attorney Rafa Goldberg recommended. "Yesterday."

"And?"

"He sent a certified letter to Duck, Ezra Faul, and the president telling them he is representing me, and he thinks I've got an excellent case if it goes to court." *But it's going to break the bank just to retain him.*

"What's the alternative?"

"Well, there are several. First, there will be the university hearing before a panel of tenured professors. If they clear me, it'll stop there. Or, the university could back down and reverse their position. That's about as likely as the Pope converting to Islam. If all else fails, we either go to court or work out a settlement."

Abbie speared another olive. "I hope they clear you, and if not, I hope they settle. A trial would be a publicity nightmare, particularly if the university loses. And they'd probably have to bring the student in to testify. There's always the risk she won't be able to keep her lies straight."

"True. Their whole case rests on the word of a liar, and they know it." Sebastian stabbed a piece of feta cheese with his fork.

"How are you going to counter the racial epithet charge?"

Sebastian sipped his beer. "Well, that's a tough one. It's like fighting an imaginary foe, since it never happened in the first place. However, according to Alicia's testimony, Miles was present at the time, so I have a witness. The problem is, Miles and I discussed it the same day

I met with Q, and neither one of us can remember any incident like that involving Alicia. Students and faculty pass each other in the halls dozens, if not hundreds of times every semester. How could I possibly remember the exact day last spring, five months ago, that I passed by Alicia and another black student and made a despicable remark about them that I would never in my life say?"

"Hmm. But she also has a witness, apparently. Do you know who it is?"

"Keisha Williams."

"So, it's their word against yours and Miles'."

"That's where it stands."

The waiter brought their entrées to the table and cleared away the salad plates. Abbie picked up her fork and asked, "Who's on the faculty panel?"

"I don't know. Whoever they are, they must be tenured, but no one from the music department can serve. If they rule against me at the hearing, Martin will file suit against the university for defamation of character and wrongful termination of a tenured professor."

Abbie grinned. "I hope that'll scare the you-know-what outta them, so they'll settle."

Sebastian shrugged. "I guess we'll see."

On the night of the concert, they had separate dressing rooms backstage. Sebastian donned a tux, which was ironic because he had never before dressed so formally for a performance in Frankau Hall. About fifteen minutes before the start of the concert, Abbie tapped on the door of his dressing room.

"You look lovely," he said when he opened the door. Over a long black skirt, she wore a shimmery mauve tunic with three-quarter sleeves that set off her dark eyes and olive skin. Her cloud of springy dark hair glinted almost as brightly as her diamond pendant and matching earrings.

"Thanks, Sebastian, a beauty I'm not, but this is a good color for me. You don't look so bad yourself."

He glanced at his reflection in the wall of mirrors and straightened his bow tie. "Well, at least I can still get into my tux." Actually, he was surprised at how loosely it fit. He had definitely lost a few pounds due to fasting. "I've had the same one for twenty years. Think we'll have an audience?"

"I do. Your students, except for you-know-who, and mine and some of the faculty will come."

"Hopefully we'll see some of my colleagues from the opera orchestra. Miles and Julia will be here of course because she's catering the reception. And I know my faithful and true Aunt Nancy and Uncle Bear will be here."

"Bear? As in Grizzly?"

"As in Barrett Leaton, but she always calls him Bear. He's the nicest predator you'll ever want to meet."

"Oh, by the way, I called my friends at KUHF radio to come and record it."

Sebastian raised an eyebrow. "You did?"

"Uh-huh. Jessica let them in to set up the microphones this afternoon. Maybe they'll rebroadcast it on Houston Highlights next weekend." Abbie grinned. "Fame awaits us, Sebastian. Take that, you dumb Duck!"

Sebastian laughed. He rose and gave Abbie an affectionate hug. He glanced at the wall clock and said, "Well, my friend, looks like it's time to play some music." He picked up his violin and bow, and he and Abbie walked down a short hall that circled behind the stage to the wings. Standing in semidarkness, they could see the brilliantly lit stage and the piano with its lid extended like a bird in flight. The audience buzzed with lively chatter and laughter. "Sounds like a good crowd," she said, flexing her hands to test them for any pain. *So far, so good.*

Sebastian dealt with his own pre-concert jitters, an unsettled stomach, by mouthing a quiet prayer. Moments later, a sudden peace descended on him. To his surprise, he felt his physical distress ease, and a calm certainty arose in his heart that all would be well—not only the concert, but the situation with Omega too. He suddenly felt a great eagerness to go out onto the stage and play.

He checked his watch—it was 7:35. As agreed, Jessica dimmed the house lights. A hush fell over the audience. Sebastian leaned down and whispered, "Ready, Dr. Goldberg?"

"I am indeed, Dr. Morrow."

With one hand, he gripped his violin and bow, and with a flood of affection and a sweet confidence, he grasped Abbie's small hand in the other. "Shall we?"

They walked out to a warm, welcoming round of applause.

❧

Miles recognized the four potted palms from the set of *Tales of Hoffmann*, two on either side of the stage. It felt strange to him to see the hall from the audience's perspective. As Principal Flute of Opera D'Argento, he always sat in the orchestra. He should have been relaxed, but he felt tired and on edge after all the recent events, both personal and professional.

Simon had contracted some kind of long-term, mysterious stomach bug. Visits to two different doctors who prescribed antibiotics and anti-nausea medicine in September and October had not resulted in any improvement. The child continued to vomit almost every morning, worrying him and Julia to death. On this evening, the lone night they had gone out together, Julia's parents babysat their son. Just before they left, Simon, so wan and thin, had played them a little tune on the Brazilian flute Miles received from Duck.

Ah, dear Dr. Duck. The fact that he had caved immediately in the face of false allegations against Sebastian, Miles' closest friend at Omega, infuriated him. To help the evening succeed, Miles had done what little he could. He had asked his wife Julia, who ran Gourmet to Go, a prosperous catering business, to provide food and drink for the reception. He had tried to boost attendance at the recital by inviting all his flute students and giving his music literature class extra credit if they came. He counted heads in the audience.

"Are they here?" asked Julia.

"I see Betsy Bloom, the administrative assistant at Omega, Philip Washington, the voice teacher, and Storgis, our conductor."

"Point out Philip Washington. I've never met him."

"He's the black man two rows down across the aisle with a purple scarf around his neck. I'm surprised he's here—he's been out for a week with laryngitis."

"Good of him to come if he's been ill."

"Indeed. As for Omega students, so far I've counted thirty-seven."

"Not bad. You must have used intimidation."

He smiled at his pretty wife, a petite brunette. "Yeah, I'm a bleedin' ogre all right. But a show of force wasn't necessary. The students really like Sebastian, and they want to show their support for him and Abbie too. He's a good bloke in every way: teacher, performer, and colleague. He has the misfortune, as I do, to work for administrators whose greatest distinction is their utter moral cowardice. So, of course, those missing tonight are dear Dr. Duck and Dean Faul. Bloody Quislings."

"Here come your friends," said Julia, as a strong ovation rose and sustained itself in the hall. Sebastian and Abbie came out hand-in-hand and bowed, but the applause went on for over a minute.

Silvie de Graaf enjoyed opera and symphonic music, and organ concerts, of course, but she had never attended a recital for violin and piano only. When she told that to Leo on the drive into Houston, he replied, "Stick with me, Mamma. I'll take you places you've never been before." She imagined he probably would. Who knew where her son's musical career would take him?

Leo was in Bullinger that afternoon for a wedding rehearsal at St. Mark's, so they drove to Houston together in Silvie's Volvo. She asked him why the concert was not at Omega University.

"When Dr. Morrow invited me, he gave me the date, but not the venue. I assumed it would be at Omega. I called the music department office for directions to their concert hall, and the woman who answered told me the venue had changed from the hall on campus to Frankau Hall, where we saw *Tosca*. When I asked why, she told me Dr. Morrow was currently on leave from the university and had chosen a new venue for his recital."

"Why is he on leave?"

Leo shrugged. "I have no idea."

As they drove through the sprawling, endless suburbs, Silvie knew if it hadn't been for Leo's revelation about Lucas, she would have traveled into Houston that night to a museum with him instead, the lying wretch. The thought depressed her. Four days earlier, she had emailed Lucas the infamous photo, with the note:

Here's a photo I thought you might like to see, taken by my son during your last business trip to Dallas. (Directly after the extended, sloppy kiss at the steakhouse bar.) You evidently handled a lot more than bakery problems on your visit. I won't be going with you to the Pompeii exhibit Friday, but if the photo is any indication, I'm sure you won't lack for company.
I can't abide liars, so please don't ever contact me again. I also wish to terminate my contract with Hlavicek's Bakeries.
Silvie

She shook her head in a conscious attempt to drive the thought of him away. To divert herself, she asked Leo if he had met any interesting girls at the University of Houston.

He smiled. "As a matter of fact, I have—a violinist named Stephanie Curtis, and I hope she'll be there tonight to hear Dr. Morrow." He grinned at his mother. "I strongly encouraged her to come."

"Well, point her out to me if she's there."

She was glad Leo had a love interest. Handsome though he was, he had never had a steady girlfriend. Of course, he had just turned twenty, and he had plenty of time. But she had met Edward, her future husband, at age nineteen.

Silvie sighed—her musings had come full circle, back to herself. She fervently wished she could pack her burdensome, unwanted thoughts in a weighted suitcase and toss it into the Brazos.

When they arrived at Frankau Hall, Leo chose seats downstairs on the left so he could see Abbie's hands at the keyboard. There was a moderately sized crowd, with many young people. Leo scanned the audience, looking for Stephanie Curtis, Silvie presumed. After a few minutes, the lights dimmed, and then applause rose when Sebastian, looking thinner, but very elegant in his tuxedo, and the pianist came out of the wings. Silvie had forgotten how handsome he was.

He had an obvious affection for Abbie Goldberg, so much so that Silvie wondered if the bond between the two musicians might be romantic. She recalled he had introduced her as his "friend" at Leo's pre-competition recital. The audience's warm, prolonged applause before the musicians played a single note proclaimed their affection for the pair.

After Abbie settled herself at the piano, they opened the program with a Mozart sonata. The cleanness and transparency of the music and the perfect teamwork between piano and violin was refreshing. The music reminded Silvie of a bubbling brook—crystal clear, with nothing hidden. It helped wash away the thought of Lucas.

She was impressed by the playing of both musicians, but she was especially touched by the sweetness of Sebastian's sound. The tone, so rich and vibrant and singing, went right to the heart. She wondered if the warm, beautiful sound of the violin was created by the particular instrument, or the player, or some combination of both. She decided to ask Leo later.

The Mozart had only two movements, and as the musicians played the second one, Silvie closed her eyes. The gentle, dancelike lilt brought to mind the image of children playing in a field of flowers. A feeling of peace stole over her, and she felt her depression lift. She wanted the music to go on and on. She was sorry when it came to a close.

During the applause for the Mozart, Leo said, "They're both wonderful. They must have played together for years—they're like one being."

"Are they married?"

"Musically, yes." He grinned at his mother. "Well actually, she is married, but not to him. Her husband is Rafael Goldberg, the heart surgeon. I think Dr. Morrow is single."

Silvie smiled. *Nice to know.* They continued the concert with the Brahms Hungarian Dances. Sebastian and Abbie played with such fire and flair it sparked Silvie's imagination. The zesty, mercurial music reminded her of the gypsy women in Stockholm, with their laughter and bold, dark-eyed glances, their gold bangles and the colorful skirts that swayed seductively as they walked, broad-hipped through the streets of the capital.

❧

The concert couldn't begin soon enough for Nancy Leaton; it meant an end to Bear's incessant talk about Australia. He was a travel nerd who had been almost everywhere save The Land Down Under. Now that the continent was in his sights, he wasn't going to give up until they visited it. His mind hopped like a runaway kangaroo from the Sydney Opera House to the Great Barrier Reef to Ayers Rock. Nancy had tried distraction and diversion every time he broached the subject. Since those strategies failed, she had moved on to discouragement. She had more objections to Australia than Sebastian had to dating. She repeated them like a negative litany: too far, hugely expensive, upside-down seasons, weird and untrustworthy wildlife, not to mention the language barrier.

"Language barrier? Woman, they speak English!"

"Well, between their impenetrable accents and peculiar words, who can understand them?"

She desperately needed a break from buzzing digeridoos and endless documentaries on the Outback. The applause for Sebastian and Abbie finally overwhelmed Bear's discourse on Aboriginal rock paintings, and Nancy sat back with a sigh to enjoy the concert.

Finally, some real music. She enjoyed the Mozart and the Brahms, but her favorite piece was the Debussy Sonata. In parts, the music, luminous and still, seemed like moonlight translated into sound. In other sections the mood was agitated, impetuous, romantic.

Romantic. Now there was a word. When would Sebastian find a good woman? With Mary Catherine gone (and what a heartbreak she had been), he could remarry and make a new life for himself. She glanced at her husband of forty years, who sat transfixed by the music. What would she and Bear do without each other? Privately, she thought she would be lonely, but she would survive. Bear would be lost. A man, more than a woman, needed companionship, a lover, and a friend. After all, that was why God made woman in the first place. It was not good for the man to be alone.

For reassurance, she glanced at the images of Adam and Eve in one of the stained glass windows. Taking into account the place where she sat, she decided to add one more prayer to all those that had been uttered in this once sacred space: *All right, Lord, Sebastian needs a woman. Help us out here.*

CHAPTER 26
RECEPTION

ince Frankau Hall had very little foyer space where people could gather during intermissions, Opera D'Argento customarily utilized the outdoor courtyard adjacent to the hall to sell concessions. The large area, formerly a children's playground, had been landscaped and redone. High brick walls bounded it on three sides, while the street side was enclosed by a tall iron fence with a central archway and gate. The center area had been paved with brick in a herringbone pattern. All around it lay raised beds of begonias, ferns, irises, chrysanthemums, and azaleas, interspersed with wooden park benches. Two large, old sycamores stood sentinel inside the fence on either side of the gate.

At night, crisscrossed overhead with strings of small twinkling lights, the courtyard was a charming, magical space. Fortunately, the late October evening, cool, clear, and breezy, was perfect for an outdoor reception. Julia's Gourmet to Go crew had set up two long, narrow rectangular tables in the center area. They loaded one table with platters of small chicken salad sandwiches, cheeses, a giant bowl of fruit, cream puffs, éclairs, and brownies, and the other with coolers of bottled water, sodas, and a large coffee urn.

At the end of the program, after another extended ovation with shouts and whistles from the students, Sebastian had invited everyone to the outdoor reception. When Silvie rose to leave the hall, an animated Leo tugged on her sleeve and pointed to the far aisle. "Mamma, Stephanie is over there. See the girl in the green jacket with shoulder-length reddish hair?"

"Yes."

"I'm going to catch her before she leaves. I'll meet you at the reception." Leo disappeared with the speed and unerring accuracy of Cupid's arrow.

Abandoned, she made her way out the front doors and down a few steps to street level. She followed the exodus of people down the sidewalk to the left and then left again through an arched gateway. Silvie decided to get something to eat and drink at the tables set up in the center of the quadrangle while she waited for Leo.

Naturally, the first people to the food tables were the fleet-footed, ever-ravenous students. Miles and Julia did a brisk business serving them and refilling the platters, while the crowd waited for Abbie and Sebastian to appear. After fifteen minutes or so, they entered through a door at the back of the courtyard. When the crowd saw the two musicians, there was more applause, and their eager fans engulfed them.

As the knot of young people around the tables loosened, Silvie found herself standing beside an older couple in front of the fast-disappearing cream puffs. The small, bespectacled woman gave her a bright, friendly glance and said, "Wasn't that a wonderful concert?"

"Oh, yes. I enjoyed it very much." Thankful there was not a kolache in sight, Silvie put a sandwich, two strawberries, and an éclair on her plate.

"I have to say I'm very proud of the violinist. He's my sister's son." The woman beamed and her dark eyes twinkled.

"Oh." Silvie paused with the sandwich halfway to her mouth. She suddenly remembered her conversation with Sebastian the day she had the flat tire. "Mrs. Felicity Morrow."

"Yes!" the woman exclaimed. "That's my sister. Did you know her?"

Silvie smiled and shook her head. "No, Sebastian mentioned her to me once. He called her his darling mother."

"And she *was* a darling, both as a mother and sister." She smiled and held out her hand. "I'm Nancy Leaton and this is my husband Barrett."

Barrett was a portly man, taller than his wife, but several inches shorter than Silvie. He was making quick work of the cream puffs and sandwiches piled on his plate. Silvie decided Sebastian's height and blue eyes must have come from his father's family, although he and his Aunt Nancy had the same dark, abundant hair shot with silver.

Silvie replaced her sandwich on the plate to free her hand. "I'm Silvie de Graaf." She shook hands with Nancy and Barrett.

"How do you know Sebastian?" Nancy asked. "Are you also a musician?"

"No, I'm not. We . . . uh . . . ran into each other in my bookshop in Bullinger."

Just as Silvie tried again to eat her sandwich, she felt a hand on her shoulder. She turned to find Leo standing behind her with the auburn-haired Stephanie.

In the meantime, Nancy Leaton noticed that Silvie didn't wear a wedding ring. "Bear," she whispered, leaning close to her husband, "wouldn't she be a nice match for Sebastian?"

He pursed his lips and shook his head very slightly. "Nancy, my dear, now is not the time. Although cavorting with the opposite sex is never far from a man's mind, I'm sure Sebastian is focused on what he's facing at Omega." He hurled his empty paper plate into a trash can with more force than necessary and muttered, "Those damn idiots." He seized his wife by the hand, and led the way. "C'mon, woman. Let's go congratulate him on his playing."

After Leo introduced Stephanie to his mother, Silvie asked her if she had enjoyed the concert.

The young woman's shoulder-length auburn hair contrasted beautifully with her fair, almost transparent skin that bespoke the British Isles. Slender, quite attractive, and wearing a green jacket over a cream-colored blouse and a long black skirt, she smiled up at Silvie. The top of her head just reached the level of Leo's shoulder. "Oh, yes." Her hazel eyes flashed. "I was especially interested in the Debussy because I'm studying that piece now. Dr. Morrow's an excellent violinist, and he has such a beautiful sound."

"I noticed that, too," said Silvie. "Do you think that comes from the particular instrument or from the player himself?"

As she pondered a reply, Stephanie wrinkled her nose in such a way that her freckles slid together and her upper lip puckered slightly. "Well, I think it's a combination of both. The quality of the instrument makes a huge difference. That's why the Stradivarius and Guarneri violins are so prized. But I think, ultimately, a player's sound reflects his own qualities."

"What do you mean by that, Stephanie?" Leo asked.

"Well, for example, two of my fellow violinists at school are both very fine players, with violins comparable in quality. But one is a brash, outspoken person. He produces an edgy, harsh sound. The other is a more introverted, nerdy type. His sound is smaller, but much more refined."

"Interesting," said Silvie, thinking of the great sweetness of Sebastian's tone. "I suppose our unique personal signatures carry through everything we are and all that we do, from fingerprints and DNA to the sound of our voices—even a person's touch on a musical instrument." She thought for a moment. "So would you say a musician's playing reveals his character in sound?"

"To a certain degree, I think you're right, Mamma. The trick is recognizing and interpreting that signature."

Which is exactly what you're able to do, isn't it, Leo? Silvie kept her thought to herself, and instead changed the subject. "Have you eaten and spoken to the musicians yet?"

"Eaten, yes." They spoke simultaneously, glanced at each other, and laughed.

"Food always comes first, Mamma; you know that. But let's go speak to them now," said Leo. "Remember they both came to hear me play my competition pieces before I went to Dallas?"

"I certainly do," Silvie said. As she ate the sandwich and strawberries on her plate, she noticed Leo held Stephanie's hand.

"How did you meet them, Leo?" asked Stephanie.

"Sebastian's a member of St. Mark's Catholic Church, where I work in Bullinger. I invited him to hear me play my preparatory recital, and he asked Dr. Goldberg to come, too. She teaches piano at Omega University, where he works." Leo corrected himself. "Or worked. Apparently, he's on some kind of leave. Anyway, Dr. Goldberg jotted down some helpful comments as I played and gave me the sheet afterward."

"Is she an organist, too?"

"Actually, I'm not sure, but her comments weren't really about organ technique. They were musical suggestions that had to do with tempo and phrasing. They really helped. So, let's go over there—I owe them."

As they walked toward the back of the courtyard, the small ruddy-cheeked man who tended the food table apologized for stepping rapidly in front of them. He bore two heavily laden plates. "Sorry," he said in a British accent, "I'm bringing sustenance for my friends, those hard-working musicians."

"Excellent idea," said Silvie, "Sebastian looks like he could use a good meal. I'll get them something to drink." She picked up two bottles of water from one of the tables on her way.

The Brit bearing loaded plates handed one each to Sebastian and Abbie. "Bless you, Miles!" Abbie beamed. "And bless Julia for catering! I'm cross-eyed with hunger."

"Me, too! Thank you, Miles," said Sebastian. He wolfed down an entire finger sandwich at one go.

Miles bussed Abbie on the cheek and shook Sebastian's free hand. "Absolutely brilliant playing, both of you. What a wonderful recital, and you got a professional recording of it."

As Abbie munched on a cream puff with eyes closed in bliss, Sebastian said, "That was Abbie's idea."

"Well, tell me when KUHF is going to broadcast it. In the meantime, I must return to my post. Sorry," he said as he walked past Leo and Stephanie. Silvie stood just behind them holding the bottled water.

"Leo!" Sebastian exclaimed. "So glad you came." He glanced down at Abbie. "Remember our amazing organist friend, Abbie?"

She smiled. "I never forget excellent musicians."

Sebastian held his plate with one hand and shook Leo's hand with the other. Before Leo could utter a single compliment, Sebastian added, "And who's this?" He nodded toward Stephanie.

As Leo made the introductions, and Stephanie conversed with both musicians, drawing all their attention, Silvie observed Sebastian and Abbie. Their unfeigned interest and clear delight in speaking to the young people warmed her. Abbie, a chubby teddy bear with a halo of dark, curly hair, wore rimless spectacles that magnified her keen, intelligent eyes, deep brown and shining. The smile lines fanning out from the corners of her eyes testified to her good humor. No camera in the world could have done her justice, for a photograph could not capture the beauty of her spirit, which radiated in her eyes and through her expressive, animated face to transform her plain features.

Sebastian, tall and lithe as an athlete, stood at her side. It was a pleasure to watch him. His face was a photographer's dream, but his body too, wide at the shoulders and narrow-waisted, seemed to be of perfect proportions. A lock of wavy, almost black hair with silver points fell over his brow, a startling contrast with his deep blue eyes. He had a strong, straight nose and sculpted cheekbones, but he seemed thinner, more worn and gaunt than she remembered. There were deeper lines in his forehead and around the corners of his wide, mobile mouth. He had a shadowed, troubled air, as if he bore some burden. Perhaps he was just tired from the stress of the concert.

Suddenly, she heard Leo say, "And my mother is here, too."

Startled out of her reverie, Silvie stepped forward with the bottles of water. "For you," she said, handing one each to Abbie and Sebastian.

They both thanked her, but Sebastian couldn't quite hide his surprise. Although he said, "Silvie, I'm so glad you came," he looked as though he really meant *I can't believe you're here.* He drank the water thirstily. "Hot work, playing."

"Well, it was wonderful playing. This is the first time I've heard a violin and piano recital, and I enjoyed it so much." Silvie extended her hand to Abbie. "I'm Silvie. We met at Leo's organ recital." As she shook Abbie's small hand, she added, "I hope to hear you play another time."

Abbie smiled. "Thank you. It's a pleasure to see you again," she said. "Leo, I see where you get your good looks."

Leo blushed as Silvie and Stephanie smiled.

Silvie turned to Sebastian and shook his hand. As she complimented his performance, she was taken aback by his cool manner toward her, much more subdued than his way with Leo and Stephanie. She wondered why. He had been cordial at Leo's recital as well as the day he put the spare tire on her car. He had been so warm, charming, and engaging during their lunch. Now he seemed tense; he gave monosyllabic replies and avoided eye contact. Instead of focusing on her, he kept scanning the crowd. She found it maddening and quite rude.

Immediately after they spoke to the musicians, Silvie, Leo, and Stephanie left the reception. Leo walked Stephanie to her car, and then returned to drive his mother home. Since he had to play an eleven o'clock wedding the next day at St. Mark's, he was spending the night in Bullinger. During the long drive, Silvie's irritation with Sebastian, bothersome as low-level static, underscored her conversation with Leo. Her son, rarely loquacious, chattered happily about the concert and Stephanie, oblivious to Silvie's mood, and this exasperated her even more. Provoked and peeved, she could hardly concentrate.

It was very late by the time they arrived home. Silvie drank a smidgeon of red wine and then got ready for bed. Still wondering why Sebastian had seemed so distant, she slid under the covers and reached to turn out the bedside lamp. What was different about the time she had eaten lunch with him and tonight? They had enjoyed each other's company thoroughly then; she had felt very comfortable with him at the restaurant, at least until Lucas appeared.

She turned out the lamp and lay on her back with her hands behind her head. Why had Sebastian acted so aloof—why hadn't he even looked at her? He had certainly been looking for someone.

Herre Gud—he had! It suddenly dawned on her—Sebastian had been scanning the crowd for Lucas.

CHAPTER 27

PREDATORS

Sebastian didn't bother to change out of his tuxedo for the trip home. Miles' petite wife Julia (bless her) had urged more food on him. "Here," she said, "you need some more meat on your bones." She handed him a wrapped plate of sandwiches and fruit and a cup of coffee for the road, to keep him awake for the ninety-minute drive. As he drove north and west of the city, he sipped the coffee and ate two more chicken salad sandwiches, some strawberries, and chunks of cantaloupe and pineapple. By the time he eased his hunger and wiped his sticky fingers on a napkin, he had just passed the 610 Loop. Most of the drive remained, and he had plenty of time to think.

He was a little worried about his chickens. He had heard coyotes howling in the area the last few nights, but so far Penny, his Great Pyrenees, had kept them away. Although she was as gentle and sweet-natured as a lamb, her deep, ferocious bark sounded like Cerberus, the Hound of Hell. When Sebastian left for the concert, around 4:30, the sun was still fairly high in the sky. Penny kept watch while the chickens chased grasshoppers and foraged. They should have gone to roost about a half hour before sunset, shortly after six o'clock. The coop door was open, and he hoped they were safe. By the time he got home, it would be midnight. He would check on them first thing.

The recital had gone well, and he looked forward to hearing the recording. It had been gratifying to see all his Omega students, minus Alicia. They told him they missed him and asked him when he would return. Even Betsy Bloom came out. She updated him in her typical way, "The sad news is that Pinocchio's nose has grown so long, she can only ride in a convertible now. She can't even fit into the classrooms. Tsk, tsk. More Ds on the way."

It pleased him greatly that Philip Washington came despite his laryngitis. He was the first in line to congratulate them after the concert. In his raspy, hoarse voice, he confined his remarks to the performance and made no mention of the racial brouhaha at Omega. Nonetheless, for Sebastian, his presence was testimony that he bore no ill will.

Like a tonic, the support and good wishes lifted his spirits.

It had been an unexpected pleasure to see Leo de Graaf and meet his friend Stephanie, who was studying the Debussy Sonata herself. With all the drama at Omega, Sebastian had forgotten he'd invited Leo. The real shocker had been Silvie, the fair Nordic queen, with those arresting blue-violet eyes. The moment he saw her, Sebastian had been on the lookout for Lucas Hlavicek. Wherever she went, Sebastian imagined, the Kolache King would not be far behind. Although he kept scanning the courtyard, Sebastian hadn't seen the man, not that he really wanted to.

Since the day in the restaurant when he had seen Lucas kiss Silvie with the stamp of ownership, he knew full well they were on intimate terms. Sebastian had no claim on her, but the knowledge of her sexual relationship with Lucas made him feel constrained and awkward in her presence. She was the first woman who had interested him in ages, but of course she was taken. Why wouldn't she be, a beautiful woman like that? If he wanted peace of mind, the best thing to do would be to shut her out entirely. It was the equivalent of excising half his heart, but what else could he do? He sighed. Like a lifer in prison, he was resigned to it—a prolongation of the emotional vacuum he had inhabited for ages.

He passed the exit sign for Omega University. Good, he would be home in thirty minutes. Dear Omega. Would he still work there three weeks from now? Did he even want to? If it came to a trial and he won, he might be reinstated, but would he stay? Maybe he would work there until he could find a job elsewhere. But tenured positions were not that easy to come by, and a new job might very well entail leaving the Houston area. He would have to sell his house and land and get back the grand total of $8,400 in equity he had accrued in the past year.

Well, first things first. On Tuesday, he had to go before the faculty panel for a hearing. In a way, he looked forward to testifying; he could put his case before someone other than Duck. He had documentation to prove Alicia had not performed up to par and deserved the D. On the other hand, the racial slur he was alleged to have made could not be proved or disproved. Hearsay was not evidence, so he hoped that part would be thrown out.

He gave a great yawn. Well, no point in getting that far ahead. His eyelids drooped and he shook his head to stay awake. He had come down from the performance high. He yawned again as he turned off the highway. There were no houses and no streetlights in the first stretch of the farm-to-market road. The night was overcast, with no moonlight or stars. Perhaps it was his fatigue, but he had the sensation of driving into a palpable darkness.

The pitch-black night brought to mind the reading he had done on the demonic, and he felt his stomach muscles tighten, as if he faced an imminent threat. Demonic entities . . . the forces of malice that sought to destroy human beings were legion. *The number of devils active in the world is greater than all the people who have been alive since Adam.* So said Padre Pio. Sebastian imagined hordes of ugly creatures with leathery wings, swarming like locusts in the darkness.

He crested a hill, and in the distance, he saw a house with a single lighted window. It comforted him immensely and his muscles relaxed. There was no real contest between light and dark; the deepest, blackest darkness could be vanquished by even the smallest light.

Almost home.

By the time he pulled into the yard, he was quite drowsy. Wagging her feathered tail, Penny emerged from under the house (her den) and trotted over to greet him as he got out of the car. The three cats lounged on the front deck. "Hello, Penny girl. Did you guard the house and take care of the cats and chickens for me?" She gave a great doggy grin with her tongue lolling out of the side of her mouth. Sebastian stroked her head and shoulder, and she leaned against his leg, ensuring that his tux trousers would be coated with blond, wiry hair. She shed year-round. Well, he didn't care; he'd have to get the tux cleaned anyway after all the sweat from the concert.

He patted her head one last time and then brought his violin into the house and laid it on the piano. He grabbed a flashlight and went back outside to see about the chickens. The coop, a little house on stilts, sat a few yards behind the cottage on the south side. He and Kieran had enclosed the legs of the coop in hardware cloth to keep out predators. A narrow ramp led up to the small square opening which allowed the chickens to come and go. For human access, Kieran had installed a tall, narrow door to the right of the smaller opening. Inside, there was a flat U-shaped deck about waist high with three nesting boxes at the back. The roosting bars sat two feet above the deck.

As Sebastian opened the door, he directed the flashlight up toward the roost and counted: "One, two, three, four." No coyote casualties. "All present and accounted for." Relieved, he watched them affectionately for a moment. They perched wing-to-wing in a bunch: Newt, the big white rooster; Buff, Antonia, and little Olympia. He loved the quiet little clucking noises they made as they blinked in the light and shifted positions slightly on the bar.

As he lowered the flashlight, something caught his eye. He noticed a thick black cable hanging from the roost, touching the wall near the rooster. It puzzled him for a moment. Tired as he was, he couldn't remember putting it there. Then the cable moved. Sebastian trained the light on it and found himself inches away from a large and powerful snake. An adrenaline rush shot through his entire body.

The snake, intent on climbing onto the roost bar, appeared to ignore Sebastian. As he watched in fascinated horror, it raised its head and the upper third of its body, cobra-like, above the bar until it was higher than the rooster's head. It leaned toward Newt and then lowered itself onto his back. With lifted, swaying head, it glided over the rooster's back toward Buff and the other two hens. The snake, thick as a bicycle tire, must have been about five feet long. The night-blind chickens, though nervous and restive, didn't squawk or protest. They didn't know what was touching them.

Sebastian had seen enough. He turned and ran to the thicket of trees on the far side of the coop. He searched on the ground with the light until he found a fallen tree branch about four feet in length and thick as his thumb. He grabbed it and tested it to see if it was sturdy. Then he ran back to the coop. The snake had straddled Buff and Antonia and moved toward the smallest hen, Olympia.

He felt his stomach roil with atavistic revulsion. He wanted to bolt, but he couldn't leave the chickens defenseless. If the snake wrapped itself around Olympia, it could squeeze the life out of her.

He had to do something. Adrenaline took over. He raised the stick, feeling afraid and ridiculous at the same time. There he stood in his tuxedo, close onto midnight, going head-to-head with a snake in the close and odorous confines of a chicken coop.

Holding the flashlight in his left hand, he kept the light on the snake. He intended to prod the reptile and dislodge it from the roost. But things didn't go as planned. The snake struck first; it lifted its head and attacked the stick with bared fangs. He cried out in surprise—he felt the force of the strike all the way to his elbow. That set the chickens off. They suddenly squawked, flapped their wings, and moved sideways on the roost. The noise alerted Penny, who rushed over, stood just behind Sebastian and barked, practically deafening him.

In the midst of the cacophony, Sebastian tried twice more to hit the snake, but the snake kept striking back. On the fourth strike, its fangs caught in the wood. With a swift movement, Sebastian backed away and pulled the stick toward himself, with the snake attached. In mid-air it released its grip and fell onto the coop floor with a heavy thump, wriggling wildly toward the door opening. Sebastian yelled and jumped backward. The snake shot past him on the ground while Penny barked furiously. It slithered away into the thicket of trees.

Feeling hugely relieved, but weak in the knees, Sebastian slid a thin wooden panel into place to close off the small opening to the coop and shut and latched the door. Meanwhile, Penny had followed the snake's trail and sniffed the ground by the trees. "Penny, come." The last thing he needed was for the dog to get bit. A snake that big could do serious damage. Thankfully, Penny obeyed him and walked with him back to the house.

Inside, he quickly stripped off his tuxedo and took a long, hot shower. Afterward, he changed into a T-shirt and pajama bottoms and poured himself a shot of scotch. He found his book on Texas snakes and sat down in the recliner with his feet up. He suspected the snake was a non-venomous rat snake, but it was hard to identify in the darkness. Before he opened the book, he took a sip of scotch which warmed him wonderfully from throat to stomach. "Ah," he breathed and closed his eyes momentarily.

He turned to the chapter on rat snakes. The first thing he read was: *Texas rat snakes are among the most aggressive non-venomous serpents in the state. If threatened, most bite readily.* Well, he could vouch for that. The biggest specimen recorded was over seven feet long. They averaged between three and a half feet to six feet. "Sounds right." *Prey is primarily warm-blooded birds and their nestlings, rodents, small mammals; animals too vigorous to be swallowed without resistance are first squeezed in a loop of the well-muscled trunk.* Ugh, he tried not to visualize that. Thank God he intervened before the snake crushed Olympia.

Texas rat snakes were agile climbers and could even swim well. Tonight's snake certainly had no trouble climbing up into the coop, which stood about four feet off the ground. Either it crawled up the ramp, or it climbed one of the wooden supports. Once inside the coop, it traveled another two feet to get to the roost.

He took another sip of scotch. Rat snakes mainly killed rodents, which was fine with Sebastian, just so long as they stayed away from his chickens. He knew snakes weren't inherently evil; they hunted to survive. And most snakes were not aggressive; they avoided con-frontation and only fought in self-defense when cornered. The snake hadn't attacked him until he poked the stick at it.

Suddenly drained of all energy, he set the book aside and leaned his head back. Snakes were what they were—predators—no dissem-bling there. On the whole, serpents in the animal kingdom were highly preferable to their human counterparts. The human sort tended to be much more subtle and often more dangerous. Self-centered masters of guile, driven by their desire for power, they often held high positions and masqueraded as paragons of virtue. But beneath their carefully maintained exteriors, they harbored the deadly venom of malice.

His thoughts turned to the day he had told Duck he would not change Alicia's grade.

"Well, I'm quite sorry to hear that, Dr. Morrow," Duck said, with a scarcely concealed look of triumph. "In that case, you are hereby suspended with pay. Dean Faul and I will take the matter to the provost and the president, and we will decide whether or not to terminate your employment in the next few weeks. Please remove any personal effects from your studio, since we'll use it for your replacement."

The little speech was delivered in a pleasant, matter-of-fact tone of voice, as if it had been well-rehearsed. Duck smiled cheerfully and glanced at his manicured nails. "And now, if you'll excuse me," he gestured toward his office door, "I have work to do."

Sebastian wanted to punch the bastard. He was booted out by a man who wasn't even qualified for his position. Duck wouldn't have been department head at all, except for the betrayal of Dean Faul and Roscoe's behind-the-scenes political manipulation. Ferris Duck dismissed him, a senior professor, with all the concern of a man brushing a speck of lint off his shoulder. It galled Sebastian mightily that after his twenty-two years of excellent work, the dean, who had hired him, hadn't stood up and supported him. No one had fought for him. He left the music office flushed with anger, both ears buzzing—he literally saw red.

Just remembering the scene burned him. He took another sip of scotch. In his mind's eye, he pictured Ferris Duck and Dean Ezra Faul.

Yes, indeed, given the choice, he'd be much happier dealing with rat snakes.

CHAPTER 28

SUNDAY

After he played the 9:30 Mass, Leo dashed down the stairs from the choir loft to the men's room. He only had fifteen minutes before the eleven o'clock. On the way back from the restroom, he met Sebastian in the narthex. "Dr. Morrow, good to see you this morning! Congratulations again on your wonderful recital Friday."

Although the violinist smiled and seemed glad to see him, Leo observed his slumped shoulders and the dark circles shadowing his eyes. He looked so drawn and worn, Leo wondered if he might be ill.

"Thanks for coming and bringing your mom and Stephanie. It's always a pleasure to perform with Abbie. She's a wonderful pianist, and we really know each other's playing."

"Oh, I could tell that. Mr. Shakespeare said it better: it seemed that between your musical mind and hers, there was no impediment." The remark, Leo was glad to see, elicited a big smile from Dr. Morrow.

"Let me not to the marriage of true minds admit impediments," quoted Sebastian. He nodded. "It's true. When I'm onstage with Abbie, we anticipate each other musically in a marvelous way."

Leo hesitated, and then decided to satisfy his curiosity. "Dr. Morrow, when I called Omega to get directions to your recital, the woman I spoke to told me you were on leave. And I wondered, uh . . . well, is it medical leave? Are you all right?"

Sebastian ran a hand through his hair and furrowed his brow. Leo hoped he hadn't overstepped his bounds.

"Yes, my health is fine. It's not medical leave." With his lips pressed together, he drew in a deep breath and released it. "A student levied a false accusation against me, and the administration chose to suspend me almost immediately, even though I've worked there for more than twenty years without incident."

Leo was nonplussed, and his face must have showed it, because Dr. Morrow smiled and clapped him on the shoulder to reassure him. "Don't worry, Leo, there'll be a hearing soon, and I'll present evidence to defend myself. It's a long story, and I probably shouldn't talk about it until after the hearing."

"I understand," Leo said. "Gosh, I'm sorry to hear that. I wish you the best of luck in clearing your name."

"Thanks. See you next Sunday." Sebastian turned to go.

"Oh, I almost forgot!" blurted Leo. "Mamma said if I ran into you, to ask you to lunch with us."

"She did?"

The wide-eyed look of surprise on Dr. Morrow's face was almost comical. "Yes, you won't regret it. Besides being a good business-woman, Mamma is also a very good cook. Kristin didn't come home for the weekend, so it'll be just you, me, and Mamma."

No Kolache King? Sebastian had fasted before Mass and his stomach was a yawning, empty cave. The thought of a home-cooked meal was quite appealing. Spending time with Silvie was even more appealing, but he didn't want to tantalize himself when she already had a boyfriend. He wanted the boyfriend to be T.

Sebastian Morrow and nobody else. *Of course, the odds on that were as likely as a mule winning the Kentucky Derby.*

Seeing Dr. Morrow's hesitation, Leo prompted him, "We surely look forward to having you come."

Well, he really liked Leo and Kristin. He could still be a friend of the family, as long as he didn't have to come into contact too often with lovely Silvie. And now, in light of his Omega troubles, he might need a whole raft of friends. Ah, what the hell. "All right, thank you, Leo. What time should I come, and what's the address?"

"Good. Come at 12:30." After Leo gave Dr. Morrow the address and they said their farewells, he vaulted up the stairs to play the prelude for the eleven o'clock Mass.

✦

Silvie's menu ran through her head as she drank her second cup of breakfast coffee: *svenska köttbullar med lingonsylt, potatis med dill, gurka salad.* For dessert, *semlor med kaffe.* Not those damn kolaches.

She enjoyed cooking and entertaining. How odd that in the nine months she had known Lucas, he had only come to her house for dinner once. It wasn't for lack of invitations. Either he was too busy and away on business, or he wanted to eat out; there was always some new restaurant he wanted to try. In hindsight, Silvie wondered if he had avoided situations where Leo and Kristin might be present. Maybe he had never wanted to know her family. Not to mention the dog. Sage hadn't let Lucas into the yard. He had barked ferociously and bared his teeth like an attack dog. Silvie had had to put him on a leash and restrain him so Lucas could get into the house. She smiled. *What good taste you have, Sage, my darling.* Animals weren't fooled. Neither was Leo. If she had listened to her son, or trusted his instincts, she could have saved herself a lot of grief.

Well, Lucas and his desires were now history. She slapped her hands together to punctuate the thought. Gone, period. New start. She donned her apron and set to work. She wanted this to be an excellent meal, and she hoped Sebastian would come. It would do him good. His new gauntness reminded her of an illustration from a child's book of poetry—Jack Sprat who ate no fat. Given a chance, she would take care of that.

When she told Leo to invite the violinist if he saw him at Mass that morning, her son replied, "Excellent idea, Mamma. Now you're on the right track."

If he hadn't dashed out the door so fast, she would have swatted him.

❧

The house was located on the northern outskirts of the town. Similar to many of the houses in Bullinger and Sebastian's own home, 707 Thayer Street had been built in an earlier era with quality workmanship and materials. A pale green, two-story, wood frame house with white trim, it sat behind its picket fence on a large, shaded lot. Leo's black Jeep and Silvie's blue Volvo were parked in the driveway to the left of the house.

Sebastian parked behind the Jeep. When he cut the engine, he heard the church bells of St. Mark's chime the half hour. As he glanced up at the bright blue sky with its scudding clouds and felt the gusty wind buffet the car, his heart beat ridiculously fast. *What a fool I am.* He took several deep breaths to calm himself and picked up the carton of eggs he had brought from home.

He let himself in through the gate. As he turned to latch it, he sensed the dog before he saw it. A young black and silver German Shepherd came around the corner of the house. It approached silently. Sebastian waited at the gate. The dog came to his side, sniffed at his trousers and carefully considered him. Then it sat down expectantly and cocked its head sideways, as if to say, *All right, you may pet me now.* Sebastian spoke quietly, "You're a self-contained one. Do you smell my dog Penny?" He stroked the dog's head and shoulders for a moment. "I'm here to see Silvie and Leo." The statement was greeted by a pricking of the ears. The dog rose and led the way down the flagstone walk to the house. Bemused, Sebastian followed the German Shepherd up the wooden stairs to the generous front porch. Two large potted hibiscus plants flanked the door. Sebastian muttered a quick prayer and rang the doorbell.

Even before Leo answered the door, the drifting smell of warm food came to greet Sebastian.

"Dr. Morrow!" Leo looked so aghast Sebastian wondered if he had come to lunch on the wrong day. "You're here."

"I am."

"But Sage didn't bark."

"He came to greet me and then led me to the house."

A giant grin split Leo's face. "Miraculous, I'd say. He won't let anyone but family into the yard." His unfeigned pleasure warmed Sebastian. "Just you, apparently."

"Well, Sage, I'm honored." The dog made a small murmur and sat on his haunches with a wide grin. *I'll wait right here for you,* he seemed to say.

"Come in," said Leo.

He followed Leo's white-blond head inside. A spacious living room lined with floor-to-ceiling bookcases opened to his right. A grand piano stood against one wall, surrounded by comfortable-looking furniture. Through an open door to his left, he could see the dining room, with three windows and a wooden table set for three. The house had high ceilings and beautiful, polished wood floors. The books lying on end tables, the stacks of music on the piano, the framed photos here and there, lent the room a quality of lived-in, mild disorder. Sebastian liked it.

Leo called out, "Mamma, Dr. Morrow is here, and Sage didn't even bark."

Silvie, wearing a navy apron over a sky-blue tunic and cream trousers, emerged through a swinging door directly in front of him. He caught a glimpse of a large kitchen behind her.

"Sebastian, welcome!" She held out her hand and he stepped forward and took it in his. "You must have a way with animals. That's never happened before."

"Well, I do love animals. I have a dog too." He held out the carton of eggs. "And I brought some fresh eggs, courtesy of my three industrious free-ranging hens."

"You've got chickens?" Silvie raised her eyebrows. "What kind are they?"

"They're what's known as *determined* chickens. Their plan is to keep me from starving. They're laying so many eggs I can't keep up with them."

She laughed. "Good for them, and thank you." She opened the carton. "Oh, look, Leo. White, tan, and dark brown."

"*Determined* chicken eggs are obviously the best," said Leo.

After admiring the eggs, Silvie disappeared with them into the kitchen. "Be right back." She returned shortly with a small tray holding a bottle of Campari and three drink glasses with ice. "Lunch is almost ready, but I thought you might like an aperitif."

"I would indeed," said Sebastian. "By the way, the food smells delicious."

"Swedish meatballs," said Leo, giving the thumbs-up sign.

"Let's sit down a minute so the chef can rest her feet," Silvie said. "Leo, pour the drinks." She set the tray down on a coffee table in front of the sofa. She promptly sat down on the sofa, slid off her shoes, turned sideways and propped her long legs on the cushions. Sebastian sat in a comfortable armchair facing her, while dutiful Leo poured the drinks.

Sebastian sipped the dark red liqueur gladly. "Mmmh, I haven't had Campari for a long time." He glanced around the room. His nervousness had evaporated, and he felt comfortable in the home and company of the de Graafs. "All these books and a nice piano too."

As if to confirm Sebastian's remark, Leo sat down at the keyboard and improvised quiet background music.

"My late husband Edward was a great reader and collector of books. No surprise that he founded the bookshop. Most of these are his. But the piano is what the doctor ordered," said Silvie. "When Leo was twelve, his piano teacher told us he had to have a grand to practice on. That's when the old upright moved out and the Steinway moved in."

"His teacher was right. A serious musician has to have an instrument of quality to work with, one that's responsive with a beautiful sound."

"Your violin seems to fit that bill," Silvie said. "You get such a sweet sound from it."

Sebastian knew it was true. He had the requisite technique, but it was the quality of his sound that had won him the position in the Baltimore Symphony and the concertmaster position at Opera D'Argento. "Thank you."

"Oh," Silvie blurted, "I met your aunt and uncle at the reception last night. Nancy Leaton, the sister of Mrs. Felicity Morrow."

Sebastian smiled. "You remembered that."

"I did." Silvie swirled the ice in her drink. "I remembered it because it was tied to the remark you made about your manly honor."

"Ah, yes. Well, manly honor sometimes comes with a price." He shifted position in the armchair. "I'm finding that out in my professional life." The remark slipped out, perhaps because he felt so at ease. He couldn't call it back.

"Leo told me you're on leave from the university. What happened, if I may ask?"

The music stopped abruptly. Leo sat on the piano bench, hands clasped in his lap, with his eyes on Sebastian. Silvie swiveled on the sofa, set her feet on the floor, and straightened her back. They seemed to await testimony.

Well, everyone would know sooner or later. "A student accused me of racial discrimination."

"Oh my. Do you think it will cost you your job?" asked Silvie.

"It's quite possible." He smiled ruefully. "It's a false accusation, I should add." Sebastian drained his glass. "There's an easy way out, but my aforementioned manly honor requires me to do what is right, not what is easy."

"Do you have the support of your supervisor?" asked Silvie.

"My colleagues, yes. My supervisor, no."

Now she understood why he seemed so drawn and tired. "Are you still receiving your salary?"

He nodded. "For the time being."

A long silence followed his remark. Eventually, Silvie said, "I think it remarkable that under such duress, you played so beautifully on Friday." Her smile was a sunburst. "*Och nu, vännen, att stärka och uppmuntra dig, kommer du att få äta världens bästa svenska mat.*"

She stood up and marched into the kitchen, a Nordic queen on a mission.

Sebastian turned his puzzled glance on Leo. "What did she say?"

Leo grinned. "She said, 'And now, my friend, to strengthen and encourage you, you are going to eat the world's best Swedish food.'"

"Ah."

"Where cooking is concerned," Leo confided, "Mamma has no false modesty."

My friend, she had called him. Sebastian didn't know what to think. Silvie was so relaxed and charming with him and so damned beautiful. Her concern about his situation seemed entirely genuine. But what about the boyfriend? She hadn't mentioned the Kolache King, and Lucas hadn't attended the concert last night. As Leo led the way into the dining room, Sebastian felt new energy in his step and confusion in his soul. He felt encouraged somehow, but he didn't want to get his hopes up. Honestly, it would be torture to be Silvie's friend; he wanted so much more than that.

CHAPTER 29

THE HEARING

With velocity approaching the speed of light (at least in university bureaucratic circles), the hearing committee convened three weeks after Sebastian filed the grievance. At the request of Provost Corrotto, five individuals (none from the music department) were selected from a pool of tenured faculty. The panel chose its own presiding officer, Dr. Abe Shaheen of the math department. The racially mixed group consisted of two African Americans: Carlotta Banks, nursing, and Warren Drexel, communications; and two white faculty: Christopher Monroe, engineering, and Edith Moon, English.

Sebastian had worked on a university committee with Abe Shaheen in years past and knew the man was a stickler for proper procedure, which gave him confidence. With Shaheen in charge, the hearing would be handled correctly. Prior to the hearing, Sebastian notified Dr. Shaheen that he had legal counsel, and he provided copies of his exhibits and a witness list. Shaheen informed Sebastian that the hearing would be recorded by a court reporter.

After studying the rules governing such hearings, Sebastian was dismayed to read: *The rules of evidence shall not strictly apply.*

Apparently, hearsay evidence could be admitted at the panel chair's discretion, if deemed reliable. Unfortunately, Alicia's accusation about the racial slur could come into play. Sebastian hoped it might not matter, since it couldn't be proved or disproved. He also discovered that the hearing committee's conclusion was not necessarily final. It could be rejected by the president, who could then appeal to the Board of Regents. They would make the final decision.

The hearing was held on the chilly, foggy morning of Thursday, November fifth, in a conference room on the third floor of the engineering building. Sebastian and his attorney Martin Katzberger entered the room at 8:45. Sebastian regarded his surroundings in surprise. *Really? The College of Engineering with its megabucks can't afford windows?* The place was as cheerful as a morgue. It was a gloomy, rectangular room with dark paneling, gray carpet, a long narrow table, and two large video screens affixed to the walls at either end. The fluorescent lights, which resembled inverted ice cube trays, added a dismal, funereal touch. One of them flickered continually. It wouldn't have surprised Sebastian to see a corpse laid out on the table. He just hoped at the end of the day it wouldn't be his own.

He and Katzberger sat beside each other in the only empty chairs at the end of the table. Sebastian nodded to his adversary, the provost, who sat across from him. Emilio Corrotto was a stooped, balding man with an unhealthy gray complexion, crepey skin on his long neck, a lipless mouth, and hooded, beady eyes. Though he bore a strong resemblance to a somnolent tortoise, Sebastian knew his appearance was deceptive; his bite could be swift and lethal. Corrotto's black blazer hung open over a lavender shirt that strained to cover his drooping belly. The university lawyer, Cyrus Young, a portly bald man wearing an ill-fitting gray suit, sat beside Corrotto.

Chairman Abe Shaheen, small and olive-skinned with dark, curling hair and bifocals balanced near the end of his long nose, sat at the head of the table. Sitting with her machine against the wall, the court reporter, a thin, bony woman with an alert glance in her dark eyes, repeatedly tossed her graying brown ponytail with nervous energy.

The foxlike Martin Katzberger, with his thin, triangular face, light brown eyes, and bushy reddish eyebrows, was allowed to advise Sebastian, but he was barred from speaking. Sebastian introduced him. Katzberger smiled, revealing a mouthful of very long, very white teeth. "Good morning, everyone," he intoned in a confident baritone as he adjusted his round horn-rimmed glasses. Abe Shaheen, the panel members, and the university attorney introduced themselves in turn.

Five witnesses waited just outside on two cushioned benches left and right of the conference room door. Abbie, battling the urge to light a cigarette, found a cellophane-wrapped peppermint in her bag. With both hands hurting, it was an ordeal to unwrap it, but she finally did, and popped it in her mouth for comfort. Miles kept his anxieties at bay by quietly probing Alfred Chang's brain for the best Chinese restaurants in Houston. On the other bench, Alicia Borden and her mother, a stout, light-skinned woman dressed in a tight-fitting blue pantsuit, carried on a whispered conversation, while Keisha Williams bent her head over her iPhone as her two thumbs tap-danced busily on the keypad.

At nine o'clock, Abe Shaheen called the hearing to order in the conference room. "The university, represented by Provost Emilio Corrotto, seeks to dismiss Dr. T. Sebastian Morrow, Associate Professor of Music, on the grounds of racial discrimination against a student, Alicia Borden. The administration, as the plaintiff, bears the burden of proof.

"We have reviewed the evidence supplied by both parties prior to this hearing. The panel must decide if Dr. Morrow did, in fact, discriminate against the student by unfair grading practices and by inappropriate verbal comments." Then he produced a list of the documented evidence and a list of witnesses to be presented by each party, all of which he handed to the court reporter for insertion into the record.

"In addition, we have issued an instruction barring the witnesses from talking to each other about their testimony. Any witness who does so will be excluded from testifying. We will call the witnesses, one at a time, and the panel will question them. They may be cross-examined by the panel and the opposing party. After all the testimony, each party will make closing statements. The administration, represented by the provost and attorney Cyrus Young, will present its case first."

Sebastian inhaled deeply. *Here we go—let the inquisition begin.*

Provost Corrotto called Alicia Borden as the first witness. When she entered the room, Shaheen instructed her to stand and address the panel from the far end of the table. A buxom, pretty girl with dark, liquid eyes and a cropped afro, she wore a light blue dress with a navy blazer and black flats.

"Please state your name, current level, and major," Shaheen said.

"My name is Alicia Borden, and I'm a sophomore music major." She maintained a respectful and quiet demeanor, and she spoke clearly and well.

"In your written statement, Ms. Borden, you asserted that your violin instructor, Dr. Morrow, discriminated against you on the grounds of race. Could you please explain that for the panel?"

Alicia nodded and studiously avoided Sebastian's eyes. He sat a mere three feet to her right.

"He gave me low grades for my violin lessons during the semester and a final grade of D. I'm his only African American violin student. All the white students got As or Bs. He also put me last chair in the orchestra, with all the white violinists ahead of me. When he used a racial slur against me and another African American student in the hallway of the music building, I knew without a doubt his grading was racially motivated."

Alicia swallowed and cleared her throat. "I was with my friend Keisha Williams, who also heard it. He walked past us and said real loud, 'I *hate* those damn niggers!'" Her voice wavered slightly as she said it.

Carlotta Banks sighed audibly and shook her head, while Warren Drexel, the other black member of the panel, remained impassive.

At that point, Martin Katzberger whispered something in Sebastian's ear and made a note on a legal pad.

"It shocked me and made me angry," Alicia continued. "I didn't expect to hear something like that from a university professor. That's when I realized that a teacher with that much prejudice could never grade me fairly. The bad grades he gave me had nothing to do with my playing and everything to do with my race."

After a long silence when no one spoke, Shaheen asked her a series of questions. "Did you prepare for your violin lessons as well as the other students?"

"Yes, I did."

"How many hours a week did you practice?"

"At least ten hours a week, which is what was recommended in the syllabus."

"Did the other students practice ten hours a week?"

She shrugged. "Some did, and some didn't."

"So, some practiced less than you?"

The corners of her mouth turned down and she answered emphatically, "Yes."

"And they got higher grades?"

"Yes, they did."

"Do you think the other students got higher grades because they played better than you?"

"Well, some of them played better, but that's just because they're juniors and seniors."

"Did you feel that Dr. Morrow assigned you music of the appropriate level?"

"No, he gave me pieces that were too difficult for me. Then when I tried my best to play them, he gave me low grades."

Abe glanced at his notes. "Did you attend all your lessons?"

Alicia wet her lips with her tongue. "Well, there were times when I got sick and couldn't. But I attended most of my lessons."

"Did Dr. Morrow treat you respectfully in the private lessons?"

"He often seemed irritated and unfriendly. I could tell he didn't like me, and he was very critical of my playing."

"I see," Shaheen said. "How did the D in violin affect your grade point average?"

"It brought it down below a 2.0, which was the minimum level to keep my academic scholarship. I asked Dr. Morrow to change the grade, because he gave it to me on account of my race. But he refused. So, then I spoke to Dr. Duck, the department head."

"How will the loss of your scholarship affect you, Ms. Borden?"

"I'll have to drop out of school."

"Thank you, Ms. Borden."

"May I go now?" Alicia asked Abe Shaheen.

"Not yet." He glanced at the other members of the panel. "Do any of you have questions for Ms. Borden?"

Edith Moon spoke up. "Yes, I do. Good morning, Alicia." She smiled and tucked a strand of sandy hair behind one ear.

Alicia raised her chin, set her jaw, and faced Dr. Moon. "Good morning," she murmured.

"Did Dr. Morrow ever suggest a way to help you improve your grades in violin?"

"Well, he said I should practice more."

"And did you increase your practice time?"

"I practiced at least two hours a day, just like his other students."

"So, you did not increase your practice time."

"No."

"Did Dr. Morrow give you a syllabus with his written expectations and grading criteria for the course?"

"Yes, he did."

"Did he require you to play one piece from memory?"

Alicia pursed her lips. "Yes, but the piece he gave me was too difficult to memorize."

"So, you did not play it from memory?"

She shook her head. "No, because it was too hard."

"What was the name of the piece?"

"It was the J. S. Bach Concerto in A Minor, the first movement."

Abe Shaheen interrupted. "Dr. Morrow, could you please pass out copies of the syllabus for everyone?"

Sebastian opened the folder he had brought and gave everyone a copy.

Holding the syllabus in her hand, Edith Moon pointed out, "Ms. Borden, you said you were a sophomore, but I see that the Bach A Minor Concerto is listed as a freshman-level piece."

Alicia bent her head and studied the list but said nothing.

Dr. Moon continued, "So he actually gave you a piece *less* difficult than a sophomore would normally play."

Alicia sniffed and shook her head.

"Ms. Borden, you received the D in violin at the end of the spring semester, but you didn't discuss the matter with Dr. Morrow until this fall. If the low grade in violin and the incident in the hallway upset you so badly, as you stated, why did you wait four months to discuss it with Dr. Morrow or Dr. Duck?"

"Well, Dr. Morrow doesn't work in the summer. He's not at school at all. And Dr. Duck was just hired."

"You're allowed to email or telephone your instructors, aren't you?"

"Yes."

"Your grades for the other spring semester courses you took were a B, three Cs and two Ds. The other D was in English Composition, correct?"

"Yes."

"May I ask a few questions?" Warren Drexel, a large, imposing black man with a completely shaved head, raised his hand. "Ms. Borden, let's talk about the incident in the hallway. What was the date and time Dr. Morrow made the alleged statement?"

"It was in May, at the end of the spring semester, after finals, so it would have been about May twelfth, in the afternoon."

"*About* May twelfth?" Drexel echoed. "You're not sure of the date?"

"I don't remember what day of the week it was."

"That surprises me a little, since the incident upset you so much. Are you certain he said those exact words?"

Alicia leaned forward and raised her voice. "He said it—I heard him!"

"All right, Ms. Borden, calm down." He waited a beat before he continued. "So this fall, when you realized you were no longer eligible for a scholarship, you took action. Do you think the D your English instructor gave you was a legitimate grade, or was it also racially motivated?"

"There are several black students in her class. I'm the only one taking violin lessons." Alicia scowled. "Dr. Morrow made it obvious by using the racial slur against me."

No one else on the panel had questions, so Abe Shaheen asked Sebastian if he wished to question the witness.

Before Sebastian could answer, Martin Katzberger asked if he and Cyrus Young might confer with Abe Shaheen.

"Well, yes. Come forward, please."

Martin leaned in close and whispered, "Dr. Shaheen, the statement about the alleged racial slur is hearsay and unreliable. It should not be admitted as evidence."

Cyrus retorted, "It is not hearsay. It meets an exception—it is the statement of a party opponent and therefore admissible."

"We will allow the statement," said Shaheen.

Cyrus Young wiped his brow with a white handkerchief as both lawyers returned to their seats. Sebastian told Dr. Shaheen he had no questions.

Corrotto called in Keisha Williams next. A tall, heavyset girl dressed in a black skirt and a pink blouse, she verified that she had heard the same statement. She added, "Mr. Greenfield, the flute instructor, was with Dr. Morrow, and he laughed when he heard what Dr. Morrow said."

Warren Drexel asked her to name the date and time of the alleged statement.

"Well, I think it was around May twelfth, since it happened at the very end of the spring semester."

"So, it might have been May eleventh or May thirteenth?"

"Maybe, but I think it was May twelfth."

"And the time of day?"

"It was late in the afternoon."

Martin Katzberger raised his hand and asked for another conference. He and Cyrus Young huddled with Abe Shaheen. Martin's lips contracted into a thin line and he whispered, "Dr. Shaheen, I ask that Ms. William's testimony be struck from the record. It is obvious the two students discussed their testimony beforehand. Neither one could remember which day this event supposedly happened, yet they somehow chose the same date by chance. That is simply not believable. They have clearly agreed on a date, no doubt as they sat outside in the waiting room."

Cyrus retorted, "The testimony should be allowed. They certainly could have narrowed the date down to a single day independently of one another. As far as what they actually discussed in the waiting area, well, it could be anything—the weather, the last football game, boyfriends—who knows?" He shrugged and smiled dismissively. "Naturally, they talked with each other about the event many times since it happened, but they were instructed not to discuss testimony before this hearing, and I'm sure they complied."

After pondering the attorneys' words, Abe Shaheen said, "It does appear they have collaborated, but I don't see that we can prove or disprove what they talked about in the waiting area. Therefore, we will let the testimony stand."

"Thank you," Cyrus Young replied.

As the attorneys returned to their seats, Abe asked, "Any other questions for the witness?"

If he had been on the panel, Sebastian had to admit to himself that he would have believed their testimony about the racial slur. Even if they weren't sure of the date, both girls seemed entirely sincere and convinced that he had used the N-word. If they were lying, they were consummate actresses. It completely confounded him.

When Keisha Williams left the room, Abe asked Sebastian to present his defense.

Sebastian stood and cited Alicia's poor lesson grades, her jury sheets, and her spotty attendance record. He called the cellist Alfred Chang as his first witness.

Sebastian seated himself, and Shaheen began the questioning. "Mr. Chang, could you please describe Ms. Borden's playing during her spring jury exam?"

Alfred Chang stood and gazed steadily at the panel through his thick-lensed glasses. A middle-aged man with large hands and a benevolent expression, he answered in a firm voice, "It was a poor performance. She really couldn't play her assigned pieces with any degree of competency. It was quite obvious she hadn't properly prepared." He ran a thick-fingered hand through his abundant black hair. "I also gave her a D for the exam."

"Do you think the piece she played was too difficult for her?"

"Not if she had practiced sufficiently. It's one of the easiest concertos."

"Was she seated unfairly in the orchestra?" asked Shaheen.

"No. Dr. Morrow and I always hear the orchestra auditions together. Ms. Borden played poorly. She was clearly the weakest violinist, so we agreed to place her in the last chair."

Shaheen asked Chang if he had ever known Dr. Morrow to seat students or grade them on the basis of race. He shook his head. "No, he always grades and seats students fairly, based on their performance."

Sebastian called Abbie Goldberg next. She stated her name and position as Professor of Piano. Though she faced the panel confidently, her expression appeared strained, and she winced occasionally and flexed her fingers. To his dismay, Sebastian realized her hands were hurting.

Shaheen began the questioning. "Dr. Goldberg, how long have you worked at Omega University and what are your duties?"

"I've worked here for thirty years. I teach piano, music history, and serve as an accompanist for student recitals and juries."

He asked Abbie to describe Alicia's playing in the jury exam. "Well, she played poorly. The other violinists were prepared and played their études and solo pieces very well. Ms. Borden stopped repeatedly in the étude and solo piece, and she failed to play her solo piece from memory, a requirement all the other students fulfilled."

"Did you accompany all the violinists that day?"

She adjusted her glasses. "Yes, the violinists and all the string students."

Shaheen asked, "Dr. Goldberg, how long have you worked with Dr. Morrow?"

"Twenty-two years."

"In all that time, have you ever known him to grade any student on the basis of race?"

"Never."

When Abbie left the room, Sebastian called Miles Greenfield.

Miles, looking like the dapper British gentleman he was, wore a gray wool three-piece suit with a red tie one shade darker than his ruddy cheeks. After Miles stated his rank as Assistant Professor of Flute and his time of employment as six years, Dr. Shaheen asked him if he had ever heard Sebastian use any racial epithet on or off campus.

"No, never. Dr. Morrow is on very good terms with music students of all ethnicities, and to my knowledge, he has never shown any racial bias toward any of them. We also work together at Opera D'Argento, where many of the singers and some of the staff are black, and he has never shown any bias there either."

"Can you tell us what happened on the day Dr. Morrow is accused of using the racial slur, when you were with him in the hall?"

"No, I cannot, because the incident never happened. A statement like that would have been so utterly out of character for him, I would remember it. I've walked the halls with Dr. Morrow many times and laughed at his remarks, but had he said something like that, I would have been appalled and reported it myself."

"Any questions from the panel members?" Abe peered over the top of his bifocals at his colleagues.

When no one spoke up, Shaheen excused Miles and said, "Dr. Morrow, please tell us your side of the story now."

Sebastian took a deep breath, rose, and faced the panel. "First of all, I did not use a racial epithet against Alicia Borden. I have never used racial slurs like that in my life. And furthermore, I didn't use the word *hate*. I don't hate any of my students." Sebastian gazed steadily at the members of the panel.

"Ms. Borden accused me of making the racial slur only after I refused to change the grade. When she first came to me about the D in violin, she never mentioned the so-called racial remark. I found out about it the next week when Dr. Duck called me in and asked me to change her grade. He read her written statement about the alleged incident in the hallway to me then."

"So, the issue of the racial slur came up only after you refused to change the grade?" Shaheen asked.

"Correct."

"Did Ms. Borden have a music scholarship?"

"No, she did not. I was unaware that she had any scholarship at all until Dr. Duck informed me about her academic scholarship when I had the conference with him. It was the Isaiah Yates Scholarship for African American undergraduates, one I had never heard of."

"Why do you think she raised the accusation of racial discrimination against you in the first place?"

"I honestly don't know, because I didn't treat her any differently than my other students."

Shaheen adjusted his glasses. "Why did you give her a D when you gave all your white students higher grades? What is it you are asking the panel to understand here?"

"It's simply this—I grade solely on the basis of merit. Her race played no role in this at all. Had Alicia Borden prepared properly and played well, *with improvement*, she would have received an A or B, but she did not. Only when she realized the consequences of her actions—in other words, that she would lose the scholarship—did she make the accusations against me. Instead of being honest and taking responsibility herself, she charged me with racism, so the blame fell on me. I had the choice of changing the grade or losing my job.

"The easy way out was to give her a higher grade, but I refused because there is no legitimate reason to change it. She earned it fair and square. And as you heard earlier, both Dr. Chang and Dr. Goldberg agree that she deserved the grade, due to her lack of preparation. In addition, most of her absences from violin lessons and orchestra were unexcused. That also indicates her lack of commitment."

Carlotta Banks raised her hand. "Dr. Shaheen, I have some questions for the witness." A statuesque black woman with a closely cropped afro, she wore flamboyant hoop earrings and a slightly irritated expression.

She fixed Sebastian in a steely gaze. "Don't you think, Dr. Morrow, that Ms. Borden may have been afraid to broach the subject of the racial slur when she was alone in your studio with you?"

Before he could answer, Katzberger whispered something to Sebastian. He nodded and addressed her. "Dr. Banks, that implies physical intimidation, which has never been an issue in this case."

Abe Shaheen replied, "That is correct." He addressed the court reporter, "Please strike the question from the record. Proceed, Dr. Banks."

Carlotta Banks sighed and pursed her lips. After a moment, she said, "Ms. Borden has testified that you were often irritable and unfriendly in her private lessons. What was your reaction when she accused you of grading on the basis of race?"

"I was shocked. Then I explained that race had nothing to do with it. I also tried to reason with her and encourage her. I told her she had the potential to be a fine violinist, but that potential needed hard work to develop, and up to that point, I hadn't seen any improvement in her playing. The university and I, as the violin teacher, have certain performance standards that students must meet to graduate. The professional music world is highly competitive, and it's my responsibility to prepare all my students to compete in that world."

"How many African American musicians are there in your professional opera orchestra?"

"None."

"How many African Americans play in the Houston Symphony?"

"I think there is one."

"You played in the Baltimore Symphony before you came to Houston. How many African Americans were in that orchestra?"

"None at the time I worked there."

"Why is that, do you think, Dr. Morrow?" she asked.

"I suppose it has to do with the high cost of instruments and training for classical musicians. The successful ones usually begin private lessons when they are five or six years old, as I did. Many black families don't have the financial resources to provide lessons and good instruments for their children. But I also must point out that classical music in general has not been a traditional part of black culture, which can account for so few entering the field."

"I see," she said. "So, would you agree that aspiring classical musicians, who are black, are often ill-prepared when they get to the university level?"

"Yes."

"Shouldn't they be particularly nurtured and encouraged by their teachers? Shouldn't they receive extra help and understanding? Shouldn't they be given some slack if they play freshman-level pieces in their sophomore year, as Ms. Borden did?" Carlotta Banks smiled wryly. "I mean, after all, Omega University is not Juilliard."

"No, but we still have to keep our standards high. I think black musicians should be encouraged and helped as much as possible. However, black students are not the only ones ill-prepared on entering university. There are also white students, Hispanic, and Asian students who are not as prepared as they should be. They *all* have to rise to the expected standard of performance. If the standard is adjusted for each of their insufficiencies, then we have no standard. High standards are critical—the higher the bar, the greater the improvement in quality of performance will be."

"Perhaps your zeal for high standards and your life experience in all-white orchestras clouded your judgment and caused you to grade unfairly in the case of Ms. Borden."

Sebastian chewed on his lower lip and tried to gather his thoughts. After a moment, he said, "If I were a football coach, I would choose the very best players for the varsity. I'd identify the highly motivated ones who had an overriding desire to succeed. My criteria would be motivation, improvement, and performance ability. If a player had all three, I wouldn't care if he was black or white or any shade in between—he'd be on my A team." He drew in a deep breath. "I assure you, as a professional musician I can spot those same qualities in my violin students. I don't care what race they are; I can see their drive and their desire to succeed. With those two qualities, they will improve dramatically. Honestly, Ms. Borden showed little of either, and consequently, she made no progress."

Dr. Banks challenged him. "She practiced as much or more than your other students."

Sebastian shrugged. "So she said, but no one monitors the practice rooms. Had she truly practiced all those hours, there would have been some noticeable improvement, but I can assure you, she was consistently unprepared for her lessons. That is why, at the end of the semester, she played her pieces as if she was still sight-reading them."

"No more questions."

Sebastian sat down, and Abe Shaheen asked for closing statements.

Provost Corrotto rose and addressed the panel. "The university cannot tolerate racism in any form, and this is why we seek to dismiss Dr. Morrow. Although his record has been clean, the racial discrimination he has shown this year cannot be overlooked or go unpunished. As evidenced by his remark in the hallway, he harbors a deep, ugly bias against African Americans. We believe he gave the D and refused to change the grade in the hope that the student would lose her scholarship and be forced to withdraw from the university. It was an indirect method of getting rid of Alicia Borden because of her race.

"We believe Dr. Morrow's lifelong experiences in the elite, almost exclusively white, world of classical music have also prejudiced him against aspiring African American musicians. He made no effort to help Alicia Borden improve; he behaved with impatience and frustration when she struggled to play what was a difficult piece for her, and he refused to help her when she came to him in desperation over losing her scholarship—a scholarship, ladies and gentlemen, that was the only way she could finance her education.

"As representatives of a state university, we are pledged to educate and protect the rights of students of all ethnic backgrounds. Dr. Morrow's deeply offensive and outrageous statement, his use of the N-word, clearly demonstrates a deeply ingrained prejudice. That prejudice motivated him to grade unfairly and thus jeopardize Alicia Borden's chances of obtaining an undergraduate degree. This we cannot allow. Dr. Morrow should be immediately dismissed from his position at Omega University."

Then it was Sebastian's turn. Martin Katzberger had prepared him well for his closing statement. "I'm glad Provost Corrotto brought up the student's scholarship. The idea that I covertly schemed to make Alicia Borden lose her scholarship is pure bunk. At the time I gave the grade, I didn't even know Ms. Borden had a scholarship.

"I believe the student asked me to change the grade without telling me about the scholarship because she didn't want to reveal her actual motivation—money. She made it sound like the issue was an unfair grade based on her fine performance, supposedly equal to that of the other students. As both my colleagues testified, that was decidedly not the case.

"Furthermore, what would I have to gain by forcing her out of school due to some mythical animus? Academics, as you on the panel know, are constantly under pressure to recruit students and retain them. The state legislature looks at numbers of graduates when they consider funding for universities. For me to alienate students and force them out of school would be working at cross-purposes with myself. My job is to keep them in school and help them graduate.

"As far as the racial slur is concerned, there was none. I never made that statement and never would. If you recall, Ms. Borden said I made the statement *loudly*. Why would I jeopardize my reputation and employment with such reckless behavior? Why shout out such a slur in front of many witnesses?" Sebastian shook his head. "Wholly unbelievable. It just doesn't make sense.

"I think Ms. Borden and her friend manufactured the whole incident to cement the charge of racial bias." Sebastian smiled. "Furthermore, to imply that my professional experience in orchestras, which include Asian, Hispanic, *and* white musicians, somehow biased me against black musicians, is ludicrous. The professional music world is color-blind.

"And so am I. I bear no hate for my students, and I do not label them with ethnic slurs. I wish them well, Ms. Borden included. I tried to encourage and help her. I told Ms. Borden on several occasions that she had good potential as a violinist, but in order to develop that potential, she had to work hard. She chose not to.

"May I also point out that though Ms. Borden is the only black student in my violin studio, there are many black students in my theory courses and in the orchestra I direct. None of them ever accused me of discrimination. If I were a racist, it is certain other incidents would have cropped up in twenty-two years, but they never have. In all that time, my record has been completely untarnished. I hope you will act in a fair and impartial manner to dismiss these false charges and reinstate me so I can return to the job I love."

Abe Shaheen adjourned the hearing at 11:45 and dismissed the witnesses. "We'll take a lunch break and begin deliberations at 1:30 this afternoon. Once we reach a decision, I will text you. Please stay in the vicinity so we can convene quickly at that time. And just a reminder that our decision is not final. It must be reviewed by the president and the Board of Regents. If the president rejects the decision, he can appeal to the Board of Regents, who will make the final judgment."

By the time Sebastian left the conference room, all the witnesses had gone. He knew Abbie, Miles, and Alfred Chang had afternoon classes and students to teach. With no place to go, he walked slowly out the door toward the elevator just as Alicia Borden and her mother emerged from the ladies' room. As they walked quickly past him, Mrs. Borden shot him a disdainful, furious look. Her angry "*Hmmmph!*" impaled him like a spear; Sebastian felt the impact in his gut. He watched them stride away, leaving a trail of resentment in their path, as palpable as dust and ashes.

No matter what the verdict, he knew in their eyes he would always be guilty. To avoid further contact, he bypassed the elevator and took the stairs. He wondered if he would still have a job by the end of the day, or if destiny decreed he would be fired, lose his income, and subsequently drown in debt.

CHAPTER 30
THE BATTLE

Sebastian figured he had at least two hours before the panel would come to a decision. He drove back to Bullinger and parked on Zeiss Street, across from de Graaf's Bookshop. He turned off the engine and looked at the cheerful yellow façade of the nineteenth-century building, the brightest spot in the cloudy, overcast day. His stomach was knotted so tight, he didn't think he could eat lunch, but he decided to visit Silvie and get some coffee and a snack, as long as it wasn't a kolache.

As he was about to exit the car, he remembered he had promised to call Helen. He rang her up and described the hearing quickly, as she was in the middle of her busy day as a vet. "Call me back when you know the decision," she told him. "I'm praying for you, Dad."

He thanked her; he certainly needed prayer. He left the car and crossed the street to the bookshop. The jangling bell announced his entrance.

"Sebastian!" Silvie exclaimed. She sat behind the counter next to the cash register. "What are you doing here, all dressed up, so early in the day?" Her smile was open and beautiful to behold, but he couldn't bring himself to smile in return.

"Oh!" She read the heaviness in his gaze. "Was the hearing today?"

He nodded.

Her brow furrowed and she put one hand to her cheek. "What did they decide?"

"They haven't yet. They heard all the testimony and they're breaking for lunch now. The panel will reconvene at 1:30 to deliberate."

He looked so dejected and thin, it worried her. At the rate he was losing weight, he might soon disappear. She came out from behind the counter. "Have you eaten?"

"No. I thought I'd have a cup of coffee and something to go with it. Just not a kolache."

"I'll make you a latté." As she walked to the coffee bar, she pointed to the sofa. "Sit down and try to relax." She glanced at him quizzically. "You don't like kolaches?"

"I don't like the kolache-maker." It was true, but Sebastian hadn't intended to utter it; the remark just popped out of his mouth.

She turned her head sharply. "Lucas Hlavicek?"

"Correct. I only met him once, but that was enough."

"When did you meet him?" Silvie already knew the answer, so she bent her head to hide her smile and busied herself making the latté.

"The day I helped you with the flat tire, remember?"

"Ah, yes, at the restaurant." She poured the steaming brown coffee into a white ceramic mug. "Sebastian, I no longer sell kolaches here. I severed all ties with Lucas, both professionally and personally earlier this fall."

Sebastian's pulse jumped. To him, her speech was pure poetry, surpassing Shakespeare.

She brought his coffee and something wrapped in a napkin. When she sat beside him on the sofa, her eyes were merry. "Have a scone, Dr. Morrow, and you need not search in my vicinity for that dishonest Czech pastry-maker ever again. I gave him the boot, and I'll never in this life eat another kolache."

He raised his eyebrows. "Well, no matter what else may befall me in the next few hours, that statement made the day a resounding success."

Touched by the light that kindled in his eyes, Silvie's smile radiated pleasure. "I wanted to tell you earlier, but this seemed like the right moment."

Sebastian set his mug down and took her hand in his. He searched her eyes intently with a gaze both gentle and grave. And then something happened she could never have foreseen. She felt herself irresistibly drawn to him, and in their shared and open glance, a marvelous unveiling occurred. Aware of nothing but each other, their souls, laid bare, seemed to intermingle timelessly. Without a word spoken, trust and mutual accord arose between them, and love unfolded its petals like a perfect flower.

A customer entered, and the bell brought Silvie back to herself. So transfixed had she been she had forgotten where she was. Still touched, but suddenly self-conscious, she drew her eyes away and gestured toward the cup. "Drink," she said.

Sebastian bent his head and sipped the hot, strong coffee.

"Tell me how it went, Sebastian," she said, "the hearing."

"It's hard to say. My witnesses made it quite clear that the student deserved the grade."

"Oh, excuse me a minute." Silvie rose to check out a customer who stood at the counter holding three books in her hands.

In the meantime, Sebastian tasted the blueberry scone and sipped the coffee. He had skipped breakfast, and the food and hot drink boosted his energy. The best tonic, though, was simply to be with Silvie and far away from Omega. He gazed at her as she helped the customer. Her warm, open expression, the full-lipped smile, and the glorious blue eyes lifted his heart.

She returned and sat beside him. Her orange blossom scent washed over him—light, sweet and fresh. "Do you think they might rule in your favor?"

The luminous quality of her loose, white-blond hair was almost as beautiful as the concern in her eyes. "I really don't know. The worrying part is the accusation that I used a racial slur. I didn't, but the two girls insist that I did. Miles Greenfield, the Englishman you met at the reception, was also implicated by them. He testified that it never happened. Unfortunately, it's just 'she said' versus 'he said.' It's not provable either way, but both girls spoke so forcefully, I'm afraid they just might sway the panel." He shook his head. "I guess we'll find out shortly."

The bell jangled again, and they turned their heads. "Leo!" said Silvie.

"Hey, Mamma, you look surprised. Did you forget I had to play the funeral this morning?" His charcoal gray sports coat set off his corn silk hair and pale complexion.

"Not really. Sebastian distracted me. He's just come from the hearing at the university."

Leo came over and shook Sebastian's hand. "Glad to see you here, Dr. Morrow."

"Thanks, Leo. I may be in Bullinger permanently if they fire me."

"Let's hope they have better sense than that," said Silvie. "Excuse me again."

A white-haired, heavyset man wearing jeans and a maroon Texas A&M sweatshirt approached her and asked if she had books on gardening and military history. "Those are on opposite ends of the second floor. Come with me, and I'll show you."

Leo watched his mother and the customer mount the stairs. He sat down beside Sebastian and said quietly, "The opposition has raised its head."

"The opposition?"

"Yes, the ones we battle against."

"Alicia Borden?"

He shook his head. "No, the ones who work *through* people. Principalities and powers."

Startled, Sebastian felt the hair rise up on the back of his neck. Leo's statement transported him back to the moment when he had seen the demon looking out of Mary Catherine's eyes. He replied, "I learned a long time ago, by personal experience, that such entities exist, but what I don't understand is why they would come against me."

"They have assignments to destroy human beings any way they can. Sometimes they work through our weaknesses—appetites, pride, sexual sins, fears, and so on. But sometimes they work through the actions of other people. They especially target people who make spiritual progress, those who draw close to God. Padre Pio, for example—he was physically assaulted by the devil."

Sebastian dared not compare himself to Padre Pio, the pinnacle of spiritual advancement. If the good priest was the mountain's summit, he was the base. But he had to agree; Leo had just echoed the conclusions of the exorcist and the pastor, whose books Sebastian had read during the summer. He looked at the boy in wonder—he was only twenty years old—how did he have this spiritual knowledge; how could he make his pronouncements in such a calm, matter-of-fact way? It was as if an angel spoke, or as if one of the church fathers had been resurrected in twenty-first century Bullinger.

"Simply put," Leo added, "Satan and his demons hate us."

Sebastian knew it was true. He shuddered involuntarily as he remembered the astonishing malice in the demon's eyes. "But why?"

"Because they hate God, and we're made in His image." Leo's brow wrinkled, and the intensity in his eyes pierced Sebastian. "We're in a battle, Dr. Morrow. That's why God gave us armor and weapons: the belt of truth, the breastplate of righteousness, the shield of faith, the sword of the spirit. Those who are unaware are in the greatest danger."

Silvie returned at that moment. "Leo, have you eaten anything?"

He stood up. "No, I'm meeting Stephanie for lunch in Houston." He grinned. "But I'll have a latté and a cookie for the road." When Silvie turned toward the coffee bar, he said, "Sit down and talk to Dr. Morrow, Mamma. I can make it myself."

Five minutes later, Leo bustled out the door bearing a paper cup of coffee and a chocolate chip cookie in his hands. "He strikes like lightning from the east," remarked Sebastian. "The Swedish-American version of *blitzkrieg*."

"That's my son."

"He's an unusual person, Silvie."

"Yes, he always has been. He's very sensitive, and, uh, what's the word . . . discerning. When he was younger, he used to make dramatic statements, and the other children teased him. I found his pronouncements annoying sometimes because they were so strange. I wanted him to be like other children, you know—normal. But he never was, and his classmates mocked him so much that he almost stopped talking. For a time in his mid-teens he got into a number of fistfights at school over it. There were one or two bullies he had to face, but when they found out he wasn't afraid to fight, they eventually left him alone. After that, he withdrew; he kept to himself and funneled all his energy into playing piano and organ. He's become a person who speaks little, but when he does, watch out!"

Indeed. "What sort of things did he say when he was younger?"

"Well, he saw colors swirling around people's heads and bodies. He thought, naturally, that everyone saw as he did. But others couldn't see the colors, so when he described what he saw, no one believed him. Some thought he had an overactive imagination, but others thought he was lying."

Sebastian remembered his experience with the child Sasha in the restaurant, when the young boy had gazed at him so raptly. "I wonder if all children can see those colors and then lose that faculty when they get older?"

Silvie shrugged. "I don't remember anything like that myself, but we forget so many things as we grow up. Perhaps it's only the purest souls who carry that faculty into adulthood." She leaned forward and rested her chin in her hands. "I worry about Leo. This world is not kind to the pure of heart."

Sebastian sighed heavily. "Or to those who tell the truth." *The blood of the martyrs, the blood of the innocent ones cries out from the ground.*

Just then, two more customers entered the store. At the same time, the portly man in the Aggie sweatshirt descended the stairs with his books. "Found what I wanted," he called out to Silvie.

She rose and Sebastian rose with her. "Thank you for the coffee and scone, Silvie. I'd better go."

"Wait." She walked to the counter, took one of her business cards, and wrote something on the back. She gave him the card. "That's my mobile number. Let me know the outcome."

Sebastian put the card in his breast pocket. "I will."

As he left Bullinger, he turned on the windshield wipers in the light rain, thinking of Leo's words. *The opposition has raised its head.* That was surely true. He was engaged in a battle, and who knew what the outcome would be? Exoneration would lead to reinstatement and a return to work. If the panel ruled against him, a court battle loomed. Martin would sue the university for wrongful termination and defamation of character.

The clouds grew increasingly darker as he neared Omega, and the rain fell with greater intensity. As he drove, he mentally replayed his conversation with Leo. For years, ever since he had seen the demon in

Mary Catherine, he had kept the encounter secret. But now, because of Leo's understanding and explanation, Sebastian didn't feel so alone. And in large degree, the boy had de-mystified the foe.

A comforting thought came to Sebastian—the power of the enemy, no matter how great, could not compare with the power of the Almighty. All created beings, from Homo sapiens to the nine choirs of angels, were lower than their Creator and subject to Him. And the Creator had promised protection: *And He shall give His angels charge over thee, to keep thee in all thy ways.*

He took the exit for the university as the wind increased and heavy rain lashed at the car. It would be easy to resent his accuser and his enemies, but he knew resentment could grow like a cancer to consume those who harbored it. That was a price he would not pay. He had done no wrong; he had graded fairly, and he had treated his students, all of them, with respect. Let come what may, he would simply stand firm and face whatever future Providence might provide.

He parked and sat secure in the car as the rain and wind assailed it. He prayed for calm and strength. Five minutes later, his mobile phone beeped as a text came through from Abe Shaheen: *Please return immediately to the conference room. We've reached a decision.*

CHAPTER 31
EVIDENCE

The academic life is a cerebral one; the head rules over the heart. Unlike lesser beings, academics pride themselves on controlling the passions. Conscious of their intellectual prowess and specialized knowledge, their formidable achievements and many degrees, they have little choice but to assume their superior roles. In their black, billowing robes and oddly shaped caps, they are marked out as a secular priesthood, ranked in glory (in their own estimation) just a little lower than the gods.

When everyone reconvened in the sepulchral conference room, it appeared to Sebastian that the panel had dined on sawdust. Their dry, unemotional eyes and aloof glances, coupled with a faint air of indigestion, told him nothing. Their demeanor did not surprise him. A committee member on various occasions himself, he had interviewed job candidates and auditioned prospective students, all the while maintaining a mask of indifference. He knew what they were doing, but he wished they hadn't done it so well. He couldn't read them at all.

Fortunately, he didn't have long to wait for their decision. He stood beside the stooped, tortoise-like Dr. Corrotto as they faced the panel. Despite his resolve to retain equanimity, Sebastian's knees felt rubbery, and he wondered if his pounding heart might burst open his chest and ricochet around the room.

Abe Shaheen spoke solemnly, "Although the vote was not unanimous, we have decided in favor of Dr. Morrow."

Corrotto gave an audible huff and crossed his arms over his chest. Sebastian closed his eyes and exhaled through his mouth. Then he drew a deep breath in relief.

"We'll make our recommendation to President Reynolds this afternoon." Abe fixed Sebastian directly in his sights. "Dr. Morrow, before any action can be taken to reinstate you, we must wait for the president to concur with this decision. However he decides, the matter will still have to go to the Board of Regents. As you know, the final judgment will be theirs. Hopefully, we'll hear from the president by late tomorrow. I think it prudent to wait until we get notification from Dr. Reynolds before we discuss the outcome with anyone. I've already given the panel members the same instructions. Any questions?"

"No." At the moment, Sebastian's only desire was to exit the room like a shot.

Abe glanced at the panel members. "Thank you all for your time and work. This hearing is adjourned."

Dr. Corrotto stroked his crepey neck and smiled at Sebastian with the tenderness and warmth of a reptile. "Congratulations, Dr. Morrow; enjoy it while you can. I highly doubt this decision will stand. Good day." He turned on his heel and marched away. Before he got to the door, he was punching numbers on his mobile phone.

Everyone knew Corrotto had a close relationship with the president. Sebastian was fairly sure Luther Reynolds would know the decision in the next two minutes. Despite his desire to bolt, he walked to the front of the room and thanked Abe Shaheen first, and then every member of the panel before they disappeared to their various offices.

Dodging sidewalk puddles, he jogged back to his car through a light, chilly drizzle, all that was left of the storm. His pleasure in the decision was undermined by uneasiness. He knew there would be a backlash from Alicia Borden's mother and activists in the black community if it appeared that racism had gone unpunished. Mrs. Borden had already threatened to create a media storm.

Sebastian didn't know what to expect from Luther Reynolds. The man had a politician's easy smile and bonhomie, but that certainly didn't guarantee integrity in action. The president's two main interests seemed to be money and football, with any concern for academic excellence left in the dust of their passing. Sebastian knew that any university president would flee scandal, or at least cover it up. Reynolds had managed to do that with Scott Woolrich, the former head of the music department, who embezzled funds. When the theft was discovered, instead of filing charges and creating a hullabaloo, Reynolds disguised Woolrich's firing. He concocted a story that the man's diabetes (which was real) had worsened to the point that he had to retire immediately (patently false). They gave Woolrich a nice send-off, with the rumored agreement (confirmed by Betsy Bloom, who prepared the paperwork) that the university would garnish a certain amount from his monthly pension until the debt was repaid.

Technically, in the matter of Omega University vs. T. Sebastian Morrow, Luther Reynolds was a member of the opposing team. Yet he had the power to challenge the decision, and Provost Corrotto would no doubt urge the president to do just that. It wasn't a good sign either that the vote had not been unanimous.

Sebastian knew his daughter, his colleagues, Silvie, and Leo waited to hear from him, but he felt too mentally exhausted to speak to them. He decided to go home, take a nap, and eat dinner first. His only meal had been coffee and a scone. Maybe later he would have the energy to explain the situation to everyone.

Once home, he made himself a three-egg cheese omelet. He added toast and jam, a green salad, and a hefty glass of red wine. Thanks to the chickens, he was becoming an expert omelet-maker. After the meal, he put the recliner in max-recline position, filled it with his long-legged frame, and immediately fell asleep.

When he awoke, it was almost dark. He went out to the coop to check on the chickens. He gathered three eggs, counted heads on the roost, and shut them in for the night. The sky had cleared, swept clean by a very welcome Canadian cold front. A single silver star kept the crescent moon company.

Penny stood out in the yard, barking at the woods, and Plush the cat, begging for food, rubbed herself against his ankles. It was past time for their supper. Sebastian fed the menagerie, and then changed into jeans, a sweatshirt, and sneakers. He added a light jacket and sat outside on the big deck. He called Helen first.

After he explained about the decision and its possible reversal, Helen asked, "Well, at least you won the opening battle. That's a hopeful sign. But how are you, Dad? What have you been doing to keep busy?"

"Well, I bought a park bench and set it down beside the pond. I put up a bird feeder, a birdbath, and a hummingbird feeder. Sometimes I sit out here on the deck and watch the egrets and great blue herons hunting on the edge of the pond." *And I pray mornings and evenings, and fast.* "I'm also practicing a lot for the opera. But, at this point, I'm running out of home improvement tasks. Honestly, being unemployed makes me jittery, and I don't know how much longer this is going to go on."

"When is the next opera?"

"Thankfully, rehearsals begin next week."

"What is it?"

"*Madama Butterfly.*"

"Oh, that's cheerful."

Sebastian laughed. "Yeah, what would opera be without that winning combination of callous betrayal and suicide?"

"Poor old Cio-Cio San!" Helen laughed. "Well, Dad, in all your free time, you could take some pictures of Penny and the chickens and send them to us."

"Don't forget about my three refugee cats."

"That's right, they showed up after our last visit. We haven't seen them."

"Didn't I send you some pictures of them?"

"No, the last photo I got was your eaten-up arm with all the chigger bites."

Sebastian smiled. "Oh, Miles took that last spring just prior to a committee meeting at Omega."

"See, Dad, that was six months ago. You've been delinquent. Go out into the yard and take some pictures."

"All right." Sebastian smiled. Whether it was her purpose or not, she had succeeded in lightening his mood.

After he spoke to Abbie, Miles, and Alfred Chang, he went back inside to retrieve Silvie's business card so he could call her. She didn't answer her phone, so he left a brief message. To keep his mind off himself, Sebastian spent the rest of the evening listening to his 1955 recording of *Butterfly* with the marvelous Maria Callas and Nicolai Gedda.

Abe Shaheen called at two o'clock on Friday. "Dr. Morrow, I'm sorry to inform you, but President Reynolds rejected our decision. He examined the evidence and the transcript of the hearing, and now he's in the process of writing his recommendation for dismissal.

He'll submit everything to the Board of Regents on Monday." Abe paused. "I think his haste is due to the planned demonstration."

"What demonstration?"

"Oh, I thought you knew. It's supposed to take place Monday at noon here on campus, a protest rally sparked by this whole affair. The group that organized it is called Students for a Racist-Free America."

Sebastian was taken aback. "Dr. Duck did tell me that Alicia's mother threatened to call in the national media. *Hmmph*, I imagine the local news networks will be there."

"Probably so." Abe sighed audibly. "I'm sorry, Sebastian."

"Ah, well. Thank you for all you did, Abe. By the way, what was the final vote yesterday?"

"Three to two."

"Not good."

"No. The racial slur issue split the panel. I believed you when you denied ever saying that, but the girls were very convincing."

"Convincing, but mistaken. Do you know when the Board of Regents will meet next?"

"Yes, on Monday evening, November 16. I'm sure they want to resolve this dispute, so, hopefully, they'll add it to the agenda."

"Am I allowed to be present with my attorney to defend myself?"

"Yes, of course. They can also request other important witnesses to appear."

"All right, Abe. Thanks again." Well, Sebastian mused, he was down, but not out. Not yet. Luther Reynolds might be the president, but he didn't have the last say. He had decided for dismissal, in all probability to placate the students, alumni, and public opinion. The Board of Regents, like the panel, was a group, and Sebastian thought he had a much better chance with a jury rather than a single judge. If they decided in his favor, that would be final. If he won, he won, no matter how close the vote; the decision couldn't be overturned.

Now he had to inform everybody all over again. But he decided that could wait. He wanted to get out of the house and walk. He put on his boots and slipped his phone into the pocket of his jacket. Once he was outside, Penny, invigorated by the cold snap, wagged her feathered tail and invited Sebastian to play, feinting this way and that with her head and front paws. Her back legs had strengthened with exercise, and she didn't move like an old dog anymore. Sebastian took out his phone and snapped a few pictures of his Great Pyrenees for Helen. Then he made a circuit of his property, striding rapidly and enjoying the exercise. He ended up beside the pond, where he sat down on the park bench.

Orange, brown, and yellow leaves floated on the ruffled surface of the pond. They sailed in circles like tiny rudderless boats on the blue water, a mirror of the clear sky. Sebastian leaned back on the bench, crossed his long legs, and listened to the rustle of the dry leaves on the ground, blown about by the north wind. If he had to be jobless, this was a much better place to be than back in the gritty Houston barrio.

He glanced up at his cottage. He had moved in seventeen months ago, and he wasn't ready to move out. He loved the little house, the quiet pond, and the spacious, hilly property. If he got fired, he would find other employment, even if he had to work outside his profession.

He blew out an explosive breath. What a turn of events. Once he had gotten the house and property under control, his professional life had fallen apart—an irony he could have done without.

All three cats appeared in single file, walking delicately through the fallen leaves, tails held high. Plush hopped up on the bench and crouched on her haunches beside him. She waved her duster-like orange tail and purred. Little Tortie and Jemmers, the tuxedo cat, walked to the edge of the pond and lapped up water, side by side, like miniature lionesses. Sebastian took the opportunity to capture the moment. Then, Plush the huntress leapt off the bench to attack her prey, a swirling mass of leaves. "Photo number three," murmured Sebastian and clicked.

The iPhone made it so easy, he wondered why he so seldom took any pictures. Penny interrupted his thoughts. Facing the road, she gave several short barks. Shortly thereafter, the yellow school bus lumbered past. "Four o'clock. School's out."

School might be permanently out for him. He had to consider what he would do if he lost his job at Omega. He could probably get an adjunct position somewhere. In the Houston area alone, there were six junior colleges and four universities with music programs, and there were dozens of high school orchestras that might have open positions.

The sun was setting earlier now, and the wind grew colder. Sebastian walked back up the hill to the house to feed the animals. They followed him, the cats scampering here and there while Penny brought up the rear. The chickens still foraged, but they had moved closer to the coop. They would soon go to roost.

After dinner, Sebastian called Helen and his friends to tell them the news. Each one commiserated with him and offered suggestions, some more vehemently than others. Abbie declared, "If in the end they fire you, I'm going to return fire. One well-placed cigarette and the whole effing place will burn down. We'll dine on roast Duck." Helen and Kieran lobbied for him to come to Lancaster and work with them as either a vet assistant or a drywall installer. Alfred Chang offered to testify before the board if necessary. Miles sputtered with anger, "That bloomin' idjit Luther Reynolds. He must be related to Ferris Duck and the stinkin' brown sludge at the bottom of a latrine. Spineless cowards both."

Silvie related Leo's comment. "Whatever happens, Mamma, he's already won because he did what was right in the first place, and he stood by it."

"What will you do if they fire you, Sebastian?" she asked.

"There are other string instructor positions locally. Houston has gobs of colleges and universities."

"Will they be reluctant to hire someone accused of racial discrimination?"

Sebastian rubbed his eyes. "Huh, good question. If they fire me, it will send ripples of fear through the whole academic community, and it may well stain my reputation forever. I don't know. I just hope I don't have to run that gauntlet."

After his conversation with Silvie, Sebastian felt chilled by the damp cold in the house. He turned on his heaters for the first time that year. The big heater in the living room produced a cheery, open flame that curled up and flickered around several ceramic logs. It was almost as atmospheric as a fireplace, and Sebastian quite enjoyed it. He set the smaller one in the bathroom on low. In five minutes, the chill was gone.

After he showered and put on his pajamas, though it was still early, Sebastian went to bed. The day had taken its toll, and fatigue settled on him like a great weight. He lay flat on his back for a minute, and then spoke into the dark, "Lord, what am I going to do? How can I prove my innocence?"

In the next instant, he realized he hadn't sent Helen the photos he had promised. "Oh, hell. I'd better do it tonight." He threw off the covers and sat up on the edge of the bed. Suddenly, with the impact of a roaring freight train, it struck him: "Oh, my God!" he blurted, "I *can* prove it." What a dunderhead he was—he had had the answer all along.

He raised his glance to the ceiling. "Ha! Thank You, Lord, and thank you, Helen!" All his energy returned in a rush of adrenaline. He sprang up, a determined man on a mission. He would send the three photos and locate the incontrovertible evidence that was all the proof he needed.

CHAPTER 32

BLOOD AND GUTS

The argument began when Stephanie wanted to see the latest movie on the occult, *Portal of Power*, while Leo wanted to see a film about WWII. They sat facing each other over their loaded trays in the university's busy underground dining hall. Stephanie had come from the orchestra rehearsal, and she had propped her bulky, rectangular violin case in the chair beside her. They were in the process of devouring giant cheeseburgers with no pickles (on that they agreed) and big crinkle-cut fries.

"Why don't you want to see *Portal of Power*?" She sipped her root beer.

"Well, the writer of the original novel is a Wiccan, and her stated purpose is to indoctrinate people into her agenda. I don't want to see a film about the wonders of witchcraft." Leo took an enormous bite of his cheeseburger.

"Leo, it's not real—it's fantasy. Anyway, it's good witchcraft versus bad witchcraft." Stephanie bit triumphantly into two ketchup-coated french fries at the same time, confident she had scored a point with that remark.

"It's billed as fantasy, all right, but witchcraft and sorcery are real, and their origin is satanic. Do you know what witchcraft is, Stephanie?"

She stopped chewing and stared at him. "The use of magic and spells."

"Yes, and the invocation of demons and familiar spirits."

"You're kidding, right? There is no such thing."

"No? Hollywood sure thinks so. They've made fortunes many times over with films on the demonic."

"Yeah, but those are just movies, not real life."

"Stephanie, the film *The Exorcist* was based on an actual case of demonic possession. The family called in a Catholic priest to cast out the demon."

"Maybe the person was just mentally ill, like the so-called demon-possessed people in the Bible. Those were most likely schizophrenics."

Leo drank some of his milkshake while he tried to figure out the best rebuttal. After a moment, he said, "You know, the Pharisees, the learned men of Israel, doubted Jesus' divinity. Even His own disciples weren't sure of it. But the demons knew exactly who He was. They called Him by name. Once, when He was in a synagogue, a man there had an unclean spirit. And the man said . . . wait a minute." Leo grinned at her. "Well, he didn't actually say that. I'm saying it. Let me look this up so I get it right." He wiped the ketchup off his fingers and put his iPhone on the table. After searching a minute, he found the reference. "Ah, here it is, the first chapter of Mark in the noble King James Version, my personal favorite." He read aloud:

> *And there was in their synagogue a man with an unclean spirit;*
> *and he cried out, saying, "Let us alone; what have we to do with*
> *thee, thou Jesus of Nazareth? art thou come to destroy us? I know*
> *thee who thou art, the Holy One of God." And Jesus rebuked*
> *him, saying, "Hold thy peace, and come out of him." And when*

*the unclean spirit had torn him, and cried with a loud voice,
he came out of him. And they were all amazed, insomuch that
they questioned among themselves, saying, "What thing is this?
what new doctrine is this? For with authority commandeth he
even the unclean spirits, and they do obey him."*

"See, the demons spoke through the man, directly to Jesus. There
were more than one, since they said *us* and *we*. But the man himself
was ignorant of Jesus' identity. That wasn't schizophrenia, Stephanie;
it was evidence of possession by supernatural beings with spiritual
sight. They saw and recognized Jesus from that perspective."

"Well, those were demons. What's wrong with witchcraft?"

"Witchcraft brings people into contact with demons. It gives
demons an opening into a person's life. The problems for the boy
whose story forms the basis of *The Exorcist* began when he played
with a Ouija board. It seemed innocuous at the time, just a fun
game, but that's how the demons gained entry. Once it grew into
full-fledged possession, his life became hell."

"But Leo, *Portal of Power* isn't like that. I've heard it's a little scary
sometimes, but a lot of it is funny and charming."

"Serial killers are also funny and charming. In the beginning."

"You!" Stephanie gave up. "All right, I'm tired of arguing. Let's go
see a WWII film about blood and guts."

"And sacrifice and true valor." Leo grinned at her. "Thank you,
Stephanie." He picked up her hand and kissed the palm. "You're a
sweetheart, but you taste like ketchup."

She couldn't help laughing. His kiss pleased her, but she tried not
to show it. "What time does it start?"

Leo checked online. "In twenty-five minutes."

"Oh, I won't have time to drop off my violin at the dorm."

"You can take it with you."

"I'm sure I can," she agreed. "Since everyone else will be watching *Portal of Power*, my fiddle can have its own seat."

⁂

Stephanie found the WWII film touching, but being stubborn, she didn't want Leo to know how much she liked it. "Well, it wasn't too bad," she said airily as they walked out.

"Uh-huh, I saw you cry when the lieutenant was killed," replied Leo with a grin. "I think it was a lot better than you expected."

"Oh, no!" she exclaimed when they emerged from the cinema in a popcorn-scented cloud. Rain poured down with the force and noise of a waterfall.

"Give me the violin," said Leo. As soon as he had it in hand, he cried, "Race you to the Jeep!"

Stephanie bolted into the parking lot so suddenly she left him open-mouthed and flat-footed on the curb. He ran after her, dodging puddles and cars until they got to the Jeep. Leo put the violin in the backseat, and they piled in, wet, breathless, and laughing.

"Ha-ha, I won!" Stephanie crowed.

"You sure did. Honestly, I think one of your forbears must have been a racehorse; you shot out of the gate like Seabiscuit."

She laughed and responded with a high whinny. "Naaaaaaay, I just like a challenge."

Leo's reply was swift. He leaned over and kissed her. It felt so good, he did it a few more times. Being a generous soul, not to mention a hot-blooded young girl, Stephanie returned the favor. Their give-and-take continued for several minutes until she murmured, "Leo, we can't spend the night here."

"Ah, what a pity." Unfortunately, she was right. He had to take her back to the dorm and then travel all the way to Bullinger so he could play Sunday morning Mass. Reluctantly, he started the engine, and they headed back. On the way, he called his mother. "Gotta let her know my ETA," he informed Stephanie. "On Saturday nights she always waits up for me."

Parking at the university was a study in frustration. The ratio of students to parking spaces was as lopsided as the gender imbalance of men to women in China. Naturally, all the Visitor spaces were taken in the lot across from Stephanie's dorm. After searching up and down the rows, Leo finally found a spot at the very back. Stephanie retrieved the violin from the backseat and carried it with the sturdy strap over her shoulder. The rain had stopped, so they ambled slowly, hand-in-hand between the cars, to delay their moment of parting.

All the vehicles had flyers on their windshields. One had blown off, and out of curiosity, Leo picked it up. He used the light from his mobile phone to read it.

> ***Take down the racist clown!***
> ***Morrow has got to go!***
> ***Protest Rally @ Noon***
> ***Monday, Nov. 9 - Omega University***
> ***Students for a Racist-Free America***

"Oh, no," he groaned and handed it to Stephanie.

"They can't mean Dr. Morrow, the violinist."

"I'm afraid they do," replied Leo. "A student there accused him of racial discrimination, and the university put him on leave. That's why he gave his concert at Frankau Hall. They may even fire him. There was a hearing about it at Omega day before yesterday. This is really bad for him."

"Surely he didn't do it."

"No, he didn't, but these days, just an accusation is enough to mar someone's reputation."

Stephanie wadded up the flyer in her hand and threw it on the ground.

"Why is it so dark out here?" Leo muttered. He scanned the perimeter and saw two of the tall overhead lights nearest them had burned out. He thought he glimpsed the outline of a huge, dark, birdlike figure perched on one of the lampposts. If it was a vulture, it was the biggest one he'd ever seen. Or was it something else? An oppressive feeling, a terrible premonition overtook him. He glanced to either side, gripped Stephanie's hand, and quickened his pace. "Let's hurry."

"Oh, so you want to get rid of me now?"

He shook his head emphatically. "No, I—"

Suddenly, two black men in dark clothes sprang out from behind an SUV. The smaller one with dreadlocks lunged at Stephanie and grabbed her by the wrists, while the big man purred at Leo in a low, musical voice, "Hey mon, gi mi ya money, so we don hurt di gal."

Leo's heart froze in fear for Stephanie. As he reached for his wallet, everything happened at once. Stephanie screamed, "Let me go!" and kneed the smaller man in the groin. As he dropped her wrists and bent forward, she hit him in the head with the violin case and knocked him to the ground.

Simultaneously, with all his force, Leo threw a desperate punch at the big guy's jaw. The man's head snapped back and he cried out, but he retaliated, striking Leo hard in the gut. Leo doubled over in pain and collapsed onto the asphalt. Stephanie's earsplitting scream unnerved Leo's assailant—he turned tail and ran.

Then she shrieked at the top of her voice, "Help, help, help!"

The smaller guy grimaced and growled at Stephanie. "Fuckin' bitch."

When he spoke, she noticed the glint of two gold teeth.

He picked himself up off the pavement and hobbled away after his accomplice into the darkness. She watched him go, knees trembling in reaction. "You coward." Then she knelt beside Leo. "Are you okay?" Her voice shook.

He moaned in pain. He lay on his side in the fetal position, hands clutched over his stomach.

"Can you get up, Leo?" She put her hand on his and felt a warm, sticky wetness. "Oh, my God, you're bleeding."

"Call 911," he managed to say. Then pain and darkness engulfed him.

⁂

At 10:15, Silvie got a call from Leo. "Mamma, I'm going to drop Stephanie off at her dorm, and then I'll be on my way to Bullinger."

"See you soon." She figured he would arrive around 11:30. She didn't want to go to bed until he was home. To pass the time, she read a novel about a female espionage ring during WWI. The head of the spy ring was a Frenchwoman from an aristocratic family who was also fluent in English and German. Silvie was able to understand all the German dialogue, since it was so close to Swedish.

An hour later, the ring of her mobile phone woke Silvie out of a deep sleep. At some point, she had dozed off on the sofa. She glanced at her watch. It was 11:40—Leo would arrive shortly. She sat up and reached for the phone which lay on the coffee table. She saw her son's name on the screen. "Leo?"

She heard a baritone voice with a strong Texas accent. "Is this Mrs. de Graaf, Leo de Graaf's mother?"

Confused and groggy, Silvie answered, "Yes."

"Ma'am, this is Dr. Rob Truett at Methodist Hospital. Your son was mugged tonight on the University of Houston campus. He was brought here to the emergency room."

Confusion became ice-cold fear. She was immediately wide awake.

"He was stabbed in the abdomen, and we need permission to operate immediately."

"Oh, God." She felt a quaking through her whole body. "Yes, of course."

"Thank you, he's on his way to the OR right now. The surgeon, Dr. Heinz, will determine the extent of the damage, and then take whatever steps are necessary. Your son couldn't be in better hands. It would be good if you could get here as soon as possible."

"I'm leaving now, but I'm in Bullinger. It'll take me about an hour to get there." Thankfully, she was still dressed. She grabbed her keys and her purse, threw on a jacket, and rushed out the door.

Late at night, the roads into Houston were clear. People took advantage and drove well over the speed limit. Silvie got behind a white pickup truck doing eighty and kept up with him. Her mind worked in overdrive. She had to tell Kristin, but that could wait until Sunday morning when she knew more. The dashboard clock read 12:10. She realized it was already Sunday morning. She called Sebastian.

The phone rang several times before he answered, sounding surprised, "Silvie? Is something wrong?"

"Yes." She felt the prick of tears. "Sorry if I woke you, but Leo was mugged tonight. Someone stabbed him in the abdomen and he's in surgery in Houston."

"Oh, no." A sense of foreboding descended on Sebastian.

"Sebastian, can you contact the priest at St. Mark's and tell him Leo won't be there in the morning?"

"Yes, I'll do that."

"I'm sorry to call you so late, but I just found out a few minutes ago. I'm driving in now."

"Which hospital?"

"Methodist."

"Silvie, I'm going to drive in and meet you there."

"Oh, would you?" Her voice broke. It was at times like this that Silvie missed the presence and calm of her late husband Edward. She didn't protest. "Thank you, Sebastian. I know I'm going to need support." His kindness breached her self-control, and the tears she had managed to suppress until that moment spilled over.

CHAPTER 33
TRUE MEDICINE

By the time Silvie arrived at the hospital, filled out insurance and consent forms, and found her way to the OR waiting room, it was almost one o'clock in the morning. She found an exhausted, distraught Stephanie there. "Oh, Stephanie, are you all right?" Silvie went directly to the girl and embraced her.

"Yes, I'm fine. A little shaken up and tired is all."

Silvie sat down beside her, but before she could say another word, a doctor, still in green surgical scrubs, entered the room. "Mrs. de Graaf?"

Silvie nodded and they both rose. "I'm Leo's mother, and this is his friend Stephanie."

"I'm Dr. Matt Heinz, the surgeon." A thin, tall man with angular features, close-cut black hair, and large brown eyes behind his glasses, he gave them a quick, warm smile. "Nice to meet you both. First, let me say the surgery went well, and Leo is in recovery right now. The stab wound was about four inches deep in the lower left quadrant of the abdomen." He placed his left hand on his own abdomen to show them. "The knife perforated the colon and pierced a large vein, which is why he lost so much blood. The good news is that we were able to cut out the affected portion of the intestine, about four inches, and then reattach the ends. Sometimes with a perforated colon we have to do a temporary colostomy, but it wasn't necessary in this case."

Silvie's brows furrowed. "Is his life in danger or will he be okay?"

"Well, if it was only the perforated colon we had to worry about, he would be in the clear. We repaired the colon, but when he was stabbed, the bowel contents spilled into the abdominal cavity. That creates the risk of a very serious infection, which is why we rushed him into surgery to repair the damage as soon as possible. Now we're going to treat him aggressively with antibiotics. We're also giving him blood. We'll keep him in ICU and monitor him around the clock, until we feel the risk is past."

When Silvie looked crestfallen, Dr. Heinz tried to reassure her, "His youth and health are in his favor. Young guys like that are healing machines. If you have any questions, please ask the nurses in ICU to contact me. And by the way, those nurses are excellent. They'll monitor him very closely. As soon as he's out of recovery, one of the staff will notify you."

Dr. Heinz had no sooner left the room than Sebastian entered.

"Silvie, how is he—oh, and Stephanie, the violinist." He was surprised to see her and her canvas-covered violin case resting beside her. "Hello! How is Leo?" He hugged them both briefly.

Silvie recounted Dr. Heinz's report. Then, while they waited for Leo to come out of recovery, Stephanie described the events of the evening. "The big guy told Leo they wouldn't hurt me if he handed over his wallet. When the smaller one, the dreadlocks guy, grabbed me, I just reacted without thinking. I couldn't stand him touching me, so I screamed, kneed him in the groin, and then hit him as hard as I could with my violin case. It knocked him down.

"At the same time, Leo slugged the big guy. He hit back, and I thought he punched Leo in the stomach with his fist, but apparently, he had a knife. Leo doubled over and collapsed. At that point I screamed for help and they ran off." She shrugged. "I guess they didn't expect any resistance."

Sebastian spoke. "Stephanie, did you notice them following you?"

"No, the lights had burned out in that area of the parking lot, and they wore dark clothes, black or navy blue, and jeans. I never saw them at all until they sprang out right in front of us. I think they were loitering in the parking lot, waiting to mug someone. Leo and I just happened to be there at the wrong time."

"Do you think you could identify them?" asked Sebastian.

"Maybe. The dreadlocks guy's two front teeth were gold. The other one had a sing-song accent—Jamaican, maybe."

"What happened when they left?" asked Silvie.

Stephanie sighed. "Leo lay on the ground, curled up on his side, holding his stomach. When I asked him if he could get up, he just groaned. I touched his hand, and it felt wet and sticky. I was shocked when I realized he was bleeding. He told me to call 911, which I did immediately, and then he passed out.

"There was a lot of blood. I lifted his shirt and pulled down his jeans on that side so I could locate the wound. Blood just gushed out. I applied pressure to the wound with both hands and prayed. All I could do was wait. It was cold and the asphalt was wet from the rain. I was very afraid the men would come back while Leo was helpless.

"Then I heard footsteps, and suddenly two more black men appeared, and the scary thing was, they were bigger than the one who stabbed Leo. They could see Leo was hurt and I was in distress. I must've looked petrified, because one of them said, 'It's all right. Don't be afraid.' After he said that, I didn't relax entirely, but I wasn't scared anymore. The one who spoke asked what happened, and I told him. 'I called 911, and they're sending an ambulance, but he's bleeding badly.'

"Without saying a word, they took off the jackets they wore, and then they stripped off the red and white UH sweatshirts underneath. One of them eased a sweatshirt under Leo, to cushion his back, and he rolled the other one into a pillow for his head. The second man said, 'Be right back,' and ran off. The one who stayed with me laid the jackets over Leo's chest.

"Then the other man returned with a red wool blanket. I guess he got it out of his car. He spread that over Leo as well. 'Don't worry,' he said, 'we'll stay with you until the ambulance comes. You're doing the right thing—keep pressure on the wound.' It was damp and chilly, and at that point all they had on were white undershirts and jeans. It was so kind of them, and I was so relieved they were there. I thanked them several times.

"They were so big and muscular and dressed alike. I guessed they were athletes. I asked if they were on the football team, but they said no—lacrosse. I didn't even know UH had a lacrosse team. We didn't talk after that. They just knelt beside me and waited.

"A long, awful time went by; it seemed interminable, but finally I heard the ambulance siren. The men stood up and waved their arms so the driver could find us. The EMTs jumped out and put some kind of gel in the wound, covered it with a dressing, and applied pressure. They lifted Leo and put him on a gurney. At some point, while I was distracted, the two men who had helped me left. I didn't even see them go. It was almost as if they disappeared, and their clothes and blanket vanished, too."

"Maybe they were angels," mused Sebastian. "Where Leo is involved, I wouldn't be surprised. God protects His own."

"Their appearance was certainly providential," remarked Stephanie. "They seemed completely focused on the task at hand—no small talk." She shrugged. "Whether they were angels or not, I'm so thankful they came."

Frowning slightly, Silvie remarked, "I'm sure they were students, just like they said."

Both Sebastian and Stephanie heard the disapproval in her tone, and an awkward silence ensued.

After a moment, Silvie pushed a lock of hair behind one ear and asked, "Well, what happened next?"

Stephanie cleared her throat and replied, "Inside the ambulance, the EMTs covered Leo with more blankets and gave him oxygen. One of them called ahead to the hospital to give the ER doctor a heads-up. They started the siren and tore out of there. They wouldn't let me ride with them, so I took Leo's keys and followed them in his Jeep.

"I guess the 911 people sent a policeman to the hospital. He asked me questions and made a report while the ER doctor called you, Ms. de Graaf, and you know the rest."

Silvie put her arm around Stephanie. "You had the guts to fight back, and you tried to stop the bleeding. You're a brave girl."

Tears came to Stephanie's eyes. "Yes, but if I hadn't screamed, maybe they would've just taken Leo's wallet and run. Maybe he wouldn't be hurt now."

Sebastian replied, "Or maybe they would have stabbed you both or stabbed Leo again and killed him on the spot. There's no telling what could have happened."

"Stephanie, you should go home and go to bed. Get some rest and come back tomorrow. Let's get you a cab." Silvie searched in her wallet, took out two twenties, and handed the money to Stephanie. "That should cover it."

Stephanie held up one hand. "I can drive Leo's Jeep back to the dorm."

"Absolutely not. I want a cab to deliver you right to the door."

She accepted the money and gave Silvie Leo's keys. "Thank you,

Mrs. de Graaf, but do you mind if I stay until Leo comes out of recovery? I'd like to see him before I leave."

"Oh, yes, of course."

Shortly thereafter, a nurse notified them that Leo had awakened. Silvie entered the Intensive Care Unit alone. At the center of what seemed like a metallic forest with hanging drip bags and blinking monitors, Leo lay covered to the chest in a narrow bed. His fair skin, an unhealthy white, seemed blanched of all blood. His eyes were closed. His long blond lashes made a feathered shadow on his cheeks, and the sight sent a swift flood of memories coursing through Silvie's mind, as she recalled the moment she first held him: Leo the baby, the little boy, the adolescent, images from his childhood to the present.

She noticed a dark bruise across the swollen knuckles of his right hand. "Leo," she said softly.

His eyes opened and he blinked a few times. He turned his head toward her. "Hey, Mamma."

His voice sounded hoarse, but Silvie felt a surge of relief just to hear him speak. She gently clasped his bruised hand with both of hers and fought back tears.

"Is Stephanie all right?"

Silvie nodded. "Yes, she's fine. She and Sebastian Morrow are waiting outside."

"Good." He swallowed with difficulty. "My throat feels sore." He licked his lips and smiled wanly. "I had a fight, Mamma, and it looks like I lost."

Silvie smiled as a tear ran down her face. "It was an unfair fight, darling Leo. But by the looks of your hand, you did the best you could."

"I was so afraid for Stephanie, I hit him with everything I had. And he obviously retaliated. Then I passed out, and I don't know what happened after that."

"Stephanie called 911 and they sent an ambulance. They brought you here to Methodist Hospital." Silvie explained about the wound, the loss of blood, and the surgery. "The only thing to do now is rest and recover. The doctor told me young guys like you are healing machines." She leaned forward and kissed him gently on the forehead. "Would you like to see Stephanie and Sebastian?"

"Stephanie first and then Dr. Morrow."

As Silvie left to get Stephanie, the nurse told her to keep the visits brief—five minutes only. While Stephanie visited with Leo, Silvie waited outside in the hallway with Sebastian. "It reassured me to talk to him, but I'm so afraid he might get an infection," she confided.

He put an arm protectively about her shoulders. "Well, we'll fight fear with prayer and take it one day at a time."

"Sebastian, Leo is such a good person. Why do you think God let that man attack him?"

Sebastian scratched his head. "Who can say? I don't think for an instant that God wanted someone to attack Leo, but God allows people free will, even malicious ones. His ways are marvelous, and I know He can bring good out of evil."

"I can't imagine what good can come of this," Silvie muttered.

When Stephanie emerged from ICU, Sebastian said, "Wait here, Stephanie. When I come out, I'll walk you down to the entrance and make sure you get a cab."

When Sebastian entered, he was disappointed to find Leo sound asleep. His face resembled a mask, its pasty-white relieved only by the bluish circles under his eyes. The chilly room, the harsh fluorescent lights, and the lateness of the hour made the scene surreal. As he watched over the injured boy, he felt an icy cold in the pit of his stomach. Sebastian sighed. The opposition had truly raised its head again. The principalities of this fallen world, so rich in malice and evil, knew exactly how to single out the innocent and desecrate the beautiful. The battle never ended.

He had to admit to himself, despite his confident assurance to Silvie, he too wondered what good could come out of this. The cold room and the maze of medical equipment brought back unpleasant memories of Mary Catherine's hospital stay the previous year. Even though she had never taken care of herself, she had lived most of her allotted threescore and ten, but Leo's adult life was just beginning. Just as in Mary Catherine's case, Sebastian dearly wished he could help. At the moment, the only thing he knew to do was to whisper a simple prayer for Leo's complete and rapid healing.

At 2:15 a.m., the nurse in charge told Silvie she could stay, but it might be best for her to get some rest and come back in the morning when Leo would be awake. "He'll be fine tonight; he'll sleep most of the time. We're keeping a close watch on him; he won't be alone for an instant." Sebastian agreed with the nurse and convinced Silvie to get some rest. After Silvie gave the nurse her mobile phone number, they left.

They put Stephanie in a cab and Silvie made her promise to text them when she got back to her dorm room. Sebastian asked Silvie if she was going to drive home. "No, I'm going to Leo's garage apartment in the Heights. I've got a key. Sebastian, you're welcome to spend what's left of the night there. He's got a big sofa you could sleep on. You can follow me there."

"Well, if you don't mind, I will. Thank you. I don't want to doze off on the way to Bullinger."

⁂

Sebastian's deep sleep was troubled by a nightmare. In the dream, Mary Catherine sat straight up in her hospital bed, and pointed an accusatory finger at him. "*You*—you did it. It's *your* fault the healer sent a goddess. Did you know that? A goddess in a red gown came flying through the window that day and touched me. Any desire for alcohol left me in the instant." She threw back her head and cackled.

"You, a Roman Catholic, a so-called Christian, resorted to witchcraft. But guess what—it didn't work. The goddess chased out the demon, and then he returned with seven others more powerful than he! Hee-hee-heeeeee! It might as well have been a curse—I only got worse and worse." Her eyes narrowed and she lowered her voice. "Witchcraft, Sebastian, witchcraft! It's all your fault!"

He woke in a sweat, heart hammering, confused for a moment by his strange surroundings and the sound of a woman's voice. Mary Catherine? Then he realized it was Silvie speaking on the phone to her daughter Kristin, and the events of the previous night all came back to him. As Silvie told Kristin what had happened, Sebastian tried to calm himself. It was only a dream, only a dream. Despite the fact that he had long since confessed it to a priest, the dream brought back all the old feelings of guilt and remorse.

Feeling stiff from his night on the sofa, he stretched and got up, still completely dressed. He went to the bathroom, peed, and washed his face. When Silvie ended the phone conversation, he said, "Let's get something to eat. There's a great kosher deli about five blocks from here."

Fifteen minutes later, they got a table by the window at Sol's Deli and ordered lox and bagels with coffee. The place was already filling up with Heights residents. Sebastian poured a generous amount of cream into his coffee and drank. He closed his eyes and murmured, "Ah, that may just revive me!"

Silvie nodded and sipped her coffee, too. Her blue-violet eyes, tinged with worry and sadness, were underscored by plum-colored smudges of fatigue, and deep lines ringed her mouth. She was still the flaxen-haired Nordic queen, but one whose only son had been felled in battle. As Sebastian rested his eyes on her, he wished he had the power to bring it all to rights—to restore the son and bring gladness back to the eyes of the mother.

"Did you get in touch with St. Mark's?"

"Yes," he said, "I left a message at the rectory last night. They'll probably call in the retired organist who lives in town. But who's going to mind the bookshop while you're with Leo in Houston?"

"Kristin will take a couple days off from school. She's coming to the hospital to see Leo today. She'll stop by the house on the way from Austin and pack a bag for me with clothes and toiletries. I also have a part-time employee, Margie Ramble. She's a retired school librarian who usually helps on weekends and during the Christmas rush. Hopefully, she'll be able to work full-time for a week or two—however long it takes for Leo to get discharged from the hospital."

The waiter brought their food, and Sebastian's mouth watered just looking at the lox, cream cheese, the red onion slices and the sprinkling of capers on his onion bagel. He squeezed a little fresh lemon juice on the lox and then dug in. Silvie came close to matching his intensity, and he was glad to see her eat well. She was going to need all her strength in the days to come.

After a speechless interlude while they both sated their hunger and drew energy from the food and hot coffee, Sebastian offered to help out at the bookshop if needed. "I'm still unemployed, you know. And I'll be glad to go back with you to the hospital after we eat."

"Thank you, Sebastian. Could you just stay until Kristin comes? She'll probably be here around midday."

"Sure. Leo was asleep when I went in last night. I'd like to talk to him a little today."

Sebastian left his car at Leo's place and rode with Silvie in the blue Volvo. "At least I can spare you the cost of parking," she said. "We'll come back at lunchtime."

"I can drive Leo's Jeep back to the apartment," he suggested. "If we leave it in the medical center garage much longer, you may have to pay the parking fee in installments."

"Good idea." As Silvie drove the fifteen-minute route to the hospital, she realized she knew very little about the man she had just spent the night with. She glanced at him. "Do you have children, Sebastian?"

"One child—my daughter Helen. She's thirty-two."

"Does she live here in Houston?"

"No, she and her husband live in Lancaster, Pennsylvania. She's a veterinarian."

"And Mrs. Sebastian Morrow—her mother?" Silvie smiled and gave him a sidelong glance.

"Mary Catherine died last year in June."

"Oh, I'm sorry! What happened?" Silvie blurted in surprise. "She couldn't have been very old."

"Well, she was sixty-four, eight years older than I am. She had a stroke and went into a coma. But she was an alcoholic with a history of poor health in her later years."

Perhaps it was the fatigue that lowered his guard, or the shared intimacy of the night they had endured together, but he wanted Silvie to know who he was—he decided to trust her with his story. He told her more about his personal life than he had ever told anyone else. "We separated when Helen was five. My daughter and I moved to Houston from Baltimore, so I could get a doctorate."

"So you were a single father?"

"Well, yes and no. I raised Helen on my own, and we lived apart from her mother, but Mary Catherine and I never divorced." Sebastian smiled and shrugged. "The consequences of a Catholic upbringing."

She turned left and merged onto I-10 into light Sunday-morning traffic, the same route Sebastian had taken the night his house was moved. "Did Helen see her mother often?"

"Not really. Maybe twice a year. I wouldn't leave her alone with Mary Catherine. I couldn't trust my wife, so Helen and I visited her together at Christmas and sometimes for a week or two in the summer. One summer, Mary Catherine came to Houston to visit us, but I wouldn't let her drink at all while she was here, so she never returned."

"It must have been difficult for Helen."

"In more ways than one. When we left Baltimore, Mary Catherine's parents, her father in particular, stopped speaking to me. They also cut Helen off. My parents were gone, so she lost the only grandparents she had. Thankfully, Aunt Nancy and Uncle Bear stood in the gap. We spent many holidays with them out in the country."

Silvie took the downtown exit, threaded her way through the urban maze, and turned south onto Main. As they neared the hospital, her stomach muscles tightened, and her blood pressure rose. "I'm so worried about Leo." He had always seemed too good for this world, and now it was as though all her fears for him had materialized. She had lost her husband two years ago, and she would do whatever she could to make sure she didn't lose her son. "I wish I could wave a magic wand and make him well."

"I know about that impulse. I tried it with Mary Catherine, and I can assure you it doesn't work."

Silvie turned her head and gave him a questioning glance. "What do you mean?"

Sebastian told her how he had asked a distance healer to help his wife. "At the time, I didn't understand healers like that practice a form of witchcraft. They project a very real force. It seemed to help Mary Catherine at first, and then her alcoholism took an even greater hold on her. Consulting the healer was one of my worst mistakes, and one of the several ways I failed Mary Catherine. I actually had a nightmare about it last night." Sebastian shook his head. "So, from my own bitter experience, I know the one way we can help Leo, aside from medical treatments, is through prayer. There is no other."

Although his words were sincerely and earnestly spoken, Silvie had her doubts. She had been raised in the Lutheran Church, but there seemed nothing dynamic or transforming about the Christianity she knew. Did any power lie in whispered words, in pious formulas? Or did those prayers simply comfort those who prayed? Leo needed stronger medicine than that. She didn't tell Sebastian, but if she had to bet, she'd put all her money on physicians and modern medicine. Never mind the prayers.

CHAPTER 34

THE LIE, MAGNIFIED

Abbie stood at her studio window on the second floor of Berman Hall, lighted cigarette in hand, to watch the mob. Had Ferris Duck entered and beheld the voluminous cloud of smoke, he would have guessed the piano was on fire. But there was no danger of discovery, as Abbie well knew. Duck, that slimeball extraordinaire, had been summoned across campus to an "emergency meeting" with the president, the provost, the dean, and all department heads.

"Tell me," she muttered to herself, "where are the people of character, courage, loyalty, and integrity?" Why didn't one of the whole craven crew stand up for Sebastian? At least Abe Shaheen had tipped the scale when the panel stalemated at 2-2. Despite the sharp pain in her hand, Abbie ground out the cigarette in a styrofoam coffee cup with force, wishing the cup were the forehead of an administrator—any administrator, she didn't care. She immediately lit another cigarette, her fifth in a row, and took a deep drag.

Righteous Social Justice had invaded the campus and Major Absenteeism had followed in its train. Very few students had shown up for classes—not a single one of her piano students. They were all out there milling around in the mob or enjoying the spectacle of a massive demonstration (with TV coverage by the major networks, no less) at sleepy little Omega U.

And spectacle it was. The focal point was a speaker's platform set up near the lake. Standing at the podium, a young black man revved up the mob's energy, shouting slogans into the microphone. The raucous, eager, sign-waving crowd of maybe five hundred young people responded. They raised their fists, waved placards, and chanted, "*Take down the racist clown! Morrow has got to go,*" in a communal frenzy.

The crowd of students was ringed by campus police, three mounted state troopers, television cameras and crews, and reporters. A few stalwart music students counterprotested. They had made their own signs—*We want Sebastian Bach!* She was proud of them for the effort, but they covered as much space and caused as much disruption as a pimple on a giant's ass. Abbie counted six buses parked at the edge of the road, evidence that many protestors had been transported to the site. The demonstration was organized by an off-campus organization, Students for a Racist-Free America. Their signs were legion.

In principle, Abbie agreed with them. She loathed racism, but this whole uproar was based on a lie. The student's charge of racial discrimination was simply a ploy to protect herself and manipulate the system. Abbie's anger and dismay grew minute by minute; even chain smoking didn't calm her down. How easy it was to smear an innocent man. Sebastian hadn't done anything wrong; that had been evident when the faculty hearing panel had ruled in his favor. Then Luther "Spineless Wonder" Reynolds, had caved in to pressure and reversed the decision. Now the case had to go before the Board of Regents for the final ruling. Today's demonstration was meant to sway public opinion and intimidate the administration. Unless the Board of Regents had more backbone than the campus administrators, Sebastian would be fired.

She opened the window and turned her portable fan on high speed to clear out some of the smoke. There was a knock at the door. Abbie didn't bother to extinguish her cigarette before she opened it. "Come in, Miles."

"Good Lord, Abbie!" He waved his hands at the smelly cloud and coughed. "You must be smoking two at a time. We're going to rename you Chimney Goldberg."

"My mother wouldn't approve, but it's not a bad idea. Smoking gives me something to do. Practicing is out—I can't concentrate with that going on." She gestured at the window. "And I haven't taught at all today; I had three no-shows."

"Likewise. Too bad there's not a pub in Berman Hall. I could use a pint." He walked over to the window to get some fresh air. "You have a great view of Much Ado about Nothing."

She joined him and waved her cigarette hand at the shouting crowd. "There we have the power of the lie, magnified by a mob and recorded by the salivating media."

"All to bring a just man down."

Abbie nodded. "The world is so reassuringly consistent in that regard." She averted her head and blew out a cloud of smoke. "You know who's really responsible for this?"

"Alicia Borden?"

"No, she's just a young, scared girl who tried to cover her own faults. I don't think she truly foresaw what would happen, at least I hope not. She lied all right, but the real perpetrators are the administrators who didn't stop this at its inception. Duck or Dean Faul, either one could have put it to rest if they had supported Sebastian and stood up against the pressure. When that didn't happen, the panel did the right thing at the hearing. It could have stopped there, save for another administrator, our dear president, who kowtowed to intimidation and reversed the ruling."

"Who do you think called out the dogs?" Miles asked, pointing his thumb at the mob.

"Probably Alicia's mother. She threatened to do that at the outset." Abbie tapped her ashes into the styrofoam cup.

Miles pointed. "Look at that commotion at the back of the crowd." They watched as two young black men were chased briefly by the mounted state troopers, apprehended, and arrested. "Wonder what that's all about?"

"Who knows?"

Noticing how discouraged and fatigued Miles appeared, Abbie veered off topic to ask about his main concern. "How's that little guy Simon doing?"

He shook his head. "Vomiting every day. They've tested him for diabetes, leukemia, parasites, food allergies, and illnesses I've never heard of, and they still don't have a diagnosis. The stress is wearing us out."

She had raised two sons, and she knew how upsetting it was to have a sick child. In a low, comforting voice, she tried to reassure him, "The doctors will figure it out, Miles. Try to be patient." She sighed. "Well, to return to the subject at hand—do you think we'll get Sebastian back?"

"We may know sooner rather than later. Betsy Bloom just told me the Board of Regents was supposed to rule on his case next week, but due to this demonstration and all the media coverage, they've scheduled an emergency meeting for Wednesday, day after tomorrow. Betsy informed Sebastian today."

"Sounds like the mob is the piper, and the Board is going to dance." Abbie dragged on her cigarette. "Doesn't bode well."

"No, not at all."

Betsy Bloom called Sebastian at home and notified him about the Board of Regents' emergency meeting on Wednesday. Then she described the ongoing demonstration on campus. "Watch the evening news if you want to see it. All the students are out there, but whoever organized this brought in a whole lot of outsiders, too—six busloads. Dr. Morrow, you gotta be proud—the orchestra, except for Pinocchio, is counter-demonstrating for you. I'm dying to go out there myself, but I can't. I'm alone in the office and I have to man the fort."

"Thanks for letting me know, Betsy. Oh, and could you send me a scan of the minutes from the search committee meeting on May thirteenth? I'm going to need it for the Board of Regents' hearing."

"Will do." Evidently in a chatty mood, she continued, "When you left, Dr. Morrow, you pulled the plug on peace. It went down the tubes, and now we got chaos here. The students hate the grad student who's teaching your theory courses, and the orchestra is talking mutiny. They don't think Q has the musical chops to conduct a kazoo band."

Sebastian laughed.

"We sure miss you. And you're not the only one; Mr. Washington has been out so much with laryngitis, we had to hire a sub for him. I opened his studio for the new guy and got creeped out by that ugly wooden bust on the piano—the one Q brought back from Brazil. It's a man with a big open mouth and red threads wrapped around its neck." She laughed. "At first I thought it was a voodoo doll. Ha! Actually, it wouldn't surprise me a bit if Q's squeaky-clean exterior is a front for some real kinky weirdness. He gives off strange vibes. I should know—I'm the one who's around him the most. Of course," she laughed, "I only get to tell the bald truth when he's out of the office. Well, come back to us soon, Dr. Morrow!"

The remark about Q surprised Sebastian, but he smiled as he clicked off the phone. Betsy Bloom was the home of unadulterated honesty. She always managed to cheer him up.

Then, with a sense of urgency, he phoned his lawyer.

Martin checked his schedule. "Sorry, Sebastian, I have to be in court on Wednesday. There's no way I can appear at the meeting in person or by video conference. But if you can meet me here at my office tomorrow afternoon, we can go over your presentation for the hearing."

They agreed to meet at 4:00. Martin continued, "I'll contact the Board of Regents to let them know you'll testify. We can go over any other witnesses we should call tomorrow."

Sebastian told him about his new evidence.

Martin laughed. "That's great! Send me copies of everything ASAP and make enough copies for every member of the Board and anyone else who might be present—Corrotto and any attorneys. You know, Sebastian, if they have any sense, this should clinch it for you. If not, we'll sue their asses from here to Kingdom Come."

As soon as he clicked off the phone, it rang. Silvie gave him an update on Leo, who was still stable, but feeling a little worse. The surgeon, Dr. Heinz, had reassured her that such a downturn was expected for the first three days after surgery on a perforated colon. The body had to deal with the toxins released from the rupture, but soon the antibiotic would kick in and work its magic. If all went well, Leo might be able to leave the hospital after another week to ten days.

For a Monday, Sebastian thought, it was a very good day. Let the mob demonstrate all they wanted. The important thing was that despite the downturn, Leo was stable. For himself, the change of date for the Board of Regents hearing suited him just fine. Let it be resolved sooner rather than later. If he got reinstated, he could finish out the last five weeks of the semester. It was more complicated if he got fired. First, he would have to wait out the results of a lawsuit. If he won, he would have to decide whether or not he wanted to return to Omega. If he lost . . . hell, he didn't want to think about it.

Anyway, at this point, he was getting way ahead of himself. His immediate job was to make copies of his new evidence. But first, he had to call Miles.

Miles answered quickly. "Sebastian! You're the subject of our conversation. Abbie and I are here in this smoky tobacco den she calls her studio. We've been watching the campus drama—the demonstration inspired by you and the scourge of our time, Political Correctness. In capital letters, of course."

"Well, my friend, I think I've found the key to shutting down all the PC."

"And what might that be?"

Sebastian told him about the new evidence.

"Ha! Well blow me down! That's perfect—why didn't we think of it before?"

"Exactly. Miles, could you testify at the Board of Regents' meeting, Wednesday at 4:30? It'll be on campus in Goodwin Hall."

"With pleasure. I want to see the looks on their faces."

CHAPTER 35

GOLD

On Sunday evening, in addition to his morning and evening prayers, Sebastian had begun a three-day, water-only fast. Having never tried such a thing before, he had no idea of what effect, if any, it would have. He prayed diligently for Leo's recovery and for himself, that his accusers would know the truth—he had not discriminated against Alicia Borden.

On Tuesday afternoon, before his appointment with Katzberger, he visited Leo and Silvie at the hospital. Leo, treated with powerful antibiotics, was still in ICU, monitored around the clock. He could only have liquids, and he had considerable pain and swelling in the abdomen. "I'm going to have a very impressive scar," he told Sebastian, "a permanent reminder of my brief but dramatic knife fight. I guess you could say I'm not your typical organist."

Sebastian laughed. "Yeah, not too many of them are street fighters."

He spoke very softly. "I had a few battles with bullies in school when I was younger, but this time I learned something. When one goes to a knife fight, one should bring a knife."

"Good point."

"Although Stephanie managed pretty well with a violin case."

"That she did," Sebastian agreed with a grin. "What a girl."

Leo nodded. "I know how to pick 'em, don't I?"

"You sure do," Sebastian laughed. "Well, Leo, you're minus some blood and a chunk of intestine, but I'm glad your sense of humor is still intact."

Leo smiled wanly, blinked slowly a few times, and fell asleep. Sebastian whispered to Silvie, "I'll be glad when he's up and about with his old energy. While he's sleeping, let's get some coffee downstairs before I go."

In the ground floor cafeteria, sparsely populated at 2:30 in the afternoon, they sat at a window table. Still fasting, Sebastian drank a glass of sparkling water, while Silvie worked her way through a yogurt and berry parfait. He told Silvie about the new hearing date set by the Board of Regents.

"Tomorrow? Are you prepared for it?"

Sebastian sipped his bubbly drink. "Well, I will be shortly. The demonstration on campus and the adverse publicity scared them. They want to get this resolved as soon as possible, so I'm meeting with my attorney later this afternoon to prepare."

"By the way, I saw pictures of the demonstration on the Monday night news, and there was an article about it in today's *Chronicle*." Silvie smiled. "Who'd have thought you'd cause so much trouble?" She ate a bite of the parfait.

Sebastian nodded. "Yep. I tend to go whole-hog."

She smiled and stirred her coffee. "Do you think all the publicity will influence the Board against you?"

"That is very likely the point, but I hope they remain impartial. I grew up believing that mob justice is not the American way. Whoever screams the loudest is not necessarily right—I mean that's why we have laws. The thing is, I have new ev—"

"Oh, I forgot to tell you!" Silvie interrupted. "The Houston police called Stephanie today, and asked her to make an appointment to come down to the station. They rounded up a couple of suspects for her to identify. Guess where they caught them."

"I have no idea."

"They arrested them yesterday at the Omega demonstration. They were pickpocketing people in the crowd, and they apparently fit her description in some way."

"Does she think she can identify them?" Sebastian drank the last of his water.

"She's not sure, but she said she'd call me once she's seen them."

"Well, keep me informed." Sebastian glanced at his watch. He really didn't want to leave Silvie, but he had to meet with Martin. "I guess I'd better go now. The appointment with my attorney is at four. I'll try to come by tomorrow evening after the hearing."

"I'll walk you to the entrance."

"No, sit—you haven't even finished your parfait." He rose, and hesitated for just a moment. Then he leaned over and kissed Silvie gently on the lips. "That's something I've wanted to do for a long, long time." She lifted her face to his, and Sebastian thought the ocean itself had not the beauty or depth of her blue-violet eyes.

Without a word, she grasped his hand and held it to her cheek. With that simple gesture, a whole new horizon unfolded before him: a fresh beginning with the promise of peace, an end to his interminable days in the howling wilderness. It unlocked the gates of exile and pointed him home, exactly the place he had so long sought. He kissed the top of her head and inhaled her fresh, sweet scent. With the greatest reluctance, he forced himself to leave her there alone.

Gold is remarkable and rare, the noblest of metals. Lustrous and beautiful, it is unique among the elements. It is one of the most stable metals, virtually indestructible, and it never rusts or tarnishes. Ductile and malleable as no other metal, a single ounce can be drawn into a wire five miles long, or it can be hammered into sheets so thin as to be translucent. Like the sun, gold symbolizes the sacred, the ineffable. On the earthly plane, it is the symbol of kings.

In the elevator on the way back to the Intensive Care Unit, Silvie fingered the gold wedding band she wore on a chain. With Leo hospitalized, she had kept the ring close as a comfort, a way of summoning Edward's presence. But now she felt uncomfortable wearing it. She unclasped the chain and put it and the ring in her pocket. Time to lay the past to rest.

Suffused with a deep, unaccustomed calm, her thoughts revolved around Sebastian. Though she relived his kiss like a smitten schoolgirl, in her innermost core she rested in an ark of certainty: her absolute trust in Sebastian. She had never felt such a degree of confidence in any man, not even her husband.

She recalled Sebastian's confession about his alcoholic wife that first morning after Leo's surgery. In truth, the story had jarred her, but it was his way of opening up and laying everything bare. Even in the absence of hope, he had been faithful to Mary Catherine for decades. Though his every attempt to help his wife had failed, he had kept trying all those years. Silvie personally knew no case comparable, nor could she think of any other example of such loyalty and patience. He was handsome and talented, but in fidelity and virtue, he was gold.

Leo's eyes were closed when she entered the room. She wasn't sure if he was sleeping or not. She gazed thoughtfully at her only son.

Somehow, with his unerring instincts, he had recognized Sebastian's qualities from the very beginning. She smiled as she recalled Leo's words when she had asked him to invite Sebastian for lunch. *Excellent idea, Mamma. Now you're on the right track.*

He opened his eyes, so like her own. Silvie reached out and smoothed the hair from his forehead. "Were you sleeping?"

He shook his head. She smiled broadly at him. "I just had coffee with Sebastian. His final hearing takes place tomorrow. He wanted to stay longer, but he had to meet with his lawyer to prepare."

Leo nodded, but his eyes were troubled. "Mamma, the pain in my abdomen is worse, and I'm nauseated. I've been having chills and then feeling hot."

Worried, but trying to keep her face impassive, she simply said, "Let me get the nurse." She walked to the nurses' station and told Sean O'Leary, the day nurse. Sean, whose outward appearance belied his name, was a small man, with black hair, fine features, and dark brown eyes.

He came immediately to Leo's bedside and checked his temperature and pulse. "It's 101 and his heart rate has increased," he told Silvie. "Leo, let's get a reading on your blood pressure." He logged the results and said, "I'm going to let Dr. Heinz know." He walked quickly back to the nurses' station to contact the surgeon.

After a few minutes, the nurse returned carrying an empty vial. "Dr. Heinz ordered a blood sample." He quickly drew the blood and took the vial away. Leo sat up, ashen-faced, and with a note of panic in his voice, said, "Mamma, I'm gonna throw up!"

Silvie grabbed a plastic bin from his bedside table and held it in front of him just in time. He leaned forward and threw up a stream of pinkish-tinged liquid. He'd had nothing solid to eat since the stabbing. He closed his eyes, took a breath, and then gagged and vomited again.

Sean returned with a fresh drip bag and a damp cloth to wipe Leo's face. He noticed the contents of the plastic bin, and said, "I'll take that, Mrs. de Graaf." Leo drank some water to rinse out his mouth and spat it into the bin. Then he wiped his face and laid back with a pinched look. Sean changed out the half-empty drip bag for a new, full one.

"What's that?" Silvie asked.

"This is an antibiotic, but more focused to a specific type of bacteria than the other one, which was broad-spectrum."

Silvie pondered it all and wondered if an infection had set in. She knew Dr. Heinz made his rounds between seven and eight, and she intended to be there when he came by. In the meantime, she smoothed the hair off Leo's clammy forehead and told him to rest. She tried to keep her fear and worry at bay with a self-encouragement litany: *The nurse wasn't at all panicked. The doctor will handle it with the right drugs. Leo is young and strong, a healing machine. Modern medicine can cure just about everything. It will be all right. It will be all right.* Repeating the words with growing intensity at Leo's bedside, she unknowingly davened like a Jew praying at the Wailing Wall.

Leo lay back and closed his eyes. Silvie tried to pass the time by reading a *deckare*, a Swedish detective novel, but she couldn't concentrate. She gazed at her sleeping son and wondered if his body had become a battleground where every passing minute, swarming bacteria festered and multiplied. She glanced up at the antidote, the plastic bag holding the new antibiotic. She watched the drops fall in a slow, steady rhythm. All her hope focused on that clear liquid. Surely the medicine would win the silent warfare.

That evening, Dr. Heinz confirmed Silvie's fears. "Yes, he has an infection, but it's not out of control." He read the worry in Silvie's eyes. "We're on top of it, Ms. de Graaf. The antibiotic should take care of it. Try not to worry."

"But I thought he was past the risk. Why is this happening now?"

"A lot of time transpired from the moment Leo was stabbed until we got him into the operating room. It was right at one hour. That was a long time for the toxins to be in his system." His kindly brown eyes gazed into hers. "We've shifted to a powerful drug now. It can kill the bacteria, but it takes time. We'll monitor him very closely and we'll see how he is in twenty-four hours."

After the doctor left, Silvie tried to ignore her fears by reading the novel. At some point she fell asleep with the book in her hand. She awoke to find the night nurse, Brenda, recording Leo's vital signs.

"Ms. de Graaf, you should go home and rest. If there's any change for the worse, we'll call you." A stout, middle-aged woman with a streak of white in her crinkly brown hair, she gazed at Silvie with concern in her blue eyes. "He'll probably sleep through the night. You can come back early tomorrow morning."

Silvie rose, stretched, and yawned. She felt bone-tired. "All right, but please call if there's a change."

CHAPTER 36

RULING

The Omega University Board of Regents consisted of nine members, but only seven were able to meet at such short notice. That number still qualified as a quorum. Chairman Bradley Andrews presided over the meeting. Present were the Vice Chairman, Elaine Tupek, and five other members, their General Counsel, Max Rehburg, as well as Provost Corrotto and a recording secretary.

Sebastian and Miles entered the conference room on the first floor of Goodwin Hall ten minutes before the hearing was scheduled to begin. The university had obviously reserved its showcase conference room for the Regents. An oblong mahogany table with cushioned chairs stood in the middle of the room. The floor was overlaid with a huge and beautifully patterned red and blue oriental rug. The bone-white walls gleamed in the bright lighting, and the three large windows revealed a small courtyard enclosed by a brick wall. It was landscaped with beds of purple and white chrysanthemums, ferns, and bright green hostas. At the center was a cascading fountain in a circular stone pool.

As soon as Chairman Andrews called the hearing to order and made the introductions, he got right to the point. "Dr. Morrow, the Board has read the transcript of the previous hearing. We have also read President Reynolds' dissenting opinion and his rebuttal." He paused and eyed Sebastian over his half-glasses. "Your attorney, Mr. Katzberger, informed us that you have some new evidence. Let's begin with that."

Sebastian handed out copies of two documents and one color photograph. "My attorney and I read Dr. Reynolds' decision also, and we noted that his greatest objection was over the alleged racial slur. The evidence I've handed out includes copies of two emails, one from my colleague Miles Greenfield to me, and the other from me to my daughter Helen. Both were sent on Wednesday, May thirteenth of this year. I've highlighted the dates and times. The second document contains the minutes of a search committee meeting on the same date. The photograph was taken by Mr. Greenfield, who is present today to testify.

"I would like to begin with the photograph. It's a picture of my forearm. As you can see, there are numerous red lumps on it. Those are chigger bites I got on my property in Helprin County. Miles took the picture just prior to the start of a search committee meeting in Berman Hall here on campus."

"Excuse me, Dr. Morrow, but what has this to do with anything? Please don't waste our time."

"I assure you, Chairman Andrews, this is highly relevant."

"I certainly hope so, for your sake." Andrews frowned and pushed his half-glasses higher on his nose. "All right, continue."

"Chigger bites, as you probably know, itch horribly at times. And just as that meeting ended, the itching flared up again. I had numerous bites on both arms and legs. As Miles and I walked out into the hallway, I scratched my arm and complained loudly. I said, 'I *hate* those damn chiggers.'"

Sebastian gazed at the Board members to gauge their reactions, but he got only puzzled looks and silence.

"And your point?" asked the chairman.

"That was the moment we passed the two black students in the hall. They misheard what I said—they thought I used the N-word. The whole misunderstanding was based on the fact that *chiggers* sounds like, well, the N-word.

"I asked Miles to send me the photo that day, so I could forward it to my daughter who lives in Pennsylvania. The first document shows Miles' email to me at the top and my email to my daughter below." Sebastian paused while they read.

Sebastian,
Here's the photo I took of your war wounds. Don't go too heavy on the Benadryl.
Miles

Dear Helen,
It's already chigger season in Texas! I found out the hard way. I thought it started in June, so I didn't use any bug spray when I went outside. The photo shows 37 bites just on my forearm, but I'm covered in bites everywhere. I'm plastering myself in calamine lotion and chugging Benadryl to get relief from the itching. Believe me, I won't make the same mistake next year. I'll stock up on bug spray in April. Hope all is well with you and Kieran.
Love, Dad

"The second document includes the roll and minutes from the search committee meeting the same day. I highlighted the date, the time, my name and Miles Greenfield's name."

Bradley Andrews said, "I have some questions for Mr. Greenfield."

Miles rose.

"Did you take this photograph?"

"Yes, with my iPhone."

"What was the purpose of the search committee?"

"We were seeking a new department head after Dr. Woolrich, uh, well . . . retired."

"Do you remember Dr. Morrow's remark in the hallway?"

"Yes, that is exactly what he said."

"And what was your reaction?"

Miles' ruddy cheeks burned a deeper red. "I laughed, and then I said something like, 'Those beastly little buggers,' which could have been misinterpreted as well."

"Thank you, Mr. Greenfield. Please have a seat." Bradley Andrews turned to Sebastian. "Dr. Morrow, why have you waited so long to present this evidence?"

"Because I never connected it to Alicia Borden's accusation. Just last week my daughter asked me for more pictures of my new home. She mentioned this photo to me as the last one I had sent her back in May. I'd forgotten all about it, but then it suddenly dawned on me what had happened. I remembered what I said in the hallway. It was just a fleeting remark with no significance other than to vent my irritation. The chigger bites healed, and I forgot about it. When Alicia Borden made the accusation four months later, my remark about chigger bites certainly didn't come to mind. I honestly thought Alicia and her friend had fabricated the story about a racial slur to strengthen her case for discrimination.

"I did wonder why both students were so adamant that I had used a racial slur when I knew absolutely that I had not. But this explains everything. They misheard what I actually said and believed I had used the N-word. It also clarifies why Alicia said I spoke loudly. That was true; I did speak loudly in frustration at the horrible itching. But, as stated in the previous hearing, I would have been stupid and foolhardy to shout out a racial slur in a hall full of witnesses. That is not what happened. I made an innocent statement that was misinterpreted."

"Do you have any questions, Mr. Rehburg?" Bradley Andrews glanced at the General Counsel.

"Why, yes, I do." Max Rehburg's bushy black mustache couldn't hide his oily smile or the large gap between his yellowing front teeth. He stood up and unfolded himself to the height of at least six-seven, Sebastian estimated. *All the better to intimidate.*

He ran a hand through his thick black hair and lanced Sebastian with small, pale eyes of indeterminate color. "Dr. Morrow, what strikes me about this so-called new evidence is how convenient, how pat it is. Your memory of it comes just prior to this hearing, which will decide your future at Omega University. How timely." He let the words hang in the air.

"I see how the students could have misunderstood what you said—that is, if you said it at all." He gazed at the Regents and then again at Sebastian. "You have given us a photo of chigger bites on someone's arm." He smiled. "You see, we don't really know if it's your arm." He tapped a pen three times on the table and then continued, "You have given us two emails which prove that Miles Greenfield sent you the picture, and you forwarded it to your daughter. The search committee minutes prove that you were working in Berman Hall on May thirteenth. But none of that actually proves you made the statement in the hall, 'I hate those damn chiggers.' You could just as easily have said, 'I hate those damn—'" He broke off abruptly to let the unsaid word resonate in their minds. Rehburg showed his yellow teeth in yet another smile and said pleasantly, "Quite a clever defense, Dr. Morrow. Isn't that your strategy?"

Sebastian drew in a deep breath and exhaled it. "First of all, Mr. Rehburg, my testimony is true—I don't need a clever strategy. Secondly,

I know I can't prove my statement conclusively without a video or audio recording. But given the preponderance of the evidence which occurred that day, as well as my untarnished record at Omega, with never even a hint of racial discrimination, I think it reasonable for the Board to believe I'm telling the truth. I've certainly shown more proof than the plaintiff, who, by the way, bears the burden of proof, and who has a compelling reason to lie. And as for timing, please remember it was she who waited four months to lodge a complaint."

Sebastian dropped his gaze momentarily to the shining, dark surface of the mahogany table, and then he lifted his head and met the eyes of each person in turn, first Max Rehburg and then each regent, resting his gaze finally on Bradley Andrews. Standing straight, he spoke with a firm and measured tone, "I'll say this one more time, and I swear by God that I'm telling the truth: I did not use a racial slur on May thirteenth. I am innocent of the charges against me. I rest my case."

Following Sebastian's testimony, he, Miles, and Provost Corrotto left the conference room. No one other than the Regents, their legal counsel, and the secretary was allowed to be present during the deliberations. In the anteroom, Sebastian and Miles sat side by side in comfortable chairs where they also had a view of the courtyard and fountain. Corrotto continued out into the hallway. They could see him through the glass door, pacing slowly and talking on his mobile phone.

Gesturing at Corrotto, Miles said, "Every time I see him, he looks less human and more tortoise."

"I have to agree. The bad thing about tortoises is they have very small brains, but exceptionally long life spans."

Miles nodded. "He could be 150 years old."

"At least. It may be the vegan diet: grass, leafy greens, and malice."

"If that's the key to longevity," Miles stated, "I'm ready to die young."

Sebastian laughed. "Miles, thank you for coming to testify, but it's not necessary for you to stay."

"Bollocks. I'm not leaving you alone with the reptile—I'm here for the duration, mate. And I should say, you made a brilliant case for yourself in there. Well done. If they don't exonerate you, they're either daft or thick as pig shit."

For a while, they sat silently and watched the busy fountain sending up its cheerful spray of water. Then, to keep his mind off himself, Sebastian told Miles about Leo de Graaf's stabbing and hospitalization. "He's an excellent organist, and I'm very fond of him. Abbie and I heard him play a preparatory recital for a competition this fall, just before they suspended me. He's only twenty years old, and he won third place competing against organists ten years older."

"What's his prognosis?"

"It's a bit dicey. The intestine has been repaired, but there's the risk of infection, so they're keeping him in ICU. So far, so good, and this is the fourth day. Hopefully, all will be well. I'm going to visit him this evening."

And then, knowing Miles was a friend he could trust, and perhaps because his defenses were worn down by the repeated accusations thrown against him, Sebastian began to unload his tightly held secrets.

"Did I tell you my wife died last summer?"

Miles raised his eyebrows. "No. You mean your ex-wife?"

"No, my wife. She was an alcoholic. We lived separately, but we never divorced."

"Oh. So you weren't an eligible bachelor after all."

"Not gay either."

When Miles laughed, Sebastian said, "Yeah, I know people suspected it. I haven't been interested in anyone—until now."

Miles folded his arms across his chest. "Ah, and who might that be?"

"Leo's mother, Silvie de Graaf. They came to my recital at Frankau Hall. You might remember them, both Scandinavian types, tall, good-looking with white-blond hair and blue eyes."

"Is she a musician also?"

"No, she owns a bookshop in Bullinger. You know, Miles, I never thought I would want another relationship ever again. But, amazingly, now I do."

"Well, blimey, St. Sebastian, your days of living like a monk may be swiftly coming to an end."

Sebastian smiled. "But it's complicated by this situation. If I lose my job, how can I support a wife?"

"Sounds like she's doing a bang-up job supporting herself, exactly like my Julia with her catering business. And honestly, Sebastian, if the necessity arises, an excellent musician like you will find another position, even if it takes time. If you've latched onto a good woman after all these years, don't let anything get in the way."

Sebastian noticed the dark circles under Miles' eyes, and he suddenly remembered the cause of his friend's fatigue. "Is Simon better now? Abbie told me he'd been ill."

"No, he's not. He's been vomiting almost every day since the beginning of the fall. They've tested him for everything imaginable, but they haven't been able to diagnose him. He's lost a quarter of his body weight. Julia and I are ready to tear out our hair."

"I'm very sorry to hear it."

"And then at work, it seems like the whole department is falling apart. After you were suspended, Philip Washington got laryngitis and hasn't been able to shake it off for two months. He can't teach or perform. He's never experienced anything like it in his life."

"Betsy Bloom told me. And Abbie has got shooting pains in her hands. Sometimes it's so bad she can't play."

"Really? She hasn't mentioned it to me."

"No, she's a stoic, that one."

Their conversation ended abruptly when the conference room

door opened, and Vice Chairman Elaine Tupek announced, "Dr. Morrow, we've reached a decision. Please come in." She beckoned to Provost Corrotto. Surprised by the speed of the verdict, Sebastian and Miles exchanged glances full of hope and fear, and then Sebastian rose and went to meet his fate.

CHAPTER 37

MAGIC

As he drove westward into the fading November light, Sebastian felt a deep calm come over him. The matter was resolved. He had texted Martin as soon as he left the building. In the end, the outcome was less important than the fact that he had stood his ground. Now there was no more he could do, and it was time to get his mind off himself. After he fed the animals at home, he would drive to the hospital in Houston to lend his support to Silvie and Leo.

As he crossed the Brazos, he recalled the day he threw Duck's gift, the green stone frog, out the passenger window. He was glad he had done it; he imagined it lying on the bottom of the river in mud and darkness. A fitting place for it.

He switched on his headlights and thought about his colleagues' troubles, his friends from the music search committee. What had happened to them this fall? Miles, who had sat faithfully with him during the deliberations of the Board, had a child chronically ill with a mysterious malady. Abbie carried on without complaint, though she knew her career could be threatened by the recurring pain in her hands. And Philip's marvelous voice had been silenced by prolonged laryngitis.

Betsy Bloom had told him about poor Philip. What had she said when she entered his studio? *It creeped her out.* She had thought the ugly male bust was some kind of weird voodoo doll. He smiled.

And then his jaw dropped.

Light suddenly exploded in Sebastian's mind. With instant clarity, he realized what had happened, and the malice of it took his breath away. Ferris Duck's gifts were all handmade in Brazil. *Macumba! Brazilian magic with great evil power.* He had read about it in the exorcist's book. All the sudden illnesses suddenly made sense. He knew their origin—if he was right.

But what if he was wrong? Would Duck really go to such lengths to harm them?

There was one way to prove it. He called his friend immediately. "Miles, it's Sebastian. On the way home, I was thinking about events at Omega, and I want to ask you a question. Do you keep the wooden flute Duck gave you in your studio?"

"No, it's just a toy, really. I gave it to Simon."

Sebastian's pulse pounded in his ears. "Then I know what's wrong with your son."

"What do you mean?"

"If you trust me, Miles, do exactly as I tell you. Take the flute outside and burn it. Collect the ashes and throw them into the sewer—don't take them inside the house."

There was silence on the line. "But Simon likes it. He can play a few notes on it. And anyway, what does the flute have to do with his illness?"

"Miles, listen to me, the flute came from Brazil. Abbie's mermaid, Philip's wooden sculpture, and my green stone frog did too. We were all on the search committee. We eliminated Duck and he knew it—I'm sure Roscoe told him. I think he decided on revenge. Because of his wife, he spends a lot of time in Brazil, where black magic and witchcraft are commonly practiced. I believe Duck had those objects cursed by someone in Rio, a witch doctor probably. They've been infested with demonic power and the specific intent to do harm. That's what's causing the illnesses in Simon, Abbie, and Philip."

"Are you serious, Sebastian? You received a gift and you're not ill."

"No, because I got so angry at Duck I threw it into the Brazos River back in September."

Miles was silent.

"Witchcraft has true power, Miles—it can do great harm. I know it sounds ludicrous, but why not burn the flute and see what happens? You've spent time and money on doctors and medicines to no avail. It's a simple fix. You can always replace it with a real flute. If there's no change in Simon afterward, you can prove me a fool."

Miles spoke slowly, finding his way. "Simon's illness began in September. That's when I brought the flute home."

Sebastian waited while Miles worked it out.

"It's just so hard to believe. Could Duck really be that malicious?"

"All we know about him are the stated facts on his résumé and what he's done since he came to Omega. Who can read the heart of a man? He certainly hasn't been a friend to me," added Sebastian. "In fact, when he suspended me, his delight was plain to behold."

"If your suspicions are correct, do you think he knew exactly what effects the . . . uh, cursed objects would have?"

"I think it's likely he directed the shaman or witch doctor to curse the objects in specific ways. The ill effects seem targeted to each person's career: Abbie's hands, Philip's voice. He probably didn't expect the flute would end up in the hands of a child, but even so, it's achieved its purpose—to harm Simon is to harm you. If you had retained the flute, you might be the one vomiting."

Sebastian thought for a minute. "Maybe I'm being too harsh.

Maybe he thought it was just a prank, and he didn't expect the effects would be as dire as they are. I don't know. Maybe he thought it was risk-free revenge. He knew it would cause some sort of harm, but he would never be implicated. It's a perfect setup. If we accused him, he would deny it and call us delusional, and everyone would believe him. After all the misery he caused, he'd laugh in our faces."

"There's really no way to prove it, is there?" said Miles. "Except by the trial of fire." He blew out an explosive breath. "Well," he declared, "I'm gonna take that blasted flute outside and burn it tonight. Let's put it to the test."

"Don't forget to throw the ashes down the sewer."

"Will do, and thanks, my friend, for raising the alarm."

When Sebastian arrived home, he fed the cats and Penny, and then closed the chickens into the coop. He didn't eat, since he was still fasting, but he drank a tall glass of water. He took a quick shower, changed clothes, and then drove back to Houston to the hospital. On the way, he called Abbie and Philip.

First, because she asked immediately, he told Abbie the Board's decision, an outcome she said she'd expected. "But that's not the point of my call," Sebastian said, and hurried on to tell her his suspicions about Ferris Duck. Her skepticism was not as deep as Miles'.

After he related Betsy Bloom's "voodoo doll" comment, Abbie said, "Let me find that mermaid and look at it." She retrieved it from her cloth bag while Sebastian stayed on the line. "Oh my gosh, both wrists are so tightly bound with black threads, I can't even get my fingernail under them. That's exactly where the pains start, and then they shoot through my hands into my fingers. Ha! I never made the connection—but why would I? Who would have thought it?"

"Abbie, the reason I did is because I had an experience with the demonic in my personal life many years ago. It made me aware that such dangers exist. I've read the experiences of an exorcist and a pastor who deal with deliverance, and the exorcist specifically stated the types of sorcery with the greatest evil power are African, Haitian, and Brazilian. Brazilian black magic is called *macumba*. Those are the toughest curses to break."

"Cursed—what a diagnosis! But it's a fact that the X-rays, MRIs, and blood tests I've taken haven't shown any physical problems at all, and yet the symptoms persist. Rafa's been baffled by it."

"That's because the cause is spiritual."

"Apparently so. It will be my unadulterated pleasure to burn this infernal object," said Abbie. "I'll do it tonight. But there's one other thing I want to say. If this is true, we may not be able to bring Q to justice."

"I think not."

"Nevertheless," she added, "we have hope for retribution. In my opinion, evil people like him are stupid. He will do other things that cross the line, and in the end, his own arrogance will bring him down. I think it's just a matter of time."

Philip's voice was a scratchy whisper of its old, resonant self. Sebastian did most of the talking. He repeated Betsy's account of entering the singer's studio and her "voodoo doll" remark. Sebastian reminded Philip of the male figure's open mouth (like a singer) and the red threads tightly wound around the throat—the exact location of his inflammation and problem.

Like the others, Philip had sought medical help and found no cure, but unlike them, he had relatives in Haiti and was familiar with voodoo culture. He instantly recognized the truth. "I believe it, Sebastian," he whispered. He said he would drive to Omega that night to retrieve it from his studio and burn it. He thanked Sebastian profusely, and he wanted to talk about the whole racial discrimination incident, but Sebastian put him off. "Let's talk when you've got your voice back, Philip. There's plenty of time."

Sebastian drove on into the city in hope. Maybe, after three decades, he had begun to harvest the fruit of the demonic experience with Mary Catherine. In order to fight demons, one had to know they existed. He prayed the knowledge he had just transmitted to his friends would heal them and set them free.

CHAPTER 38

BATTLEGROUND

By late afternoon on Wednesday, Leo was sweaty, restless, and incoherent. His eyes looked panicked as he struggled to communicate, but his words spilled out like pick-up sticks, randomly, without meaning. "I yellow . . . sing tractor. Fish . . . glide metal . . . yes." He had a fever of 103, and his heart and respiration rate had steadily increased. In the meantime, his blood pressure dropped. His condition had slowly worsened. With mounting panic of her own, Silvie realized the worst-case scenario had come to pass: Leo was fighting sepsis.

To counteract the low blood pressure, Dr. Heinz ordered the medical staff to give him a shot of epinephrine. Along with the antibiotic, he added saline and blood. For the time being, that was all they could do. Before the doctor left, he told Silvie they might have to intubate Leo if he had trouble breathing. "The nurses will keep me informed."

Silvie and the medical staff watched and waited.

Sebastian arrived around eight o'clock. Silvie's face, an unnatural white, telegraphed her fear. She ran to meet him and clung to him with both arms in a viselike grip. "Sebastian, he's going downhill," she whispered. "It's sepsis. The antibiotic doesn't seem to be working the way it should. His fever went up, and he had trouble breathing. They had to—" Tears filled her eyes and she couldn't go on.

Sebastian embraced her wordlessly. He tried to appear calm, but his pulse spiked with alarm. They had intubated Leo. He lay connected to a ventilator, like a fish, hooked and dragged out of water, with his mouth open around the tube. With his eyes closed and skin pasty-white, he breathed mechanically. Three drip bags dispensed their liquids: two clear ones, the saline and the antibiotic, and the red one holding blood. They had catheterized him as well. Sebastian saw the urine bag hanging off the side of the bed.

Sepsis, the poisoning of the blood by toxins. He knew antibiotics were the only cure, and if that failed . . .

"If they can't get it under control soon," Silvie whispered, "he's going to die."

Sebastian squeezed his eyes shut momentarily. He found it hard to comprehend that Leo's young life—one of great promise—now lay in jeopardy.

And that promise had been stolen from Leo by a knife-wielding thug. A rush of anger washed over Sebastian. How much money had he thought he would get from the boy—twenty bucks? For that, he would kill? Sebastian rubbed his eyes. Had the attacker been under the influence of drugs? Had he been Satan's pawn—a means of murdering Leo?

Sebastian thought it possible. Demons destroy people. He had looked into the eyes of one; he had seen the malice, the consuming hatred. They succeeded in destroying Mary Catherine. Sebastian himself had endured their oppression—the lies and false accusations hurled against him. But the absolute worst blow would be Leo's death.

Silvie still clung to him, and he kissed the top of her head. He gently pried her away from him and gazed into her eyes. "Silvie, let's pray for Leo. Let's each take hold of one of his hands." Sebastian moved to the opposite side of the bed and took Leo's hand in his. They joined their free hands across his body, and Sebastian prayed, "Dear Lord, we thank you for Leo's life and all his gifts and talents. By your great power and mercy, please heal him. Cleanse the infection from his blood and grant him a rapid and complete recovery. In Jesus' name. Amen."

"Thank you, Sebastian." Unshed tears stood in Silvie's eyes, magnifying the blue-violet irises, and then they spilled down her cheeks, but she made no move to wipe them away.

Sean, the dark-haired nurse, came over to take Leo's vital signs. Sebastian suggested to Silvie, "While he's doing that, let's step outside for a moment."

They walked out of ICU into the waiting room. Silvie took a tissue out of her pocket and wiped her eyes and blew her nose. "I'm sorry, Sebastian, I forgot to ask you how the hearing went."

"Ah, the hearing." Sebastian smiled ruefully. "Well, I gave such a brilliant defense of myself, they fired me. I'm officially unemployed."

"Oh, no."

"I'm afraid so. But it's not over yet. Tomorrow morning, my attorney will file suit against the university."

"Good."

The dark circles under her eyes, her slumped shoulders, and her look of deep fatigue and worry concerned him. "Silvie, have you eaten anything?"

"Breakfast."

"Good Lord, that was at least twelve hours ago. Let's go down and get something from the cafeteria." He didn't tell her his own fast had lasted almost seventy-two hours. Aside from weakening him physically, he perceived no other effect. A gray despondency settled on Sebastian. Apparently, his attempt at spiritual discipline had failed.

"My stomach's in such a knot, I don't know if I'll be able to eat anything. And I don't want to leave Leo."

He took Silvie's hand in his. "Well let's ask Sean if he thinks we can leave for half an hour. If so, we'll go down to the cafeteria and see if you can eat. They may have some hot soup that will do you good. And I'm hungry too."

Sean reassured them, "His temperature is down to 101, and he's been stable the last couple of hours. It's a good idea to get some hot food while you can. Gotta keep up your own strength. Give me your mobile number, and I'll call immediately if there's any turn for the worse."

In the cafeteria, Silvie ate most of a bowl of chicken and vegetable soup with a cornbread muffin, and Sebastian broke his fast with a tuna salad sandwich. They both had coffee afterward, and Silvie ate a couple of bites of his apple pie.

"I'm beginning to see a little color back in your face," he said. The food bolstered him as well, and his spirits lifted.

"Yes, I feel better. I was hungrier than I thought. I'm so glad you came, Sebastian."

He took her hand in his. "I don't want to be any other place than here with you. As my friend Miles said to me at the hearing, 'I'm here for the duration.'"

With a beseeching look in her eyes, she said, "Sebastian, what am I going to do if Leo dies? I don't think I can bear it."

He squeezed her hand gently. "Silvie, we're not there yet. We'll take it minute by minute, and we won't give up hope. Never give up. He's young and strong, physically and spiritually. I believe he'll pull through. You'll see."

Internally, Sebastian fought to believe his own words. With his other hand, he caressed her cheek gently. "Let's go back. I know we'll both feel better if we're in the room with him."

For the next three hours, Leo's condition remained about the same. But from 11:00 p.m. on, the momentum of the battle changed. The infection gathered all its forces for a final assault. Leo's temperature spiked to 103, then 104, 105, 106. His blood pressure dropped drastically, resulting in inadequate blood flow—and therefore insufficient delivery of oxygen and nutrients to the heart, brain, and kidneys. No matter how much saline, fluids, or drugs they gave him to raise his blood pressure, Leo's body did not respond. Multiple organs, including his kidneys, failed.

Silvie, Sebastian, and the medical staff watched helplessly. The point came when the battle was lost—the fight ended. Leo's heart stopped and he left them. At one in the morning, the doctor pronounced him dead.

The nurses quickly extubated him, disconnected all the intravenous tubes, the monitors, and the catheter. They cleaned him, and then the medical personnel left, leaving them alone with the body. The night nurse closed the drapes around the bed to give Silvie and Sebastian privacy for their final farewells.

Silvie laid her upper body over Leo's, pressed her cheek against his, and embraced his limp, still-warm torso. Between bouts of shuddering sobs and silent weeping, she spoke quietly to him in a stream of melodious Swedish.

Sebastian's mouth tasted of ashes. He wished he'd thought to call a priest for last rites, but it was too late now. Though he stood inches away from Silvie at Leo's bedside, the blood ties of mother and son and the foreign language formed a barrier that separated him from them like a wall of glass. With vague surprise at himself, he felt no impulse to comfort Silvie. It was her son he thought about. His mind filled with images of Leo playing the organ, Leo holding hands with Stephanie, Leo's astonishing pronouncements about the spiritual world.

Leo, whose spiritual eyes were open from infancy, had helped him understand the direct but unseen action of the spiritual world on the physical. Perhaps that was why the young man had come into his life.

When the veil had been lifted from his sight and he saw the demon manifested in Mary Catherine's eyes, the unseen world became real to him; Sebastian never doubted again. But his knowledge had seemed pointless, of no use, until Leo made him understand the ongoing war, the daily battle against those invisible entities, the principalities and powers who seek to destroy human beings.

Leo had also seen a magnificent light surrounding him, perhaps confirmed by the child Sasha. There had to be a purpose for those experiences, that knowledge.

Sebastian's mind whirled, trying to make sense of it all. The adversary had won every battle. Through alcoholism, he had destroyed Mary Catherine. In the last weeks, he himself had been slandered and fired. And now, in a moment of great triumph, this same foe had caused the miserable, untimely death of this gifted boy.

Suddenly, out of the blue, Sebastian found himself standing in a green and pleasant meadow ringed by trees and covered with a profusion of flowers in the most vivid, beautiful colors. And there was Leo—smiling widely and striding quickly toward him across grass of the greenest green—the epitome of strength and confidence and life. His blue eyes shone and his hair, radiant as light, ruffled in the wind. Sebastian's back straightened and his heart pounded with joy.

And then the vision ended.

He was suddenly back in the cold hospital room, confronted again with the heartbroken mother and the dead, shattered son. The scene he witnessed was altogether wrong—it should not be.

It would not be.

Energy shot through Sebastian like an electric charge, and he acted. With his weight on the balls of his feet, he leaned forward and touched Silvie's shoulder. "Silvie, come away."

Something in his tone caused her to obey without hesitation; she stood up and stepped back.

Focused solely on Leo, Sebastian stood to his full height as the power within him rose in a mighty crescendo and burst out in a war cry. "Listen to me," he shouted to the invisible foe, "Leo is *not* dead. He is going to live. He is going to live, *in the name of Jesus!*"

Silvie gaped at Sebastian as if he had lost his mind.

And then she gazed upon the lifeless body of her son. "*Herre Gud! Han andas, Sebastian!*" She burst into tears. "He's breathing."

"Yes, he is. Thanks be to God." Sebastian had never felt so alive in all his life. His chest expanded with warmth and energy. So buoyant and light was his body that he felt he might rise up in the air at any moment.

He watched Silvie cradle her son's head in her hands with the utmost delicacy, tenderness, and wonder. "O, my darling Leo," she whispered. Leo's eyelids fluttered and opened, and life—comprehending, incomparable, divine—shone in those blue-violet irises.

❦

Much later, after the dumbfounded medical team returned to attend to her son, Silvie held Sebastian's hand and whispered, "How is this possible? He was dead for almost thirty minutes. I don't understand what happened here."

It suddenly occurred to Sebastian that maybe his fast had done some good after all, but he kept that to himself. From a place of utter peace, he smiled. "Well, Silvie, like Stephanie, I think we surprised the enemy. Clearly, he didn't expect any resistance."

CHAPTER 39

THERE

Despite the dire warnings that Leo would likely waste away for years in a coma or a vegetative state with permanent brain and organ damage from lack of oxygen, he went home five days later with no ill effects. His recovery remained a mystery and astonishment to all, save Leo himself and Sebastian. Discharged from the hospital on Monday, November sixteenth, he was overjoyed to go home to Bullinger. He had to avoid heavy lifting and strenuous exercise, but he could eat normally, and he was free of pain.

Stephanie made a special trip that evening to see him and to bring him all his textbooks. Needless to say, she delivered a careful hug and a quantity of heartfelt kisses as well. "Mmm," murmured Leo, after an especially long and satisfying one, "love, being the motive power of the universe, is the very best medicine."

"In that case," replied Stephanie, "let me provide a little more." And so she did.

He told her his plan to spend the next two weeks reading and making up all the work he had missed. He fully expected to take his finals in early December. Tobias Mortensson had informed him that the competition performance sufficed to exempt him from the organ juries. "That was a blessing," said Leo, "since playing organ taxes the abdomen, due to all the pedal work, and I won't be able to practice for a few weeks."

Their parting was reluctant, but Silvie invited Stephanie for Thanksgiving the following week.

On Tuesday morning it rained, and Leo was alone for the first time since his hospital stay. In the stillness of the house, and over the quiet ticking of the rain, he heard the church bells of St. Mark's chime the hour. He closed his eyes and let himself drift, as he sometimes did. He breathed slowly and hoped for a glimpse of the place he sometimes visited in dreams. *There.*

And then it all came back to him. He relived the twenty-seven minutes of his own death.

The moment he left his body, he experienced a feeling of lightness and expansion; he floated in marvelous freedom. As he surveyed the scene below him, he saw his body in the hospital bed, the efforts of the medical staff to revive him, and the distress of his mother and Sebastian, but he remained curiously detached from it all. He felt himself drawn upward, rapidly through the night. He traveled with great velocity toward a light, a light he powerfully desired to reach.

And then he was *There.* He felt a sense of wonder as he walked in a field where the grass, flowers, and trees glowed with color, life, and an active, responsive vitality far surpassing anything known on Earth. Every blade of grass, every flower, leaf, and tree sang a wordless song. Like dancers, they moved and swayed of their own accord, the literal fulfillment of a verse from Isaiah:

> *For ye shall go out with joy, and be led forth with peace: the mountains and the hills shall break forth before you into singing, and all the trees of the field shall clap their hands.*

The vivid colors had a cleanness and purity about them, a transparency as if they were light itself. In the distance he saw majestic snow-capped mountains. He heard an unseen choir singing music with harmonies and moving lines, unmatchable by any instruments or voices on Earth. From low to high, he heard a richness of pitches and frequencies new and wondrous to him, far beyond anything he had ever heard before. Later, he could not exactly recall or imitate it, but he knew the music's purpose was praise to the Creator.

Then a man with dark, wavy shoulder-length hair and a neat beard, came walking across the field to meet him, hailing him with one hand raised, "Leo." He wore a long shimmering white robe, with a wide gold belt at the waist. He smiled and embraced Leo, and at his touch, it was as if every longing, every desire in Leo's life was suddenly fulfilled. He felt healed and cleansed, immersed in love. He had come home, and he was possessed of such peace he never wanted to leave.

"Leo," the man said, "you are present now in the place you saw only in glimpses before: the place you call *There*."

"I am, but I never imagined even a jot of this beauty and this peace."

"No one on Earth can." He gestured to the landscape before them. "There is this and so much more." He smiled. "Your eye has now seen, and your ear heard, a small portion of what has been prepared for you. You will see and hear it all when you return."

Return? That implied going away. Leo's heart sank. "Must I leave so soon?"

He gave no answer, but Leo suddenly thought of his mother, his sister, and Stephanie. He wanted badly to stay, but he didn't want to leave them alone in the world.

"Will you go or stay?"

In the distance, he clearly heard someone calling his name, and it decided him. "I'll go back."

The man nodded. "It is the right choice. Tell them, Leo, tell them."

Tell them? Tell them about this experience? Yes, he would, but there was another level of meaning in the words that mortified Leo. He suddenly realized how selfish he had been to conceal his spiritual knowledge. In order to protect himself from ridicule and disbelief, he had kept his insights to himself, like a miser hiding all his gold in a dark room—so much gold. Kept under lock and key, it did no good for anyone; no one could see its shine and its glory. He felt a wave of shame, but the look in the man's eyes was so loving and so understanding, it buoyed him up. Leo felt an overwhelming desire to redeem himself.

The next thing he knew, he was back in his body in the hospital bed, feeling heaviness and pain. His mother leaned over him to embrace him, and he felt his cheek warmed and wet with her tears. Beside the bed, Sebastian stood tall and proud as a conqueror, with a look of triumph in his eye.

The day after Leo recalled his near-death experience, Sebastian came to visit him. It was the violinist's only day off that week from the opera. The company was in the midst of its run of *Madama Butterfly,* which would end the weekend before Thanksgiving. Even though Leo had been admonished to tell others about his otherworldly experience, he hadn't yet told his story to anyone, even his mother. He decided to try it out on Sebastian first, man-to-man. They sat facing each other in the living room. Leo rested on the sofa with his feet up, and Sebastian sat in an armchair.

"Dr. Morrow, my spirit left my body during the time I was dead," Leo began, "but what I experienced only came back to me yesterday morning." He recounted the tale, while Sebastian listened with rapt attention. Leo kept his eyes on Sebastian's face, watching carefully for any signs of skepticism. Sebastian heard him out but said nothing.

"Well?" said Leo.

"I believe you, Leo. It's just a lot to take in. And I wonder, is your spiritual sight always on?"

"No, it comes and goes. I really don't have any control over it. For long periods it can be dormant, and I don't even think about it. And then, suddenly, I can have a remarkably vivid experience. That's how it was when I saw you at the Baptist wedding."

Sebastian opened his mouth to speak, but Leo held up his hand. "And here's something I never told you. When Mamma and I went to see *Tosca* last year, I saw an immense angel stand beside you when you stood up to tune the orchestra. It was a brief but very powerful vision. The angel was magnificent. And, for an instant, he looked at me."

"Huh. What do you make of that?"

"Well, first of all, the angel knew I could see him, and in a way I can't explain, his glance instantly imparted the knowledge that you and I were linked. I knew without a doubt there would be some tie between us. Then we met at the Baptist wedding in Houston and again at St. Mark's." Leo grinned. "And as you can see, here we are."

"You know, Leo, what you said that day after the wedding completely puzzled me at the time, but ultimately, it made a life-and-death difference." Sebastian leaned forward and rested his elbows on his knees. "Let me explain what happened while you were absent from your body."

"I saw some of it from above, while I floated near the ceiling. The medical staff worked on me. You had an arm around Mamma, and she looked so afraid."

"That's right. But the important part happened after the medical staff gave up and the doctor pronounced you dead. They removed all the tubes and equipment. They cleaned your body and let your mother and me remain with you for a little while. She cried a lot and held you in her arms and spoke to you in Swedish. Of course, I had no idea what she said. As I looked at your body, I recalled our conversation about the opposition. Remember?"

"Yes, in the bookshop."

"You made me aware of the daily battle between human beings and the unseen powers who hate us and strive to bring us down. I realized it was those powers that inspired and encouraged evil in the heart of the man who stabbed you. I haven't told you about my wife, but she had a long, losing battle with alcoholism, which caused her early death. Then there were the attacks on me, the false accusations. I also remembered what you told me about a magnificent light around me. I hoped that signified I could do some good."

Sebastian looked into Leo's blue-violet eyes. "And then, I think perhaps because I had been on a long fast, I had a sudden vision of you, alive and well, smiling and confident, in a field of the greenest grass and most beautiful flowers I'd ever seen. I was overjoyed. Then like that," Sebastian snapped his fingers, "the vision disappeared, and I was back in the hospital room watching your mother grieve over your dead body.

"It seemed so wrong—I had just seen you alive and well. Suddenly, an unstoppable energy rose up so powerfully in me I had to act. I drew your mother away from you, and with a force and intensity I've never felt before, I shouted, 'Leo is *not* dead. He is going to live. He is going to live, *in the name of Jesus!*'"

Leo sat up straight. "It was *you* who called my name. I heard it! I wanted to stay, but when I heard you call, I decided to return. I could have stayed there, and believe me, I very much wanted to. But I thought about my family and Stephanie, and I told the man I would go back. He said it was the right choice, and the next thing I knew, I was back in my body."

"Who was the man?"

"It was the Lord," Leo answered. "It couldn't have been anyone else. The love I felt emanating from Him . . . it's indescribable; I never felt anything so powerful. It comforts me still."

At that moment, the front door opened, and Silvie came in. "Hello!" She walked directly to Leo, kissed him on the forehead, and then took Sebastian's hand in hers. "I'm glad you're still here. You'll stay for dinner, won't you? But I'm afraid it's only leftovers."

He couldn't help smiling; his heart lifted at her touch and her nearness. "Yes, thank you. Your leftovers, Silvie, are probably worlds better than my most inspired culinary creations."

Over dinner, which turned out to be pork loin with lingon jam, boiled potatoes with butter, and a green salad, Silvie asked Sebastian if his lawyer had filed suit. She sat at the head of the table with Leo to her left and Sebastian on her right.

"Wait," said Leo, holding one hand in the air like a crossing guard, "first catch me up on the hearing." He spoke to Sebastian, "When Stephanie and I were in the parking lot, just before everything happened, we saw flyers advertising a big demonstration against you at Omega."

"Yes, that happened, all right, but I wasn't on campus to see it." Sebastian then told Leo about the faculty hearing which ruled in his favor, followed by the president's reversal, and the emergency Board of Regents' meeting. "When the Board of Regents ruled against me, I lost my job. My attorney filed suit against Omega the very next day."

"Why didn't they believe your story about the chigger bites?" asked Leo.

"Oh, I think they probably did, although they would never admit it. Their knee-jerk reaction was to hide behind the mask of political correctness. And political correctness, like a high-ranking Pharisee, is always the enemy of the uncomfortable truth. They simply caved in to social pressure; they didn't have the guts to fight it.

"The other big reason, which trumps everything, is money. If they didn't get rid of me, the university could be sued for discrimination and possibly lose federal funding. It was safer and more profitable for Omega to fire me than to risk the loss of federal dollars. They can always hire another violin instructor."

"Do you think you'll win the lawsuit?" Silvie asked.

"I believe so—I have to clear my name. What university is going to hire a professor who was labeled a racist and subsequently fired? If I'm going to have a future in college teaching, I have to be exonerated, and the decision of a court of law carries more weight than a Board of Regents' hearing."

"Are you looking for another job?" she asked.

Sebastian swallowed a bite of pork. "Mmmm, delicious. Not yet. I'll do that after the first of the year. I'm all right financially for the time being."

In truth, his financial situation was so dire, Sebastian didn't want to talk about it. With the November opera, his final Omega paycheck, and the upcoming Christmas gigs, he figured he could make it through February. He was too embarrassed to tell them he had not a cent in savings, and he was still mired in massive debt. He had very large balances on three credit cards from the work on the house, and then he had the monthly payments on his home equity loan and looming property taxes. He rarely had more than fifty bucks in his bank account at the end of the month.

Academic job openings for 2010 had begun to be been posted, but most positions, if he could even land one, didn't begin until August or September. From March to August he would have only the opera and occasional freelance jobs to sustain him—income insufficient to pay all his obligations. Even if he sold the house, he only had about ten thousand in equity. And if he lost the lawsuit, he would have to pay court costs and astronomical attorney fees.

All his financial worries could have been a recipe for high blood pressure, insomnia, and peptic ulcers, but Sebastian's experience with Leo had given him an entirely new perspective. He figured a God whose very name could raise the dead would find it child's play to supply his needs. He would do his part; he would look for a new position. But from the present to the point when his employment and financial issues resolved themselves, he would simply take it one day at a time, give thanks for all his blessings, and trust his life to the care of the good Lord.

"Have they set a court date?" Leo asked.

"We hope it will be sometime in December or January. Martin thinks we have a very good case."

"If you win," asked Silvie, "will you return to Omega?"

"Good question. My inclination is yes—I don't want to harbor bitterness or resentment toward the student or the administrators. I love teaching, and I would miss my colleagues terribly, especially Abbie and Miles." He drank a sip of his red wine. "I guess if it all works out, I would like to return."

"Speaking of court," said Leo, "I've got a case coming up myself."

Sebastian stopped with his glass in midair. "Did they find the two guys who mugged you?"

Leo smiled. "They caught them pickpocketing people at the Omega demonstration."

Sebastian set his glass down. "Silvie mentioned that."

"Yes. Once they had them in custody, they noticed the similarities to Stephanie's description in the police report she filed. She went down to take a look, and out of five photos of men with similar characteristics, she was able to identify both of them. And guess what—the big guy faked the Jamaican accent, but he couldn't hide his broken jaw. I guess I did better than I thought."

"Good for you, Leo. No wonder your hand was bruised. Have they been charged?"

"Yep. The police went to the DA's office and got a warrant for aggravated robbery. They got it approved by a judge, and they served the warrant to the fake Jamaican dude and Mr. Gold Teeth in jail."

Sebastian raised his glass. "Well, I'll drink to that!" He drained the last of his wine. "Will the punishment fit the crime?"

Silvie answered, "I'm glad to say it does. It's a first-degree felony and they could get five to ninety-nine years or life." Smiling broadly, she raised her glass. "And wishing to be as vindictive as possible, I sincerely hope it's life."

"Mamma, have a little mercy!"

"Well, all right, ninety-eight years." She drank and told Leo, "You'll understand me better when *you* have children.

"But enough about court cases, let's discuss Thanksgiving. It's only eight days away, and we have a lot to be thankful for. I hope you don't have any plans, Sebastian, because I'd like you to spend the day with us. Kristin will be home from UT, and we've invited Stephanie."

"Well, thank you for the invitation, but my daughter Helen and her husband Kieran are coming to visit me. I haven't seen them since July, and they want to provide moral support. I'm going to invite Aunt Nancy and Uncle Bear too."

"Why don't you bring them all?" suggested Silvie. "We'd love to meet the rest of your family. I've already met your aunt and uncle. It would be great fun."

Sebastian hesitated, "I don't know—it'll be quite a sacrifice. I'll have to give up my yearly wrestling match with the turkey."

She laughed. "Oh no you won't—you can wrestle with mine."

"All right, it's a deal." A great warmth washed over him as he reached out and shook her hand. He would spend Thanksgiving with all the ones dearest to his heart.

"Sebastian, *vi är så oerhört tacksamma för det du gjorde. Det var helt otroligt!*"

Sebastian shot a mock-serious glance at Leo. "There she goes again. Translate, please."

He laughed. "In my role as prognosticator, I have the feeling the study of the Swedish language is in your future."

"Is that what she said?"

Leo laughed again. "No. She said, 'We are so extremely thankful for what you did. It was totally incredible.'"

Silvie, whose blue-violet eyes were magnified by tears, spoke directly to Sebastian. "*Du uppväckte min enda son från döden.*"

"You brought back my only son from the dead," Leo translated.

Sebastian took her hand in both of his. "Silvie, I only said the prayer. It was God who brought Leo back from the dead." As the tears spilled down her cheeks, Sebastian added, "And that son of yours has quite a tale to tell you." Sebastian gave Leo a meaningful glance.

He rose. "Thank you for the best leftovers this man has ever eaten. I must go and feed all my animals now and make a brave start on housecleaning for Helen's visit."

Silvie brushed away her tears and rose also. "Let me walk you to your car." Once they were outside, she took his hand. The chilly, damp night did not affect the inner warmth she felt as Sebastian's hand closed around hers. Sage materialized at their side.

Sebastian reached down to pet the German Shepherd. "Do you think it necessary to escort me to my car, Silvie?"

"Not really. After what happened in the hospital, I rather suspect one like you may very well walk with angels."

Sebastian glanced down at her quizzically.

Silvie frowned. "I really came out here because you forgot something."

"Did I? What was that?" They had reached the car, and they stopped to face each other.

"You forgot to kiss me."

Sebastian nodded. "That is a grave error on my part."

"I would have to agree, and one you'd better correc—"

He made amends posthaste, taking his time to do a thorough, and in Silvie's estimation, quite outstanding job.

When she returned to the house, flushed and bright-eyed, Leo had begun to clear the table. She asked her son's opinion. "Do you think Sebastian will be vindicated in court?"

"Mamma, despite all the accusations and the rulings against him, he did nothing wrong. Whether it happens within the legal system or not, his vindication is absolutely certain. When or how it will occur, I don't know, but justice will prevail."

Silvie felt reassured. "I hope so. Now, what was Sebastian talking about—what story are you supposed to tell me?"

"Oh, that. Umm, let's leave the dishes for now," said Leo. "Come in the living room, Mamma. You might want to hear this sitting down."

CHAPTER 40
LESSONS IN THE WILD

They sat at either end of the sofa. Silvie listened to Leo's story attentively, but with a tension she could feel in her whole body. She knew her son was not a liar, but she found his tale disturbing and difficult to believe. The truth was, she really didn't want to believe it.

After Leo finished, there was an awkward silence. He watched her expectantly and a little anxiously. Silvie felt an unwanted stab of jealousy that Leo had confided in Sebastian first. She didn't know where to begin, but at last she seized on the man's admonition to Leo. "*Tell them*, the man said. What sorts of things have you been withholding, and why didn't you . . ." She glanced down at her clenched hands. "Well why didn't you want to confide in me?"

"Mamma, I was mocked and ridiculed so much when I was younger—not by you, but by the kids at school. And, well . . . sometimes you seemed so impatient, almost irritated, when I tried to talk to you about what I saw. It was as though you really didn't want to hear what I had to say at all." He ran a hand through his hair. "It made me turn inward. It seemed safer to keep my spiritual sight a secret from everyone. And honestly, at the beginning, I just enjoyed seeing the swirling colors surrounding people. As time went on, I gained experience and began to understand what the colors meant. They do not lie. From the colors I see, I can tell many things. Your sadness and depression after Pappa died was like a muted gray veil around you. But I know you're better now—it's almost entirely gone. You have pink and blue around you—light, clear, pastel colors.

"Lucas' aura was ugly—murky green and brown—the colors of a liar. That's why I never liked him. I know you have the right to find another man and marry again. I never wanted to interfere with that; I just didn't want you to be involved with a deceiver."

"That he certainly was," Silvie agreed. "And what about Sebastian?"

Leo's furrowed brow relaxed, and he sat back for a moment before he answered. "The first time I ever saw him was at *Tosca*, and a strange thing happened. While the orchestra tuned, I saw a tall, brilliant angel stand beside him for just a few moments."

Silvie leaned forward and interrupted, "I didn't know you could see angels."

Leo smiled. "It happens occasionally."

"What was that about?"

"Well, the angel looked at me, and somehow, without a word spoken, I immediately knew there would be some kind of link between Dr. Morrow and me. That was in April. A few weeks later, I saw him at a friend's wedding. He played with a string trio at the front of the church. Watching him, I almost forgot about the bride and groom— that's how striking and unusual his aura was—very large and shining, golden. When the wedding was over, I ran after him. I felt compelled to tell him." Leo laughed softly. "And he had no idea."

"You never told me any of this, Leo."

"No. But now you know why I trust Sebastian, and why I confided in him."

Silvie dropped her gaze and cast her mind back across the years. She had to admit to herself that her attitude had been precisely as he described. He had sensed her reluctance all along. She hadn't wanted to hear about anything that smacked of the supernatural or spiritual. She had always been practical-minded, grounded in this world. Like Edward, she had been a true believer in science and reason, in things that could be measured, codified, and above all, controlled.

Leo's spiritual sight threatened that explainable, ordinary world. She had trusted in science and modern medicine to heal him, and both had failed miserably. But Sebastian had believed in something else—something immeasurable and powerful, impossible to control, something far surpassing the bounds of human reason. And against all odds, against all logic, by faith alone, he had called Leo back from the dead.

Together, Sebastian and her son had proved her wrong. Leo had shaken her worldview, and Sebastian had shattered it. "Leo, I'm sorry." Haltingly, she tried to explain herself and apologize. It was time to grow up. "Honestly, in the realm of spiritual matters, our roles seem reversed. You are the adult and I . . . well, I'm like a child. I have a long way to go, much to understand." She smiled crookedly as tears started in her eyes. "There is no Santa Claus."

Leo laughed and embraced her. "No, Mamma, but there is something so much more wonderful, the source of all life, all joy, all love."

She nodded. "It's a miracle, Leo."

"What happened to me, or what's happening to you?"

She laughed through her tears. "Both."

As Sebastian drove home in the dark, thinking about the de Graafs, it seemed to him that his role in Leo's return to life was redemption for all the failures and mistakes he had made with Mary Catherine. He sorrowed still over his wife, but because of her—and his talks with Leo—he had learned to know the enemy and how to fight him. And he had enabled his friends to do the same.

To his great satisfaction, Miles, Abbie, and Philip had burned the cursed objects Duck had given them. Perhaps because of his strong belief, Philip recovered the quickest. He went back to work two days later, energized and in fine voice. The pain in Abbie's hands lessened to mere intermittent twinges, and finally ceased altogether after a week. Simon stopped vomiting, but continued to have stomachaches until Miles called an Anglican priest to come to the house. The priest anointed the boy with oil, prayed over him, and blessed every room in their home. The stomachaches ceased, and Simon's return to health was complete.

Miles was overjoyed, but his anger toward Ferris Duck swelled. He wanted all involved to confront Duck *en masse*, but he was overruled by the others. Abbie explained it would only give Duck more satisfaction; they couldn't prove anything, and he would simply laugh in their faces. She explained her theory on the stupidity of evil. "Like Lucifer, Q is guilty of pride and arrogance. He thinks he's far superior to us common mortals, and like his angelic predecessor, pride will lead to his damnation. Mark my words: he's going to overstep his bounds and cause his own ruin." She smiled. "All we have to do is watch and be patient."

Thinking on it all gave Sebastian a measure of peace and a deep gratitude.

He drove for a while with a quiet mind—until he remembered Silvie's invitation. He decided he'd better call Helen and Aunt Nancy sooner rather than later. It made him nervous, since telling them about the change of plans for Thanksgiving dinner would expose his budding relationship with Silvie. He wondered what they would think. Aunt Nancy, the lone, renegade Episcopalian in their Catholic clan, had always wanted him to remarry. She would no doubt be delighted, but Helen might not be so quick to approve. What would she think of Silvie, who was a mere fourteen years older? Leo and Kristin could be her future half-siblings—what of that?

"Well, it's about to be a whole new world," he said to himself. A Shakespeare quote leapt into his mind: *What's past is prologue.*

He made a mental reckoning of the past, which he seemed to have trekked through with singular style and flair. He had moved to the country and promptly set his house onto someone else's land, plunged into major debt, lost his estranged wife of thirty years, got fired for being a racist, met a clairvoyant organist with a gorgeous, sexy mother, and called said organist back from the dead. Hair-raising, yes—safe and idyllic, not quite.

He turned onto the access road and accelerated onto the highway for the fifteen-minute ride home. "I seem to recall that my original plan of moving to the country was supposed to keep me *out* of harm's way," he muttered under his breath. He tapped the steering wheel with his thumbs. Hmmm, maybe Houston was the safer environment after all. Should he have stayed, remained a renter with no debt, gone on the same way as always?

That question begged another: why had he never divorced his wife? Was it out of loyalty to Mary Catherine and the church's teaching on marriage and divorce? Or had he actually withdrawn from life in order to protect himself from further emotional hurt, like a small, frightened animal cowering in its hole? Perhaps he had simply taken the easy, do-nothing course: drifting without effort or direction, floating here and there on the sea like a spar from a shipwreck. He hoped he had been morally upright, but he feared he might also have been an emotional coward, frozen in stasis.

He turned onto the farm-to-market road, still pondering the past. His marriage had conveniently barred him from all other romantic attachments; it was a ready-made excuse to deflect any interested women and his friends' well-meaning attempts at matchmaking. Over the years, the flirting and efforts at seduction by the opposite sex had lessened. Either he had grown less attractive or he projected some sort of negative signal like an invisible No Admittance sign, a force field that rebuffed all comers.

Silvie's entrance onto the stage changed everything. He could no longer be an observer, waiting in the shadowy wings. He had just bounded onto the boards himself, to take his place beside her in the story. And, for good or ill, that was exactly where he wanted to be. Dangerous territory, but exciting. Were the rewards worth the risk? Those kisses were rather rewarding; he hadn't kissed a woman so thoroughly in decades. Sebastian smiled; he had forgotten how much he enjoyed it. But if he opened his heart to love, he opened himself up to hurt.

He felt his muscles contract in response to the thought of pain. Even so, he couldn't go backward—he had to take what life offered. To release his tension, he slapped the steering wheel. Let come what may, he'd take it like a man. Time to summon up some emotional courage.

With one thing leading to another, he wondered if he could live with someone again. There was some truth in what he had told Aunt Nancy—he was set in his ways. Did he want to barter his freedom for intimacy and companionship? Could he adjust? Did he want to take on the responsibility and burden of two stepchildren, even if he was fond of them and even though they were both poised to leave the nest?

As he turned onto Vogel Lane, his mind returned to those kisses, and then to the thought of complete intimacy with Silvie. He felt pulse and breath quicken, surprised at the strength of his desire. Somehow, it would be all right. Seeing her in his mind's eye, he responded like the musician he was; without thinking, he began to hum a tune. After a moment, he realized it was "Where'er You Walk," an aria from Handel's *Semele*. Opera D'Argento had given the Houston premiere last season. In the story, Jove sings it to his lover Semele. In a clear baritone, Sebastian sang it as his own love song to Silvie:

Where'er you walk,
Cool gales shall fan the glade;
Trees, where you sit,
shall crowd into a shade.

Where'er you tread,
the blushing flowers shall rise,
and all things flourish
Where'er you turn your eyes.

As he released the last note, he turned into his yard and smiled; as usual, music had restored him. In his customary, solitary way, he spoke his thoughts aloud, "Well, Silvie, you've made me flourish like a barren tree come back to life. Not being dead yet, T. Sebastian Morrow is still a man, pledged to love, cherish, and protect a woman." He turned off the ignition and added, "And after all this time, as Miles would say, that qualifies as a bloomin' miracle."

❧

Standing in the kitchen, Helen clicked off the phone, poured two glasses of red wine, and went to find Kieran. She sat down beside him on the sofa and handed him a glass. "Curiouser and curiouser."

"What is?" He looped an arm around her shoulders and pulled her close.

"When we go to Texas next week, we're having Thanksgiving dinner with the de Graaf family."

"Who are they?" He tasted the wine.

"Friends of Dad's who live in Bullinger, apparently. He's never mentioned them before, although he did talk about their bookshop. There's Silvie the mom who owns it, her son Leo, the organist who plays at Dad's church, and daughter Kristin. Leo was stabbed in a mugging recently, but he's home now and on the mend. Dad said he visited him in the hospital and provided moral support for Silvie."

"What about Mr. de Graaf?"

"No mention of him. But Aunt Nancy and Uncle Bear will be there too." Helen sipped her wine and smiled. "You know what, Kieran? I think Dad has a girlfriend."

"Well, darlin', I certainly hope so—it's about damn time." He raised his glass in a toast. "Here's to Sebastian and Silvie."

❦

Bear laid down his book and petted the Siamese cat reclining on his lap, but his real attention was fixed on Nancy and her half of the conversation as she spoke on the landline.

"Sebastian! Bear and I are fine. I'm knitting and he's reading a travel guide on Sydney and the Great Barrier Reef, what else?"

Nancy pursed her lips and drew her brows together, listening. "Who?"

"Oh, yes, I remember meeting her at your concert in Houston.

Very tall and blond—so pretty."

There was a long speech on the other end. Bear scratched the purring cat behind its ears.

"Oh, he's her son. I never made the connection. How is he now?"

"Thank heavens."

Another extended speech.

"She did? Where do they live?"

"I see. Well, of course we'll come. Will Helen and Kieran be there too?"

"Excellent! I was going to bring one pecan pie, but now I'll bring two. Let us know all the details later. Bye." She set the receiver down with an impish grin on her lips.

What happened next became Leaton family legend. Bear's eyes grew wider than those of the cat, as he watched his wife of forty years lift up her arms and spin like a whirling Dervish, all the while whooping like an Aggie after a touchdown. Still shrieking, she ran across the room in his direction. From four feet out, she launched herself into the air and landed beside him on the sofa with a thump. The impact lifted him vertically off the seat and dropped him back. It was too much for the cat, who shot out of his lap and rocketed upstairs to the bedroom to hide from the madwoman.

He gaped at her in disbelief. "Woman, have you lost your mind? What the hell's wrong with you?"

Nancy Leaton laughed and hugged her husband. "Nothing's wrong—everything is finally right, Bear. I thought Armageddon would come before I would ever see this day. Sebastian has a *girlfriend*! We're invited to her house for Thanksgiving."

"Who is it?"

"Silvie de Graaf—we met her at his concert. Remember the tall, beautiful blond I hoped might be a good match for him?" Her laugh was exultant. "Hahaha, she's the one!"

"Did Sebastian say she was his girlfriend?"

"No, but I feel it in the center of my matchmaking soul—just wait and see. Her son was stabbed and almost died in the hospital, but he's home now and recovering. Sebastian visited him in the hospital and helped Silvie during that time."

"Well, maybe she's just grateful and wants to thank him by inviting him to dinner."

"Nope, it's more than that. I could hear it in his voice. I feel it—I know it. Trust me on this, Bear."

He lifted his eyebrows and tilted his head at her. "Wanna make a little wager?"

"Sure."

"I say she's only being nice, and she's not his girlfriend. If I'm right, we go to Australia next August."

She screwed up her face—he'd been going on about Australia for months, despite all her objections. She thought quickly. "Okay, Bear, but if I'm right, we spend a month in the Scottish Highlands instead."

"A month! You're going to bankrupt me."

"I sure am, 'cause I'm right." She extended her hand and challenged him with her eyes. "Shake, if you accept the terms."

He grasped her hand and grinned from ear to ear. "Ayers Rock, here we come."

2010

EPILOGUE

The wilderness, whether it be a place or a state of mind, is the womb of statesmen and saints. It may be a wasteland inhabited by owls and bobcats that prowl by night and blink at the cold, pearly shine of the moon. Or a man may walk alone in the streets of an overcrowded city and find there a wilderness, barren of friendship or kindness or love. Whether for forty days or forty years, to wander in the wilderness is to undergo trials and testing and long deprivation.

In the latter half of 2010, Sebastian came to the end of his long wandering. In May, after months of negotiations with Martin Katzberger, the university settled the lawsuit out of court. They agreed to reinstate Sebastian and pay him all back wages, court costs, and attorney's fees, plus $150,000 in punitive damages for defamation of character.

Justice prevailed at Omega as well. Alicia Borden changed her major to financial management. She gave up the violin to spend her life fiddling with other people's cash. Eighteen months later, Ferris Duck was fired and prosecuted when a tech in the university IT department discovered pornography on his work computer.

In June, over the course of twenty-four hours, Sebastian paid off his house loan and all three credit cards. He opened a savings account with the goodly remainder of the settlement. On August sixth, the Feast of the Transfiguration, he bought a sapphire ring that matched the beautiful eyes of Silvie de Graaf. That evening, he asked her to marry him, and of course, she did.

Leo recovered completely, got engaged to Stephanie, and won the next organ competition he entered. Kristin got a job with Martin Katzberger's law firm and found her best friend in Helen. In September, in honor of her father, Helen and Kieran named their first son Theodore.

Of course, Aunt Nancy and Uncle Bear spent a month in Scotland. But being by nature merciful, and unable to resist Bear for long, she promised to go to Australia the following year.

Volcanoes continued to erupt, nations fought against nations, and the earth shook all around the Ring of Fire. Hailstorms, blizzards, and tornados wreaked havoc, while corruption ran rampant in the halls of Congress. But, despite the world's alarms, in the house of Sebastian and Silvie, a cottage on three and one-half acres somewhere in Central Texas, there were books, there was music, and there was peace.

ACKNOWLEDGMENTS

All Bible quotes from the King James Version.

"Where'er You Walk," from G. F. Handel's opera *Semele*. Text by William Congreve.

Adoro Devote Benedictine Plainsong, Mode V, 13th century; text from St. Thomas Acquinas, c. 1260, Episcopal hymnal version, 1939.

Shakespeare quotes:
"He has a lean and hungry look." *Julius Caesar*, Act I, scene 2.
"Let me not to the marriage of true minds admit impediments." *Sonnet* 116.
"What's past is prologue." *The Tempest*, Act II, scene 1.

Many thanks to attorney Elizabeth Zwiener for advice on legal issues and Dr. Matthew Heinz for medical information. Any errors I have made on legal or medical matters are my own. And thanks to Daniel Bergin for help with the Swedish language.

I am grateful to my patient and helpful readers: Nicholas Bergin, William Gilbert, Annette Stadelmann, and to Nicholas and William for additional editorial help.

This book would not have been possible without the help of Gordon McLellan, Katelynn Watkins, and the staff of DartFrog Books.

Warm thanks to the excellent workman, Faustino Armijo, my model for JR, and to Betsy Faden-Qureshi, who inspired the forthright character Betsy Bloom. Special thanks to the generous, persistent silent auction bidder who won the opportunity to be a character in this novel: Nancy Leaton (and to her husband Barry, who somehow or other got dragged into the deal).

REFERENCES

Amorth, Gabriele. *An Exorcist Tells His Story*, translated by Nicoletta V. MacKenzie. (San Francisco: Ignatius Press, 1999).

Amorth, Gabriele. *An Exorcist: More Stories*, translated by Nicoletta V. MacKenzie. (San Francisco: Ignatius Press, 2002).

Dresden Frauenkirche. https://en.wikipedia.org/wiki/Dresden_Frauenkirche

In articulo mortis. Latin poetry from an arrangement of *Nearer My God to Thee* by BYU Vocal Point: https://lyricstranslate.com/en/byu-vocal-point-nearer-my-god-thee-lyrics.html

Padre Pio in pictures and words https://www.youtube.com/watch?v=-xMxPLxSyes

https://www.padrepio.catholicwebservices.com/ENGLISH/The_Devil.htm

Prince, Derek. *The Basics of Deliverance, How to Identify the Enemy*, part 1.

https://www.youtube.com/watch?v=Yzivz7gcMtE

Prince, Derek. *The Basics of Deliverance, How to Expel the Enemy*, part 2.

https://www.youtube.com/watch?v=3CsiGNxexRc

Tennant, Alan. *A Field Guide to Texas Snakes.* (Houston: Gulf Publishing Co., 1985).

ABOUT THE AUTHOR

Wendy Isaac Bergin, a Louisiana native, is a lover of language and music, and the genre that combines them both: opera. She gets to indulge her passion regularly as principal flutist of Houston's Opera in the Heights Orchestra. A seasoned veteran of the halls of academia—another hotbed of high drama—she has served on the music faculties of Prairie View A&M University, the University of Houston-Downtown, Blinn College, and Lee College. She is the author of two other novels—*The Piper's Story: A Tale of War, Music and the Supernatural* and *The Threshold of Eden*. Wendy has lived in Brooklyn, Stockholm and Houston. Now, she enjoys the adventures of bucolic life among bobcats and coyotes in the almost-hill-country of Texas.

More about the author and her work can be found on her website, www.wendyisaacbergin.com. Her two previously published books can be found on her Amazon page: https://tinyurl.com/wcu3egj.

In this age of social media sharing, without social proof, an author may as well be invisible.

So if you've enjoyed *Lessons in the Wild*, please consider giving it some visibility by reviewing it on Amazon or Goodreads. A review doesn't have to be a long critical essay. Just a few words expressing your thoughts, which could help potential readers decide whether they would enjoy it, too.